"Find the reliquary. Return it here, to me. It is a test that would prove either of you more than worthy, and a more consequential duty than any I have ever asked of my children before."

"Yes," Nolan says with urgent, devoted passion. "Whatever you wish, mother."

"Whatever you wish," I echo. And it's actually the truth. The opium smoke of the Goddess's divinity has me ready to hunt, to kill, to stand on my head and recite dirty limericks if that would earn me more of their favor. I take a gulp of air, thick as syrup, trying to settle the yearning ache for more, more, more of them. At least that cursed desire muddies the profound giddiness growing beneath it.

Emmaus might have been weak, but *I* am not. *I* have already survived the divine gift. And Tempestra-Innara has just asked me to track down the one weapon I need to finally free myself from this drowning servitude.

Now I know how to hurt them.

Now I know the weapon of a goddess's destruction.

And not a godsdamned thing in existence is going to keep me from finding it.

## By Lyndsay Ely

**DIVINE THRALL**

*The Lost Reliquary*

*Gunslinger Girl*

*Five Nights at Freddy's: Escape the Pizzaplex* (cowriter)

**OVERWATCH TIE-IN NOVELS**

*Overwatch: Deadlock Rebels*

*Overwatch 2: Heroes Ascendant: An Overwatch Story Collection*

# THE LOST RELIQUARY

## Divine Thrall: Book One

# Lyndsay Ely

LONDON   **NEW YORK**   TORONTO
AMSTERDAM/ANTWERP   NEW DELHI   SYDNEY/MELBOURNE

AN IMPRINT OF SIMON & SCHUSTER, LLC

1230 AVENUE OF THE AMERICAS, NEW YORK, NEW YORK 10020

For more than 100 years, Simon & Schuster has championed authors and the stories they create. By respecting the copyright of an author's intellectual property, you enable Simon & Schuster and the author to continue publishing exceptional books for years to come. We thank you for supporting the author's copyright by purchasing an authorized edition of this book.

No amount of this book may be reproduced or stored in any format, nor may it be uploaded to any website, database, language-learning model, or other repository, retrieval, or artificial intelligence system without express permission. All rights reserved. Inquiries may be directed to Simon & Schuster, 1230 Avenue of the Americas, New York, NY 10020 or permissions@simonandschuster.com.

This book is a work of fiction. Any references to historical events, real people, or real places are used fictitiously. Other names, characters, places, and events are products of the author's imagination, and any resemblance to actual events or places or persons, living or dead, is entirely coincidental.

Copyright © 2025 by Lyndsay Ely

All rights reserved, including the right to reproduce this book or portions thereof in any form whatsoever. For information, address Saga Press Subsidiary Rights Department, 1230 Avenue of the Americas, New York, NY 10020.

First Saga Press trade paperback edition October 2025

SAGA PRESS and colophon are registered trademarks of Simon & Schuster, LLC

Simon & Schuster strongly believes in freedom of expression and stands against censorship in all its forms. For more information, visit BooksBelong.com.

For information about special discounts for bulk purchases, please contact Simon & Schuster Special Sales at 1-866-506-1949 or business@simonandschuster.com.

The Simon & Schuster Speakers Bureau can bring authors to your live event. For more information or to book an event, contact the Simon & Schuster Speakers Bureau at 1-866-248-3049 or visit our website at www.simonspeakers.com.

Interior design by Lewelin Polanco

Manufactured in the United States of America

1 3 5 7 9 10 8 6 4 2

Library of Congress Cataloging-in-Publication Data is available.

ISBN 978-1-6680-8031-3
ISBN 978-1-6680-8032-0 (ebook)

This book is dedicated to B-Spec, my writing group, in thanks for the many years they've put up with my first drafts and semi-autocratic writing retreat bedroom assignments.

# The Lost Reliquary

# One

*When they whisper, we wake...*

---

Every divine execution begins pretty much the same: with me, bored and sweaty, staring down at the worn patch that sits before the altar of Tempestra-Innara, last living goddess of the Devoted Lands.

I hate that spot.

Even from the highest gallery of the Cathedral, it stands out like a stain, darker than the stone surrounding it, burnished smooth over centuries by the knees of countless devoted, conquered, and condemned. The Cathedral's apse curls around it like an embrace, oil lamps on spidery chains flickering among the golden, bejeweled bones that line the walls. Some of those bones' owners knelt too. I'm not sure they would have taken it as a compliment, having their flesh stripped away, skeletons gilded and set with gemstones, but that's the honor the Goddess bestows upon their worthiest of enemies: a tacky eternity as the Cathedral's most striking décor. From this angle, I can't quite see my favorite skull—the one with its front teeth missing and jeweled daggers in its eye sockets—but it's there. I named it Alastair.

Like the apse, the Cathedral is crowded with bodies, but fleshy living ones, which is why I am melting like a damn cake left in the sun.

Even as high above them as my fellow Potentiates and I are, practically wedged into the skeletal ribbing of the vaulted ceiling, there's no relief. It must be worse in the gallery below ours, which, despite the upcoming entertainment, remains sparsely occupied by our superiors in the Orders—some huddled Priors oozing bureaucracy, a pair of Bellators in their snappy military garb, one rather wilted-looking Cleric of the Blood. And I can't imagine the pure torture on the floor, where a lagoon of onlookers churns endlessly, their perfumes and sachets long ago congealed into a smothering overripeness that I can practically taste.

Somehow the corporeal bouquet does nothing to temper the unwashed-armpit smell of my helm. We may not put on our ceremonial armor often, but the least the Dawn Cloister attendants could do is give it a good airing out before we do. Unlike those in the Orders, *we* don't get a choice in attendance. For Potentiates, an execution is a requirement. But for the devoted, it's their lucky day, the culmination of a pilgrimage to the holy city of Lumeris—garish, throbbing heart of the Goddess's empire—and that slight chance to find themselves in Tempestra-Innara's revered presence. Thousands of the less fortunate wait outside the sprawling Cathedral complex, prayers on their lips, regret for not successfully talking (or bribing) their way past the guards in their hearts, and still hoping, hoping, hoping for a glimpse of the Goddess's glory.

"At this rate," I say under my breath, shifting uncomfortably as a trickle of sweat runs down the small of my back toward my swampy nethers, "we'll be dead before the condemned is."

To one side of me, Jeziah lets out a brief yip of laughter, as fox-like as the creature his helm depicts. On the other, Morgan is silent, but I can sense the simmering annoyance beneath her hawk, which stares unflaggingly at the Cathedral's apse. It would probably take me literally exploding into flames to break her focused, ever-obedient attention.

"Lys!"

I turn my head slightly at the hiss of my name, down the line of my fellow Potentiates to where a warning expression flashes beneath Prior Petronilla's hood. There and gone, her face shadowed again, but the message is clear. Especially when her attention snags fleetingly on the gallery directly across from us, where the Potentiates of the Dusk Cloister stand: *Do not embarrass us.* But if the Dusk Potentiates or their Prior noticed my indiscretion, they give no indication, as straight and still as the statues honoring our distinguished predecessors that line the halls of the Cathedral complex.

We are a mirrored set, the gold-trimmed ebon gray of their armor contrasting with the polished red and gold of ours in a perfect theatrical duality. I don't know the names or faces of the Dusk acolytes, and they don't know ours. There are only helmed facades: raven, wraith, weasel, serpent, and, at the very end, a demon, with horns that curl as delicately as seashells. Until we join the higher Orders, we are nameless, faceless things to everyone outside our Cloister, our sole purpose to train and learn to serve the Goddess to the highest degree. Within the Dawn, competition to be the best is fierce. But Prior Petronilla never lets us forget that, no matter how we excel, the Dusk Potentiates might be that much better, that much more devoted. I expect her counterpart seeds the same expectation about us, forcing not an ounce of potential to go unrealized.

But anonymous or not, pitted against one another or not, we are all the children of Tempestra-Innara. Their Chosen. Every one of us once knelt on that infamous spot below and received the gift of the Goddess's blessing: our communion of blood.

A shiver runs through me. But not from the memory.

Tempestra-Innara has arrived.

Instinctively, I stand straighter, discomfort forgotten as a sudden, diminishing sensation takes me. I am small, smaller even than when I first beheld them, when their gift trickled its way over my lips and into my veins. That shared blood sings now, their holy presence like a rush of fever as the bones in the apse shift, revealing the hidden door to the Goddess's sanctum in the Cathedral spire. Below, the crowd cries out with pleasure, fear, awe. They clutch the reveries that hang around their necks—tiny representations of the holy flame wrought in gold, silver, marble—and reach out for a touch that will never deign to grace them. There is no acclimating to the arrival of the Goddess, not even for those with their divine gift. I've stood in their presence countless times, and still it overwhelms, turning my mouth dry and making me ache to throw myself down onto the weathered stone below, to supplicate myself. To bask and bathe in their godly power.

They glide forward. At the edge of the dais that marks the boundary between the apse and the Cathedral's nave, the Goddess stops and raises their hands. Flames appear, filling their palms with a clean, white blaze. I feel the trembling in my legs again. Many in the crowd fall to their knees. I hear whimpers. I see tears.

I get it. For most, it's their first time this close to the Goddess's glory. Do they see the same thing I do? The unnerving amalgamation of flesh and divinity, familiar and alien at the same time? Describing Innara, the chosen vessel, is easy enough: tall and slight of frame, with a light complexion and brown hair.

But that is not a description of Tempestra.

They tower.

They radiate.

They glow with the cold brightness of a full moon, their tresses flowing with the power of a river swollen by spring thaw. And their flames . . . even from a distance the flickering tongues of divinity feel hungry with a need to cleanse the impure.

*When they whisper, we wake . . .*

The prayer begins without need for a cue, a rising swell of voices.

*At their command, we follow. In their light, we are seen . . . we are judged . . .*

My lips move automatically, reciting words I've known longer than I can remember, brought to my village by soft-tongued clerics long before a Bellator's forces arrived to deliver their enlightenment in a more bellicose manner.

*May their blessed flame find purity of faith, or else leave cinder and ash.*

Jeziah once told me he thought the air seemed thinner at the end of a prayer. Lighter, as if something has been burned out of it. I agreed at the time. But it was a lie. The air seems as thick and cloying as it did before. No matter how fervent the delivery, prayers are just words dressed up fancy. And as this one tapers off, Tempestra-Innara lowers their hands, letting their flames extinguish before they address the crowd.

"Bring forward the condemned."

They don't waste time getting down to business. Which I appreciate, since the initial shock of their arrival has faded, and now I feel the sticky sweat again. The quicker this is over, the better.

The massive doors at the front of the Cathedral swing open, admitting a welcome rush of cool air. The condemned in question has probably been waiting just beyond them for ages, but there's an order to these sorts of things. An anticipatory fear that needs to be constructed, a level of threatening theatricality that must be reached. After all, anything less than a showy execution is simply an invitation for further insurrection.

The man's name is Emmaus. He stumbles as he's dragged down the center aisle by the rope around his neck, hampered by chains binding his ankles and wrists. The restraints hardly seem necessary; even from a distance, he moves feebly, bruises covering his exposed skin, barely keeping upright. Not that it earns him any sympathy from the onlooking crowd. They hiss and spit, rancor as thick as their perfumes. Because common criminals don't get divine executions. Because Emmaus is more than that—he's a heretic. And a proficient one at that. He has preached against the Goddess and distributed sacrilegious tracts. He and his coconspirators have murdered magistrates and clerics, and eluded the Goddess's forces for nearly two years.

Until they sent Andronica.

One hand gripping Emmaus's rope, Andronica saunters her way to Tempestra-Innara, not a trace of humility in her razor-sharp gaze. As the Goddess's Executrix, such things are below her. My fellow Potentiates and I briefly break our static vigil to tap the sigil of the Dawn Cloister on our shoulders. Respect for the Executrix, who was once one of us. They are the Goddess's right hand, their hunter, their blade. Prior Petronilla absolutely puffs with pride as Andronica stops before the Goddess.

We are all stronger, faster, more resilient than a normal person, thanks to the Goddess's gift. Our senses are sharper, our wounds quicker to heal. We can call the divine flame (some, like me, with less competency than others). But of all the paths a Potentiate will follow—Bellator, Prior, Arbiter, Cleric of the Blood—the position of the Executrix is the most revered. The most desired. And utterly out of reach. Andronica is still in her prime, radiating with vitality. But nothing, save the Goddess, lasts forever. The gift of Tempestra-Innara's power is given in youth; and like youth, it fades. Eventually, Andronica's strength will wane; when that happens, another young Potentiate will take up the Executrix mantle.

But long before that, I will be assigned to an Order. An irritating thought. Within months, maybe a year, Prior Petronilla will choose my fate. And it won't be in Lumeris, where the best of us strive to remain, constantly awash in the Goddess's light. Nor any of the Ordained Cities, farther from their radiance, but still pampered pillars of their empire. No, if I know Petronilla, she'll shunt me off to the farthest posting from the Goddess she can manage, the sort of position usually reserved for Chosen in their waning years. And I'll accept it like the good, obedient child that I am, because what other choice is there?

Andronica yanks the rope, sending Emmaus to his knees. There's no fight left in him, his head hanging heavy to his chest. A reverie escapes his tattered shirt, a simple painted plaster pendant in the style favored by the lower classes. And by heretics. Easy to smash quickly if one needs to hide their spiritual inclinations. That Andronica has allowed Emmaus to keep wearing it is a clear mockery. Even with my divinely assisted eyesight, I can't tell which dead god Emmaus is so devoted to that he risked ending up exactly where he is now, but it doesn't matter. One is as damning as another.

And ridiculous. There are no other gods, not anymore. Tempestra-Innara killed the last of their siblings well over a century ago. All that's left are beliefs that refuse to die too.

"Mother." Andronica bows. "As you commanded, as you entrusted me to do, I have brought you the heretic Emmaus."

Tempestra-Innara inclines their head slightly. "And for that, my daughter, you have my thanks and love. Emmaus." The Goddess speaks the name with a measure of respect. More than he merits, but it's there nonetheless, a minute concession from a victor whose triumph was never in question. "You are guilty of treason and heresy. For that, you will die with greater honor than you deserve, by the hand of divinity."

Emmaus laughs, a creaking, defiant sound that sends a ripple of offended gasps through the crowd. "You may be divine . . ." I'm damn near impressed by the venom he summons. "But you are *not* my goddess."

More scandalized murmurs, cut off by a single word from Tempestra-Innara.

"*Heretic.*" The sound shivers through the Cathedral, curdling my guts. Even Morgan flinches a little. The humanity in Tempestra-Innara's features slips away, turning as cold as a marble statue's. "I am the *only* goddess."

No one, save Andronica, is unaffected by the declaration. She smirks a little, beaming with devoted pride. Then, almost indifferently, she turns and kicks Emmaus in the side. He lets out a cry of pain, worse than the blow warranted, which makes me suspect it's not the first kick his ribs have taken lately.

"I should have cut out his tongue to gift you, Mother," Andronica says. "If he speaks again, I will."

But Emmaus doesn't quiet. Instead, he reaches for his necklace and wraps his hand around the pendant. His lips begin to move, and though he speaks too quietly to make out, I know a prayer when I see it. I almost laugh. *Fool.*

I'm not the only one who anticipates the Goddess's rage. The whole Cathedral collectively holds its breath, waiting for the inevitable execution, which, if it might have been merciful before, sure won't be now. *Now* the Goddess will undoubtedly want to make an example of an example. Which means things are about to get graphic.

Divine execution might be an honored way to die, but it's not a pleasant one.

Displeasure hardens the Goddess even further as they raise their hands again. But Emmaus doesn't falter when the flames reappear. He continues to pray, rocking slightly as he brings the necklace to his lips and kisses it. Making peace with the last moments of his life.

At least, that's what I think. Until I see his fist tighten. Until I hear the faint, chalky crunch an instant before Emmaus throws his head back.

It all happens so quickly. Even Tempestra-Innara doesn't have time to react.

Suicide by poison. A syrupy moment passes as Emmaus stands and smiles—no, *grins*, lips blackened by whatever was secreted in the necklace. Mocking. Triumphant. I smirk beneath my helm. Maybe Emmaus isn't as much a fool as I thought. To escape the wrath of Tempestra-Innara's flame, in full view of hundreds of their followers and chosen gifted—heretics have certainly rallied behind less compelling tales.

Silence falls on the Cathedral. Not even Andronica moves, waiting, prudently, for the Goddess to react, to say something. This execution has turned into a colossal fuckup. Someone will have to bear the fault of it.

Tempestra-Innara does not speak. Nor do they move. And for the first time, I glimpse something I've never seen on the Goddess's face. Something that must be anything else, because it can't *possibly* be what I think it is.

*Fear.*

The Goddess strikes—a divine blow, unnatural in its speed. A blow that should leave Emmaus in as many pieces as his reverie.

A blow that Emmaus blocks.

Cries erupt from the crowd as Emmaus grips the Goddess's wrist with one hand and snatches their neck with the other. He begins to squeeze. A blade swings—Andronica's—but Emmaus glides beneath it, landing a kick that sends the Executrix flying. With unsettling vigor, Emmaus laughs. Impossibly, his bruises have disappeared, and he doesn't move like a man with shattered ribs. Instead, he stands tall as his fingers tighten further. A truncated cough escapes the Goddess.

Then, abruptly, he begins to wheeze. To choke.

The heretic pitches forward, eyes squeezing shut as he loses his grip on Tempestra-Innara. Freed, the Goddess stumbles backward, the look on their face . . .

I don't need to see it clearly to know something is truly wrong.

Especially not when Emmaus's eyes open again. All humanity there is gone. In its place is blackness, oily and fetid. A darkness that spreads, bubbling over Emmaus's face, pouring from his nose and mouth in a hideous gush. One that starts to consume him. To *change* him. Emmaus raises his arms, flesh disintegrating as spears of the grim effluvia burst from what used to be his hands, sharpening to a point as they plunge into Tempestra-Innara's shoulder, stomach, thigh.

The Goddess screams, a sound that grates across my soul.

The world upends, turns fragmented. For a moment, I think I am impaled too. But when my vision clears, I am uninjured, and have moved without realizing it, hands now gripping the stone balustrade of the gallery. I cannot look away from the horror below, blood pounding in my ears even as it seems to drain out of me.

What I am seeing shouldn't be possible. *Cannot* not be possible.

And yet, the blackness continues to grow. Faster even than my stunned disbelief as I watch Emmaus about to succeed in doing what I have secretly dreamed of since the first time I knelt on that worn Cathedral floor:

Killing Tempestra-Innara.

# Two

*Into the light, we are reborn.*
*Within the flame, we are reforged.*

—SHARED MOTTO OF THE DAWN AND DUSK CLOISTERS

**T**WO THINGS I LEARNED early and keep close: Everyone has secrets, and every secret has consequences.

Some of those consequences are merely embarrassing, like how peaches make Morgan fart like a draft horse. Others would mean punishment if discovered—Jeziah's trysts with the Cloister attendants springs to mind—but are still forgivable.

My secret would be an instant ticket to an exceedingly-painful-and-probably-not-quick execution.

I've forgotten the particulars of the first time I truly imagined killing Tempestra-Innara, only that I conceived the fantasy not long after arriving at the Dawn Cloister. And since then, my repertoire of daydreams has grown like a well-tended garden. The swift, brutal efficiency of decapitation. The slow sensuality of exsanguination. Defenestration (through the Cathedral's stained glass windows, of course). Evisceration. Immolation. Stuff there isn't a fancy word for. I've even dreamed of blanketing their bound and helpless form with angry scorpions—indulgent and impractical, but what fantasy isn't?

Especially as none of those things would kill a goddess.

But that sensibility never limited my imaginings, the treachery I keep deeply interred in the soil of my thoughts. A secret, with consequences, that I always knew to be impossible.

Until now.

I remember thinking at my communion, as Tempestra-Innara readied to bless me with the gift of their divinity, that it made no sense that a goddess could bleed. But they can, and they do—in great dark torrents, crimson sheeting from their wounds to the Cathedral floor.

I want to smile. To *laugh*. But . . . consequences.

Screaming, on the other hand, is just fine. *I* don't scream, but others certainly do, chaos spreading as quickly as the dark pool at the Goddess's feet. Yet, none of the devoted run. Whether it's loyalty or simply shock winning over fear in their meaty little minds, I don't know, but the crowd is nearly frozen in place as Emmaus continues his assault. I count the Cathedral Guard among them, not exactly surprising, their ranks being almost as ceremonial as our armor.

"Protect the Goddess!"

Prior Petronilla's desperate command is the blade, honed by years, that finally cuts through everything else. Instinctively, I draw my sickles from their scabbards on my back. Unlike my armor, they are most definitely *not* for show, curved silver with ebony hilts, not even a hint of flashiness. I tear off my ridiculous, vision-limiting helm and toss it away as Morgan appears beside me, spear raised and ready. But it's the Demon of the Dusk Cloister who attacks first, absolutely heedless as they launch themselves over the balustrade. Morgan does the same, with me in her wake. For a heartbeat, there is only the plunge to the Cathedral floor, and the horrific creature that waits below.

Emmaus is gone. His body is blacked, completely enveloped by the greasy darkness he released. Too late I realize it's sprouted more grisly appendages, barely missing one as my feet strike stone. I roll out of its reach; a cry tells me Morgan isn't so lucky. Oh well. In the Cloisters, there is no room for weakness, and I wouldn't have wasted the time to check on her if I had it.

Which I don't. Another black tentacle slices in my direction. I leap aside and collide with a stone pillar as I make my own cut, blades plunging into the darkness. Foul fluid sprays, coating me. The rational part of my mind tries to make sense of the creature—looks like sludge, cuts like flesh, and smells like death in a trash pile at the height of summer. I choke, unable to breathe through the reek of it, twisting around the pillar in a desperate attempt at reprieve.

I'm going to puke.

Then I'm going to *die*, loosing my guts onto the floor of the Cathedral. A ridiculous way to go. But even that embarrassing coherence slips away as I frantically wipe at the nasty ichor with the backs of my hands. Every second carries the tight expectation of a blow, or straight up death, but when I finally clear enough of the fluid away to take an almost-clean breath, I'm still alive. I breathe through my mouth, suppressing the indescribably foul taste of it on my tongue as I peek around the pillar. On the dais, the horrific darkness has coiled itself around Tempestra-Innara's neck, but the Goddess is fighting back now, fingers clawing, skin pale as old snow.

They live. They still fight.

Which—*fuck*—means I have to too.

My hands tighten around my sickles as I step out from behind the pillar. Slaughter spreads before me, bodies strewn across the floor—devotees, Cathedral Guard, two Priors, a Dusk Potentiate. More that I can't see. The rest of my blood brethren stand to fight, though the crowd has snapped out of their shock, screaming in terror as they rush the doors. But the Cathedral exit is locked, trapping them.

"Protect the Goddess!" Prior Petronilla's cry comes again, a reminder that the crowd is not my concern. Still, I lunge as a dark appendage wraps around a nearby devotee. I am too far away to reach him before it contracts, rending the man in two, releasing a wet slop of viscera. I slash at the tentacle. It retracts briefly before attacking again. Not me, though. One of the Dusk Potentiates—the Demon. They evade it easily, dismembering the unctuous blackness almost casually before pressing closer to the apse, and the Goddess.

But they don't see the other appendage replacing it, coming from behind.

"Demon, look out!"

By some miracle, they hear me and react, throwing themselves to one side. The tentacle scores only a glancing blow, connecting with their helm and sending it flying, revealing a dark-haired, pale-complexioned young man beneath. His face is calm, determined—way more than it should be given the nightmarish scene. Singularly focused, he cuts the second appendage away and twists back toward Tempestra-Innara.

I don't get a chance to do the same. Another tentacle appears, forcing me to vault over the gutted devotee, putting me closer to the Emmaus-monster. I don't bother with the flailing limbs. They seem mindless, and endless. Their source is the real enemy. Except how can I kill something when I don't have the slightest clue what it is? *Where was the lesson for this?* I want to throw at Prior Petronilla. Over a decade of learning and training, and right now, all of it seems as helpful as the wet entrails caking my boots.

Through the melee, I catch a glimpse of Morgan. She is on her feet but barely, putting no weight on her left leg as she stabs desperately at the dark entity with her spear. To me, her survival rates about as highly as the Goddess's, but two can do more damage than one, so I work my way in her direction.

Then, I am struck. I fly through the air, something at least semi-vital crunching as I collide with a pillar and fall to the floor.

The world blacks for an instant. Or maybe longer, I have no damn idea. When the fuzziness subsides, I am staring into Jeziah's face.

But he's not staring back. His eyes are blank with death, blood pooling beneath his dislodged fox helm.

*Dammit.*

I need to get up. Need to fight. But understanding floods me. Whatever horror Emmaus has unleashed, we are powerless against it. *Weak.* We cannot save the Goddess, and we can't save ourselves.

Which leaves two options: Keep up a futile defense and die. Or don't, and also die.

Shit choices. I pull myself up, mainly because it will piss me off for eternity if Jeziah's corpse is the last thing I see in this life. Back on my feet, I raise my blades again and take a steadying breath.

Then I let go. The pandemonium fades into a muted buzz as I allow my body to do what it's been molded to do. My eyes find the one thing in this world that matters: Tempestra-Innara.

My Goddess.

My blood mother.

My godsdamned curse.

A third choice emerges, one for me alone: the desire to see them fall before I do.

But the Goddess doesn't succumb. Despite the darkness piercing them, attempting to rip their body to pieces, Tempestra-Innara no longer looks wan—they look *pissed*. Their hands have ceased their frantic tearing, righteous anger blossoming on their delicate features. As I watch, the light of them grows from an intangible aura to a true one, and I sense what is coming just in time to abandon my current plan and attempt to get as far away as possible.

Emmaus's corpse wasn't slated for decorative purposes. Had the execution gone as planned, Tempestra-Innara's divine flame would have engulfed him, consumed him until there was nothing left but ash. The Goddess turns that power on the monster Emmaus has become, starting with the appendages assaulting them. The flame ripples down those dark tentacles like fire over an oil spill, spreading with a desperate fury unlike any I have witnessed before. I stumble back, nearly blinded by the brightness, pain exploding as my skin begins to singe. A new scream sounds. It is not human. I don't know what it is, except that it comes from the roiling darkness, and that it comes as a relief.

Human or not, I know a death cry when I hear it.

When the flames subside—only after the scream does—I am on the ground again, dizzy with the energy still crackling in the air. Where Emmaus used to be there is nothing but a smoking pile of pallid gray ash. And standing above that heretic-turned-horror-turned-dust-pile is Tempestra-Innara. They appear calm, save for their breath, which is slightly faster than normal. Their formerly white garment is shredded and looks as if it's been used to mop the floor of a slaughterhouse. For a long minute, they stare at the ash. Then down at their wounds, which are still bleeding freely.

By the normal conventions of flesh, such injuries wouldn't be survivable. But divinity has its own rules. As I watch, the Goddess takes a deep breath and closes their eyes. A moment later, the wounds begin to close. Soon, they are gone completely.

During the healing, the crowd has ceased its panic, cautiously loosening again. The faces among it are a mélange of confusion, fear, relief, and pure, completely unhindered devotion. I see similar expressions on my blood brethren. The ones who are still alive, at least. I can't help but glance back at Jeziah, and spot Morgan, only steps away. She's on the ground as well, face covered in blood, with what appears suspiciously like a bit of bone poking through her left shin. Catching me looking, Morgan sneers.

She's fine.

Getting to my feet again, I seek out the Demon. He's alive, on his feet, and ridiculously unruffled despite being as painted with gore as I am, with eyes only for our blood mother.

A relieved silence settles throughout the Cathedral.

Tempestra-Innara's divine light still burns.

*Yay.*

I shove the disappointment as deep as it will go, sure the Goddess will look my way and spot the betrayal in my face. But they only gaze over the crowd of survivors, most of whom have fallen to their knees, whispered prayers forming on their trembling lips. The people wait; for what, I'm not sure. An explanation, a blessing, a dinner recommendation for one of Lumeris's many fine establishments . . . it doesn't matter, so long as it comes from the Goddess.

Instead, framed by the golden wall of bones, the Goddess sighs sadly and raises one hand. "I am so very, very sorry."

I don't understand what is happening until I hear the first choking gasp. Within heartbeats, it spreads, racing through the crowd, an unstoppable wave of death.

And I can only watch as, one by one, the devoted drop to the ground, dead.

# Three

The truest moment of devotion comes in our very last, when Death arrives, but faith in the flame still burns bright... Not darkness, but light, will ferry us into our peaceful rest.

—FROM THE WRITINGS OF CLERIC LEANDRO,
HIGH CLERIC OF THE BLOOD

**T**HE RIDE BACK TO the Dawn Cloister is awkward, to say the least. Especially given the complete lack of explanation that precedes Prior Petronilla ordering us away from the massacre and into our carriage. Three were needed to carry us to the Cathedral; one suffices now, though it's a tad snug.

And smelly. Morgan and I are caked with the remains of the encounter, and even with the windows thrown open, it's nearly unbearable. I almost feel bad for the younger Potentiates, whom Prior Petronilla held back from the fight, preventing what would have surely been more empty seats. Almost immediately, Reia, the youngest allowed to attend today, begins to cry.

Morgan slaps her, the sharp snap of flesh on flesh breaking the heavy silence.

"Stop sniveling." It's impressive how intimidating Morgan manages to make herself while pale and sweating, leg wound hastily bandaged and probably pure agony. And yet, no obstacle to being a colossal bitch. "You're lucky the Prior isn't here to see you."

"Don't listen to her." I don't look at either of them as I speak, watching out the window as the skeletal stretch of Cathedral complex recedes behind us: its skirt of imposing bone-white walls, around which the gilded structures of Lumeris cling; the pointed tower where the Goddess dwells; and the fire that glows at its golden pinnacle—always lit, always burning. The Enduring Flame. "The smell would make anyone's eyes water."

"What . . ." Reia, barely fourteen, sniffles. "What *was* that?"

Morgan raises her hand again, but I grab her wrist and hold it, eyeing her askance. *Daring* her. Scowling, she shakes free, but doesn't try to strike again.

"Heresy." I reply to Reia's question the way the clerics would. That handy, all-purpose answer that explains exactly fuck all about what just happened. Because there's only two things I'm sure about right now.

The first—a conclusion punctuated by the corpses of a few hundred devotees—is that Reia is better off not asking questions. That whatever happened wasn't meant to be seen.

Which also serves to confirm my second conclusion: that Emmaus not only tried to assassinate Tempestra-Innara, but nearly succeeded.

The Dawn Cloister is as heavy and dark as Lumeris is ethereal and light. And yet, a welcome sight. The moment we stop, I throw open the door of the carriage and begin shedding the pieces of my armor in the stable yard—leaving them for the attendants to gather, clean, whatever—driven inside by one thought and one thought only:

A bath.

My sickles I keep close, though, sheathed on my back, despite an itch to hold them. Once I'm through the nearest archway, thick stone walls douse the noise of our return with cold silence. Unlike the gilded, ornate Cathedral and matching sprawl of Lumeris, the Dawn Cloister is austere in decoration. Still, plenty of statues of my Potentiate predecessors lurk in niches and corners throughout. They have nothing to say as I blow past them, lucky enough to be immune to the pungent scent I bring. I bypass the wing that houses our cells, the classrooms and training halls, not slowing until I feel the air around me begin to turn warm and damp. Isolated in the hills, a few hours' ride from the Cathedral, the Dawn Cloister doesn't have a lot of amenities one might call luxurious. But there is a system of natural hot springs that feed its baths. Minerally steam fills my nostrils as I enter a bathing chamber, making sure to bar the door before stripping off my ruined uniform and plunging into the heated waters.

There, finally, I begin to shake.

Today, I almost watched the Goddess die.

For some indeterminable amount of time, this is the only thought in my mind as I stand in the center of the sunken pool, hypnotized by the tendrils of steam snaking off the water's surface. Only when the smell begins to get to me again do I reach for a bar of soap and scrub furiously until the last of the foul ichor is gone. Then, slowly, I sink, descending until entirely submerged. Strands of wine-red hair swim across my blurred vision, a reminder of my gift. I'd begun dyeing it years ago, inspired by devotees I'd spied during a period when the color was in fashion. Eventually, I stopped, but it kept growing that hue all the same, a quirky—but far from unique—side effect of being one of Tempestra-Innara's Chosen. Jeziah arrived at the Dawn Cloister with wrists ringed by vivid black tattoos that betrayed an origin among the nomads of the northern Riverlands. If he'd remained with them, those tattoos would have climbed until they reached his collarbone. Instead, as time passed, the ink faded to the barest ghosts, though he still covers them when he can.

*Covered* them. My gut clenches briefly, but whatever grief I owe Jeziah can't stand against the confounded numbness.

The divine gift can affect us in the same way the Goddess can affect the world—altering it, molding it, locking the only door to safety—albeit in simpler, smaller ways. But I'd never imagined anything—divine or created by human hands—resulting in what happened to Emmaus. My hand goes to my reverie, made of solid gold, still yoked around my neck by its chain despite the tumult of the battle. What could possibly turn someone into an unimaginable horror in a matter of seconds, while be secreted in such a small vessel? Why would Emmaus ingest it willingly?

And—most important—how powerful was it to make Tempestra-Innara *afraid*?

I surface on my back, floating as I scour the events of the execution as thoroughly as I did my skin. The battle and subsequent slaughter are insignificant.

Emmaus's change.

Tempestra-Innara's fear.

These are the moments I come back to.

These are the moments that set me shaking again. Not because of what Emmaus did, but because it *could* be done. For years, I've imagined inflicting every sort of death imaginable on the Goddess, knowing all along that my thoughts were impossibilities. That nothing I could do would even scratch their power. The Goddess was untouchable—endless—and because of that, so was my fealty to them.

I sink beneath the water again.

For years, I'd secretly denied my inescapable servility. Loathed it. And then finally, despite my plentiful murderous daydreams, I'd accepted it. Now Emmaus had gifted me with the one thing I'd never been able to imagine: hope.

Tempting, teasing, impossibly cruel *hope*.

And because of that, shrouded within the warm, wet womb of the bath, I begin to scream.

# *Four*

There is no greater honor in this existence than to be chosen by the Goddess to become part of them, one of their own. We are their children. They are our mother. They care for us. We serve them. There is no greater honor.

—THE SAME SPEECH PRIOR PETRONILLA
GIVES ALL THE NEW POTENTIATES

I WAS A GIFT.
 A fucking *gift*.
Presents should be things like a knit sweater or a really good knife, not a dozen shivering children torn from their homes, kneeling on a cold stone floor before a golden ossuary. But that's what we were, each plucked from obscurity by one of the Goddess's Chosen—in my case, a Bellator whose name I never learned. My journey to the Cathedral? Barely remember it, a blur that only came into focus once I was added to the pack. I was heavy then, a creature of clay, hollowed out by the circumstances of my acquisition.

That at least meant I was quiet. Others were less stoic—there was a fair amount of sobbing and snot, though a few were ensorcelled by the sheer grandiosity of the Cathedral. As we waited, some part of me clarified, the idea of escape flickering, probably my first sharp thought in days. Which led my gaze to Alastair, the skull with the daggered eyes.

I wondered if the blades came free, and how far I might get wielding them. Stupid thoughts given the Chosen still surrounding us, any one of whom could have cut me down in the blink of an eye.

Then, Alastair began to move, the wall of bones sliding aside like a curtain.

I'd heard the stories of Tempestra-Innara, of course. But a goddess a thousand leagues away is not the same as a goddess so close you could spit on them. And as soon as they appeared, I understood. For the first time in my short, sheltered, upended life, I understood: I was a heretic. A sinner. And that the Goddess was truly, exceptionally divine.

It was an understanding that pissed me off like nothing since. Even more than when Morgan used to sneak shards of glass into my boots.

There were no introductions. No pesky orations about the offerings being made or where we came from. Only us, lined up before the apse like dolls, and Tempestra-Innara's penetrating presence. The Goddess examined each of us in turn, gliding down the row, silent as they gazed down at the terrified children at their feet. Most trembled. A couple fainted.

When they reached me, I expected death. That Tempestra-Innara would see the rage beneath my awe, the hate beneath the reverence.

But the Goddess only smiled. Reached down to brush the strands of filthy hair from my face. The brief contact nearly toppled me, their power a flooding, welcoming light out of the darkness, the warmth of the sun after a long, cold night. For the span of that brief caress, my fear, hunger, pain . . . gone. There was only the Goddess.

There was only their love.

The other children were taken away. I never saw any of them again.

And then, following my divine communion, I was ferried off to the Dawn Cloister.

The slamming of a door jolts me awake even as the dreamy sensation of godly fingers brushing my cheek lingers.

Night has fallen. I am in my cell, alone. The door is locked and bolted.

I hadn't expected to fall asleep.

I probably shouldn't have. I don't need as much sleep as most, but years of structured training has conditioned me to take rest, sustenance, and advantage whenever I can.

I throw my blanket aside and pad across the worn carpet.

Someone is in the corridor, their steps as angry as they are uneven. I slide open the door's narrow viewing port. The hall is dim, only a few oil lamps lit this late at night. A figure cuts across my view: Morgan. Wherever she's come from, she's pissed. So much so that she doesn't catch me spying as she stops abruptly before her door and slams a fist against the wood. It creaks painfully. When her arm drops, there's a fresh, fist-sized divot in it. Only then does Morgan wrench the handle open and enter, the next slam likely waking whoever the first one didn't.

There's only one place she could have come from at this hour, in that mood.

Prior Petronilla must be back.

Questions.

After the shock of the execution, after my thoughts stopped being wild things rampaging through my mind, that's what I was left with: questions. None of which I had answers for.

But I knew who might.

I knock on the door to Prior Petronilla's office. At first, there's no response, but a thin line of light betrays the room's occupancy. As does the smothering incense the Prior insists on burning day and night. Burnt orange and peppery clove. Wood resin. A scent that I will associate with being in trouble until the day I die.

Finally: "Enter."

The Prior blinks at me as I do. "Lys." Her voice is flat, betraying nothing. "I didn't call for you yet."

Yet? *Shit.* That means she already planned on summoning me, something that, historically, has never been to my benefit. Still, I smile. "Thought you might want some company."

She sighs with irritation. "Sit."

I plunk onto the hard wood bench set before her desk. The one that completes the sensation of impending punishment. Prior Petronilla's office is the most unwelcoming yet warmly appointed room I've ever been in. Thick, hand-knotted rugs, a wall of books, exquisite tapestries—it's like camouflage for a snare. There is only one thing I like about it, one part I've even, on occasion, manufactured my own chastisement in order to see: the huge framed map on one wall, the most detailed I have ever seen of the Devoted Lands.

Lumeris sits southwest of center on the lumpy potato of a continent, the Ordained Cities forming a rough circle around the capital. Aerdis for the Bellators, Pirga for the Priors, Siscia, where the Clerics of the Blood commune, and—smallest of them all, more fortress than city—Osturan, where the Arbiters reign. I'd find myself in one of them soon enough, baptized into whatever Order Petronilla decides to burden with me, before being shuffled off to one of the countless smaller cities and towns scattered beyond. These thin out the farther the map reaches, leading to a jagged diagonal of islands along the southern coast, tangled river marshes to the north, the swells and clefts of countless valleys and hills, and, finally, to the very fringes of the Devoted Lands, including a cluster of sharp peaks where a Bellator once kidnapped a broken little girl.

But it's not what I can see on the map that sparks my interest, but rather what I can't—the world that lies beyond its edges, in those sparse, vaguely sketched spots slipping beneath the polished wooden frame. Places untouched—unfettered—by the Goddess's light, beyond their reach.

And mine.

Unbalanced by my semi-expected arrival, I sit in silence and wait to be addressed, but the Prior only stares at me, expression one part contemplative, one part sourpuss. If she'd already planned to have me here, it *must* be about what happened in the Cathedral. And yet, I get the sense she's disappointed. As if *I've* disappointed her. Not sure how, though. I survived, didn't I? That's one up on Jeziah and the others.

I get tired of waiting. "I want to know what happened this morning."

She leans back in her chair, exhaling bitterly. "Of course you do."

No explanation follows. "Do *you* even know?"

That snaps the fire into her eyes, more the Prior Petronilla I'm used to seeing on the other side of that desk. "Tread lightly, Lys. Your insolence is the last thing I need right now." But her anger recedes almost immediately. "A tragedy. That's what happened this morning. The heretic, prior to his execution, managed to release a powerful poison into the Cathedral. Only those with our blessing survived it."

It's exactly the sort of horseshit explanation I was expecting regular folks to get, but not me.

"Oh, of course. One of those rare, dismembering poisons. *Hate* those."

Her annoyance flashes again. "This is no joking matter, Lys. What happened was . . ." She stops, unsettled. Which is unusual enough to unsettle *me*. "This is what is important right now: Andronica is dead."

"Yeah, I saw the pieces."

"Andronica is dead," she repeats more forcefully, "which means the Dawn Cloister needs to put up a candidate for Executrix."

"Already? You'd think they'd at least give her body a chance to cool—"

"Quiet." She doesn't sound mad now. More . . . tired. "There will be mourning, but the Goddess has requested candidates *immediately*." Her eyes lock with mine. "Jeziah and the other senior Potentiates are dead. Morgan is injured, and the others are too young and untrained. That leaves you."

I laugh, a little snort, totally unintentional. Partially out of surprise, more because that's the last godsdamned thing I care about right now. Though it does explain Morgan's tantrum. "So put up Morgan. She'll be kicking down walls in a week, maybe—"

"This isn't a request, Lystrata." The words snap like a switch. "There is no time to wait for Morgan to heal. Tomorrow you will accompany me to the Cathedral. There, you will conduct yourself as nobly as a Potentiate of the Dawn Cloister should, and serve the Goddess as they order."

Resignation sneaks into her tone by the end. I sympathize. The only person who wants me to be the Cloister's candidate less than Prior Petronilla is *me*. And maybe Morgan.

"No," I say.

"Excuse me?"

"No. Not until you tell me what really happened."

Silence simmers. I try to read her eyes, but I'm not sure I like what I see. It's more than the usual frustration, for sure. But then again, I did just refuse to serve the Goddess, which definitely borders on sacrilege. There are plenty of lines I've crossed since coming to the Cloister, but for the first time, I wonder if I've gone a smidge too far.

Then, the hardness in her gaze softens. "Why do you let Morgan beat you?"

"Excuse me?"

"In your training. You almost always let her win. Why?"

I cross my arms. "Don't know what you're talking about."

"You do. As much a pain in the ass—in *my* ass—as you are, Lys, you are a more than competent Potentiate. Impressive, even. But you hold back. You *hide*, both in your physical training and in your educational examinations. I tolerated it because your potential didn't make up for your insolence. And because I never expected to be in a position like this."

"Morgan beats me fair and square all the time." But not always. It's a lesson I learned early on—being the best means you're the one everyone is trying to knock down. We all serve the Goddess, but that doesn't mean we aren't encouraged to try to serve a little better than the next Potentiate. Failure results in punishment, sometimes even death. But so does success. Jeziah and I both understood that, which was about two-thirds of the reason for our "friendship." Best to be near the top, but not *on* top. Not if you wanted to survive long enough to leave this place. "She's a better fighter than me. If anyone should be Executrix, it's her."

"Yes." The Prior folds her hands in front of her. "But that's not a possibility right now, and this is not a negotiation. And, frankly, if I could punish you for turning it into one, I would. But I don't have that luxury. So, know this: If you wish to learn more about what happened at the Cathedral, you will accept this path. *This* is your responsibility. *This* is the Goddess's will. There is no other."

Her meaning is crystal clear. To refuse again will be regarded as blasphemy. At least this shows that she doesn't suspect me of anything more than my usual obstinance, that she hasn't picked up on my penchant for imagined deicide any more now than in the past.

I let out a breath. "The Goddess's will it is." The words taste sour in my mouth.

*Executrix.* Bound even closer to Tempestra-Innara than I already am. Not exactly what I had in mind.

Assuming I get the job. Because the Dusk Cloister will be putting up a candidate too, and there's no telling how good theirs will be. The two of us will be tested, pushed to our limits, pitted against one another—and probably end up with a few chances to whittle two candidates down to one. More often than not, the choice for Executrix isn't really a decision—it's based on whoever is left standing. But this is how I've been tasked to serve the Goddess.

It is also, apparently, my only chance to learn how to escape them.

"Cheer up," I say to Prior Petronilla, who still looks like she's had to swallow something rotten. "At least this means you'll be rid of me, one way or another."

# Five

Prior. Bellator. Arbiter. Cleric of the Blood. Each calling has its own esteem, its own distinctions. But Executrix—its call must be answered by only the finest of our blood brethren. For they serve at the Goddess's side, acting as their hand, their blade, and, when necessary, their executioner.

—*EDICTS OF THE BLOOD*, 3RD EDITION

**I AM EVER SO KINDLY** allowed the last few hours before dawn to prepare myself. Which means I'm ready to go early, since there's nothing for me to do besides put on a clean uniform and give my sickles one last going over to make sure there's no crusty bits of Emmaus left on them. (There are a few. Ick.)

The Cloister stable yard is shadowed and silent, save for the faint tread of my steps across the cobbles, enough to alert the horses, who nicker a faint greeting as I enter. Stall by stall, I pat their muzzles as I pass, choosing two of the draft horses to draw the carriage Prior Petronilla and I will use. Attendants' work, but I'm not cruel enough to wake them hours before they need to gather for morning prayers. My fellow Potentiates will follow suit a little after that . . . or not, I suppose. I picture that daily gathering, erasing familiar faces I've seen strained with effort, twisted by anger, broken and bleeding. When I get to Jeziah, his features are laughing. A lump forms in my throat. I swallow it and get the horses hitched, even if it risks a chastising from the Prior for "lowering myself."

I lead them into the yard to wait. The silence turns immediately oppressive, my thoughts flipping to and fro between getting stuck as the Dawn Cloister's candidate for Executrix and the possibility that it will lead me to answers about how Emmaus nearly eviscerated Tempestra-Innara. A smile touches my lips. At least *that* thought is a warming one.

Instinct throws me to the side a split second before a spear embeds itself in the wood of the stable wall next to me. There, it quivers with disappointment.

I draw my sickles and calmly turn toward its source. "The proper response is 'Congratulations.'"

Morgan is about as furious as I've ever seen her. Which is saying something. "*I* should have been offered."

"Yeah, well, next time our blood mother is attacked, make sure not to choke during the rescue."

"I didn't—" She wisely cuts herself off. Morgan may have dumped me on my ass in training plenty of times, but she knows better than to engage me in a war of words. "You don't deserve to be a candidate for Executrix."

No, I don't. "Take it up with Prior P. Or try to kill me again. But I'm warning you, I'm gonna make a run for it. Think you can keep up on that leg?"

For a moment, I *do* think she's going to come at me again. She's practically vibrating with fury, not the focused, calculating Morgan I'm used to facing here in the yards. I almost consider telling her that I agree with her. But she did just try to kill me, so fuck her feelings.

"Go back to bed." I lower my sickles but don't put them away. "You do your holy duty and I'll do mine. Just like we're supposed to, right?"

Morgan scowls, but she's done. The decision made is the Goddess's will, and one murder attempt is as much insurrection as she plans today. "May the Goddess see the truth about you—your weakness and unworthiness." With that, she turns away and limps back into the Cloister, and the night.

But her words hang in the air. *May the Goddess see the truth about you . . .*

I hope not. Because if they ever do, what happened to Emmaus will look like a mercy.

In a dim chamber off the chilly corridors that worm their way beneath the Cathedral complex, the bodies of the divine dead lay on stone tables, shrouded in white linen. All except for their faces, where a single thin strip has been laid across their eyes. There's something impossibly still about them, less than even meat now, no more life in them than the statues in the Cathedral's halls above. The twinge in my stomach has returned, digging deeper this time. With the exception of Jeziah, I can't claim to *care* about the deaths of my fellow Potentiates, but there's an unfairness that nags. An injustice. None of them had any more choice about their fate than I did, even if they embraced it. And now they are dead before fulfilling the purpose they strove so hard for, robbed of two lives instead of just one.

The reason for that stands above them, a thin trickle of tears running down their cheeks.

I have never seen the Goddess cry. Never seen them like this. It's odd, almost obscene, an unmooring sensation that buffets me in the wake of their usual swell of divinity. I know they are our blood mother, that we are referred to as their children, but that holy parenting is mostly absentee, the Cloisters doing the real work to beat us into proper shape, both figuratively and literally. So, the tired sadness in their face is unexpectedly visceral.

A Bellator Prime, High Cleric of the Blood, Prior Superior, and a Senior Arbiter—the chosen among the Chosen—watch the Goddess. I watch them, mainly the Arbiter, whose very presence crawls through the chamber. Her eyes are milky white, the color leached from them like a cloak washed too many times, along with most of her sight. It's the effect of decades of judgements, fueled by the cordial the Arbiters drip into their eyes, the one that allows them to see truths within someone. They can't exactly read thoughts, but they can ascertain whether a person's devotion and love for Tempestra-Innara is true. Or if it's not, and that person is a heretic.

I've always found the whole concept unsettling, and right now, it's damn near unnerving. If passing an Arbiter's judgement is part of the evaluation to become Executrix, this little party may be over with real quick.

But so far Prior Petronilla's and my arrival has been ignored. The vigil continues—the Arbiter stays on her side of the room; I stay on mine.

And the Goddess mourns.

A pale, graceful hand rises and falls, brushing a cooled cheek. My innards quiver, jealous of the touch. It's a sickening bliss, the memory of which tightens around my throat. Then, my muscles stiffen as a different thought rises to combat that desire: the Goddess laid out like the corpses before me, eyes covered, marble cold. I banish it, the fantasy too dangerous to entertain. Not here, not now.

Steps approach. I practically pounce on the distraction, turning to find a robed Prior and—will today's surprises never cease—the Demon. Now the Dusk Cloister's candidate for Executrix, apparently. Up close and not covered in gore, he's what Jeziah would have called *fetching* (or perhaps *tasty*), with an alabaster complexion and dark hair swept to one side in a rakish style that doesn't quite match his quiet serenity. I scan him head to toe; he ignores me completely.

Guess he's not too concerned with his competition.

"Forgive us for making you wait, my Goddess." The Dusk Prior sounds genuinely remorseful.

Meanwhile, Prior Petronilla oozes satisfaction, as if this is the first test in choosing the next Executrix, and we've scored the point.

"Forgiven." The word is tiny, barely carrying despite the quiet chamber. Tempestra-Innara caresses Jeziah one last time before turning their attention our way. Once again, their divine light washes over me, a drink I cannot get enough of. One I would joyfully drown in. Yet, when the Goddess moves closer, out of the shadows, some cling, darkening the skin beneath their eyes with a markedly human fatigue. But the tears are gone now, disappeared, though I never saw them wiped away.

"I apologize for summoning you here so quickly," the Goddess continues, "but grave matters call for grave haste. Priors of the Cloisters—which of my children have you brought me?"

Prior Petronilla begins first, as if our prompt arrival has earned that right. "The Dawn Cloister presents your honored and gifted daughter Lystrata."

"Lys," I correct. Lystrata may be my full name, but it's not the one I hear in the few memories that remain from before I arrived in Lumeris. *Lys*, those whisper. Always just *Lys*. Prior Petronilla immediately shoots me a look of horror, as if I've just dropped my pants to shit on the floor. And maybe I have, figuratively, but if there's no unringing that bell, might as well make sure it was heard. "My name is Lys."

The Goddess smiles faintly. "Lys, yes."

I tremble as my name passes over their lips, suddenly wishing I hadn't made the correction, dipping my head deferentially to hide the discomfort.

As pissed as Petronilla undoubtedly is, the Goddess moves on without any sign they share that sentiment. "And this one?"

Now the Dusk Prior is the one who seems bloated with confidence. "The Dusk Cloister presents your honored and gifted son Nolan."

*Nolan.* He proves he's smarter than me right off by keeping his mouth shut. Instead, he gazes at the Goddess with a wide-eyed, unbroken stare, overflowing with devotion.

Great. A suck-up for sure.

The Goddess nods. "My children. A new Executrix must be anointed, and you, as the finest of your Cloisters, have been chosen to prove yourselves worthy of that appointment. In the past, this has meant setting your abilities against one another." They pause. "But I am afraid the events of yesterday have invariably altered that course. Now, contrary to the usual evaluations, what I must ask you to do now is something entirely different: to work together."

My jaw tightens. Work... together? What does *that* mean? Winning the position of the Executrix has always meant exactly that—winning. Being stronger, faster, stabbier. I have *many* questions, but the Goddess's mention of the slaughter in the Cathedral keeps them tangled up on my tongue. It also confirms that Prior Petronilla was playing straight with me when it comes to learning more about the whole affair. So, I muster one of my least practiced skills: patience.

Which is a good thing because, once again, no explanation follows. Instead, the Goddess heads for one of the arched doorways. "Follow, please."

We do, a line of somber ducklings in order of importance, the silent quartet of my most senior blood brethren falling in behind the Goddess first, then the Cloister Priors, and finally Nolan and me. I steal another look at him, but his attention is still for the Goddess and nothing else. A sword is belted at his waist, a heavy, brutal thing without an ounce of subtlety. It's the same weapon he used against the Emmaus-monster, and he seemed to be handy with it, so I'm not exactly disappointed that we aren't headed for hand-to-hand combat.

As to where we *are* headed . . .

The deeper we go into the Cathedral, the more the ornate trappings fade, the lower the vaulted ceilings grow. They press down, ancient and heavy, chalky spots of niter clinging to the bare stone, a vague dampness scenting the air. It's too dark here for even our divinely blessed eyesight, but the Goddess has that covered. Lamps set into niches light as we pass and extinguish behind us. Black in front, black behind, our steps barely echoing, as if the darkness is absorbing all signs of life down here. It's enough to make me miss the corpse room.

Finally—a door. Solid iron, it's heavily riveted, with no handle, no keyhole, and absolutely nothing to indicate what might lie behind it. The Goddess presses a palm to it; the heavy clunk of some mechanism disengaging follows, and the door creaks open. Slightly anticlimactically—beyond the portal is even *more* darkness.

The Goddess enters. Nolan and I wait for the others to follow, but instead they step aside.

"Come," the Goddess calls. "They will wait."

Definitely not the most encouraging of invitations. What's inside that a couple of lowly Potentiates are allowed to see, that the most elevated of the Goddess's Chosen aren't? I risk a glance at Nolan. There's no fear in his features, no emotion at all save for a slight thinning of his lips to show he might be having some apprehensive thoughts too. Which is only smart, given we're being invited into the sort of chamber that feels as if an exit isn't always guaranteed. But that's where the Goddess is, and the Goddess has answers.

Fuck it.

I go ahead of him with a haste that I'm sure makes Prior Petronilla proud, letting the darkness swallow me. I hear Nolan follow. He's savvy enough in the dark to make his way to one side of me, the sound of his breathing the only orientation I have.

Again, the door creaks, and what's left of the light disappears as it closes behind us.

# Six

No, we don't render aid, more than a bit of water, and I'd call even that an indulgence. If they are strong, our mother has chosen well, and they will survive. If not, they are weak, and have no place among us.

—FROM THE PERSONAL CORRESPONDENCE OF PRIOR GREIN
(DUSK CLOISTER) TO PRIOR ILUA (DAWN CLOISTER)

**D**IVINITY CAME IN THE drowning deluge of a thin trickle. The moment it touched my lips, it surged into my base, human blood, blazing through my veins, leaving not a single corner of my flesh unchanged. And like a wildfire, it did its godsdamned best to destroy me. Being chosen wasn't a guarantee of elevation—there was also the trivial part about actually surviving the Goddess's gift, a trial no one bothered to warn of beforehand.

But I survived, waking to a feeling not unlike what I experience in the pure blackness of the Goddess's secret mystery chamber. Their presence saturates the air, turning the darkness into something almost alive, seething with power. It is disorienting, upending—only the sense of solid stone below my feet and the vague presence of Nolan keeps me grounded.

Then, light. Lamps, hundreds of them, ignite, their combined flickers sun-strong as they illuminate the chamber—round, domed, and larger than expected. Also, empty, save for a single pedestal in the center. On it sits the fanciest bottle I've ever seen, clear glass veined with delicate whorls of gold, and a stopper that appears to be a single ruby cut into the shape of a flame. No, not glass—rock crystal, utterly flawless. It's small, the sort of vessel that might hold perfume or scented oil, but I doubt the Goddess has dragged us all the way down here to show off their signature scent. Especially since the liquid it contains is a deep, vibrant red.

"There are secrets best kept hidden," Tempestra-Innara says, gliding over to the pillar, "and pieces of the past better off forgotten."

Oh, good. Another useless "explanation."

The Goddess picks up the bottle and it begins to glow, a cool, diffuse light that leaves no doubt that its source is rooted in the divine. But it isn't until the Goddess plucks the ruby free that I begin to understand.

Blood sings to blood.

"This, my children," they continue, complexion cooled by the otherworldly illumination, "is a reliquary." They speak the word with a mix of reverence and apprehension. "An ancient vessel created specifically for the blood of a divinity—*my* blood. A rarity now, but once quite numerous, long ago when my siblings still walked this land."

That gets my attention. Speaking of the old gods, except in regards to their defeat, isn't the usual casual conversation. And never once have I heard Tempestra-Innara bring them up. The last, Arcadius-Viktori, the Green God, was defeated by the Goddess over a century ago, in a battle that leveled the god's temple and most of the city around it, and whose ruins remain extremely *ruined* even now.

Tempestra-Innara returns the stopper to the bottle and the bottle to the pedestal. As soon as they release it, the glow fades. "We spread our blessings foolishly in those days, sending our reliquaries far and wide to share our gift. Unfortunately, there were those that saw that generosity as something to take advantage of, and consequences that we did not consider. Even after we became more . . . judicious in our gifts, divine blood was no longer the only coveted rarity. As you know, divinity does not fade with the death of the body. And there are some that practice a most vile form of heresy."

They don't say the word aloud: Renderers. I know all about those. It's practically a time-honored tradition for the older Potentiates to threaten the younger with giving them over to the Renderers. Hunters of the living blessed. Scavengers of the divine dead. A length of old bone, a flap of desiccated skin, coveted fresh blood—all rendered into concoctions that impart a taste of godliness to anyone willing to pay the price. Never mind that the effects are temporary, and punishable by things much less appealing than death.

"Our gift was not meant to fall into unworthy hands." The Goddess turns grim as they continue their increasingly opaque explanation. "I'd thought them all found, destroyed. It seems I was wrong." They reach out again, one finger caressing the crystal reliquary. "What power remains in the body of a god's Chosen is less than what they were gifted. And a vacated avatar is reduced to nothing more than ash by the changing. But it is not the same for the pure, collected blood of a living divinity. And while the blood does change when its god dies—decays in its own way—the raw power remains. Do you understand?"

Finally, enough points for me to draw the lines between. So that's how Emmaus nearly felled a goddess—takes one to kill one. Somehow, he got his hands on a reliquary, hid some blood in his reverie, and waited until he was within striking distance to chug it. My stomach tightens with disappointment.

"But . . ." I surprise myself by speaking, a papery whisper nearly lost in the expanse of the chamber. "What it did to him . . ."

Tempestra-Innara nods, mistaking my distress for horror. "Not all survive the gift of divinity when it is given true. Even less so when it is . . . polluted. But despite the corruption, it is still a powerful weapon. I suspect Emmaus fully knew what he was committing to, and that he did not expect to survive his act. I also suspect the power overwhelmed him faster than he thought it would. But though Emmaus was too weak to see the deed through," the Goddess finishes, "that does not mean the next assassin will be."

A shiver runs through me. *Weak.* With that one word the Goddess reignites my hope.

I start to speak again and stop, frozen by a new sight. A blossom of red has appeared on the Goddess's white gown, above one breast. As I watch, it spreads. From the slight tensing of the air beside me, I know Nolan has noticed it too.

Tempestra-Innara follows my gaze and lets out a small noise of annoyance. "It is a particularly wicked heresy to use such a foul weapon to strike. And yet, its damage is potent, and lingers." They raise a hand over the patch of blood. When it drops again, the stain is gone. "My children, as long as our enemies have the reliquary, they are a greater threat than ever before. But they will be wary now, keep it well hidden. Armies could tear apart the lands for years and find nothing. And so, instead of blades and bludgeons, I will send you."

For a moment, there's silence. Then Nolan shifts beside me and clears his throat, the most liveliness he's shown since arriving.

"Forgive me, Mother." He's almost sickeningly deferential. "But why us? You have many more experienced children."

"Whose name and faces may be known by our enemies," the Goddess replies. "As Potentiates, you are unfamiliar, and your youth means your gifts are still in their prime. Furthermore, you've both seen the tainted blood's power, fought against it, and survived. There is no one better suited to this task. So even though you would normally be rivals to become Executrix, I ask you to work together on this, as family." Tempestra-Innara moves closer to us, so close that their divine power is an engulfing bonfire. "Find the reliquary. Return it here, to me. It is a test that would prove either of you more than worthy, and a more consequential duty than any I have ever asked of my children before."

"Yes," Nolan says with urgent, devoted passion. "Whatever you wish, Mother."

"Whatever you wish," I echo. And it's actually the truth. The opium smoke of the Goddess's divinity has me ready to hunt, to kill, to stand on my head and recite dirty limericks if that would earn me more of their favor. I take a gulp of air, thick as syrup, trying to settle the yearning ache for more, more, more of them. At least that cursed desire muddies the profound giddiness growing beneath it.

Emmaus might have been weak, but *I* am not. *I* have already survived the divine gift. And Tempestra-Innara has just asked me to track down the one weapon I need to finally free myself from this drowning servitude.

Now I know how to hurt them.

Now I know the weapon of a goddess's destruction.

And not a godsdamned thing in existence is going to keep me from finding it.

# *Seven*

In death, in life, brethren.
Lay bone and blood together
With ash, and with all.

—FROM "AT REST," BY THE POET ANDRALLES

---

WHEN I DIE, I will be honored. No matter where the spark of my life is extinguished, tears will fall, garments will be rent, and my body will be prepared and borne to a place of honor: Cineris, the necropolis of the divine dead.

Of course, that's assuming I don't die a traitorous heretic, an increasingly likely possibility.

When the next morning arrives, I am still at the Cathedral, trussed up again in ceremonial armor and ready to help ferry my fallen brethren to their eternal rest. The armor has, thankfully, been cleaned, but there's enough of a lingering hint of monster goo that my breakfast churns. I adjust my rat helm, hoping for a little fresh air, but given the corpse-laden carts behind me, it's wishful thinking. The demon helm turns ever so slightly in my direction, and I wonder if that's Nolan's way of quietly admonishing my restlessness. Like me, he sits astride a horse, waiting for the funeral procession to begin.

After our little jaunt to the reliquary chamber, we didn't return to the Cloisters. Instead, Prior Petronilla deposited me in one of the

Cathedral guest wings, filled in a few logistical blanks about my new mission, then departed with a pleading "You must not fail" and an expression that definitely conveyed something more along the lines of *Don't fuck this up.*

So far, so good.

Nolan was already waiting when I arrived at the stables. There was a small fountain in one corner for the horses to drink from, and Nolan stood by it with his head bowed, reverie clasped in his fingers, lips moving silently in prayer. Only when I came within a few paces did he acknowledge me.

"Hey." I didn't know what else to say. I'd never spoken directly to anyone in the Dusk Cloister before—my shout of warning during the attack doesn't really count—and anyway, what's the proper greeting for someone you're about to embark on a quest for a god-slaying weapon with? "Ready to get this funeral rolling?"

That earned me a strange look followed by a carefully cordial "Good morning." Even stranger was waiting with him as the attendants fussed over the last of the equine preparations. He didn't seem inclined to conversation, and even if he had been, I don't know what could have been said.

Under normal circumstances, I'd expect attempts to unnerve me, maybe even a full-on goading. He'd likely have tried to find out every scrap of information about me—what areas I excel at, what weapons I handle best—as I did the same. Anything that might result in an advantage. Instead, we'd been given the same task, the same instructions, probably even the same breakfast. I wasn't sure where that left us. I hated that there even was an *us*. Only one of us could be Executrix in the end, and I couldn't help but be curious about what Nolan thought about that. Fortunately, once we took our position in the procession, small talk wasn't required.

Around us, in the shadow of the Cathedral, thousands of mourners had gathered, some clearly having traveled all night. More, I'm sure, would be on their way; after all, nothing spreads faster than bad news. No doubt Lumeris would be covered in a veil of mourning for days, if not weeks, to come, before it returned to its usual devoted, decadent self.

All of our blood brethren are honored in death, but the level of fanfare has risen to match the scale of their tragic ends. The Order of Cineri arrived sometime this morning, one representative for each body. They escort each cart, in black cassocks, black hoods, and bloodred masks molded with the vaguest of human features. Like Potentiates, they are anonymous, but in a much creepier way.

This is the only other path open to me, the only Order I can choose myself: babysitter of the dead. Never to leave Cineris, save to collect the occasional corpse. Not a chance. I can't imagine who would willingly put themselves in an even smaller cage. Already, the notion of being turned out into the Devoted Lands unsupervised has me itching with anticipation.

Nolan and I have been set at the front of the line of carts, an honor guard to represent our respective Cloisters. Beyond the carts is a contingent of Cathedral Guard, then a group of clerics—not of the Blood, but from the regular, lower orders, their hierarchy too convoluted to bother sorting out—praying like it's going out of fashion. The common mourners will be allowed to follow behind them, to show their respect as we escort the dead to their final place of rest.

Somewhere in the Cathedral, a horn sounds—a low, mournful note that spreads like a fog.

That's the signal.

We urge our horses forward. The pace we set is a slow one, respectful as we pass through the high gate of the Cathedral complex, into the streets of Lumeris. The city of light. Of the Flame. Nowhere else in the Devoted Lands does one find the beauty and artistry that makes up Lumeris. Poets have written entire tomes about the sweeping splendor of its streets, the sunset tones and gilded ornament of its buildings. I hate it. It is a predatory magnificence, a fat tick that feeds off an endless flow of tribute, drinks dry the pilgrims desperate to feel the warmth of divinity on their skin. I want to dig my heels into my horse, gallop out of the city and into the open landscape. But that's not exactly proper funeral etiquette. So, I keep in line with Nolan, gaze straight ahead, the creak of the wheels behind us a haunting reminder of when I first arrived at the Cathedral.

I was carried on a cart too. Alive, but barely.

There's not a soul in Lumeris who isn't on the streets watching us. A lot of hard, melancholy faces. A lot of tears and prayers. And a lot of empty rooms in the guesthouses we pass. My hands tighten on the reins. Somewhere, more bodies are lined up, hundreds of them, beginning to blacken, bloat, and leak. They won't be carefully washed and shrouded, or receive processions. They won't have mourners lining the streets for them. I wonder if any of them would be happy that they died in service to the Goddess, even if that service was only keeping a dangerous secret.

Probably. And that likelihood singes my very core.

I used to think about running. About leaving Lumeris and the Cloisters as far behind as I could. I'd remember the world beyond them, as little as I knew of it, and think: *They'd never find me.* I could disappear in the middle of the night, hunt and steal my way beyond the Devoted Lands, build a new life somewhere the addictive, toxic light of Tempestra-Innara couldn't touch.

I even tried it, once. A few years after I arrived at the Cloister, our training went thus: Enjoy a several-day ride in a cramped carriage, here's a knife, now go into the mountain woods for a week and don't die.

A perfect opportunity.

I felt the pull earlier than I realized. Really, within hours of leaving the land I knew behind, but it was so faint at first that I attributed it to nervousness, and later to the fact that I was trying to live on a diet of scavenged berries and bitter greens. But it grew, and I began to find myself looking backward, toward the way I'd come from. Toward the Cathedral. By the time the feeling reached an urgent sensation I simply couldn't ignore, I understood: I'd been bound to Tempestra-Innara in more ways than one. The farther away I got from the Goddess's light, the worse this feeling would grow. And that my blessing was more than a gift—it was a tether.

To this day, I wonder whether that test had less to do with survival than it did with the lesson I learned. Maybe I wasn't the only Potentiate who quietly balked against the lot that had been cast for me. Or maybe it was simply a demonstration of what we'd all have to contend with eventually, when we left the bosom of Lumeris for the Orders.

I wasn't foolish enough to ask. But it was about that time that my fantasies of deicide really began to flourish. Impossible, yes, but the last measure of satisfaction left to me. Because I finally understood that my only escape from the Goddess was that last, final escape whose procession I am now leading.

Thankfully, once we are beyond the city, we pick up the pace. A lightness takes me, still tinged with anxiety, but this is it—the beginning of *outside*. My divine shackles haven't been struck away, but the chain holding them has been let out a bit. It is very nearly the sense of freedom.

But not. And I can't let myself be fooled into thinking it is.

Cineris.

My first look at it is from a distance, sitting beneath a woolen ceiling of cloud that's appropriately somber for the occassion. The journey from the Cathedral to the necropolis takes most of the day, hours that pass with nothing but prayers and wails and the growing desire to violently silence both. So, it's a huge relief when I spot what appears to be a cluster of jagged black teeth punching up out of an unnervingly flat stretch of land.

The high, uneven walls of Cineris are obsidian dark, rough cut, and frankly unwelcoming. There is only one way in, a reinforced steel door that appears as if it would scoff at any battering ram in existence, even on its worst day. This is where the bodies of those blessed by Tempestra-Innara have been brought for centuries. It is a fortress of the dead—and a vault for the power still contained within them. Cineris doesn't pay even a passing thought to Renderers, even if they were so foolish as to creep this close to the Goddess.

At a certain point, the Cathedral Guard stop the crowd behind us from advancing any closer. Nolan and I continue, along with the Cineri and their carts. Only the divinely blessed—dead or alive—are allowed within the walls of Cineris. Nolan and I have barely stopped when the door opens. Beyond it are more of the necropolis's keepers, gloved hands folded in front of them. With a solemn gait, we move to either side of the entrance as, one by one, the wagons and their cargo enter. When that is complete, one figure steps forward.

"May the Flame warm you." A masculine voice sounds from behind the mask. "Before you enter, you must prove your divinity."

"The outfits aren't enough?" I knew what to expect, but it comes out anyway, because I am cranky after the ride and tired of chaperoning corpses. I also know this is part of the plan, that the Cineri has been prompted to admit us. Later, two riders wearing our armor will exit and return to the Cathedral. As far as anyone knows, all remaining Cloister Potentiates will be home by tomorrow, safe and accounted for.

The masked figure twists their fingers anxiously, thrown by my response.

Nolan comes to his rescue. "Of course." He holds up one hand and takes a breath. An instant later the flame appears—larger than any I've ever seen from a Potentiate, blazing nearly a foot off his palm.

"Impressive size," I say, to exactly zero reaction. Only a sense of annoyed impatience as Nolan extinguishes the display and the Cineri turns to me. "Okay, okay. But stand back and shield your eyes."

I hold out my hand and call. A rush of energy surges through me, every inch of my skin prickling with warmth as the light appears. What there is of it. It's an unimpressive flicker at best, rippling over the skin of my palm. Calling the flame is one of the few areas where I never have to feign ineptitude, but lucky for me, size doesn't matter when it comes to proving divinity.

The man moves aside. "Welcome, blood brethren."

And with that, I enter Cineris in the last way I ever expected to: alive.

# Eight

The fade is slow. But as it does for all things of bone and blood, it inevitably arrives. For flesh, though made divine, is still human. And divinity burns so brightly that to transition to a new vessel leaves the first spent. Reduced to ashes, to dust, to a memory of glory. An avatar is divine. But Tempestra, only, is eternal.

—THE WRITINGS OF HIGH CLERIC OF THE BLOOD PALDRA

**B**EYOND THE GATE OF Cineris is a large half-moon courtyard, avenues leading off it like spokes from a wheel, long, narrow corridors of black stone. Once we are closed in, it feels almost oppressively silent, a sensation like lying inside an open grave. I immediately hate it. I'm not supposed to be here. Not yet.

"We have been prepared for you." Our host gestures to the avenue farthest to the right as we dismount. "Rooms are waiting with your supplies. You may leave your horses here; others will be furnished when you depart in the morning."

I start to follow.

"Wait." Nolan removes his demon helm. "The interments. Are they taking place now?"

The Cineri nods and points. Down one of the corridors, I spot the tail end of the cart train.

"I would like to pay my respects," he says. I want to tell him the show is over, but Nolan sounds genuinely emotional. "If that is allowed."

"Of course," says the voice behind the mask. "When you are ready, take the path I indicated. It will lead you to the living quarters."

Nolan begins walking without asking if I want to join him. As if I couldn't now, without looking like a jerk. I remove my helm and toss it to the attendant, then rush to catch up. Nolan doesn't slow. Quiet *and* rude, apparently.

"I suppose it wouldn't hurt to make sure Jeziah is really put to rest." My words sound too loud here. "He always was a bit of a prankster."

Nothing for the span of several more steps. Then: "I didn't realize the Dawn Cloister had time for jokes amid their training."

Sarcasm. Finally, a sign of humanity.

"We had time for both, I guess, if you count the time Jeziah poisoned my tea with an infusion we'd studied that week." It's not really funny—I was puking for two days straight—but I chuckle anyway. Nolan doesn't. Apparently, the Dusk Cloister kept things tight. "I got back at him by 'accidentally' breaking both his wrists during a sparring match. After that, we called a truce, more or less. Pranks from then on were less . . . incapacitating." Something tightens in my chest. "The Dusk Potentiates who died, were you . . . friends?" I'm not sure of the right word. Jeziah and I weren't really friends. But we weren't enemies either. Allies, maybe. Or familiar constants, who could fill each other's time with things other than attempted murder.

Again, Nolan doesn't respond right away. "Their names were Deena and Malachi. We were companions, in training and in study. That's all."

Of course not. No friends in the Cloisters. I take that measure of him and stick it away for future reference.

His step slows. "But both were smart, intensely devoted to our blood mother, and good soldiers. Their loss is a loss for all of us."

"Oh. Sorry." I fumble the second word, letting the silence return.

The thick walls of the corridor stretch high around us. Before we go far, inscriptions appear, set at regular intervals. I stop to examine one. Nolan is curious enough that he does the same.

*Ephrainn*, I read. *Fulfilled their duty in the thirty-eighth year of the incarnation of Tempestra-Oren.*

Crypts. We're surrounded by them.

"There's so many," I breathe. Hundreds in this corridor alone. Is this what the Goddess meant when they said they shared their gifts more freely in the past? I'd imagined hundreds, maybe even thousands had fallen in service to the Goddess . . . but this? When they said Cineris is a city of the dead, they weren't exaggerating.

"Yes," Nolan says simply. "Our honored brethren."

The corridor spills out into another spoked courtyard, smaller than the one by the gate. Here, the wagons have stopped. Two are already empty, and Nolan and I watch as the Cineri move with practiced efficiency, gingerly bearing a third body over to an open slot in the wall. After the journey with the tediously loud mourners, I expect some kind of prayer, but they work in utter silence, sliding the corpse into their final resting place before replacing the outer stone slab, sealing them up forever.

Nolan takes a deep breath and lets it out. "They didn't deserve to die like that."

"They fell in protection of our Goddess. There's no higher honor." A lie, each and every death a waste. I say it because it's the sort of thing I'm supposed to say, though for the first time, Nolan looks at me as if he actually sees me. "But yeah, Jeziah and the others didn't deserve it either."

A faint sheen of reverence appears. "As you said, they did their duty. May the flame of their memory burn forever."

*With who?* I swallow. We were only known to each other, and that barely. Still, as another body disappears into its niche, I wonder if it's Jeziah. Whose abrasive laugh I'd never hear again. Who I'd never steal another bottle of wine with or stand lookout for while he slipped horse apples under Morgan's pillow. What little we had, I wish we still did.

Though then he'd be standing here with Nolan, instead of me.

We watch quietly until the last of the bodies is interred. By then, the sun is getting low in the sky, its light washing the walls of Cineris in a warm, bloody red. When the Cineri finish, they lead the wagons away, leaving Nolan and me alone with the dead.

"They'll need our armor," I say. "We should go."

Nolan shakes his head slightly. "One more thing."

He doesn't offer more, and I don't ask, only follow when he leads back into the corridors. I'm about to ask him if he has a destination in mind when I see it: the Cathedral tower. Not the one we left behind, but a perfect copy, only smaller. And missing its flame. There's no living divinity here. Beneath this diminutive reminder of Tempestra's city lies ashes, all that remains of their previous avatars. Like with our fallen blood brethren, when Tempestra makes the transition from one flesh to another, the Cineri come for their remains and ferry them back to their final resting place. But unlike our blood brethren, no power lingers. No divinity remains to be protected by Cineris's walls. Their interment is purely sentimental.

Nolan doesn't say anything, only stares at the monument. Then, with a soft, slow movement, he goes to the tower and clears the handful of stray leaves that have gathered at its base.

"Okay," he says.

"Okay? Are you sure? Don't you want to pick out a niche before we do? That wall over there looks like it has a good view."

Not even a hint of a smile. "I don't intend to end up here anytime soon."

"Neither do I, but after what happened at the Cathedral—" I cut off the spill of words, not wanting to sound weak. Or scared. "Just saying we have our work cut out for us. Dead gods' blood . . ." I don't exactly broach the topic gently. "Don't suppose that ever came up as a topic of conversation at the Dusk Cloister?"

He shakes his head. "We never studied such things." A pause. "But you're right. Seeing what it did to the Goddess . . . the damage that remained . . ."

I can tell he's thinking of those blossoms of blood slowly spreading across the Goddess's garment. Is that why he wanted to visit the ashes of past avatars?

"Do you think it's bad enough that . . ." I trail off, not sure if I'm misreading this.

"I think," he says, "that we have our task and should focus on it."

As he begins to leave, I step in front of him. "Oh no, you can't crack that particular nut halfway."

He stares, studying me. But whatever he's thinking, it's locked away tighter than the corpses surrounding us.

"Yes," he says finally, the word tight and curt. "I think Innara is dying."

Avatars die. It's what they do. What all humans do. It might take a heck of a lot longer when they are fused with a divinity, but even that doesn't grant immortality. It's anticipated. Planned for.

Unless something unexpected happens.

"You saw the blood," he continues. It's not a question.

"I noticed." Maybe I'm not the only one who has been pondering the particulars of what we don't know. "But *they* didn't seem concerned."

"And yet . . . Innara has been Tempestra's avatar for over a century." His words are cool, entirely analytic. "She was chosen after the battle against the Green God, after Enoch."

"I sat through the same history lessons you did."

"Do you actually remember them? If you exclude the avatars involved in the battles between the gods, where they were more likely to be 'damaged,' Innara is approaching the end of their average life cycle."

*Oh.* "You think Tempestra-Innara is weaker than they usually are. And you think the heretics think that too."

"Killing a god isn't easy. If I were planning to try, I'd want to make sure there were as many factors in my favor as possible."

I arrange a suitably concerned expression on my face and smile on the inside. If Tempestra-Innara was weak before, I have an even better chance now. Except . . .

The elation fades. The Goddess can take another avatar. But while they might be able to bond with anybody, they won't. Most burn out quickly, which would leave Tempestra vulnerable again; only a suitable avatar connects with divinity in the right, harmonious way. How, why . . . not knowledge shared with the likes of us Potentiates. But the search normally takes time. Time, Nolan is clearly thinking, Innara may not have. And that I have to hope she does. Because there's one thing I *do* know about the taking of a new avatar: The Goddess will go into seclusion right after, in order to fully cement the fresh bond. I have no idea for how long; when Enoch was traded for Innara, it was a matter of weeks. But Tempestra-Innara emerged into the world as the last of their divine siblings, triumphant, without a single known threat that might stand against them, even in a fragile new body.

If Innara were not the stronger, safer option still to weather a second attack, the Goddess would have immediately swapped avatars. But as soon as they find a better replacement, that will change. Which is bad for me. A new, fully minted avatar could easily surpass whatever power the reliquary blood imparts, closing what window of opportunity I had.

We need to find the reliquary *fast*.

"Innara is not our concern, though." He turns away. "Lumeris can protect the Goddess for now. Our goal is to secure the reliquary, pull the heretics up by their roots, and salt the ground so they can never try something like this again."

Not exactly a priority to me, but I nod. "Try not to sound so enthusiastic about our little team up."

He sighs. "And here I was beginning to think you could manage to speak without being frivolous."

A Cineri pounds on my door at dawn, much to my dismay. Not that I'm not used to rising early; training began before sunrise at the Dawn Cloister. But I am sleeping in an unfamiliar bed, in an unfamiliar place for the first time in a very, very long time, and for some reason, it agrees with me. After a simple, silent dinner with Nolan and the attendants in a simple, silent dining hall, we retired, and I was asleep within minutes of lying down on my utilitarian yet surprisingly comfortable cot. Maybe it was the sheer weight of Cineris's dark silence that did it, the necropolis sharing a taste of what it had to offer, but I am so startled out of slumber by the attendant's banging that it takes a solid minute to remember where I am.

When I finally gather myself, a pair of horses are waiting in the courtyard. They are lovely creatures, broad-chested chestnut geldings with dark manes and tails. Soldier's horses, because that's the fiction we'll be playing—blades for hire, making our way between contracts. I jump to claim the horse with a white star on its forehead, though I doubt Nolan would have cared either way. He certainly doesn't object, and as we managed to be cordial enough yesterday, he even adds a faint nod of acknowledgment as he mounts. The Cineri have already readied the animals with our supplies, so there's nothing for me to do but follow suit.

Then...

I stare at the gate. The last few days have been, to say the least, odd. And yet, they played out in familiar spaces, padded by familiar ritual. But not today. Today, my sickles are strapped to my back as usual, but I wear a stranger's clothes. Dark fitted pants, a matching collared coat tapered at the waist and trimmed with gray embroidery... common garb, but so different from the Cloister uniform that it is as if I've been stuffed into the skin of some unfamiliar beast. Gone is my fancy gold reverie, replaced by a simple lump of flame-shaped lead. Nolan is dressed similarly, transformed from Potentiate into a figure that could be found on any street in Lumeris.

He doesn't look the least bit uncomfortable.

The Cineri take our lack of orders as a cue to open the gate. They creak. Or maybe it's something in me. Before yesterday, I had never been inside Cineris. But it was an anchor point, a part of the world I know. Beyond it... still the Goddess's world, but not in the way the Cloisters and Lumeris are. And for a brief moment—no, more than that—I hesitate to leave that familiarity behind. *An opponent you don't know is more dangerous than one you do.* Did Prior Petronilla say that? One of our other instructors?

As I search for that marble of memory, my horse shuffles beneath me. Chuffs. He's impatient to get started.

And then, suddenly, so am I.

After Cineris, the plan gets a little less straightforward. As far as anyone outside the surviving witnesses knows, what Emmaus did was a demonstration, targeting the devotees gathered to witness his execution. Brutal, effective, but not the least bit suspect. No one, not even our absent blood brethren, is to know that it was actually an assassination attempt against the Goddess, and especially not one that was almost successful. Which means the official-yet-still-secret story is that Nolan and I are on the hunt for the heretics who were working with Emmaus, and definitely not any mysterious, previously unknown reliquary that could be used to try to commit divine murder again.

We have exactly one lead: Andronica captured Emmaus after tracking him to a house not far from Belspire, a city a six-day ride from the Cathedral. The owner of the house was also arrested, but not deemed worthy of execution by the Goddess, so they got shunted off to be dealt with by the authority in Belspire, also known as the distinguished elder Arbiter Gottschalk. Nolan and I carry a letter of introduction from the Senior Arbiter who'd been in tow when Tempestra-Innara showed us the reliquary. It's encoded to read like a normal note of recommendation; only Gottschalk will be able to read the true message, which will give us access to the prisoner.

I don't relish that task. Not because of any squeamishness about interrogation—their lot is cast, and if they have information that will help me, I've got years of Cloister training that will help me get it. But if the prisoner is still alive, there's only one reason for it: They're going to face the Arbiter's special brand of judgement. *That* I'd rather not think about. Even without my special little secret, the thought of someone rifling through my mind to determine how much I love the Goddess turns my blood cold.

The first night, we make camp in the woods. There are towns with guesthouses along the way, attracting the fellow travelers we pass, but when Nolan suggests we avoid them, I don't argue. The shininess of my new, conditional freedom still carries a measure of apprehension. Not to mention a dire seriousness that sets in the farther we get from Lumeris: After all my years in the Cloister, I'm going to have to be around regular people again. Not shielded by armor and set up in the Cathedral for the devoted to gawk at, or on an occasional visit to Lumeris, where the inhabitants bow and scrape and keep a reverent distance. The thought keeps me up late enough that the sun has fully risen when I wake to find Nolan gone.

I'm on my feet and halfway to my horse—gear already mentally discarded—when I simultaneously register that both mounts remain where we hobbled them, and that Nolan has appeared out of the line of trees nearby.

"Good morning," he says. "Did you sleep well?"

My mouth drops open to respond, though the polite inquiry is unexpected enough that words don't come. The idea that I'd fumbled, failed to see that we were, in fact, in contest with one another and that Nolan had gained an advantage by leaving me behind, still has me in its tense grip.

But he hasn't.

"Where were you?" My cheeks flush as soon as I say it, given there are several perfectly normal things one might attend to privately first thing in the morning. But Nolan simply responds: "Praying."

Something he seems to do a lot of. "Oh. Right. You should have woken me. I would've joined you." A complete and utter lie, but I try to sound sincere.

"Really?"

He knows I'm full of it. "No. I mean, I attended prayers every day at the Cloisters but . . ." This is tricky ground. I can't sound as if I lack piety. "I do like to sleep in too. And . . . I don't know, it always seemed a bit silly to me to pray to the air when we can do so in the Goddess's presence. Where they can actually hear us."

"They feel our devotion," says Nolan. "And I enjoy it. It's an act of devotion I can do anywhere, at any time. It's calming, focusing."

"I feel the same way about sparring."

He squats down to stir the fire, pushing dirt over the handful of coals still smoldering. "Did you think I'd left you?"

I could lie. But I'm sure my true thoughts were written plainly enough on my face. "Can you blame me? This was supposed to be a competition."

"Except now, it's not. If anything, it's a test."

"Then why still pick only one of us from the Dawn and one from the Dusk?" I press, since we're suddenly on speaking terms beyond a sentence or two at a time. "You and I weren't the only surviving candidates, and as far as tests go, well, this one's pretty big. Besides, we *all* want to be Executrix, don't we?"

Nolan gives me a questioning look. "Do we?"

Is *this* a test? "It's our duty to do whatever the Goddess wishes of us."

"Yes, it is."

I can't tell if he's fishing for something, but my interest is piqued. "Putting that aside," I continue, "if the choice *were* yours and yours alone, would you have wanted the chance to become Executrix?"

Turning the probing back around clearly throws him, and he chews over an answer. I wait, making it clear I expect one.

"The truth is," he says finally, cautiously, "I never considered it a possibility. Andronica was young and strong."

"Same." It's true, so I give him that tidbit of information, hoping for more in turn. "What *did* you consider?" Again, he hesitates. Our paths are chosen for us. And Potentiates aren't supposed to talk of such things, even among ourselves. But we do, and everyone knows it. Jeziah changed his mind about his preferred path on an almost monthly basis. "I always thought I'd end up as a Prior," I offer. "Somewhere very, *very* boring where Prior Petronilla would never have to see me or hear from me again."

"I can't quite picture you crouched over letters and ledgers."

"Me neither. But if it was the Goddess's will . . ."

Nolan nods affirmingly. "I suppose"—the words come out slowly, at the pace of a confession—"I used to think I might become a Cleric of the Blood." With all that praying? *Shocking.* "But Prior Yiorgo always encouraged my skills in fighting and strategy, so I expected to be anointed a Bellator. However," he adds, "if the Goddess chooses me to be her next Executrix, I will do so to the very best of my ability."

"Well, it will be one of us, so your chances are strong. Unless we fail."

"That's not an option." A grim tone enters his voice.

"Relax. I'm not saying that's the plan."

He stands. "We should get moving. I'll saddle the horses."

"I can handle mine."

He glances at me, and I catch a hint of amusement. "I don't mind. You take care of your bedroll, make sure the fire is fully out."

*Teamwork.* Right, that's what this is supposed to be. Gonna have to work on that. "Okay, but be careful with Mortimer."

He pauses. "I'm sorry, did—did you name your horse Mortimer?"

"Sure did." I cross my arms. "Prior Petronilla wouldn't let us name the horses at the Cloister, but she's not here and my new horse friend is. Got a problem with it?"

Another probing, quizzical look. But he shakes his head.

"Good, because your horse is named Buttons." I start for my bedroll, but he remains where he is. "What?"

"Nothing... it's only that you're not quite what I expected my Dawn counterpart to be."

I can't say the same. Pious, focused, driven, *devoted* . . . Nolan is everything Prior Petronilla probably wishes she could have offered up.

"Does that make you more or less glad that we aren't going head-to-head against one another?"

But apparently, we've reached the limit of sharing, because instead of replying, Nolan turns away and begins busying himself with the horses.

# *Nine*

I found the village today, deep in the woods, over a week's journey north of Ignarin. It could barely be called a village. A settlement really, likely no more than a season or two old. I saw no one, but the hearths were still warm, so they weren't far. I waited for hours before leaving. I have marked my map. In another season, I will return, and bring the Goddess's love once more.

—FROM THE DIARY OF THE CLERIC CAROSO

O UR TRAVELS ARE, IN a word, quiet.
I don't bother trying with small talk, content to take in the sights that unfold with a pleasant newness. A bubbling stream, a large rock, a pasture of grazing cows . . . mundane as they are, they are not the gray walls of the Cloister or the oppressive loom of the Cathedral. I am not choked by the thick perfumes of the devoted or the sweaty reek of a hard day's training. I am not watched. I am not constantly measured. I breathe easier, in a way I must have known at some point but can't recall when I last experienced.

The thoroughfares we follow wind themselves through the Devoted Lands. At each crossroads, cut stones point the way: to Aerdis, to the north and west, where the Bellators gather and train their legions; east to Siscia, the city governed by the Clerics of the Blood; to the smaller towns and villages that fill in the gaps between the Ordained Cities. And always, *always*, back to Lumeris, beating heart of the Goddess's empire.

I note each option with a twinge of curiosity. I know these names like I know my own, but only as spots of ink on a map. Now, they take on a fuller existence, as tangible as the other travelers we pass along the road, who smile warmly as they call out "May the Flame warm you." It's a refreshing change from the cautious, isolating reverence of the Cloister attendants and citizens of Lumeris. I return the greetings, as does Nolan, albeit with far less enthusiasm.

The sun is high in the sky when we round a bend of road to find a small wagon leaning precariously to one side. It stands out from the surrounding forest like an exotic bird that's gotten lost; swaths of bright colors streak the exterior beneath a shockingly purple roof. Squatting by its back end is an older, bony man in a threadbare coat, leaning fruitlessly on a metal bar wedged beneath the wagon's body. Quickly, I see why: The spokes of the back wheel have splintered. A replacement sits nearby.

He looks up as we approach, cheeks flushed with exertion, smiling broadly and hopefully.

I pull Mortimer to a stop. "Do you need some help?"

Nolan stops as well, though I can tell by his bearing that he'd prefer to keep moving, as the man clasps his hands together, wringing them dramatically. "May the Flame warm you and more. The Goddess has answered my prayer!" He spins, gesturing at the mule hitched to the wagon. "Lulu and I were beginning to think we'd be stuck here all night. The ruts in these roads! They get worse every year. Can't go anywhere without half a wagon's worth of extra parts, I swear to the Goddess!"

I dismount. Up close, the colors painting the wagon are even more vivid, the abstract designs nothing like the ornate but solemn stylings I'm used to. "I love your wagon; did you do the painting yourself? It's so . . ." I search for the right word. "Alive."

"Oh," chuckles the man. "An offer of help *and* a kind lie. Too generous, my dear, but I'm certain you've seen a hundred other tinker's carts with a finer presentation than this humble pile of sticks."

Except I haven't. I smile, as if caught in a polite mistruth. If such wagons were allowed in Lumeris, it certainly wasn't anywhere close enough to the Cathedral complex for me to be familiar with them.

"But while my adornment may be lacking, my selection of goods is unparalleled in the Devoted Lands." He goes to the side of the wagon and throws open a hinged panel, revealing shelves packed full with all manner of goods. "Anything you need. Soap. Reveries. New saddle straps. Tools of both iron and steel. Authentic embroidered fabrics from the Riverlands. I even have a sauce made from peppers carried across the Unlit Seas." He leans in and drops his voice. "They say the only thing hotter is the divine flame itself."

"We don't need anything." Nolan cuts in before I have a chance to inquire more about the gourmet delicacy. His tone is curt, but he's dismounted as well, giving me a *Let's get this over with* glare as the tinker closes up his wagon again. "Lys, help me lift the wagon."

I obey, taking the end of the metal bar. We lean into it, the wagon bed creaking as it rises. Either one of us could have done this easily on our own. But the tinker doesn't seem to notice our lack of effort as he removes the broken wheel and replaces it with a practiced efficiency.

"There!" He straightens again and grins. "Only one thing eases life's trials as much as wealth, and that is the vitality of youth."

"May the Flame warm you and the Goddess's favor keep you safe," Nolan says flatly, returning to the horses. "Lys. We need to keep moving."

"Please. You must let me reward you for your kindness."

Nolan scowls. "That's not—"

"A new whetstone for your blades," continues the tinker, going up the small set of stairs on the back of the wagon and ducking through the door there. "Or here, one of my regular customers is a baker, a far too generous one." He reappears and presses a loaf wrapped in sackcloth into my hands. It's still warm. "Baked fresh this morning. Half of what she gives me ends up going stale. Better to share it around than let it go to waste."

"Really," Nolan says, "there's no need to—"

"Thank you," I cut in, accepting the bread. Though, if I were to be honest, I'm more interested in the sauce he mentioned. "Fresh bread certainly won't go amiss—"

"Quiet!" Nolan's head snaps toward the road ahead of us.

I hear it an instant later: a low rumble, and the jingle of tack.

Horses, a number that can mean only one thing. A regiment of soldiers clears the bend ahead, coming straight toward us. Three riders lead the pack; upon spotting us, one urges their horse faster.

"Clear the road!" The man is lightly armored, but their Flame insignia is clear. "Make way for the Goddess's Chosen!"

Nolan has already backed away to the tree line, but the tinker isn't so fast, stumbling as he rushes to close the wagon door and get to the driver's seat. He doesn't move swiftly enough, and the rider draws a long leather wand. Penitent's crops, they are called, used primarily in disciplining their namesakes—mainly petty criminals and other minor offenders of the Goddess's grace. I'm moving before I realize it, arm raised as I put myself between the tinker and the soldier. A sharp line of pain lights up across my forearm, though my jacket offers enough protection to prevent bloodshed.

Anger flares in the rider's eyes, but I speak first. "Hey! There's no need for that. His wagon was just barely fixed; he'll move it aside if you let him."

Again, the crop rises, but by now the rest of the legion has drawn close. Including its leader, who draws their muscled black stallion to a halt. And though I know I shouldn't, I can't resist: My gaze finds the Bellator's. There's only faint relief when I find the face unfamiliar, a woman of around Petronilla's age, nearly as pale as Nolan, with dull brown hair. Her blue eyes are icy as she takes in our gathering, betraying no emotion.

I do not know her. But I know this moment.

"Is there a problem?" The words are simple, disinterested, but heavy in a way that seems to press on my already tight chest.

"No." Her lieutenant's arm drops, but it's clear he's not done with me yet. "I can take care of it."

"You can try." The words are out before I can stop them. *Stupid*, a tiny voice says within. But it's a whisper against the rush of blood filling my ears.

The Bellator stares down at me. Now and in another time.

*Crack.*

The lieutenant raises the crop again.

"Please, wait!" Nolan jumps forward, hand held out pleadingly. "My friend chooses her words poorly, but we're only trying to assist one of our fellow devoted."

*Friend.* It sounds so sincere woven into the humble appeal.

"A thousand apologies." The tinker echoes the tone. "Bad luck hobbled my wagon but the Goddess's favor brought two fine citizens to help me. It is only for that reason that I would *ever* delay one of their children, even for a heartbeat." Without waiting for permission, he climbs back into the driver's seat and directs the wagon off to the side of the road as quickly as the mule will move. Beside me, Nolan's eyes are lowered respectively again, face carefully neutral.

I bow my head. "Like he said, a thousand apologies."

"Remorse after insolence," the lieutenant scoffs. "At your word, Bellator, I will see she is genuinely sorry."

I swallow a snicker. No one's managed that yet. But as the seconds tick by, I have to admit I could have handled this better. The Bellator would be well within her power to punish me. Which wouldn't exactly help our mission.

But she only sighs impatiently. "We've been delayed in reaching Lumeris enough. Get out of the way, girl. And if you are making your way to Aerdis, understand this first: Sharp blades are a boon, a sharp tongue less so."

A lesson I've done a poor job learning. But luck is on my side; the Bellator has mistaken us for one of the countless hopefuls who converge on their city, hoping to earn a place in a legion. That, apparently, is enough to buy me a smidgen of mercy. Eyes down, we get out of the road, my fingers twisting in Mortimer's reins as the company starts moving again. Only when they are well away does anyone speak.

"Thank you again for your help." But the earlier warmth in the tinker's words has disappeared, and he urges his wagon along, in the opposite direction that Nolan and I were traveling. Nolan also remounts and continues, not waiting for me.

"That was idiotic," he snaps when I catch up.

So much for *friend.* "There was no need to strike the old man," I counter.

"No need for you to stop it either." Nor for him to step in, but he did. A little surprising. "You understand that this isn't the Cloisters? Or Lumeris?"

More than he knows.

"We are no one out here. No one owes us respect," he continues, the words growing more heated. "You didn't pay that Bellator the deference she deserved from a Potentiate, much less some normal commoner."

"I get it, okay?" Anger flares again, if briefly. Those icy eyes, staring down . . . "I'm not used to it, that's all. I . . . forgot myself briefly."

"Make it the last time," say Nolan. "And the comment about the tinker's cart . . . do you not realize that your ignorance is as much a threat as your attitude? We need to avoid drawing any unnecessary attention, no matter how small and insignificant it seems."

"Oh, I'm sorry, I didn't realize you were such an *expert*." I'll give him attitude. "I guess that means you know all about Belspire? Been there before?"

"No."

"Have you ever stayed in a guesthouse? Or spent the night drinking and playing cards and burping and whatever else it is that people do in them? Did the Dusk Cloister allow you all sorts of freedoms to travel the Devoted Lands and learn the minutiae of how to conduct oneself as a commoner?"

Silence is his only response.

"*Exactly*," I snap. "You were as sheltered as I was."

"I'm not putting my inexperience on display."

I bristle, but it's my turn to be speechless.

We continue on a little farther. Then:

"Once."

"What?" I say.

"I stayed at a guesthouse once," he replies, "when I was very young."

I'm not sure what to say to that. Potentiates aren't supposed to talk about their lives before their choosing. Some of us barely remember it. And as far as anyone is concerned, we were all birthed anew in the Cathedral, the moment Tempestra-Innara's blood hit our lips. But he brought it up, so . . . "With your family?"

Too far. His features tighten. "The Goddess and our blood brethren are my family."

"Yes, yes," I say quickly, "but you had a life before we became their children." I should be more careful with my wording, but fuck it. If he's so concerned about the success of our cover, this is relevant. Which is probably the only reason Nolan is tolerating my near blasphemy.

He doesn't answer quickly, but eventually, it trickles out. "I... stayed in an inn once with the man who... who cared for me before I came to the Goddess. He was a bookbinder. We were delivering commissions to a client."

A bookbinder. Nolan was plucked from a town then, maybe even a city.

"No, it was a library," he corrects. "Belspire's castle is supposed to have a fine library."

He doesn't specify whether that tidbit of information came with him to the Cathedral or was picked up after. And as curious as I am, I don't press. "Good. One of us has experience with the world outside the Cloisters, at least."

That catches his interest. "Because you haven't?"

Fair is fair. He answered my question, so I'll answer his. "I'd never experienced a lot of things until the Goddess's forces came to my village, though if we find ourselves surrounded by a plethora of pine trees and snow, I'm your girl."

"You came from the northern mountains."

A statement, not a question, or an accusation. Our lives before the Goddess may be forbidden territory, but there are some things that can't be hidden. Jeziah's tattoos. Or the faint ways Morgan forms certain words that betray she came from somewhere in the east. But Nolan figures me out with scraps.

"How did you know?"

"Pine trees and snow? No guesthouses or peddlers' carts? You're clearly nervous about an unfamiliar city, which means you likely haven't seen any besides Lumeris. Which makes the far north your likeliest place of origin, in the wilds of what used to be the Storm Goddess's territory."

Used to be. And probably still is. But that's not a line of discussion I feel like following.

"The first time I saw the Cathedral, I think I blacked out a little. I didn't know anything built by people could be so *big*."

"I shook." Thankfully, Nolan doesn't press for more about my old life. "But with awe. Somehow, I knew it was where I was supposed to be."

He speaks reverently, as if ending a prayer. I don't ask Nolan what happened to his father—a word he couldn't even say—any more than I'd ask him what happened to the other children he was undoubtedly presented with. I've already trod unwelcome territory enough.

"Well, I'll leave the guesthouses to your vast experience. Any other pointers on playing normal?"

It's clear he catches the tartness in my words. Still, he replies. "Remember your etiquette lessons . . . assuming the Dawn Cloister actually had those."

I snort. "Better than your insult lessons, clearly."

"Keep an eye on how other people act and mimic it. And try not to draw attention or say anything you don't have to." He sighs. "I know that's going to be the hardest part for you . . ."

"I'll manage." I'm still clutching the gifted bread. I tear a hunk of the end. "Oh . . . oh, you need to taste this."

Nolan's brow furrows in a way that tells me he couldn't care less, but he accepts the piece I hand him. Then makes a face. "It's dry. Gritty."

"Right? Can you imagine them serving this in the Cloisters?"

"Maybe to the pigs."

I scoff. "Now who is showing their ignorance? This is what the regular folks eat, so better get familiar with it." I let a beat pass. "Wouldn't want to seem *suspicious*."

His mouth thins, but he doesn't have anything to say to that.

We don't speak again until the sun is almost down and we make camp. We feed the horses, shake out our bedrolls. I build a fire as Nolan starts on a simple, sparse meal. Nolan even serves me first, as humbly as one of the Cloister attendants. In the Cloisters, all this would be done for us. But *this* is what normal people do, when they aren't bound blood and soul to the Goddess.

The family I was born into is dead. Nolan's too, most likely. But the difference between us is that he truly sees the Goddess as his mother, the other Chosen and me as siblings. And if we do manage to find the reliquary, if by some unlikely chain of events I am able to use it to kill Tempestra-Innara, I will be taking all of that away.

But Nolan's devotion isn't my problem. Neither is anyone else's. I have seen the cost of divinity's reign, paid by both heretics and the devoted alike. The Goddess's world might be destroyed, but another one will rebuild itself eventually. It always does. And maybe, with the last of the gods nothing but memory, it will have the chance to become something better.

And if not, well, I'll still be free.

# *Ten*

An offering was made of the priests who didn't flee. Stakes driven into the ground, then into flesh, grisly rows set outside the entrance to the city. The Green Garden, they blithely called it after, when it was clear the offering had been accepted. When it was clear that the Flame Goddess wouldn't raze the city to stone and ash.

—ACCOUNT OF THE HISTORIAN ADRELLIS,
FROM *THE WITHERED CITY*

I REMEMBER THE STORM. THE way we'd hear the crash of thunder long before we reached the cliffs, following flashes of light that pierced the towering, ancient trees and their verdant canopies. The growing smell of rain-soaked air and vegetal decay. I remember emerging from the forest to the sight of those never-ending black clouds that clung to the jagged, windswept peaks, and how my mother would make her offering, opening her fists and letting the winds take it.

I remember that we were never supposed to speak of these visits.

I remember that it didn't matter in the end.

The mother who birthed me had long hair the color of buckwheat honey. Sometimes it would tickle my neck as she wrapped me in a cloak or a coat, or slipped boots on my feet if we were braving the snows of winter. Which it always seemed we were. In the northern mountains, snows came early and left late. But that, we whispered, was a gift from the Storm Goddess, a shield, because it meant the clerics who did their earnest best to sell the faith of Tempestra-Innara mostly came in the summer. The ones foolish enough to risk the snows we'd find in the spring, frozen where they fell, occasionally gnawed on by a lucky woodland creature.

On the day soldiers arrived instead of clerics, my mother and I were at the overlook committing heresy. Though the Storm Goddess was no longer with us in the way the Flame Goddess was, they still watched over us. *At least,* my mother said, *as long as we make our offerings.* We prayed to them as we made the shallow cuts in our palms or fingers, reaching over the cliff's edge to let the wind take those red drops. Blood to keep Tempestra-Innara far away, blood to make our harvests plentiful and keep our village as strong and healthy as the summer storms. We were blissfully unaware of the devastation we'd find upon our return. Devastation that the Storm Goddess had done exactly fuck all to prevent.

By the time we were close enough to hear the screams, most of the village was burned beyond saving. Smoke choked the air. Corpses littered the streets. If my mother had been a little less simple and a little more familiar with how the Bellators and their legions went about a conversion, she would have picked me up and run. But she wasn't. Or she panicked. Or, or, or. Whatever her motivation, we somehow made it back to our home unscathed. My father lay in the open doorway, my grandfather a few steps beyond. Both motionless in death. My grandmother, less lucky, was still making her way there, gasping weakly as the wound in her chest leaked. I remember my mother rushing to her side, the older woman's mouth struggling to form words.

*Lannara . . .* I hear the papery hiss of that name in my dreams sometimes.

Sometime after my grandmother's trickle of red ceased, the soldiers appeared. My mother screamed: not in fear, but with rage—the deep, primal fury reserved for cornered animals. It was enough to make the soldiers take a fearful step back, allowing her the chance to grab the knife someone had been using to chop roots and tubers. It was a stupid move. And I'm pretty certain she realized it when I made my own noise, one of pure fear. I had enough time to see her remember that I was there, that she was a mother and still bore a responsibility in this world, before the soldiers cut her down too.

It gets blurry after that, though some memories stand out. Terrified faces, some familiar—other survivors from my village. Being herded like sheep through fields and forests I don't recognize by a legion that wields the word *heretic* as freely as its blades. The bone-deep chill of the early winter storm.

And, most of all, the cracking of the ice.

Most memories of life before Tempestra-Innara become increasingly distant, threadbare, as the years pass. But not that.

Never that.

On a sullen, soggy morning that very nearly has me longing for my Cloister cell, Belspire appears—almost abruptly—in the distance. Right away, I see it's no Lumeris. There's no grace to the rising, weather-stained spires that stab at the sky, tattered wisps of fog weaving between them. No welcoming glow of the flame as in the Goddess's city. Belspire is an aging city—waning in size, wealth, and prestige—but once a place of unparalleled plenty, whose favor from the Green God meant bountiful fields, orchards, and gardens that yielded everything from fine fruits to coveted aromatic oils and tinctures used for the finest incenses and perfumes. After their fall, the city's main trade endured but was much reduced, its prior fortune never reached again. Now, it is as much known for the bells that gave the city its name, which, according to our lessons, ring with an unparalleled beauty that draws visitors from across the Devoted Lands. A real tourist attraction, for sure.

I keep my gaze on those spires, which grow larger and larger as the land around us turns cultivated. Soon we are surrounded by a sea of grains and vegetation, tended at intervals by hunched, gray workers.

No, penitents.

I slow Mortimer as I spot the overseers on horseback: sworn clerics, all of them, but of the militant variety. Somewhere there's a Bellator they answer to, perhaps even the one whose legion we encountered on the road. This is where the survivors of my village might have ended up, toiling away to prove their fealty and atone for their sins ... if. How many years punishment for a heretic late to turn their faith toward Tempestra-Innara? Five years? Ten? The offenses of the people scattered through the fields are likely more common sorts—petty thieves, drunks found one too many times passed out in the street, the occasional weirdo devotee who simply *likes* this particular brand of reverence.

I slow without realizing it, watching backs bending, turning earth, on their knees picking rocks out of the dirt. Nolan notices, but I urge Mortimer forward again before he can say anything. The work of penitents helps keep the Devoted Lands happy and fed—that was the gist of our education on this particular topic.

Our company on the road grows steadily as we draw closer to the city, turning irritatingly crowded by the time we arrive at Belspire's main gate. Mortimer gives a nervous shimmy as a wagon laden with barrels passes rudely close; I pet his neck to calm him. Inside the walls isn't much better. In Lumeris, the roads are wide and clean. The buildings shine, sometimes literally with gold. But here, streets tangle like a briar, shadows clinging to its tight alleys and doorways, and the eaves beneath hard, sloping roofs. There are piles of horse shit stamped into the cobbles. It smells—not like fresh air and incense, but the way a room does in the morning, after a night with too many bodies sleeping in it.

Still, I drink in every inch, picking out hints of prior prosperity remaining in the ornaments and stonework: flowers and fruits, vines that twist and curl. Innocuous enough symbols, too common and impotent to pose a threat to the Goddess's insignia. And while its finest days have past, the city's citizens teem with a vibrancy that seems misplaced in the shitty weather. It doesn't take long to figure out why—broadsides are pasted all around, advertising a festival to celebrate the day the city pledged its devotion to Tempestra-Innara.

Not every conversion is bloody. But Belspire's certainly was. The city was ancient enough to have been a kingdom of its own once, with the castle to prove it. And when Arcadius-Viktori fell, the royal family wasted no time in enthusiastically proving their new devotion, lining the road with a thousand heretic corpses to adorn the Goddess's triumphant approach, including every one of the Green God's priests not smart enough to flee as soon as their master fell. Excessive, to say the least, but it successfully bought the royals their continued existence.

"Seems we arrived just in time," Nolan says, eyeing one of the posters.

I catch his drift. The festival is tomorrow. And it's not a real party if there isn't some grand spectacle. Like, say, a public execution.

We'll have to make our interrogation quick.

We weave our way slowly through the crowds, making for the castle in the center of the city, passing by markets and shops, and clerics offering blessings on the street corners in exchange for prayers ... and coins, obviously. At a juncture of streets, traffic stops suddenly. A wedding party passes through, their laughter and joy wet around the edges thanks to the wine bottles they brandish. They wear the warm reds and orange of the Flame, but there are vines woven around the wrists of the young couple. Gold vines, yes, but in Lumeris, it would be linen or silk cord or even cloth of gold, if the wedding purse was deep enough.

We make it only a little farther before a sweet wind smacks me square in the face. I pull Mortimer to a stop.

"What is that smell?" It's exquisite, my mouth aching from watering.

The source is a nearby tented booth wedged between a pair of shops. A young woman tends it, rolling out thin rounds of dough that she slaps on a hot griddle. As I watch, she smears a thick jelly on a finished pastry, folds it up, and then wraps it in a bit of paper before handing it to a customer.

"I know that." Nolan appears almost surprised by the knowledge. "I mean ... I remember it. It's spiced sweet dough filled with muddleberry jam."

"Muddleberry? That's not real. You made it up."

"That's just what it's called. It's preserves made from a mix of whatever berries are in season." His face brightens in a way I've never seen. "Wait here."

He dismounts and goes over to the vendor, then pays for two of the pastries, one of which he delivers triumphantly—and unexpectedly—to me.

I can't resist. The warmth of the treat leaches through its paper wrapping. "Ooooh, are we being sinful? Deviating from our mission?"

He scowls, but only a little before a downright eager look appears.

"Keeping ourselves fed isn't a deviation. Or a sin. Though if it is, I promise not to tell if you don't. Go on," he says, and I realize he's waiting for me to take a bite.

The thin, pancake-like pastry almost melts as soon as it touches my tongue, leaving behind vanilla and spice and—I make a frankly embarrassing noise as the rich jam seeps out. It's sweet and crisp and a little sour as well, a flavor unlike anything I've ever had before. It's not that we were never allowed dessert at the Cloister, but there's something different about this. The cooks always fed us in the elevated manner that our station deserved. This is more rustic, more communal, summoning long-buried memories of fall harvests—roasted nuts and dried stone fruits and syrups gleaned from the sap of trees.

And burning flesh. Spilt blood. The pain of frozen toes. Screams, and an ensuing silence that is far worse.

I swallow hard.

"It's good, right?" Nolan says expectantly.

I won't let bad memories ruin this. The past is gone; the pastry is now. And so is Nolan, kind enough to get it for me. "I can't remember the last time I've had something so good."

He's suddenly unsure, conflicted. "Me either."

Our gazes catch for a moment, his hazel eyes locking with mine. I know *handsome*—I understand the concept—but I'm uncomfortable with that meaning I don't mind looking a little longer than necessary at Nolan. Even though he can be uptight and stodgy. Even though we've been traveling for days, and lacking regular chances to bathe, his hair is greasy, there's dirt under his fingernails, and, just like me, he probably smells like horse and unwashed feet.

I drop my gaze. "We should keep moving." Enough distractions. I've been taught better. "Can't interrogate a corpse."

Nolan mounts his horse again. "No, we cannot."

We continue, quiet as we eat our pastries, save for the crinkle of paper as I lick every last spot of jam from it. Not exactly sophisticated, but I'm commoner Lys here, not Potentiate Lys. I make sure to wipe my mouth clean, though. Meeting an Arbiter with jam stains on my face would be a little too committed to the fiction.

The city shifts as we travel, growing increasingly more affluent as we approach the castle, until the shops disappear and the homes become more like compounds. Finally, we reach a sprawling plaza. Tempestra-Innara stands in its center, hands outstretched, a stone visage towering over the surrounding buildings. Flames dance in their stone palms. A shrine like this is found in nearly every city and town, though the size of Belspire's hints strongly at the overcompensating origin of the city's devotion.

Beyond the shrine sits the front gate of the castle, where a few bored guards in garish, clearly ceremonial armor are stationed. But ceremonial swords can still cut a throat, so we approach cautiously, dismounting at a respectful distance.

"Your business?" a guard barks, with the sort of grumpiness I don't begrudge someone stuck outside on a damp day.

Nolan presents the letter of introduction. "We're to deliver this to Arbiter Gottschalk."

Another guard snorts. "A little friendly correspondence?"

But the one who spoke first eyes the seal with interest. "Give it over. And wait here."

Nolan hesitates—probably because that's what the guards would expect someone in his position to do—but obeys, returning to where I stand as the head guard takes the letter and disappears into the castle. Minutes tick by.

"So," I ask the remaining guards, bored by the silence. "They letting you fine folks off for the festival? It's shaping up to be quite the affair." Chitchat. That's what normal people do.

"Nah." A guard with a sad excuse for a mustache scowls. "It's first shift for us. But can't complain. Got a great view of the opening festivities from here." He nods back at the center of the plaza, beneath the looming statue, where a platform is being erected.

Execution confirmed.

"Lucky you." I force my tone to stay bright, then content myself with scratching Mortimer on the bridge of his nose, which I've discovered he likes.

Finally, the guards perk up as a youngish man—maybe six or seven years older than Nolan and me—approaches, clad in an Arbiter cassock. I'm too surprised to be nervous. I was expecting someone older.

He has bronze skin and short light-blond hair, absurdly neat. And slate-green eyes that haven't lost their color yet. Not much anyway.

The Arbiter stops a few steps away from us, folding his hands into his sleeves.

"Arbiter Gottschalk." Nolan bows promptly, leaving me to follow suit more awkwardly.

"No." The young man's smile is polite but cool. "Arbiter Caius, of the First Stratum Assistant to Arbiter Gottschalk. He has decided to grant you an audience."

An apprentice, or not far past it. I don't recognize him, but it's common for Potentiates that show aptitude for becoming an Arbiter to be pulled from the Cloisters early, so they can focus on their judgement training, the specifics of which are little shared outside their Order.

"Welcome to Belspire," Caius continues. There's a sharp glint in his eyes, one I'm accustomed to seeing in my fellow Potentiates, that makes me wonder if he's already been let in on our little secret. "Please, follow me."

# *Eleven*

> There are certain things that you need to learn. Things that aren't entirely pleasant.
>
> —PRIOR PETRONILLA

I HONESTLY EXPECTED MORE FROM a palace, even one whose finest days have past. It's fancy, for sure, but there's a worn feel to everything, a cobwebby cling of decline. Still, I eye every cracked sconce and chipped sculpture, delightfully garish compared to the severity of the Dawn Cloister. And oddly charming compared to Lumeris's stark luxury. Nolan doesn't seem to share my interest, keeping his gaze straight ahead, on Caius, who stops us at the kind of door that clearly has something important behind it, judging by the pair of guards that stand outside. They are a far cry from the ones we chatted up outside. There is a stern, rigid discipline in their stance, and their heavy green-gray armor appears as if it would turn a direct sword thrust into a tickle. Every instinct tells me these aren't the sort to fuck with. But one gesture from Caius, and they step aside.

Our escort doesn't bother to knock.

Inside the chamber, an old man in a cassock sits at a massive desk, drooping over an open ledger. When he looks up, a murky stare locks me in place, magnified by the thick glasses that assist in his readings.

There's no mistaking Arbiter Gottschalk this time. Pale wisps of gray hair cling to a spotted scalp above a thin line of a mouth that looks like its primary activity is sucking on sour candy. He emanates a sense of fading power, complementing the castle nicely. Still, I know better than to think him weak. There are blades in those Arbiter eyes, still sharp enough to cut.

Caius closes the door. "May I introduce Gottschalk, Arbiter of the Third Stratum, divine Chosen of—"

"Yes, yes," Gottschalk interjects. He brandishes the letter in one gnarled hand. "This is an interesting bit of paper. Am I to understand that our blood mother sent you, a pair of mere Potentiates, to interrogate a heretic who has already been interrogated?"

Matter of fact and to the point. Okay, I can do that too.

"That's the gist of it." I point to myself. "Lys, Dawn Cloister. Nolan, Dusk."

"Here to do the Goddess's will," Nolan adds, exasperated by my trite introduction.

"As I said," Arbiter Gottschalk says, sounding a bit imposed upon himself. "The heretic has been interrogated. Quite thoroughly. Arbiter Caius oversaw to that personally."

Nolan dips his head respectfully. "Of course. But following the tragic events at the Cathedral, which Lys and I witnessed, the Goddess feels there might be something more to be gleaned about the location of the heretic cell that—"

"I do not question the Goddess's will or wisdom," Gottschalk says curtly. "Not even when they send me a pair of children to do what has already been done. Caius, take them to the heretic."

Dismissed.

"He's charming," I say when we are well away from Gottschalk's study. "Must be fun at your Order's parties."

Nolan gapes at my insolence, but a faint smile spreads on Caius's lips. "Gottschalk is a paragon among our path," he says with careful respect, "but not known for diplomacy. Even when it comes to our blood brethren." Despite our cover story, he doesn't lower his voice. "Don't worry, this castle is more like a mausoleum whose occupants haven't quite figured out they're dead yet." Sourness tinges his words, making me wonder how much he cares for his current position. "And what ears are here to listen know to keep their secrets well."

"You mean those cheerful fellows outside Arbiter Gottschalk's chamber?"

Caius shoots me a wry look. "Belspire's lofted Thorn Guard. An interesting quirk of the city's history. They were the royal lines' elite bodyguard for centuries even before the gods arrived, trained to be loyal, impenetrable, and deadly. Not unlike our ilk in many ways."

"And now?" Nolan inquires.

"They still serve, though they've persisted to the point of far outshining the charges they were created to protect."

The way he says it, it's clear the royals aren't the ones calling the shots for their bodyguards these days. But even though Bellators are the only ones who command legions, it's not unusual for Priors, Arbiters, or even Clerics to have a few blade-swinging minions. Someone has to do the dirty work.

"Must be a handy perk to being positioned here. How long have you been in Belspire?"

Caius's mouth thins. "Long enough."

"Seems nice. I hope I get as fancy an assignment as this."

He scoffs quietly. "You might aspire higher than this bitter weed of a city. Though we all serve where the Goddess wills, don't we?"

Oh yeah, someone would definitely prefer to be stationed elsewhere. I can't exactly blame him. Belspire isn't far from the Goddess's light, but it isn't exactly close either. The itch of that lack has already begun, a nagging feeling in the back of my mind, like I've forgotten to do something important. Caius has had time to acclimate, certainly, but this is a middling assignment, at best. And it can't be fun playing second to a superior who basically amounts to a cranky skeleton.

"You were at the Dusk Cloister," says Nolan, with obvious intent to change the subject.

Caius glances over, as if sizing Nolan up a second time. "I thought I recognized you. You arrived shortly before I left to begin my apprenticeship." He pauses meaningfully. "You both witnessed the massacre at the Cathedral. When we received word of what had happened . . . I can't imagine."

"You really can't," I say.

Nolan gives me a sharp look. There's loosening our story a little, and there's straying too close to the truth of how those hundreds of devoted really ended up dead.

"Awful." Caius shakes his head. "We must all do what we can to ensure those responsible are brought to justice."

That's all the bonding we manage before we descend a series of stairs into the darker, danker corners of the castle. A stone arch leads into a dim corridor that ends at a thick door. After removing an iron key from his cassock, Caius opens it, revealing a winding staircase leading down into the earth. The air around us shifts, carrying a musty scent of damp stone accented by the hostile tang of human suffering. At the bottom of the stairs, there is a long passage lined with cells. Belspire's prisoners are a sorry lot, shivering in the sharp chill of the dungeon air. I try to ignore the rotten food in the prisoners' bowls, the human waste in places it shouldn't be, and the haunted hollowness of the eyes that follow us. Whatever crimes are being punished here are beyond a penitent's restitution, and a whole lot of *not my business*.

Another staircase takes us even deeper into the earth, to a tight, ancient passage with thick spots of mold clinging to its stones. The light grows almost nonexistent, only a handful of oil lamps barely flickering. If the cells we passed were a place of punishment, this was a place to throw someone away entirely. Or at least somewhere no screams will be heard.

A solitary cell sits at the end of the cramped corridor. It's so dark here that, even with my eyesight, I think it's empty at first. Then: a faint movement in one shadowed corner, from what I mistook for a pile of rags. It's a person . . . mostly. There is something off about the shape and hold of her body, and a hint of old blood hanging in the air.

"Heretic." The pile trembles noticeably at the sound of Caius's voice. "You will answer any of the questions these two ask of you." The Arbiter gestures for us to step forward, something new in his face: anticipation. Apparently, Caius doesn't only oversee the interrogations at Belspire—he enjoys the work. "Proceed."

Nolan steps forward, hands wrapping around the bars of the cell. For a moment I catch something that might be pity, but he's carefully neutral when he turns back to Caius. "We need to question her in private. Those are our orders."

*Our orders from Tempestra-Innara.* That part goes unspoken, and Caius doesn't question it, though there's a flicker of disappointment. "Of course. I will return in a while." He starts to depart, then pauses. "You will not be overheard here."

"Thank you for your help, Arbiter Caius." My formal politeness seems to assuage him slightly, and he nods to me before leaving.

Nolan and I wait until his footsteps are long gone, then turn back to the ruined form of the woman in the cell.

There were many facets to our studies at the Cloisters. Swing a blade, read a book, say your prayers—those were the easy parts. But there were *special* lessons too, ones that were as much tests of our nerve as they were additions to our education.

I can tell at once that the woman has been badly tortured. She relaxes slightly after Caius is gone, limbs loosening in the bloodied scraps that remain of her clothing. Her light skin is a mess of bruises and open wounds, a few of which have begun to fester. Even if she wasn't being executed tomorrow, she wouldn't survive another week, at least not without immediate medical attention and a shitload of luck. I trace the paths of her injuries, noting size and shape and location, a picture forming of what Caius did, or had done to her.

After all, we both received the same education.

It's surprising how tough a body can be, though. Even those not divinely blessed don't die nearly as easily as one would think.

"What's your name?" Nolan says, as if coaxing a scared puppy.

Her cracked lips move, but no sound comes out. She tries again: "Magda."

"Well"—there's a sour taste in my mouth—"at least Caius didn't cut her tongue out."

Nolan grunts in agreement. "Thank the Goddess for small miracles. Magda, we are going to ask you questions. You are going to answer them. Do you understand this?"

Two bright eyes peer up at us, and though that look is guarded, there's a sheen of defiance. A minute ago, I would have called this woman broken. Now, I'm not so sure.

"I answered all of his questions," she croaks. "Please, I told him everything I know."

"Then tell me too," says Nolan. "You were an associate of Emmaus, who willingly allowed himself to be captured in order to poison hundreds of the Goddess's devotees on the day of his execution." The lie flows so smoothly from him that I almost forget that it is, in fact, a lie. But what does Magda know? Was she even aware that Emmaus's capture was planned, and not plain misfortune? Or that Nolan's mentioning of the "poisoning" is pure horseshit? Her swollen features betray nothing. "Emmaus," Nolan continues, "who tried—and failed—to assassinate the Goddess." Magda shows surprise at that. I'm a little shocked at Nolan's bluntness myself. "Did you know about that part of the plan, Magda?"

His voice is gentle, but as Magda processes what he's said, she trembles. "When the last deity falls, when the Butcher Goddess is gone . . ." Words trickle from between her lips, thin as tissue. "They will all be remade into flesh once more."

Pure heresy. Those words alone would have earned her execution. Not that it matters now. She's already condemned, so what's a little more blasphemy? But her belief in those words is powerful, an undying whisper among the heretics. The prize that awaits them, if they simply keep the faith.

It's also, according to every scholar who serves Tempestra-Innara, utter tripe. The dead gods are *dead*. And while I don't exactly trust them to offer up a truth that doesn't serve the Goddess, in this particular case, I agree. If any of the gods were able to come back from the "dead," they surely would have done so by now.

Magda remains quiet for a few more moments. Then she shifts, shivering with the pain of that movement. "I didn't know they were trying to kill the Goddess. Had no idea they could even . . ." She stops herself. "I didn't know anything at all. I told the Arbiters, I was a waystation, that was all."

"So, what?" Nolan presses. "Someone shows up at your door, you feed them dinner and make their bed up, and that's it, no questions asked?"

"Yes," says Magda, but bitterly. "Emmaus was hiding; he knew he was being tracked. He was supposed to have moved on. But the Executrix, she . . . she arrived sooner than expected." Her voice drops even quieter. "Please, I am no one. Only the waystation, nothing more."

She's telling the truth. She didn't know Emmaus had the means for an assassination. She's no one important, at least not when it comes to any heretic conspiracy.

But she's also lying. It's there, hidden behind those truths, doing its best not to be spotted. Maybe Caius didn't see it, or maybe he simply didn't care and eventually grew bored of trying to pull the information out of her, but she is certainly, most definitely, holding something back.

"This is pointless." I push Nolan aside. "She's not going to tell us anything useful like this."

I reach for the door. It's metal, but old, corroded by centuries of damp and rust. One good yank from me and the lock snaps, the door swinging inward into the cell. Magda lets out a wretched squeak as I enter, shrinking back into her rags.

I stop a few paces away and sink to the floor. It's dirty with the sort of filth I don't want to think too hard about, but I do it anyway, crossing my legs and resting my hands on my knees. Magda blinks at me.

"This is better, huh?"

Her confused gaze moves from me to the open door, and then to Nolan before coming back to me.

"You can't run," I say. "You know that. We'd catch you before you finished deciding to make a break for it. So please don't try. You've clearly been through enough pain already." Her puzzlement remains, but she knows I'm right. "There's something you aren't telling us. Something I think can help us find out more about what Emmaus did. I get you don't want to betray your associates, but you are here, and they are not. And even if you don't help us, they will be found eventually. Right now, me and Nolan here are a surgeon's knife. We can make a few quick, clean cuts to deal with the problem. But if that doesn't happen, I can guarantee you the Goddess will send more, larger knives, and swords, and cannons. Which will mean a lot of innocent people caught in the crossfire. We'd rather that not happen—not to the devoted, nor to heretics."

I know my words have an effect because her expression hardens slightly behind her greasy strands of hair. "Don't pretend to care about anyone you consider a heretic. To you, we are rats to be exterminated."

Torture hasn't fully smothered the fire in her, that's for certain. Caius is clearly more enthusiastic about it than competent. "That's not true. I . . . I was a heretic too, once. My people gave tribute to the Storm Goddess. Prayed to them. I've seen the Endless Storm." I sense the slightest tensing from Nolan at this tidbit, there and gone. "I didn't worship Tempestra-Innara. And still, they chose me, blessed me with their divinity. The Goddess can, and does, forgive all." I can lie too, when I need to.

"No." Magda's eyes go terrifyingly distant. "No, there is no forgiveness. He judged me, saw the truth inside . . . I won't . . . can't . . ." Her words flake apart like ash.

I turn to Nolan, unsure of the next tactic. There's something strange in his face, something I can't quite read. He enters the cell and reaches for Magda. She comes alive again, a cry of horror catching in her throat, but he merely lays a hand on her shoulder.

"An Arbiter's judgement is a harsh thing," Nolan says, "but it is not nearly as bad as the divine flame." He removes his hand. "I can tell you this with absolute truth, Magda—your execution will be a hundred times worse than anything you've experienced so far. Do you understand that?"

Instead of answering, Magda looks to me.

I'm not sure where Nolan is going with this, but I nod, having seen more executions than I care to remember. "A thousand times. The flame purifies." I can tell the truth too. "And as it does that, it's going to feel like you are being spit roasted while having your skin flayed as a bunch of angry rats chew their way out of you. What I'm saying is that it's going to hurt . . . a lot."

Nolan kneels down beside me so that he is at the same level as Magda. "You don't have to die like that. Whatever you owe the people you call friends, it is not the horrible fate that is waiting for you."

Magda begins to tremble again, her veneer of strength cracking. As amazingly resilient as the human body and mind can be in the face of death, everyone has their limits. And Magda is nearing hers.

"What do you . . ." Her voice breaks. "I don't understand . . ."

"Mercy." Nolan offers the word like a gift. "Whatever you may think or believe, Tempestra-Innara is merciful. And right now, *we* speak for the Goddess. Accept their offer of leniency: Tell us what we want to know, and your final judgement can happen here, and now. No more waiting. No crowd cheering for your death. No pain." There's an ache in his voice. "I promise."

I hold still as stone as both Magda and I realize what he's offering, something I should have caught on to ages ago. Once Nolan mentioned the assassination attempt, there was no chance we'd be leaving her alive.

Her eyes flicker between us—confused, frantic. "I . . . I don't believe you. You're lying."

"I'm not." Nolan reaches for his reverie, as if swearing on it. "But do not deceive me. I'll know it if you do. This offer only works if we both tell the truth." His features are soft, glazed with a sort of tired truth. His offer is both terrible and kind, and a testament to the lengths he's willing to go in order to serve the Goddess.

Magda considers for a long time, the faint beat of her heart pounding at the cage of her ribs. She is a heretic, one who believes the fallen gods still persist somewhere, kept at a distance by Tempestra-Innara's existence, and though she's still subject to the Goddess's judgement in this world, does she believe she'll face some others' in the next? One way or another, she is going to die.

Finally, her head drops. She takes a deep, rattling breath, one that probably feels as bad as it sounds. "I don't know much. I didn't lie about being no one; all I did was like you said: hide someone, feed them . . . that's all. But sometimes, they'd talk. Or sometimes, someone else would arrive, never for more than a few hours. I always left them alone when that happened, but the walls of my home were thin. Sometimes . . . sometimes they'd talk about a meeting place, where some of our network can always be found if they are needed."

"Where?" prompts Nolan.

"They never called it by name," Magda says. "Only by vague titles— 'where the Butcher Goddess fears to tread,' 'where the stones still weep.' But once, one of them slipped, saying 'the place where the trees weep' instead of 'stones.' That was when I knew where it was."

*The place where the Goddess fears to tread. Where the trees weep . . .*

"Novena." I figure it out as she says the name, barely louder than a whisper. Suddenly, Magda's attention is only for me. "You said you've seen the storm."

Yes, I've seen the Endless Storm. I've seen a sepulchrae—the spot where a god died, where the remnants of their divine power still remain. Novena is another, where Tempestra-Enoch waged battle against their last living sibling—Arcadius-Viktori, the Green God. The city where that god once kept their temple and gardens.

"Novena," Magda says again. "That's all I know, I swear to the fallen gods."

Nolan remains silent, then nods. "Thank you."

He moves forward, taking her in his arms. She goes willingly, her body ceasing its shaking as his embrace tightens around her. For a moment, they seem like family, or even lovers, comforting each other. Then Nolan's hands move up to cradle Magda's head.

"May the lost gods forgive me," she whispers, closing her eyes.

Nolan's movement is quick, decisive. I hear a snap.

"There is no god but Tempestra-Innara," he whispers, a calm expression on his face.

But Magda is already beyond those words, body slumping into him like a sleeping child.

# *Twelve*

> My life is finished. My faith is not.
>
> —LAST WORDS OF THE HERETIC TOBIUS,
> EXECUTED IN THE ERA OF TEMPESTRA-ENOCH

I WAS TWELVE YEARS OLD the first time I killed someone, which was the age the Cloisters decided we should get that little milestone over with.

It was a frigid morning and I hated it. Hated the sharp edge of the air, the wet puffs of our breath inside the carriage, the glassy cracking of the wheels rattling over frozen puddles. We hadn't been told where we were going, but no one was shocked to arrive at the Cathedral. By then we were as familiar with it as our own beds. It was nearly as cold inside as out; if the teeth of the golden skulls had been chattering, I wouldn't have been surprised. But a far less amusing sight awaited: prisoners, five of them on their knees before the apse, naked save for the chains around their wrists and ankles.

"This is today's lesson." Prior Petronilla stopped before the shivering line. "These criminals have been condemned to die. You will carry out the sentence."

It was that simple. Five children stood before five grown adults, and it was the adults who shuddered. Their heads hung to their chests, defeat so clear that I mused over whether they'd been drugged. But then one raised his head, glaring with a defiant anger. Blood crusted his mouth and chin, and I understood that there'd be no pleas for mercy; their tongues had been removed.

"There is no ceremony here, only your task." Prior Petronilla went to a table that had been set up and pulled aside the velvet cloth covering it, revealing a selection of weapons. "Proceed."

*Or else.*

She didn't say it. She *never* said those words, but they were a blade held to our throats at all times. If we failed as Potentiates, we were weak—liabilities to the authority and prosperity of the Goddess. Such a thing was not allowed. Weak meant useless. Weak meant dead.

I scanned the instruments offered, each of which I'd used before. By then, drawing blood was nothing, a daily occurrence in our training. But I'd never taken a life.

I had, however, watched lives taken. Many of them, most notably on a morning nearly as icy as this, and it was that memory that rooted me in place so long that the first prisoner was dead before I realized we'd gotten started. It was Morgan, of course, a consummate suck-up even then. No spears yet—on that morning she chose a short sword and drove it through a prisoner's heart to the hilt. The other condemned whimpered, one even began to cry, but there were no illusions of hope. One by one, the other Potentiates of the Dawn Cloister killed them, until only a single prisoner was left.

It was the one who'd glared with such hate, left all for me.

I still didn't move. I'd gone completely cold in a way that had nothing to do with the temperature, my ears filled with a thick, rushing sound. Only when Prior Petronilla shuffled impatiently did my fugue crack. Memory had dragged me deep, but survival's roots went deeper. I went to the table and grabbed the first weapon I saw—a sickle. Then I returned to the prisoner. His heart was thumping so hard I could see it beneath the wasted flesh of his chest. But still, that insolent stare. I was glad to see it.

Even if it changed nothing.

One swing, and it was over. I stared as the blood pooled at my feet, mingling with what was already there, expecting something. A new understanding, a change within myself.

Instead, there was only a familiar sensation. One that chased away the cold entirely. I looked up, unsurprised to find that the Goddess had appeared, a smile on their face as they surveyed their Chosen's grim handiwork. It was a smile that blessed the completion of our lesson. A smile that blessed our ruthless decisiveness.

A smile that I couldn't stop myself from returning.

Nolan gently moves Magda aside, leaning her body against the wall, then stands. It's too quiet suddenly, the beat of her heart silenced. She doesn't look asleep. There's no peace in her face. She simply looks dead, a living, breathing creature full of misguided faith one minute, a sack of meat and bone the next.

Still, better this fate than the one awaiting her.

Nolan appears tired, but determined. I wait for him to say something about my little confession, even chastise me for my past heresy. But he holds his tongue.

"Next stop, Novena?"

He only nods.

"What have you *done*?"

Behind us, Caius stands in the door of the cell, looking as if we've smashed a prized toy.

Nolan's expression shifts, turning from fatigue to indifference. "What we needed to do in order to get the information we required."

"You denied the Goddess their justice. This woman was to be purified tomorrow, before the eyes of the city."

"She needed to be interrogated," Nolan says calmly. "In a better manner, apparently, than before."

Caius's eyes narrow. "What did she say? Whatever it was, it was likely a lie. Especially if this is the trade you offered her."

Nolan shrugs. "If it is, we've no less information than before."

"*What did she say?*"

Nolan doesn't flinch. "The Goddess has entrusted us to handle this matter with discretion, including among our blood brethren."

Caius is *not* happy to be denied. "No matter what you learned, this is an affront to the Goddess. And *you* will have to pay the price for it."

Nolan's gaze darkens in a way I don't like. I step between the pair. "Hey! Enough. You're fighting over a corpse." I face Caius. "You can still purify her for the festival. It'll be more like a barbecue than an execution now, sure, but you'll get your show either way." That doesn't seem to assuage him, but it's all I've got. "Sorry, but we did what was needed. We're all serving the Goddess here."

Playing diplomat is the last thing in the world I'm used to doing, but the reminder does the trick.

The anger fades from Caius's features, replaced with a practiced calm. "Yes, of course we are. But Arbiter Gottschalk is not going to be pleased."

"Then tell him to reread our letter again," says Nolan. "And if he's still feeling vexed, he can go to the Cathedral and bring it up with Tempestra-Innara themselves. But trust me, I can tell you right now how that will go."

Caius considers him coolly. Then: "You are under the orders of our blood mother, and their will takes precedence above all else. Please forgive my loss of temper. This prisoner was under my charge, and sometimes it is hard to see beyond one's own responsibilities."

The air around us settles.

"Apology accepted," I say, before Nolan can stir things up again. That's *my* area of expertise. "And you'll be rid of us soon enough."

"Not too soon, I hope." Caius clasps his hands in front of him. "We've had rooms made up for you. And Arbiter Gottschalk has requested that you join us for dinner tonight. With the princess, of course."

I'd nearly forgotten there was royalty somewhere about.

I shrug in reply. "Sure. I've never had dinner with a princess before."

"Then come." Caius leads us out of the cell, ignoring Magda's corpse. "I'll send someone along to deal with *that* later."

The bedroom Caius deposits me in makes my cell in the Cloister look like a hovel. Tapestries, carpets, a bed so soft it seems to be trying to swallow me—being stationed in Belspire may not be the pinnacle of assignments, but it's clearly not the worst either.

I know that plenty of my blood brethren live in finery. Many even better than this. Spacious residences, loads of servants, as many high-quality, artisanal weapons as their hearts desire—tribute in honor of our revered rank. But Prior Petronilla and the other instructors at the Dawn Cloisters don't preach the lifestyle. The opposite, in fact: A true devotee of the Goddess remains humble. They do not desire the gifts that come with the station her blood gift grants us.

But—surprise, surprise—plenty of us end up with them anyway.

The first thing I do is bathe. I hate admitting it, but the baths at the Dawn Cloister spoiled me. I loathe the sensation of grime on my skin, of unwashed hair, of whatever else has built up after many days on the road. I soak for at least an hour, letting the languid scents of infused oils smother what happened in the dungeon. I don't feel bad; Magda bought herself a merciful end. But her conviction gnaws at me, and no amount of lavender and rose chases away the sound of Nolan snapping her neck.

A sound like cracking ice.

Physical, if not mental, cleanliness achieved, I return to the bedroom to find that a pair of dresses as well as a tailored jacket and waistcoat set have appeared, laid out carefully on the bed. Each one is an extravagance, silk and lace and what might be real gemstones sewn into one of the necklines. I gather them up and toss them into the hall before putting on my cleanest set of regular clothes.

A timid knock sounds.

"Come in!"

A youth enters, neatly liveried and green in the face, as if he's about to tell me someone I'm fond of has died. He swallows hard before speaking. "The clothing—"

"Was too elegant for the likes of me. My travel companion Nolan might like them, though." He pales further, and I take pity on him. "I prefer my own garments, that's all. How long until dinner?"

"Two hours," he replies.

At least killing time won't leave me wanting another bath. And if I have it, I might as well put it to use. "Belspire has a library, right?"

He nods enthusiastically. "One of the finest in the Devoted Lands."

"Take me there." I expect resistance, not knowing exactly what the scope of my privileges as a guest is, but the boy seems relieved to be given an order he can fulfill.

The library is massive. It makes the one at the Cloister, which Prior Petronilla always made out to be enviable, look as pathetic as the stacks of smutty pamphlets the attendants used to smuggle Jeziah sometimes. There's row after row of shelves, the chamber opening up to reveal two more levels above us, books lining the walls from floor to ceiling. It's obviously not the excitement center of Belspire—I see no one but an older woman who appears to be the librarian dozing over a tome, a line of drool hanging perilously close to its pages—but it's clearly been cared for. There's not a trace of dust, and while the library carries a sense of age, it doesn't have the threadbare feeling of the rest of the castle.

"How do I find anything in here?" I ask.

He shows me a codex in one corner, after which I send him away. The system is easy enough, and within minutes I have pulled a stack of texts and found myself a private little niche in which to peruse them.

Research topic of the day: gods.

Magda and Emmaus both clung to their faith until the very end, believing that felling Tempestra-Innara would bring back the other gods, something they have exactly zero proof of. My reason for wanting Tempestra-Innara dead is at least tangible: I want to be free. But the heretics? Their vehemence in serving gods gone for centuries seems more mad than not, sepulchrae notwithstanding. I have seen the Endless Storm. And it sounds like I'll see Novena soon enough too. But so have countless others who've watched and waited and prayed and sacrificed and probably done a funny dance or two, all in hope of a dead god's return. And yet . . . nothing.

Still, Magda truly believed there was a way to bring the dead gods back. As did Emmaus. Would my blood brethren spin similar beliefs if Tempestra-Innara croaked? Maybe. Probably. If nothing else it would be the smart way to hang on to power and their posh lifestyles. Of course, if it happens by my hand, I don't plan to stick around to find out. Things always gets bad after the death of a god. *Real* bad. The carving up of a dead deity's former lands, both literally and figuratively... cleanup in the form of countless conversions and excessive penance... messy. Divinity is as much a poison as a blessing. The world *will* be better off without it... once it's done losing its mind.

But right now, my concern isn't what Tempestra-Innara's followers will do later; it's what the dead gods' followers are doing now, and how. I—we—need more information about the reliquaries. If what the Goddess said is true—and I'm not entirely sold on that idea—reliquaries used to be common knowledge. Which means that someone, somewhere, wrote something down about them at some point, and maybe I can find some mention in one of the countless old texts I'm currently keeping company with.

It's an idea I'm quickly disabused of.

There's no shortage of books about the gods in Belspire's library. But they are, for the most part, the same sorts I'd find moldering on the Dawn Cloister shelves, missing only the occasional dirty doodle left behind by a bored Potentiate. My best find is a large map within one folio, so detailed that I'm able to find the approximate location of my former village. It's not marked, of course, but the storm is, a seething cloud of charcoal shot through with inky lightning. There is also a sketchy patch of withered plant life—Novena. Choppy waves and the rendering of a splintered prow where the Salt Goddess fell. One sketch for each of the dead gods, except the Whisperer, weakest of the divinities and first to fall when they tried to remedy that flaw by stealing their siblings' power. Shadow, Stone, Salt, Storm, and finally the Green God. All dead from one divine disagreement or another. Only the Flame left standing.

"Find something good to read?"

I nearly jump out of my skin. *Caius.* He stands calmly at the end of the table where I've built my nest of texts. "For fuck's—do you have any idea how long it's been since someone snuck that close to me without me knowing?"

He sniffs with faint amusement. "I know Arbiters are often viewed as less capable in the physical arts, but I still remember my Cloister training. We all have our little talents."

"Clearly. Someone should put a bell on you."

He's clearly proud of having taken me off guard—which is fair enough—but is restrained enough not to rub it in. Instead, he considers my leather-bound piles. "Interesting choices."

"Not nearly as much as I'd hoped." I slam the folio shut.

"Were you searching for something in particular?"

A light, honeyed tone. Nothing like the one he used in the dungeon. I don't like the shift. It makes me wonder how much he's been pondering what Nolan and I are really up to. But putting his interest off is more likely to spark suspicion than stamp it out. "Anything about the followers of the dead gods, especially from before they fell. Trying to get into the heads of the heretics, understand why their devotion remains so strong, or where they might hide out."

"Tch." Caius frowns. "Misguided fools."

"Sure," I say, "but persistent ones. And we were always encouraged to know our enemies."

Caius's eyes pinch ever so slightly. "So we are. But I doubt you'll find anything in these texts."

Now there's a hint of allurement to his words. "You got something better for me?"

With a knowing smile, he beckons.

And, with a grateful one, I play along and follow.

# Thirteen

There are seven hundred and twenty-three steps in the Stone God's ziggurat, a feat eclipsed only by the depths of the mines that circle it. It is as if their devoted are equally intent on reaching both the heavens and the hells in their honor.

—*JOGUE'S DIARY OF A SUPPLICANT'S TRAVELS*
(RESTRICTED TEXT)

There's an iron gate in the very back of the library, swirling wrought ivy painted in shades of green, more shelves tempting from behind it.

"Decorative and functional." I touch the gate as if appreciating the detailed work. Despite their delicateness, the vines feel as unyielding as, well, iron. "So, this is where you keep the good stuff."

Caius produces a key. "Certain texts aren't appropriate for *all* eyes." He unlocks the gate, which swings outward with a reluctant groan. "After you."

I step inside. The spines within are obviously older than the ones without, and less familiar. I scan a few titles, recognizing nothing.

"You are free to peruse these, so long as they remain within this room." Caius turns to leave, then pauses. "I know the selection well. Perhaps *I* could be of help. That is, *if* you could provide a few more specifics about the information you're looking for . . . or how it might help you?"

There it is, nosiness throwing off the cloak of kindly assistance. At least it doesn't seem like he's holding a grudge after what happened in the dungeon. And it's hard to blame him; I'd probably want to know what we're up to too. But it's not like I can ask directly about reliquaries. I think for a moment. "What's the oldest book you've got about the gods? All of them."

"Hmm." Caius goes to a curved shelf in one corner. "*Jogue's Diary of a Supplicant's Travels.*"

He hands me a small book with six stars debossed into a stained leather binding. Handling it carefully, I flip it open to find handwritten text relieved by the occasional sketched drawing.

"A copy of a copy of a copy," Caius says. "But Jogue was alive when six of the gods still lived. He traveled between their centers of worship, recording his observations. I'm not sure you'll find anything to explain the contemporary heretical mentality, but there may be some information about the old ways of worship."

"Thank you. It could be helpful."

*In regards to what?* his expression reads, as if he expects me to say more. When I don't, he moves to the door. "I'll return to collect you for dinner."

Then he locks me in. I guess they're serious about keeping these books where they are.

Jogue's diary begins in a neat, mundane fashion: brief descriptions of the gods' main centers of worship—Lumeris, Novena, Cyprene, and the rest—then quickly unravels into a series of seemingly chaotic daily logs and observations: lists of festivals and practices, an account of a poorly maintained road, sketches of notable architecture, rituals that caught his eye. There's page after page of it, the script and sketches wild in some places, clear and structured in others. And detailed in a way that makes the growing hunger in my stomach disappear, and my craving for knowledge grow.

It's almost hard to believe that, once, seven gods ruled in the Devoted Lands, worshipped in tandem. Jogue describes Novena as a verdant paradise overflowing with lush gardens and groves. I mainly know it as the place where the number of divinities was reduced to one, following the biggest bloodbath in history. That's something none of the texts ever tried to sugarcoat: A conflict between gods is always catastrophic. Thousands consumed by Tempestra-Enoch's flame, or smothered by Arcadius-Viktori's earthy poisons. The battle began at dawn, and it's written that by the time night fell, the ground was so thick with the dead that the surviving forces tread on a carpet of corpses. In the end, Tempestra-Enoch backed Arcadius-Viktori into their temple pyramid, a structure that, like its ruling divinity, didn't survive the final confrontation. Tempestra-Enoch paid a high price for their victory, though. The damage done to Enoch was too extensive even for the Goddess's healing powers. They took Innara as their new avatar soon after.

Now Novena is abandoned, nothing but a sepulchrae. A place so steeped in death that most believe it to be cursed forever.

But not all. If what Magda said was true, the heretics clearly had no qualms in setting up residence there.

I flip through the booklet, skimming for more about Novena, when a drawing catches my eye: crossed lightning bolts, an old symbol of the Storm Goddess Serapia. But it's the ring of crudely sketched figures surrounding the symbol that interests me. It's hard to tell, but each one seems to be clutching something in their hands. Something that might be a box, or other small container.

Maybe even a bottle.

I scan the text around it. It doesn't seem to have a narrative, more like notes meant to be strung together later.

*... winds fierce enough to shear flesh from bone ...*

*... a tribute of jewels and silks ...*

*... keeps their vessels ...*

I stop. Vessels?

*Most recently, it's said, the Goddess has turned suspicious, keeping their vessels close at hand, never far from their divine source.*

It's only a single line, but it *must* be a reference to the reliquaries. The drawing implies there were many of them, and the note seems to say that Serapia stopped sending them out into the Devoted Lands. But who knows how many might have been lost or stolen before that happened? Or maybe the Storm Goddess hid some away—maybe *all* the divinities did—reliquaries that were forgotten or lost when they fell. It certainly explains how one could have found its way into the hands of heretics centuries later. There wasn't likely to have been an inventory, after all; even Tempestra-Innara might have missed some in a hunt for stragglers.

The diary at least corroborates what the Goddess told us, but the musings are so disorganized, so fractured, that I quickly realize it could take me days to properly read through it . . . days I don't have. So, when Caius comes to collect me, I make a show of returning the books I've pulled to their shelves, all save one, which is already secreted in my coat. And I tell myself that if Caius knew what we were really up to, he'd hand it over freely.

The dining room is like some strange dream, not quite a nightmare, but not exactly inviting either. Most of that is owing to the hundreds of preserved animal heads lining one wall of the long chamber. Beasts great and small (I even spot a squirrel), all shabby with age, their glass eyes dull and clouded. And yet, all looking disconcertingly more alive than the person seated at the head of the banquet table.

The first thing I do is confirm that the princess is still breathing. Papery skin sags below rheumy eyes half hidden behind lifeless strands of long white hair. She wears a dress of fashionable, tailored finery, which only makes the sight more uncomfortable, turning her into a dreadful sort of doll. As Caius and I approach, her gaze hangs straight ahead, the only sign of life a tip of pink tongue that darts out briefly to lick dry, withered lips. Arbiter Gottschalk is seated beside her. By comparison, he's the picture of vigor, though he doesn't stand for my arrival. Instead, he sips from a glass of wine, hand trembling slightly with the effort. Also in attendance are half a dozen of the Thorn Guard, set at intervals around the room, so still I could almost take them for being stuffed too.

A party, for sure.

I have been drilled by instructors on how to behave in countless sorts of formal situations, but I am not prepared for . . . whatever this is. When Caius pulls out a chair for me, I remain standing.

"Apologies, your grace." I don't know if that's the proper title for a powerless figurehead, but it's probably close enough. "I haven't had the chance to introduce myself."

Arbiter Gottschalk makes a sound of impatient annoyance.

Caius outright scoffs. "She can't hear you. No need for formalities here." He speaks louder. "Princess Osmunda doesn't mind skipping them, do you, my dear?"

"My name is Lys," I say anyway. The two Arbiters are clearly dug into Belspire as deeply as ticks and can ignore the usual niceties, but that only makes me want to follow them closer. "Thank you for sharing your hospitality this evening."

I don't know if my words get through, but the tongue makes another brief appearance.

I shut up and sit.

The attendant boy from earlier appears, escorting Nolan to the seat beside me. He's definitely taken the opportunity to clean up too, the dust gone from his skin and clothes. No fancy outfit for him either, but his dark hair is slicked neatly with oil. I catch a whiff of it as he approaches the seat next to me—cedarwood, and a hint of mint. Classy.

"Your grace." He bows before sitting. Princess Osmunda acknowledges him as much as she does me.

Immediately, everything is weird.

Servants rush to fill our wineglasses, a conversation substitute for a few blessed seconds. Then it's the four of us staring silently at one another, and the Princess, staring silently at nothing.

"I trust your rooms were adequate," Gottschalk grumbles, clearly filling the dead air. "Along with everything else." Caius must have informed him about the dungeon events by now. I'm not sure he would have objected, given his instructions from the Cathedral, but he also doesn't bring it up, content to let it hang around us awkwardly.

"Yes," Nolan replies cordially, as if nothing is amiss. "Lovely rooms. Too nice for us, even."

"Speak for yourself." A poor contribution, but the best I can muster.

"Lys has also taken the opportunity to visit our library." Like Nolan, Caius adopts a genial tone.

Gottschalk arches one eyebrow. "Is that so? How did you find it?"

"It definitely has a lot of books." Nolan gives me a questioning look, though I'm not sure if it's in regards to my library visit or my inept response. "I can see why it has such a renowned reputation."

Thankfully, the first course arrives: soup. A bowl is placed in front of each of us, including the Princess, who gets her own special servant to help feed it to her. The first spoonful mostly trickles down her chin. After that, I keep my eyes on my food.

The soup—velvety squash drizzled with oil and cream—is delicious, as is the butter-poached fish and sauteed greens we are served for the second course, and the wine the servants pour almost continuously. Caius and Nolan keep up the polite small talk, mostly discussing the upcoming festival: how long it runs for, what sort of non-execution entertainment there will be—topics so dull I almost long for the spectacle of the Princess's soup eating.

"How is your venison?" Caius contemplates the wine in his glass, as if seeing some vision in its redness. "Delicious, yes?"

"Your cooks should be commended." Nolan dabs at his lips with a linen napkin. His wine remains untouched.

I drain mine yet again. Prior Petronilla was always stingy with it, and the vintage being poured demonstrates that the local vines remain enviable despite the lack of the Green God's favor. The warmth of it spreads through me, taking the edge off a dinner I'm increasingly ready to be over.

"It's a shame you must leave so quickly," says Gottschalk, tone conveying the exact opposite.

"Definitely." I affect a yawn. "But orders are orders, and we shouldn't linger. Speaking of which, we should probably turn in so we can get an early start."

I start to get up, but Caius signals. "Wait, please. You can't miss dessert. We've arranged for something special for you."

I couldn't care less about whatever cake or trifle the Arbiters have had whipped up for us, but we've crossed them enough already. If the price of getting what we needed includes suffering through some buttercream frosting, I suppose I can manage a little longer.

I settle in my seat. "Who doesn't love dessert?"

"Indeed. The Belspire royals have always insisted on a full formal meal, with all the courses, when they entertain. It's considered a necessary politeness." A sly, feline smile touches his lips, then disappears. "We've done away with some of the royal formalities, but even *we* would never allow politeness to fall by the wayside. To do so would be to violate the contract between host and guest. And here . . . well, that's taken quite seriously. The host shows respect to their guests." His gaze turns to me. "And the reverse is expected."

My cheeks burn, the weight of the little tome in my jacket suddenly turning from paper and board to what feels like lead. I'm sorting through explanations and excuses to justify the theft when Caius snaps his fingers.

The doors to the hall open, but instead of servants, more of the Thorn Guard enter, escorting three women in rags. They are herded over to us, burlap bags over their heads to hide their identities. I tense, book forgotten, fingers pressing into the wood of the table, even as I manage to keep outwardly calm. Beside me, Nolan stares at the women with a worrying intensity. I look to Arbiter Gottschalk, but he keeps his gaze downcast and as distant as the Princess's.

"Not sure what kinds of sweets are popular in Belspire," I say lightly, worry worming its way through my full stomach, "but I was sort of expecting cake."

"Don't you like it?" Caius feigns innocence.

"What is *it*, exactly?"

"Like I said . . . dessert." All of his polite friendliness is gone. "Tomorrow's festival is an important one. It celebrates the city's conversion to the ways of our Goddess. But it's more than that. It must also be a reminder—of what happens to heretics, and anyone else who would cross Tempestra-Innara. But your actions earlier saw fit to deny the people that."

Nolan sits a little taller, also abandoning the guise of civility. Anger radiates off him. He turns to Arbiter Gottschalk. "This is unacceptable. We did what we needed to fulfill our orders."

But the senior Arbiter doesn't look at him either. "I do not object to your actions, as I have been instructed. The remuneration Caius calls for is something else entirely."

Then he goes back to drinking his wine, at which point I realize something very important. Something that Nolan and I should have seen earlier: that despite his clear dissatisfaction with his post, Caius is the real power in Belspire.

"We have orders too," Caius continues. "The Goddess has entrusted *us* with their justice. And it will be had."

"Knock off the dramatics." I am heartily regretting agreeing to this dinner. "What do you want?"

"It's simple. The city will see a heretic brought to the Goddess's justice. Since you two killed the one slated for that fate, we need a replacement." Caius gestures to the women. "And you get to choose who that will be."

# Fourteen

The Goddess's justice must be more than a balancing. More than a price paid. It must be the paragon of their doctrines, a lesson through which the devoted and non-devoted alike learn virtue.

—FROM THE TEACHINGS OF HIGH ARBITER DIETRELIK

I ALWAYS SUSPECTED ARBITERS WERE assholes. Now I know it for sure.

One by one, the Thorn Guard yank the burlap hoods from the women, revealing their faces. Weariness monopolizes them, mingled with fear and confusion.

I can sympathize.

"The Goddess demands justice, as do their devoted. Both will have it." Caius is clearly reveling in his control. "Choose which one will replace the heretic you killed."

Silence follows. The women stare at the floor, defeat dragging their shoulders down as they await their fate. One, with limp hair the color of muddy water, trembles slightly. But none react or resist. They are trying to be small, invisible.

I swallow, my mouth dry. "Who are they?"

Caius shrugs. "Does it matter? Heretics, murderers, thieves . . . all beyond penance, all marked for the Goddess's justice in the end."

I cross my arms. "This is ridiculous."

"This is the solution to the problem *you* created."

"We had every right to do what we did." Nolan speaks with bitter incredulity. "But *you* have no right to put us through this cruel exercise, simply because *you* feel slighted."

I almost smirk at the expression that passes over Caius's face, but something tells me that would only serve to annoy him further.

Caius stands, fingers pressing into the table so hard they turn white. "I am an Arbiter."

"Ahem," I say. "*Assistant* Arbiter." Why annoy when I can infuriate?

It works. Caius's cheeks flush, his eyes narrowing on me. "Choose."

"No. She won't," Nolan says. "Neither will I."

"What he said," I add. "We're not playing this sick little game."

"Then you aren't going anywhere." Caius turns calm. Too calm. "I'll take no pleasure in putting my blood brethren in chains, but if that's what's necessary, I will. You will remain here, under our power, until we can contact the Cathedral and have them sort this out with the Goddess directly."

"Then you are a fool." Nolan shoves away from the table and makes a move toward the door, but four of the Thorn Guard place themselves in front of it. He stops. "You can't do this. Our orders come directly from the Goddess."

"Your orders come from a letter," says Caius. "Which we will simply confirm out of an abundance of caution. And, if they prove legitimate, Arbiter Gottschalk and I will make the proper apologies and reparations as needed."

I swear silently. And then out loud. Caius and Gottschalk's resolve leaves no room for argument. I shouldn't be surprised both chose dogmatic adherence to an act of devotion over common sense; that's what we're trained to do. But making us choose a replacement for Magda... The women mean nothing to him; their deaths, nothing but a treat to be fed to the devoted masses. The absurdity of it starts something screaming within me.

Forgotten, the Princess gurgles a little, as useful a contribution as any.

"Lys." Nolan says my name quietly, moving closer. "We don't need to be pulled into this. No matter what Caius believes, his power in Belspire isn't absolute."

"No," I say. "It's not." But the longer we are stuck here, the more likely we will lose any chance to find the reliquary. We can't delay, no matter how outrageous the Arbiters' demand is. And I'm not foolish enough to think that one of those women won't end up dead meat anyway.

Caius frowns. "We won't wait for—"

"Her." I point, ignoring the churning remains of the meal in my stomach.

Caius's gaze traces my gesture, and he smiles with the sort of satisfaction that makes me want to punch the smugness from him until he begs me to stop. "Very well."

"Lys—" There's worry in Nolan's voice now. "You don't have to—"

"It's done." I drop my arm. "Can we go now?"

Another long minute passes in which Caius savors his triumph. Still seated, Gottschalk is indifferent, or maybe simply content the deed is done.

Then Caius nods. "Very well. But I hope you will reconsider leaving before the festival begins. You clearly need to be reminded of the purifying power of our Goddess's judgement."

"Oh yeah? Take a wild guess where you can shove your purification." I turn on my heel and charge the guards standing before the door. Wisely, they move aside, and I shove the doors open so hard they slam against the wall.

I drank too much wine. Ate too much rich food. I feel both thickening my blood, which is filling my head to overflowing. The castle blurs as a chill runs over my skin, scraping its way down my spine.

"Lys!"

Nolan's voice, but far away. Beneath the rushing in my ears. I ignore it. Barely paying attention to where I am going, I reach a set of stairs. Stumble. Catch myself.

The ice cracks.

"Lys!" A hand clamps down on my shoulder. "Wait!"

The world snaps back into focus as I spin, tearing free. Nolan stares down at me from a step above, eyes hard with concern, a deep furrow in his brow. My hand aches. I look down to see a splinter piercing the pad of my palm. A chunk is missing from the banister. Apparently, I caught myself a bit harder than necessary.

I take a deep breath and pull the bit of wood free. Blood beads. "Oops."

The furrow deepens. "You shouldn't have had to do that."

The kind way he says it actually manages to chase away some of the chill.

"You shouldn't have had to snap Magda's neck." Another crack echoes in memory. "We need to keep going. You dealt with her. I dealt with this. It was only fair."

His lips thin. "There was nothing fair about it." The words are quiet. I don't back away as he takes a step down so that he's standing beside me. Standing *with* me. We were supposed to be rivals. Instead, this is the second time he's defended me against our own brethren. Clearly, Nolan takes our assignment to work together seriously. "That was a decision you shouldn't have had to make."

I didn't, though. Didn't even know which woman I was pointing at. Because it's easy to condemn a person if they mean nothing to you, a lesson I learned long before I arrived at the Cathedral. I can't tell Nolan that, though. I look away, mad at myself, at Caius and Gottschalk, and, most of all, at the Goddess who has forced us into these ruthless roles. Something warm alights on my arm.

His hand. Hesitant. An attempt at comfort, if an unpracticed one.

My cheeks flush again, but not out of anger. Definitely had too much wine.

"I want to leave." I step away. "We have what we need. There's no reason to stay in this rotten place any longer."

Nolan's hand, now consoling nothing but air, drops. "The horses need rest. We do too. We did what we needed to do. Tomorrow, we can begin again. But there's nothing to be gained by leaving tonight."

He's right of course. Even though staying a minute longer makes me fantasize about tearing the castle down with my bare hands, finishing what time and neglect has already started. But I nod, swallowing my other emotions.

More anger I will put aside, store up, and save for my Butcher Goddess blood mother, Tempestra-Innara.

# Fifteen

> Within the city, the bells of Belspire sing like a glorious choir. Go beyond its gates, though, beyond its borders . . . when the wind carries that song, it can sound like cries.
>
> —FROM THE WRITINGS OF CLERIC ERIS

I **STAND AT THE EDGE** of the white river.

Wind whips and screams, needling my skin with snowflakes as chalky clouds press down from above. On the other side of the water an invisible promise beckons: freedom.

I don't want to move, but I do.

Tracks appear in front of me as I step onto the frozen river, hundreds of them, trails for me to follow. But I don't want to. I don't want to follow.

I do anyway.

In the middle of the river, the tracks disappear.

*Run.* My body betrays me again, rooting me where I stand. *Run to where they won't follow.* Liberty is right there, waiting on the other side of the river. But I can't move, and beneath me, the ice begins to crack. Liquid oozes up through the gap.

Not water.

Blood.

*Crack.*

The fissures spread, the white shattering into unsteady pieces.
*Crack.*
I am frozen in place.
*Crack. Crack. Cr—*

I wake up gasping in the hazy morning light, nearly strangled by silk sheets soaked with sweat.

A dream. Familiar and unwelcome.

I curse aloud to my empty room. Kick off the bedding and take another quick bath. Pack my things.

It's time to get the fuck out of Belspire.

Almost as soon as I'm ready, a knock sounds on my door. When I rip it open, Nolan is in the hall, pack slung over one shoulder.

"You look terrible," he says.

"Flattery will get you everywhere." I push past him. "C'mon, we've got better places to be."

We trek through the castle without saying thank you or goodbye or any other of that polite nonsense. But despite Caius's emphasis last night, no one seems to care. It's festival time, and that supersedes any bothersome hospitality. I briefly worry Gottschalk and Caius will try to delay us further, but when we arrive at the stables, the horses are waiting, ready to go. I take Mortimer's reins and check him over. Given the kind of cruelty the Arbiters show for people, who knows what they might do to innocent horses. But Mortimer appears to have been well cared for, nickering softly as I rub the star on his nose.

At the castle gate, I curse again. Thousands are already gathered in the plaza, surrounding the stage constructed in the center. I'd hoped to be gone before the festival kicked off, but no such luck. It's slow going, making our way through the press of bodies, all bright eyed and joyous at the prospect of starting the morning off with an invigorating execution. There's laughter. Singing. Vendors hawking their special-occasion foods. Yesterday, my mouth watered. This morning I want to throw up. As we move, I keep my gaze turned away from the stage set at the feet of Tempestra-Innara's statue, and the foreboding metal post at its center.

We almost make it out of the plaza before I stop.

Nolan draws up beside me. "Is something the matter?"

"No." I can't help myself. I turn back to the dais. The post. "Yes."

I swing Mortimer back so that I am facing the center of the plaza. Horsed, I have a fine view above the sea of people.

"Lys?" Nolan speaks gently, but in a tone heavy with questions.

"Just . . . wait." I don't look at him, only the post. "Please."

He doesn't say anything else. We wait.

After a few minutes, the bells begin to ring.

They start one at a time but soon overlap each other, a high, joyful chorus. I expect the crowd to cheer, but instead a reverent silence falls, seeming to spread beyond us, throughout the rest of the city. Some lips move in prayer, but no one speaks a single word aloud.

Soon, a procession emerges from the castle. Caius rides at the head of it, followed by a palanquin with gauzy curtains obscuring the flaccid figure of the princess within. I don't see Gottschalk.

Then comes the prisoner. She's on an open wagon, bound with ropes, burlap covering her face yet again. The people part to allow access to the dais. There, guards drag the woman up the stairs and bind her to the post. Only then does Caius dismount and join her.

Suddenly, the bells cease.

The cheering begins.

It hits me like a punch to the gut: the communal bloodlust that Caius was so desperate to feed. How long have Belspire's people been waiting for this rare treat, this echo of the slaughter that began their fealty? It doesn't matter that there's no real justice here, or that the woman on the dais isn't Magda. They have a body, someone to blame. To judge.

Caius holds up his hands. With his blessed eyesight, he should have no trouble seeing us. But if he does, there's no break in his ritualistic performance. This is his show, one that he must think will help elevate him, maybe even garner enough of the Goddess's favor to promote him away from Belspire. Which means he's going to lay it on as thick as he can.

The crowd quiets at his gesture.

"Belspire." His voice carries throughout the plaza. "Today we gather to remember the most hallowed moment in our history: the day when this fair city saw the true light and dedicated itself wholly to our Goddess Tempestra-Innara. May the Flame warm us all."

*When they whisper, we wake . . .*

The crowd responds with prayer. When Nolan joins in, so do I.

*At their command, we follow. In their light, we are seen . . . we are judged . . .*

I want to chew every word to a pulp and spit it onto the street with the dirt and horse shit.

*May their blessed flame find purity of faith, or else leave cinder and ash.*

"Many years have passed since that joyous day," Caius continues, when the voices have settled, "and our city continues to burn brightly under their blessings. But there are still those who deny our Goddess's enduring supremacy, worshipping gods long dead."

The crowd boos.

Caius again gestures for them to quiet. "Under the Goddess's light, the devoted must not suffer a heretic to live. But in their mercy, they do not pass sentence on one who might be saved through penance. They do not punish without first rendering judgement." He turns to the woman and rips the burlap cover from her face.

I tighten. The woman with the muddy-water hair. Her face is red and puffy from crying, and unsurprisingly, she is gagged. Wouldn't want any truth to ruin Caius's stage show.

"With the authority of Tempestra-Innara," says Caius, "I will now gaze into this woman's heart, to see if she bears any true love for our Goddess that might buy her mercy. Or, if as accused, she is a true heretic."

From a pocket, he produces a small bottle of sapphire-blue glass. I've seen such vessels before, but rarely. They hold the potion the Arbiters use in their judging, a carefully guarded recipe known only to the most senior of their Order. With an absurd flourish, Caius unstops the bottle. He raises it, allowing a single drop of the liquid to fall into each eye, then blinks. Even at a distance, the new sheen is apparent.

The Judge's Sight. An Arbiter's bread and butter.

Caius turns to the woman and reaches for her, fingers alighting on her cheek, a gesture that appears almost loving. Her features go blank.

"Lys." Nolan speaks so that only I can hear him. "You don't have to watch this."

As riveted as I am, the sensation of his hand on my arm rises in memory. A touch of genuine concern. His words are an echo of that, but I can't look at him. Can't see if there's even a hint of acceptance for this twisted ritual on his face. At least he knows it's a sham. I cling to that. Then again, if he saw the truth of *my* heart, Nolan would probably tie me to the post himself... a fact that bothers me more than I like.

I keep my eyes on the stage. "Yes, I do."

An anxious minute crawls by, during which whatever is happening before us begins to bleed its way over the crowd. It comes on like an itch, an ache, causing the onlookers to shift and mutter, though I cannot pinpoint any specific sensation. Meanwhile, the judged woman begins to tremble, and then shake, though Caius remains as still as a statue. Life returns to her eyes, which widen with pure horror as her mouth stretches in a desperate, soundless scream. Finally, his hand drops. In the same instant, the woman releases a pained, guttural cry, her whole body going limp with the exertion of the ritual.

Caius spins to the crowd, face flush. "My evaluation is complete." He stabs a finger accusingly. "This woman holds no love for our Goddess, only fear and resentment. She is a true heretic. Therefore, she must suffer a heretic's fate!"

The crowd cheers as if the announcement were ever in doubt. There are exclamations of love and devotion for the Goddess, as well as jeers for the bound woman. Caius indulges the crowd's ferocity a bit longer before turning back. He doesn't need to ask for silence this time. A thousand people collectively take a breath and hold it.

We've reached the moment.

Caius cups his hands together. Then, the divine flame bursts to life with a brilliance that seems impossible in the light of day. He holds it, almost cradles it, before stepping toward the condemned. As he does, pure animalistic fear overtakes the woman. She fights her bindings, emanating a sound that sinks claws into my guts and twists. All futile. As soon as Caius touches the flame to her chest, right above her heart, it moves quickly, racing down her torso, climbing up over her shoulders. The Arbiter's control is spent—the flame is its own creature now, one that knows only a hungry spread. But this is no divine execution. What Caius calls is only an offshoot of the Goddess's. Less pure, less powerful.

Which means it takes a very long time for the woman to die.

Her screams begin immediately, though. The gag flakes away like paper, freeing the sounds further, and I have to grit my teeth to keep myself from looking away. This is what I needed to see, to witness. *I* was the one who sent this woman to her fate. I owe her something, if only that I will have to carry this memory until the day I die.

*Leave.* My thoughts screech as the scent of burning flesh reaches me, as I hear the greasy crackle of her fat. *Go.*

I stay right where I am.

Meanwhile, Caius stands back with an appropriately pious expression, hands folded before him. I sense he's practically bursting with satisfaction, a suspicion that is confirmed when his gaze deliberately finds mine. I keep my expression neutral. Let him think he's gotten the best of me, of us. And maybe he has.

But I know how to kill his goddess.

And if I succeed, his line—our line—ends. No more Arbiter's judgement, no more divine flame.

Maybe he'd still be able to keep power. Someone always does. Still, I allow myself the fantasy of him tied to that post instead of the woman, of him screaming instead of her.

Finally, the woman's cries cease, but Caius remains staring at me. Raising my hand slowly, I flash him a rude gesture, before yanking Mortimer around and heading for the city gates. Nolan follows.

Behind us, the bells begin to cry again.

# Sixteen

When the final blow fell, when the Green God succumbed, its effects were felt leagues and leagues away. In Acerna, the petals plummeted from those celebrated rosebushes. In the orchards of Evene, rot bloomed on all the fruit.

There were no survivors beyond those first few hours. Poison pervaded Novena with such ferocity that anyone—soldier, priest, Chosen—who didn't flee immediately remained permanently, entombed in a bramble crypt.

—FROM *THE AFTERMATH OF ARCADIUS*,
BY PRIOR MATTHOS (RESTRICTED TEXT)

WE RIDE FOR HOURS before Nolan finally breaks the weighted silence.

"Caius was doing what the Goddess has entrusted him to do."

Oh, I know. How I fucking know.

"Though," he continues, "I will admit that his implementation leaves something to be desired."

"You mean the part where he clearly enjoyed roasting that woman alive?" There's a bitter edge to my words and I don't even care.

*You don't have to watch this.*

That's what Nolan said. But I did. Because I've already spent enough of my life looking the other way. For as long as I've wanted Tempestra-Innara dead, craved being free of them, I still served. Still did what I needed to survive. Still lapped up the Goddess's attention like some godsdamned thirsty kitten and . . .

And that's how I would have continued, day after day, year after year, if not for Emmaus's assassination attempt. Standing by while the Goddess and their devoted throw burn-the-heretic parties. But the fact that Nolan said what he did means he doesn't think I'm weak for not wanting to watch a heretic burn. That he doesn't revel in suffering, like Caius and so many of Belspire's residents seemed to. I like that about him.

"Yes," Nolan agrees. "But we follow the Goddess's will whether or not we enjoy the particulars of it. Magda will not be the last heretic we encounter. Would you spare them?"

"No, of course not." Where is this questioning going? "Unchecked heresy is obviously *bad*. But we weren't sent to punish heretics. We were sent to find the reliquary."

"Yes," he says.

A minute of silence passes.

"In the dungeon," he begins, as I knew he would, eventually. "What you said to Magda . . ."

"Disgusted to find out a heretic has been given the divine gift?" No point in dancing around it.

He considers for an uncomfortable measure of time. "No. Rather it . . . it makes me wonder how many more of our blood brethren might have come from a similar beginning." My shoulders drop a bit. "You were a child," he continues. "A child cannot be blamed for their parents' sins."

Tension returns in an instant. Because we both know that's not true. They can be blamed, and they can be punished. But I'm in no mood for that conversation. Time to change the subject.

"Speaking of my illicit past, look what I found in the library." I pull Jogue's diary out.

He blinks at it. "You stole a book?"

"From the restricted section, no less. And they're lucky I didn't go back for a few more after what they pulled." I return it to the safety of my jacket. "I haven't gone through it closely, but I found a picture of the Storm Goddess surrounded by followers carrying what I think are reliquaries."

"Why didn't you tell me earlier?"

"Oh, I don't know. I got a little distracted by that whole thing where we were almost forcibly locked away."

"Does it say anything about where the reliquaries were kept? Or where the heretics might have found one?"

"No," I say. "Only that the Storm Goddess kept the vessels close to her. But that was a long time ago. The reliquaries could have traveled to the end of the Devoted Lands and back since then. And honestly, it's mostly filled with descriptions of places long gone, stuff like that."

"Hmm."

"Oh, don't pout. I may find something useful yet. Or, if we're lucky, we won't need any more help than what Magda gave us."

"Yes," he says. "Novena."

"Novena," I echo quietly.

After Belspire, the distance between Nolan and me narrows, and our travels fall into an easy rhythm. Ride during the day. Camp during the night. One of us makes a fire and cooks (Nolan). One of us tends the horses (me). We buy supplies from farms that we pass, though Nolan remarks that he wishes there was time to hunt the copious rabbits we see along the roads. I tell him I don't like rabbit, but I'm happy to make time to catch a trout. The nagging feeling of being away from the Goddess's light has grown, and though Nolan must be feeling it too, he doesn't mention it, so neither do I. On the second morning after Belspire, when he's finished his morning prayers, he suggests we spar. I agree, realizing I haven't passed so many days without training in years. Prior Petronilla would be ashamed.

I know he's good with a sword; I've seen him fight. But going up against him, even mockingly . . . He moves without an ounce of hesitation. Finds every opening and presses it. Even with my two sickles against his one blade, he triumphs the first two mornings we fight. On the third, I turn his sword away with one sickle and finish with the other at his throat, but not until after he leaves a scratch along one forearm. It isn't deep, but still, he helps me wash and wrap it.

The next several mornings we have to end in a draw, or else risk losing half the day.

It's stupid, but I'm almost disappointed when we begin to get close to Novena. As little information as we have to go on, it could be where the heretics have hidden the reliquary, which means we need to be ready. And not only for whom we might find. The conflict between the Green God and Tempestra-Enoch was environmentally devasting. Poison fumes emanated from the city for years. The land grew toxic and twisted for miles around. Still almost a day away, we pass into brittle, emaciated forests where only the most tenacious plant life seems to have taken root, and the needle-eyed birds don't sing. Not exactly welcoming. And it isn't encouraging that we haven't seen another soul since turning off the main road onto the one that leads by Novena.

When we crest a hill that overlooks the city, I understand why.

I expected devastation. What we find falls closer to a nightmare. The hole left by the divine conflict is massive, a great round maw punched into the earth, gaping as if trying to swallow what remnants of the city surround it, like it did the temple that once sat at its center. What's left of the city's buildings are skeletal, blanketed by a hellish briar. Blackened vines thicker than wine barrels. Thorns the size of my forearm. At first glance, it has the appearance of life, the roots and other growths twisting menacingly before pouring over the edge of the hole. But it's clear nothing here is alive.

The Endless Storm, the hellscape writhing before me . . . it's hard to believe the heretics hang their faith on such adulterated remnants of divinity.

Mortimer shimmies uncomfortably beneath me. I pat his neck. "Looks like a fun place."

"Don't stop," says Nolan. "We're just travelers passing by, remember?"

Even though we haven't seen anyone since yesterday, that doesn't mean there aren't eyes watching. Especially if Magda's deduction is correct. We travel several leagues past the former city before tying up the horses and doubling back through the woods. If there is anyone here, we don't want them to see us, or to scare them into fleeing. By the time we get back to Novena, the sun has started to set. Sharpened by dusk and shadows, the old battleground is even more ominous, the huge, black pit frankly menacing.

When true night falls, we move. Nolan and I are shadows, silent as we make our way through the ruins. It's slow going, navigating the labyrinth of vines and thorns. And a little disconcerting. We see nothing living, not even the sort of vermin that manages to persist pretty much anywhere else.

Move, then wait. Move, then wait. We make a pattern of it, circling our way around the massive pit, keeping to sheltered nooks as we search for any signs of human trespass. Nolan is focused, intense. It reminds me of the fight in the Cathedral, his determination then—full commitment, injury or death be damned. Both of us have vowed to return the reliquary to the Goddess, but our reasons couldn't be more different, and it's gotten hard to ignore the seed of something—guilt?— that has sprouted within me. Not that it alters my plans in any way, but now success will mean sacrificing the strange, fledgling comradery that has grown between Nolan and me. Part of me regrets that.

But it's a stupid part.

As long as I'm bound to the Goddess, there is no room in my world for anything so weak and fragile as . . . whatever it is we've cobbled together.

By midnight, I'm growing wearied with our fruitless search. I suspect Nolan feels the same when his occasional shifts in position grow more frequent and noticeable. But the plan was to spend the night searching, so there's no talk of giving up. Instead, I swallow yawn after yawn and pick through what Magda said to us, looking for another explanation for what she overheard. Maybe she lied. Or, more likely, she was simply mistaken, putting together snippets of information in the wrong way.

Then, something shimmers in my vision. I blink, thinking boredom is playing tricks on me, but it remains: the faintest of glows in a building up ahead. I reach out, brushing my fingers lightly over Nolan's arm to get his attention, then point. Moving in unison, we abandon our hiding spot, slipping through the shadows as we approach the light. It's low enough that a pair of normal eyes would have trouble discerning it—nothing more than a diffuse glow around a shaded window, on the second floor of a pitted stone building.

So, we're not the only living things in Novena after all.

Nolan begins to move, but I grab him.

Footsteps.

They're faint, so faint that it's half instinct that alerted me, but as soon as I signal, Nolan indicates he hears them as well. We duck behind a crumbled wall.

Several minutes pass before their source comes into view: three figures, cloaked in black. They appear out of an alley and approach a spot in the lighted building. The wall there is partially obstructed by ruins, but as we watch, they disappear into it.

Nolan draws a rectangle in the air with one finger. *There must be a door.*

I nod. We wait a bit longer before heading toward the debris. Even up close, nothing about it seems suspect, but after a bit of searching we find what we are looking for: a gap that leads to the remains of a doorway. Nolan slips through, with me on his heels. As soon as we are inside, I draw my sickles. The room is dark and empty, save for the decayed remains of a table in one corner. But there's a stairway. Nolan takes the lead, sword drawn. The light grows stronger, and I no longer doubt Magda. Something clandestine is most definitely happening here tonight.

At the top of the stairs we find a short hallway filled with doors. Most are gone, rotted away, but there is one at the very end, around which a thin line of light escapes. Nolan and I slink to it. Voices sound from within, and I hear the faint notes of gathered bodies shifting around.

"—came as quickly as we could." A male's voice. Young, from the sound of it. "There was no time to make inquiries. And it would have been too dangerous anyway."

"She's dead." A woman's voice breaks in, sharp and angry. "She must be. They didn't burn her in front of the city, but she must be dead."

They're talking about Magda.

Heretics in Belspire. It's a lucky thing we didn't encounter them on the road; they must have left the city around the same time we did.

"Maybe she died during their questioning," says a third person, gender indeterminate.

"It doesn't matter," a deep masculine voice cuts in. "She didn't know anything useful."

Wrong. A flicker of annoyance runs through me. These are the people who came so close to killing the Goddess, who can't even keep their own secrets tight enough to protect themselves? They should do themselves a favor and hand me the reliquary right now.

"It doesn't mean they won't be hunting us still." The woman is starting to sound like the cleverest of the bunch. The murmurs that follow seem to agree. "This has all gone to shit ... If they got even an inkling of anything out of her—"

"I know," says the man with the deeper voice. "But the Goddess hides. They've barely been seen since the attack. The Priors claim mourning, but our spies in Lumeris are convinced they are afraid. The attack might have failed, but—"

"It was a foolish plan!" someone spits. "We should have gone with—"

"Emmaus *sacrificed* himself to get that close," the woman interjects. "He knew it needed to be witnessed to be believed, not happen behind closed doors!"

"But what if they remain hidden away? If there's no opportunity to strike again? This will have all been pointless."

*Strike again*. Nolan and I lock gazes. That confirms it. They didn't exhaust the reliquary's supply of blood. It's clear these heretics outrank Magda, but I don't get the impression they're pulling all the strings either. Which means the chances of the reliquary being here are slim to none. By the pensive set of Nolan's features, I sense he realizes that too.

"We were told there was a chance of failure." The young man speaks again, his counsel calm, measured. "And that if it did, to have patience. We will find another chance, or make one. The thing that there is always more of is time."

"Not for Magda or Emmaus," say a new voice, low, but tart.

"This wasn't only about the Goddess," adds the woman. "We should have been picking off the Chosen by now; my crew and I were *promised*—"

"Enough," says the deep-voiced man. "The pieces we need to be in position are still in position. We can still kill the Goddess."

"I knew you should have brought more in the first place," grumbles the woman. "It wasn't enough. I knew it wouldn't be enough."

Nolan and I both go even more still than before. There it is. She might as well have said *We should have brought the whole bottle of dead god's blood to the party.*

"And where would Emmaus have hidden it?" The young man doesn't seem the least bit thrown by failure, which makes me wonder what he knows that Nolan and I don't.

"It doesn't matter now." The other man again. "I will head to Carsaire at daylight. The rest of you lie low and spread the word about what's happened. I'll contact you when I return."

The conversation turns to useless things. Food. Sleep. Nothing more about conspiracy. By wordless agreement, Nolan and I creep back out of the building and into the ruined city.

"Carsaire," he says when we're far enough away. "We'll get the horses, keep watch. Follow whichever heretic heads in that direction."

I nod. "What about the rest of them?"

"Nothing," he says. "If they don't continue on their way, it will cause alarm."

Now that we no longer need to search, we move faster through the city, taking the most direct route back to where we've hidden the horses. It leads us close to the pit. Some of the roots here are large enough to walk like paths, which we do, to avoid the worst of the rubble. As we pass a gap in the ruins that opens right to the side of the pit, Nolan slows, then changes direction, heading to it.

"What are you doing?" I say.

"Aren't you curious?" He moves almost to the very edge and leans over in a way that makes my stomach twist. "Not all of us have gotten to see the aftermath of a god's death up close."

"Fair enough, but I didn't figure you for a tourist." Carefully, I make my way over until I am standing beside him. The chasm stretches before us. "No wonder Tempestra had to take a new avatar," I whisper. "Imagine the sort of power expended to make a mess like this. It's amazing they even survived."

"The Goddess is strong." Nolan keeps an eye on the ruins. "So was Enoch, by all reports. A well-chosen avatar."

Was that the difference in the end? Was the battle at Novena less about Tempestra and Arcadius than it was about Enoch and Viktori? And what does that say about Innara, and the damage she's taken? It's the sort of question I'll probably never know the answer to, the sort of topic that would border on blasphemy to bring up. I wish I'd had more time to spend in Belspire's library. Chosen or not, there are a lot of gaps in my knowledge about the finer points of both living gods and dead.

"How deep do you think it is?" Nolan continues. "Some scholars say it goes forever."

"Do you believe that?"

"No. But like you said, it's hard to fathom the power of the gods."

Here, so close to the pit, it seems even quieter than before, as if the cavity is swallowing what few night sounds there are. The darkness of the void is mesmerizing. "It's *almost* hard to blame them."

"Who?"

"The heretics. Seeing something like this, the other sepulchrae . . . believing that it means that the dead gods are still here, somewhere."

"They're not," says Nolan. "There is only one goddess now. And the only thing that matters is returning the reliquary to them, and what that will bring."

The shift in his voice makes me look up, and when I do, I am staring at someone I don't know. Nolan's eyes have turned hard. Ruthless.

And I have only the barest sliver of time to understand how well and truly I have been played before he shoves me into the pit.

# Seventeen

No, *I'm* the smart one.

—JEZIAH

I**DIOT THAT I AM**, I fall.

Surprise smothers any cry as the great pit swallows me, and the world turns black. Only the sensation of air on my skin tells me I'm falling. Instinctively, I twist. My fingers brush something. Then they grab, desperate and uncaring. Skin scrapes from my palms, but I slow, feel something break, and fall again.

Grab.

*Snap*.

Fall.

Grab.

This time I stop. My hands grip dry, rough tendrils—the vines, or their roots. I have been saved from death by the remnants of the Green God's defeat. My heart slams against my rib cage. Then I flush, cheeks burning as if touched by the Goddess's flame itself.

Nolan tried to kill me.

That son of a divine bitch *tried to kill me*.

I swallow the nastiest curses I know, every one of which tries to punch its way into my throat. Anger follows in a flood. I let it. Better rage than the humiliation welling up behind it. I adjust my grip, clinging to the mass of bizarre plants like the salvation it is, and look up. The night sky is a beacon in the oppressive dark. I scan it for Nolan—for his silhouette, a hint of movement, anything. If he's still there, my circumstances haven't improved much, even though there's no way he can see me this far down. Still I wait. And wait. When several minutes pass and I see nothing, I relax a little.

*That absolute piece of—*

Quiet, pious, obedient Nolan. Who was so dedicated to the task assigned to us by the Goddess, and so willing to abide by their decision about Executrix. Who stood up for me against a Bellator and the Arbiters.

Who bought me a pastry in Belspire.

I want to scream. But at myself, for being such a tremendous sack of pure gullibility. All this time, I thought *I* was the one with the secret plan, and now it turns out he was scheming too, waiting until we had a real lead on the reliquary and then taking the first opportunity to get rid of me. Or maybe he's been looking for a way to do this since we started out—to cut my throat in my sleep, or poison my dinner. Admittedly, a bottomless chasm is eloquent compared to those, with the added benefit of zero evidence. Gotta give him that.

It's only one of several things I want to give him right now. The other two are, thankfully, still strapped in their holders on my back. But my sickles aren't going to do me any good from the inside of a pit.

I start to climb.

It's slow going, navigating the sinister tangle in utter darkness, careful to only take hold of roots that will bear my weight. There seems no rhyme or reason to that—some thick roots break away at my touch, while thinner ones feel as strong as iron chains. I have to stop to rest more than I like; my limbs begin to burn with the exertion. But with aching slowness, the edge of the pit grows closer. Night has shifted to the watery gray of dawn by the time I reach a spot where I can pull myself out. Arms quivering, fingers almost numb, I wrench one last time and roll to safety on the ground outside the pit.

There, I simply stare at the sky, chest heaving.

For some reason—probably the attempted murder—I think of Morgan. She would have liked Nolan. Probably would have planned to kill him while he did the same for her, if circumstances had conspired to pair them up on this little adventure instead. A funny story I'll have to tell her someday. Maybe she'll even laugh.

But first, I'm going to find Nolan and show him what his entrails look like, the Goddess's orders be damned.

I am still trembling as I get to my feet and take stock of my circumstances. Sickles—check. The plump purse of money hidden in my coat—check. But when it comes to other supplies, I'm shit out of luck. Hours have passed. Nolan is long gone. And if I don't want to risk being spotted by the heretics, I need to move too.

The forest—it's where Nolan would have headed. But when I get back to where we tied up the horses, there's nothing. The bastard took Mortimer too.

I was already going to kill him.

Now I'm going to make it hurt.

By the time true dawn breaks, all I can think about is putting my hands around Nolan's neck, pressing my thumbs into the soft parts of his throat, and choking the life out of him. The growing stiffness in my arms would make that a trick at the moment, but I indulge the fantasy nonetheless. The sun is high by the time I make it back to the main road that passes by Novena, any hope of catching up long gone. But I know where he's headed, which keeps my step motivated. That and thinking about what I'm going to do to him. But I'm moving too slow on foot. I need to find a new horse, and quick.

Seething hours pass. I stop to drink from a stream and relieve myself. I pick a few wild raspberries from a thorny briar, then immediately spit them out. They are sour and mealy, which I suspect I can thank the Green God for. Then I walk some more.

Eventually, I realize something: I am alone.

Truly, entirely alone for the first time in as long as I can remember. Even at the Cloisters, when there was no one immediately around, another Potentiate or instructor or attendant was never far. Not like this. I don't know where the nearest soul is exactly, but it's nowhere near me. Everyone in Lumeris thinks I'm with Nolan, seeking out the reliquary. Nolan thinks I am dead.

If only I *could* be. Lystrata, Potentiate of the Dawn Cloister, would, from here on forth, be lost forever in the bottomless pit of holy wrath, never to be seen again.

But it wouldn't be long before the pull would be unbearable. Even now, the invisible threads that stitch me to Tempestra-Innara give an occasional beckoning tug, spin the temptation to return to the Cathedral using Nolan's betrayal as an excuse. Which makes me even angrier. No matter where I go, a cage goes with me. There are only two avenues of escape, and they both end in death. Either Tempestra-Innara's, or mine.

And the latter is much more likely if I don't catch Nolan.

Late afternoon, I hear the sound of a horse approaching. There's still distance between us, so I stop, listening closely to the jingle of tack and hoofbeats. It's definitely not Nolan, but it's someone with a horse. And, even better, someone alone. I wait. Eventually, a figure on a dun gelding appears around a bend in the road. He slows as he spots me.

I give him a bright smile. "Hi there."

"Hello." He eyes me with suspicion, which he is right to do. I do the same, hiding it beneath a mask of friendly coyness. A young man, brown haired and slight, with a deep tan complexion that tells me that either he came from the southern coasts or his parents did. Freckles spot his cheeks, making him appear younger than he is. But the most interesting thing about him is his clothing: He's wearing a cleric's cassock. Not a Cleric of the Blood, obviously, or even a town cleric, but one of the traveling devoted who spread the word of Tempestra-Innara to places not large enough to support their own local shrines and clergy, generally referred to as mud clerics.

He blinks at me. "Are you in some sort of trouble, miss?"

My smile nearly cracks. A second surprise: I know that voice. I didn't see the face attached to it, but there's no mistaking it—this is the calm, reasoning young man from the secret meeting in Novena.

A heretic. And a cleric.

I almost laugh at the dark irony of it. Turns out I'm not the only traitor in the Goddess's Orders. It seems impossible—this underfed mud cleric going up against Tempestra-Innara? I can't decide if this is good luck or ill, but I can work with it.

"Trouble?" I make a show of thinking, considering my surroundings. "Not at this particular moment. But given that my horse got spooked and ran on me last night, taking all of my food and supplies with it, I can't be certain that situation will hold much longer."

The young man nods, as if acknowledging my made-up story, but there's still suspicion in his eyes. "You were traveling through this area alone?"

"Sure was." I draw one of my sickles and let it spin with a bit of flair before gripping the handle and giving him a wink. "I know how to take care of myself. A far bit better than a horse, apparently. I was on my way north to find work." The lies come easy. "I thought it would be smart to take a shortcut. Turns out I was wrong."

This seems to loosen him. "Yes, that's bad luck on your part."

"Where are you headed, if you don't mind me asking?"

He shrugs. "Nowhere in particular. Or, more specifically, wherever the word of the Goddess might be needed, and welcome."

"Huh." I return my sickle to its holster. "Well, are you in the market for a bodyguard on the way to nowhere in particular? Sure, most folks know better than to touch the clergy, but you never know when you might cross paths with a desperate brigand or two. I've got a special going right now: full service, unparalleled protection for a spot on your horse, and a bit of food if you have it to spare."

At first, he looks unsure, but it's clear he's low in his Order—poor—and unlikely to be carrying any weapons larger than a cooking knife. "I have faith in the Goddess's protection."

"Sure, but maybe they sent me to be that protection." I break out my most winning smile. "And if you doubt that, just know that I could have easily ambushed you, cut your throat, and stolen your horse without breaking a sweat. No one would ever find your body. I'm simply that good." It would be a lie to say a part of me isn't considering it, but I speak with what I hope is a sufficiently joking tone.

He laughs. Guess I got it right.

"I serve the Goddess," he says. "And to serve them is to serve their followers. I'll take you up on your offer. Galeas is about three days from here. Maybe you can pick up some work and make your way from there?"

"Sounds like you've got yourself a bodyguard." And I've got myself a ride. Maybe I can catch up with Nolan after all. But, more importantly, I'll have time with this heretical cleric. He seems as low among his coconspirators as he is among the Goddess's clergy, but that doesn't mean there isn't another tidbit or two to glean from him about the reliquary. Or, at the very least, what kind of meddling he's doing within the holy order. "May the Flame warm you and find you even worthier than you clearly are, er—?"

"Avery." He bows slightly in the saddle. "Of the Goddess's humble clergy."

And secret enemy of them as well. "Avery. Gotcha. And I'm Lys. Of the side of the road where you found me."

# *Eighteen*

The Endless Storm is their promise to return.

—VILLAGER, NAME FORGOTTEN

**W**E WATCHED AN OPERA troupe perform in Lumeris once. It was a rare treat, a lesson in the arts. I remember how grandiose the story was, the ridiculous events piling atop one another, until the whole thing toppled like a cake with too many tiers. But of course, a toppled cake is still cake, so it all worked out swimmingly in the end. I can't help but be reminded of it as Avery and I ride. Me, a Potentiate of the Goddess, tasked to find heretics and bring them to justice. Avery, a heretic costumed as a devoted cleric, plotting against the very deity he's pretending to serve. Both of us with the same deicidal goal.

Surely the right composer could put that to song.

But that shared objective doesn't make us allies. Sure, I could reveal who I am, what I overheard, try to join forces with my new friend.

And then I could ride right back to Belspire and confess my sins to Caius.

Not going to happen. Whatever kind of opportunity this is, I'll bide my time in figuring it out.

Luckily, Avery likes to chat. You wouldn't think it of a secret heretic, but he clearly has a cleric's gift for gab, and the sort of personality that can walk into even the most unwelcoming place and find a seat at a table before the sun sets.

"—but of course, this far north, you can't get fresh swordfish, only the dried or salted sort, which isn't really any good at all. Except for stews. It makes a half-decent stew, especially if you can find some abalone to go along with it."

"So, you're from the southern coasts?" If his complexion hadn't tipped me off, his culinary preferences certainly would have.

"Guilty," he replies. "Have you been?"

"'Fraid not. They need bodyguards down there?"

"I'm sure there are ships or caravans that could use a good sword, er, sickle from time to time. There are pirates in the deeper waters. They hide out on the little unpopulated islands where they're hard to reach, though I can't claim to have ever run afoul of them."

"What brought you this far north?" I venture. "Clearly it wasn't our fish."

Avery chuckles. "No, definitely not. I spend most of my time in the south, but my Order encourages a pilgrimage to the Cathedral at least once in a while. I'm on my way back from that, albeit along a winding, scenic route."

The Cathedral. Could Avery have been at the execution? Not inside, clearly, since he's still alive, but maybe the heretics had other spies around, waiting to see how their assassination played out. "I heard about the massacre that happened, during that execution. Were you . . . ?"

"No." The word is quiet, soft. "I'd come and gone before that. But the tragedy . . . what a horrific loss of life." There's genuine sadness in his voice.

"Yes, it was," I say, expecting Avery to continue.

He doesn't. Maybe he and his friends hadn't considered what Tempestra-Innara might do to hide their vulnerability.

It's slow going, two on a horse, and we don't make it far before the sun begins to drag low in the sky. But the decrepit forest has thinned, finally giving way to verdant fields peppered with wildflowers and stands of young trees. We make camp in a copse, where Avery gets to work immediately, pouring water from a skin into a small cooking pot and filling it with a porridge made from dried grains, beans, and bits of meat. I take care of the horse, wishing it was Mortimer as Avery stirs the food almost lovingly, chattering about a village he visited a few weeks ago and their generous gift of supplies.

"It's almost as if they knew I'd need to feed more mouths than my own." He takes a spoonful and blows on it before tasting, then adds a bit of seasoning.

"Must be one of those blessings from the Goddess I hear so much about," I say.

"They provide for those who do their work."

He lies so sincerely. I almost wish I could tell him how impressed I am. Few would suspect a cleric turning on the Goddess, fewer still one such as him.

"After Galeas will you head back south?" I join him by the fire, already aware that he's got his orders from Novena, but the lies are entertaining, and one way to pass the time.

He shrugs, handing me a bowl of his creation. He has only one set of utensils and graciously gives me the spoon while he makes do with a fork. Fortunately, the stew is hearty enough to be eaten with either. "A wandering cleric rarely goes where they want. Instead we go where we are needed, which might change from day to day." He pauses, smiling. "Today you need me. Tomorrow?"

*Tomorrow you'll head straight for your fellow heretics.* I smile back, chewing thoughtfully. It's not the fare that came out of Belspire's fancy kitchens, but it's better than what Nolan managed over a campfire. Even the thought of him doesn't dampen the flavor.

"I see your wanderings have taught you a thing or two about cooking. This is really good."

He smiles, genuinely pleased by the compliment. "Thank you. My duty is to teach the will of our Goddess, but I learn too. I've managed a particularly extensive study of regional porridges and stews."

"What else do you pick up on your travels?" A talker will talk, sometimes saying more than they intend to, so I'm happy to keep our conversation rolling.

He thinks. "I've learned to sleep on the ground to start. And I've learned just because you can't see the bugs in the mattress, it doesn't mean they aren't there."

Great, now I'm going to worry about mattress bugs. "Here's a better question: Why did you choose to serve the Goddess?"

"We *all* serve the Goddess."

Not even a hint of hesitation.

"Of course." I keep my voice light. "But not like you do. What made you want to enter the kind of service where you get to sleep on the ground, curled up with bugs?"

His gaze drops to the coals, which glow with a velvet heat that almost looks divine. "That's not much of a story. I was an orphan," he says, "living on the streets until I was taken in by a kind merchant. He was also a scholar of sorts, with an impressive collection of clerical texts. His influence inspired me to join the clergy, when I was old enough."

How utterly normal.

"I hope to repay his kindness through service," he finishes.

"Seems like you're doing a good job so far." I scrape my bowl, the last mouthful of food helping me swallow what I'm really thinking: that being a conspirator in the worst heresy in living memory is a strange way to cover that debt.

I keep watch most of the night, then catch a few hours of sleep once dawn rolls in. Another delicious porridge greets me when I wake, this one dotted with bits of dried fruit and touched with maple sugar. One could almost feel guilty, deceiving Avery while he's being so kind. But he's deceiving me as well, so maybe it's an even trade.

Another day passes (too slowly) as we plod our way toward Galeas. Avery talks more often than not, but about nothing, innocuous topics like farming communities and the best times of the year to travel to certain areas. Even after the long hours, he's easier to chat with than I would have expected, but no matter how I try to nudge our conversation in a useful manner, I don't learn anything helpful.

This is the last day. Either he gives up some good information or tomorrow I take his horse and go. I don't feel guilty about that. Clerics are used to walking. He'll be fine.

"Tell me about the southern ports," I ask after we've made camp, the touch of early dusk glazing the forest surrounding us. It's not a clever prompt, but it's something. "Maybe once I get back on my feet I'll head that way."

Avery nods approvingly. "They're beautiful," he says. "Well, the ocean more than the ports themselves. Blue waters, breezes that smell like salt and flowers at the same time. The winters are cold, but not like they are up here, where you can freeze to death too easily."

"Yeah, seen a few cleric-sicles in my time."

He appears vaguely horrified at that. Which gives me an idea. I've been asking questions about his travels, his life, and offering lies in return. Maybe a sprinkle of truth is the way to go.

"I grew up in a mountain village," I explain. "There were always a few that didn't have the sense to know when a storm was coming."

"Ah. That must have been upsetting to see."

I snort derisively. "No . . . well, a little. I used to think they were mad, though, to die in such a silly way. And all to spread a divine word we'd already heard before. You'd think they'd want to *live* for the Goddess. Not die for them."

Avery is thoughtfully quiet for a few heartbeats. "It's an honor to die in service to the Goddess. Though I'd like to think the Goddess is kind and merciful enough not to desire a pointless demise."

My mouth tastes sour all of a sudden. And when I tap the spoon against the wood of the bowl, it sounds too much like cracking. I set the food down.

Avery's brow knits. "Are you okay?"

No. I feel angry and frustrated. And cold. "Just remembering those frozen clerics. And . . . I came through Belspire before you found me. They burned a heretic there recently." A lump forms in my throat. "It was ugly, more than it needed to be. A violent death that seemed pretty pointless to me. Sometimes . . . I wonder if the Goddess even cares."

Avery blinks at me across the fire. Interrogation might not be my specialty, but I know a little something about blasphemy.

"The flame is the punishment for heresy." Avery speaks in a carefully neutral timbre, giving away none of his thoughts.

"I know, but . . ." The fire snaps. Cracks. I lean closer, feeling its warmth on my cheeks. It doesn't reach any deeper than that. The Goddess, Caius, Nolan . . . the lives they took—or tried to take, in Nolan's case—meant nothing. And yet, each one was, in its own way, an act of piety. Of faith, that beautifully cultivated fruit that too often turns out to be poisonous to those who devote themselves to it. Or get fed it by force. That thought burns a hole in my gut, but I shrug noncommittally. "Maybe. I don't know. After all, what would I understand about the intricacies of the Goddess's ways? I'm no cleric."

"You have misgivings, though?" Each word takes its time, doesn't push. "You have doubts about the ways of the Goddess?"

Doubts? I swallow a chuckle. "Doubts" sound like tiny things—inconsequential, instead of the difference between alive and extra crispy. But asking a heretic—even one wearing the mask of a cleric—to explain the Goddess's reasonings is futile. I know those rote answers by heart already. I've heard them all from people who actually *believe* them. So why did I open this door in the first place? I try to think of the right thing to say, the words that will confirm my devotion while also drawing some intel from Avery. But whatever they are, they give way to something else. "I heard a story once . . . about a village of heretics that the Goddess's forces . . . converted."

At first, that's all I can get out. Avery puts his food down, waiting patiently for me to continue.

Which I shouldn't, but I do.

"A village near the Endless Storm. Anyone who wouldn't denounce the Storm Goddess and pledge their devotion to Tempestra-Innara was killed." And plenty of others too. "Those that did were rounded up, driven down the mountain like sheep to serve their penance in the fields and workhouses. But winter came early that year, and on their way the weather turned so cold that they were forced to make camp or freeze." Despite the heat of the fire, my skin turns icy. "As a result, supplies dwindled. So when the storm cleared, the Bellator had the people moved to the bank of a frozen river. There, he told them that, instead of penance, they would be allowed a test of faith. Cross the river, and if they reached the other side, it would mean the Goddess had decided to be merciful.

*Cross the river*, he said, making it clear this was an order, not a choice, *and be free.*

I close my eyes. But instead of darkness, I see white. "No one moved at first. But this was their salvation, their chance. The only one they'd be given. And that's what finally drove the first of the villagers forward. Once that happened . . . like I said, sheep."

I open my eyes again, but the white remains—below my feet, stretching out before me, seemingly endless. I don't move. As small as I am, I am of the mountains. I know winter. I know ice. The other villagers do too, but they move anyway. Slowly, at first, and then in a run.

*Go!* The order is for me, from one of the soldiers. *Don't you want to know the Goddess's mercy?*

But I don't go, not even when he prods me with the tip of his sword, drawing blood. It's the only warm thing I feel as I watch the people I grew up with reach the center of the river. It might seem like a gamble to the soldiers watching, but instinctively, I know better. My neighbors and friends probably did too, but hope is as powerful a drug as devotion.

First comes the cracks. Then the screams. Figures blink out one by one, swallowed by the water, pulled under ice that was too thin to hold them. Then, I see only whiteness—the unbroken snow at my feet. I wait for it to be over.

Wait for silence.

Eventually, a shadow falls across me. I look up into the face of the Bellator, which is as cold as our surroundings. Even then, I don't move. Don't run. I simply stare at him with as much hate as I can muster, and wait to die in the snow instead of the river.

But he doesn't draw his weapon, or order one of his soldiers to cut me down.

Instead, he smiles, almost kindly, and makes a gift of me.

"They swore to devote themselves to the Goddess and died anyway." I feel heavy as I finish my story, which has been carefully edited for Avery's ears. The river wasn't about low supplies. It was about the whispers among the villagers, the whispers that said the Storm Goddess had sent the snows to stop the legion. *Cross the river*, the Bellator said, *and put your faith to a true test.* Regardless, the tale's cruel core remains intact. "Where was the mercy in that? There's no penance or forgiveness in death. Only . . . death."

I've said too much. Gone further than I intended, and now Avery stares at me as if I am some strange northern fish he doesn't know what to do with.

"Maybe," he says finally, the word creeping out of him, "you're right. Maybe mercy is something only truly offered when it's convenient, or mutually beneficial. Perhaps all those who don't follow Tempestra-Innara are invariably damned in the Goddess's eyes and the eyes of their followers, and they simply don't understand that yet."

Something shifts in the air between us. *Those who don't follow Tempestra-Innara.* That's what he said. Not heretics. Not that denying the existence of the Goddess's mercy is pure, unadulterated blasphemy. Hell, he practically agreed with me.

Avery gets up. Comes around the fire and sits next to me, taking my hands in his. For some reason, I let him.

Soft blue irises envelope me. "If there's something you need to confess, Lys . . . to unburden yourself from . . ."

A hundred things. A thousand. But this isn't where I wanted this to go.

So why did I let it?

*If there's something you need to confess . . .* I'm about to ask him the same question when the nearby brush rustles. The horse lets out a nervous whinny. I am on my feet in a heartbeat, pulling free of Avery's grasp, drawing my sickles.

A figure in the trees. Too large for a wolf, too small for a bear. Hunched over.

Human.

The wind shifts, carrying the thick tang of blood. With one sickle, I gesture to Avery to move back, make space for me and for my blades. The figure takes another jerking, shuffling step forward, reaching the ring of firelight before pitching forward into it and hitting the ground like a dropped burden.

"Huh." I straighten, not letting my guard down entirely, but observant enough to know that for someone to be a threat, they typically have to be breathing. Approaching the body, I wait briefly before kicking it over. A man—scrawny, ferret-like build, hollow cheeks, and a long, deep slice down his front that has resulted in more of his blood being outside than in.

And a metal collar around his neck.

With the tip of my sickle, I trace the short length of chain running from it. The final link is broken, sheared off, as if by a blow. This man was someone's captive.

I straighten and freeze, senses straining for any signs of pursuit. But there's nothing, only the crackle of the fire he must have been drawn by and the nervous shift of Avery from one foot to the other. Satisfied, I go to one knee and continue my examination.

"Lys." Avery's voice is taut, warning. He takes a step forward, as if to stop me. "Maybe you shouldn't . . ."

"Don't worry about me. Keep watch. Whoever this is, they sure didn't do this to themselves."

"There's nothing we can do for him," Avery presses. "We should go. There might be bandits. The woods around here—"

"I can handle a few bandits," I say, even though I know this isn't the work of common thieves. The young man's jacket is thrown open. I root through it but find nothing, save for a pair of glasses with darkened lenses.

Suddenly, the corpse gasps, body spasming and eyelids flying open, revealing a gaze that is very, very wrong. Eyes lock on me, their whites shot through with hemorrhages, the skin around them bruised and raw, as if sleep was something never bothered with, but daily sand rubs were. His hands wrap around my wrists, fingers digging into them like claws as the young man lets out a breathless, feral sound.

"*Chosen.*" Barely a word, it comes out like something vital being dislodged. "*Abomination.*"

Caught by surprise, I twist my arms, snapping the young man's forearms like dry sticks, not realizing the foolishness of it until it's done. The shock of it is too much. He inhales sharply, then goes limp, his bloodshot stare fluttering briefly before it goes blank.

I scramble back, rattled. Trying not to show it as I get to my feet.

Avery is already backing away. "You . . . you're . . ."

I might have denied it if I hadn't overreacted. Trained bodyguard or not, a normal person doesn't have the strength to do what I just did. So I don't try to deny, or explain. I touch the point of one sickle to my lips. *Shhhh*. I don't want to hear him say it, and there's no point in spinning a lie. He knows, I know, and because of that, the smart thing to do right now is kill him.

Yet, I hesitate. There's war in his features as he tries to decide whether to keep up his act, and how. I could give him that chance, since he has no idea *I* know who he really is. Play along for a while longer, see what this turn of events shakes loose from him. But I've already spent enough time in the company of someone intent on betraying me, and I'm not in the mood to jump back into that so quickly.

His throat is right there. One flick of my wrist and he'd bleed out within a minute—a simple, quiet ending, better than a heretic deserves.

As he starts to speak again, I raise my sickle, and strike.

# *Nineteen*

> The Goddess, in their wisdom, may show mercy. I do not question it. But it is a weakness in lesser beings such as us.
>
> —FROM *THE FLAME'S PATH*, BY SENIOR PRIOR OLIA IN THE ERA OF TEMPESTRA-DRUSILLE

"Sorry." It's at least the third time I've said it.

I load the last of Avery's gear onto his horse as he stares with pure confusion, mouth gagged, because I can't deal with questions right now. I know what he's thinking: that as one of Tempestra-Innara's Chosen, I should have simply commanded his help when we met on the road. And if that little fact was meant to stay secret, I should have made sure he couldn't tell anyone. But since *I* know that he's not really on the Goddess's side, and since *he* doesn't know that I want the Goddess dead too...

This keeps it simple. Ridiculous, but simple. Let him wonder why I knocked him unconscious and tied him to a tree instead of dispatching him. I'll be long gone by the time he comes to any conclusion.

I *should* kill him. He's a heretic, and that's what a well-trained scion of Tempestra-Innara would do. What Nolan would do. But when it comes down to it, I simply don't want to.

So, tied to a tree it is.

There's a knife among his gear, a dull, sad little thing barely worthy of the name. He blanches as I approach with it. But all I do is stab the blade into the earth near his bound hands. Not so close that he can easily grab it, but close enough so that he'll reach it eventually, if he puts the work in. Getting through the rope with a dull knife will take a bit more effort, but that's on him, not me. At least I dragged the corpse into the brush. Seemed rude to leave it watching with that scratched-up stare.

"A lesson for you, cleric: Don't talk to strangers on the road. And a bit of advice: Forget we ever met." I mount the horse. "But thanks again for your help."

Bewilderment digs even deeper furrows in his brow. But I turn both the horse and my thoughts toward my new focus: the trail through the wood and field left by the dead man. It's easy enough to follow, even in the dark. Flattened brush and broken sticks, prints in the dirt, and blood, blood, blood. The farther I follow, the more impressive it is how long the poor guy made it before finally exsanguinating. But there was something strange about him, something besides the leash. A savage quality to those last few moments of life. And his eyes . . . even dead, the sensation of them remains. Somehow, he was able to take one look at me and know who—what—I am.

That's a mystery I can't exactly leave unsolved.

The dead man's path is a winding one. Erratic. Almost frantic. It's clear he was running away, but from what? His captors? Or another threat? Finally, I come to a path in a thick stand of forest, and the unmistakable signs of a conflict, something furious and bloody, but brief. The sequence of it is impossible to glean, but the result is clear: a group that moved off in one direction, a dying man who went another.

Puzzle pieces. But not enough of them for me to make out the picture. I need more.

The second trail is nearly as easy as the first to follow, by virtue of it being several individuals who don't seem concerned about hiding their tracks. Still, it's hours—nearly dawn—before I crest a hill that overlooks a shallow valley with an old orchard. There's a farmhouse beyond it, a barn, and several pens for animals. But the pens are empty, and everything has an overgrown, untended appearance, as if no one has lived here for years. Which leaves only one explanation for the faint seep of light escaping the barn.

I hobble the horse out of sight and watch for at least an hour, belly pressed to the damp grass. Finally, the barn door opens and a man appears. He is most definitely not dressed like any farmer I've ever seen, with two massive knives affixed to his belt and a quality coat suitable for travel but not for scratching around in the dirt. He scans the ridge where I hide, searching, then goes back inside when he doesn't find what he's looking for.

The sky is already beginning to lighten, so I take advantage of the night's dregs to circle around to the rear of the barn and find a gap in the slats. The first thing that hits me is the earthy funk of horses, mingled with—keeping with the evening's theme—blood. Then: voices, and the sound of agitated footsteps. Through my peephole I can see three figures, all men. Besides a suspiciously excessive number of weapons, they all seem innocuous enough—well dressed enough to command respect, not so well as to be particularly memorable.

Suddenly, one of the figures moves aside to reveal a fourth. My breath catches in my chest. Or maybe it's a laugh. Because seated in the center of the barn—bound with chains, gagged, and looking exceedingly put out about it—is Nolan. The mirth passes quickly. A sinking feeling hits, because outnumbered or not, Nolan should have made easy work of whoever these jokers are. Instead, he's their prisoner. And he's in chains, not ropes.

Which means they know who he is.

Another puzzle piece falls into place, and I don't like what I'm beginning to see.

"Still no one out there." I take the speaker to be the man I spotted. "This is ridiculous. We should be searching too."

"There's only so far he could have gotten." This comes from a tall man, bald and built like an ox who never had to skip a meal. Real muscle. "Van and Remus will find him."

Not if he's dead.

"Not if he's dead," the first speaker practically squeals. "There was a lot of blood, we didn't see clearly what happened, and the woods—"

"The sun is rising," Baldy snaps. "We wait. No more surprises."

Did they surprise Nolan or did Nolan surprise them? Or maybe it was a mutual surprising. Would explain the chaotic leavings I came across.

"Agreed." For the second time in two days, I recognize a voice: the woman who was in Novena with Avery. Not exactly a surprise, but this just keeps getting better. "In the meantime, we need to make a decision about what to do with him."

"I know exactly what to do." The bald man jabs a finger at Nolan. "He's already cost us our hound. We cut him into pieces before he has the chance to do the same to us."

*Hound?* So, Nolan's captors are the dead man's captors as well. Which makes it highly likely that Nolan was the source of the dead man's wound. The cut looked wild; maybe breaking his chains hadn't been intentional. At least six against one—even Nolan might have gotten a little sloppy, if the "hound" had surprised him the way he did me.

"No." The woman's voice takes on an edge.

"He's too dangerous!"

"This isn't some cobwebbed skeleton dug out of a battlefield or a decrepit Prior. He's young. He's *fresh*."

With that word, the last piece falls into place. A bilious sensation ripples beneath my breastbone, sinking into my guts. The "hound" with the altered sight, keeping Nolan alive . . .

These aren't any ordinary—or even extraordinary—heretics.

These are Renderers.

*We should have been picking off the Chosen by now . . . my crew and I were promised . . .* That's what the woman said, back in Novena. That was what would have followed a successful assignation—the methodical hunting of anyone touched by divine power. This "crew" must have been situated somewhere outside Novena, waiting for the woman, and come across Nolan. And here I thought I'd gotten the short straw; I'll take a false cleric over Renderers any time.

"You're right, he's already cost us enough," says the woman. "Taking him alive makes up for that. Or do you really want to slink back empty handed after all this, tail between your legs?"

"Fuck off." Baldy seems like the charming type. But he goes quiet for a moment. "I want an extra cut once we get back to Sethane. For the trouble."

Sethane? That's nowhere near Carsaire, where the other heretic was headed. Did he have friends there waiting on him too? It's possible. Even so, the math is simple: Renderers for sure in one direction, the reliquary and hopefully no Renderers in another. I shift to get a better view of Nolan. His attention is on his captors, a chilling level of abhorrence in his gaze. It's a good bet this isn't how he thought things would go after pushing me into that pit, and I hope there's a few regrets stewing behind that revolted stare. I hope he's imagining my body, twisted and broken in the dark, when it could have been watching his stupid, deceiving back. Then again, he was right about one thing, in his actions if not his words—this was always going to go badly for one of us.

And I know exactly what he'd do if our places were switched.

The sun is nearly up, and I haven't forgotten the other two Renderers out there hunting for their dead "hound." Maybe they'll find the body, maybe they won't. Either way, I need to move before they return and have a chance to spot my horse on the ridge. *Avery's* horse. Shit. Maybe I *should* have killed him. If they find him and he tells them that Nolan isn't the only one of the Goddess's Chosen lurking around . . .

All the more reason for me to be on my way. I spare one last glance at Nolan, once again taking in the sight of him bound and helpless. It's not quite as satisfying as it was a few minutes ago. Still . . . the edge of the pit, the look on his face in the moonlight . . . I turn away.

Sorry, Nolan, but you brought this on yourself.

## Twenty

There is no fouler sort of heretic than a Renderer. More than judgement, they warrant nothing less than extermination. But despite all efforts, their kind—and more concerning, their knowledge—persists.

—FROM THE WRITINGS OF BELLATOR HADRIANA

THERE WERE THINGS THAT we were taught at the Cloisters, and things that we were told.

*Renderer*—a word I first heard on the foggy morning I found Jeziah cornered by a trio of older Potentiates while on my way to the kitchens to steal something to eat. I'd been there just over a year; him, a little less, and our training at the time had us testing our physical limits. Three days has passed since we'd been given anything other than tepid water, and my stomach ached almost as badly as during the forced march that carried me here. I kept my distance, pressed into a curve of wall, already having experienced my share of cornerings. Best not to interfere.

The fog softened their laughter, but it still carried the tang of amusement at another's expense. Then one—an older girl named Galilea—grabbed Jeziah's wrist and wrenched his arm up so sharply he was nearly lifted off the ground. "Always wondered what these were supposed to be," she mocked, the undulating bands of Jeziah's tattoos exposed. "Worms?"

No, rivers. To the north, there were hundreds of waterways that fed into the Great Meander river—one of which I had my own history with. And thousands of folks who traversed them in convoys of houseboats and barges. They would add a tattoo of each river they'd traveled the length of, filling their arms from wrist to collarbone. But I didn't know any of that until later.

"Looks like something a heretic would have," spat one of the others.

"I'm . . . I'm not." Jeziah tried to sound brave. "The river nomads—"

"Only practically a heretic then," Galilea cut in. "You know what else is up there, hiding out in the wilds? Renderers. Oh, I bet they'd like to get their hands on you. Nice and young and plump for the cutting."

Jeziah blanched.

"They'll have him soon enough." One of the others smirked. "I've seen him in the training yard."

"No they won't!" Jeziah wasn't crying. But his composure was crumbling.

Galilea sneered, releasing him. "They really dug you out of the mud, didn't they? Go 'round the kitchens when they've got a pig hung and gutted." She leaned in so that they were only inches apart. "That'll be you soon enough." Then, she shoved him into the wall, so hard I heard the crack of his skull from where I hid.

I waited until their laughter had faded away to approach. I didn't have a reason to, could have waited until Jeziah was gone too, but I found my feet carrying me over to where he was crouched, rubbing the back of his head. I knew him, of course. I'd watched him toss and turn, lashed to a bed in our dormitory, suffering the effects of our blood mother's blessings, certain this pale, scrawny boy wouldn't be one of the ones who survived. Later, I'd trained with him. Studied with him. But our relationship began and ended at the boundaries of those lessons.

He barely moved once he noticed me, but those bright, vulpine eyes of his tracked my approach.

"What'd you do?" I told myself I was asking in order to learn. Find out what he did to piss off the older Potentiates. Not do that.

He didn't answer right away, suspicious. Then: "I accidentally fell into her yesterday. During a drill."

I remembered. It was torturous, weakened as we were, to keep up the same intensity of training. But watching my footing around Galilea wasn't the only information to be gleaned here. "What's a Renderer?"

"You don't know?"

"Wouldn't have asked if I did." Sour tone. A little threatening. To make him think maybe I'd make him tell me instead of asking. He still had the hint of frailty he'd brought with him to the Cloisters, and had yet to hit the growth patch that would leave him with four inches and twenty pounds on me. At that point in time, I still had the advantage.

But I didn't need to resort to fists. "Thieves of divinity," he said. "The older Potentiates say they hunt Chosen, flay them alive, snap their finger bones off one by one, pull their teeth and grind them into—"

"They made it up!" I snapped it with a child's defensiveness. Jeziah flinched, and a feeling of superior pride rose in me. This was weakness, this fear, exactly what we were training to leave behind. He'd been caught in it, he knew, and was probably picturing how quickly I would run to Prior Petronilla and the disciplining that would follow. And I was picturing the same, knowing it was what any other Potentiate would do, and that maybe I'd be rewarded somehow, maybe with a meal. "The Goddess wouldn't—"

"The Goddess's Chosen can't be weak."

That shut me up. The truth was, we'd both been there long enough to know that there were consequences to not performing up to expectation. And that sometimes a Potentiate simply . . . disappeared. They'd be a fixture in training, a familiar face during studies, and then . . . one day their bunk or their room would be empty. One of our earliest lessons was to never ask where they'd gone. Another blessed body would take their place soon enough, anyway.

Who was to say they weren't given to monsters?

Still, it seemed unbelievable. "Our blood mother would never allow—"

"What if she didn't know?" It was the closest thing to blasphemy I ever heard Jeziah say. "I'm not afraid to die," he continued, and I was never sure if it was a defensive statement to make himself appear less fragile, or the truth, "but I don't want to die like *that*."

He didn't. He died doing his duty to the Goddess, broken and sprawled across the bloodied floor of the Cathedral. But that day we stole bread. And stewed apples and fresh cheese. The punishment was bad enough that it was nearly a year before Jeziah and I exchanged more than a few obligatory words again. By then, we both understood that Galilea's tale was only a cruelty played out by the older Potentiates and, more importantly, that we hadn't been punished for our crime, but rather for being caught.

We learned not to get caught.

Maybe Nolan needed more lessons in that.

I've gone only a few leagues before I tug at the reins of my newly acquired mount, pulling it to a stop without a full thought as to why, as if I'd reached the end of some road. Carsaire was ahead, and the heretic on his way there had a strong head start. There was the chance to catch up, if I didn't waste time. And yet, here I was, doing exactly that. And thinking of Jeziah. His sharp-edged laugh . . . his dead stare. Rotting away now, in his nook in Cineris. The Renderers were as real and present as he feared, but they would never get him. They'd never melt down his fat, bottle his fluids, or carve those bright, playful eyes from his skull.

Not like they would Nolan.

A groan escapes, never mind that I haven't made it far enough away from the farm to feel safe. And yet, I can't bring myself to urge the horse any farther.

Because if there are Renderers about, there's no such thing as safe. Especially if their "hounds" can pick me out with a glance.

"It's a good thing you're dead," I mutter, not caring whether Jeziah can hear me in the beyond. "You would have run crying back to Lumeris the minute these freaks showed up."

I pull the horse around and retrace my path. It's stupid. I know it. Nolan deserves nothing less than to be left to the fate he made. But it's the fate itself that I can't ignore, the abhorrent, rotten gnaw of it. I know what the Chosen have done in the name of Tempestra-Innara. Been party to it more times than I can count. But none of us deserve what the Renderers have in store.

Not even Nolan.

The Renderers are still at the farmhouse when I return. Back on the ridge, I count two new additions to their ranks, but if they located their "hound" or Avery, it's not clear. Given the way Baldy stomps around with an air of annoyance, however, I'm inclined to think they didn't. The caravan wagon I saw within the barn is now outside, hitched to a team of draft horses. And, to my relief, Mortimer and Buttons are lashed to the back as well. I'd pictured them lost and afraid, turned out into the woods after the Renderers captured Nolan, but clearly, they aren't foolish enough to waste a couple of quality horses. Or maybe they're just looking for more ways to pad their lost profits. As I watch, the wagon gets loaded, the final addition an ominously large wooden crate. Something in me tightens, make me wonder whether they changed their minds, decided a dead Chosen would be easier to transport than a living one, but the holes drilled into the side for air gives me hope.

Finally, they move off. I wait before following.

This is the compromise. I could try to take them here, but given the fact that they've already managed to subdue one well-trained scion of Tempestra-Innara, that seems like a less than wise idea. And if there are more Renderers, I need to know that . . . and, hopefully, figure out a way to remove them as a threat. Rescuing Nolan—if I can manage it—well, that will be a bonus. And while losing track of the heretic heading to Carsaire needles me, the woman with the Renderers seems to know where the reliquary is being kept too. I'll just have to persuade her to tell me.

I keep a safe distance, but their trail isn't hard to follow. The Renderers aren't Chosen, though. They need more sleep, their horses need breaks. They make camp, they break camp, I follow. The forests along the roads turn vibrant and plush, a far cry from the twisted, withered lands surrounding Novena. Civilization reappears in trails of smoke rising above distant villages and the presence of other travelers on the roads. I follow closer, less conspicuous now, but still keep to myself, hood drawn most of the time.

Here, I'm not the only one.

The familiar friendliness that Nolan and I encountered on the road to Belspire doesn't extent to this part of the Devoted Lands, apparently. Eyes aren't met, packs kept close, cargo tied tight. I ask a few travelers for news from Lumeris, worried that a new avatar might already have been found, but I learn nothing I don't already know, and most folks prefer to keep to their own business. Only a few call out "May the Flame warm you," more cursory than sincere. Still, with every one, the longing that has accompanied me since leaving Lumeris behind grows more pervasive. If I were forced to describe the growing distance from my blood mother, the feeling it's imparting, I couldn't say it's a true ache, itch, thirst, or anything else. It's more like some special discomfort reserved especially for their Chosen. And given we're moving farther and farther away, it's going to get worse. I almost envy Nolan, undoubtedly subdued in some manner to be so easily transported.

The forests taper off, giving way to rolling plains with mountains in the distance. They're pale and snow tipped—almost inviting. Not the stormy, craggy spires I remember from my youth. An estimation informed by hours studying Petronilla's map tells me this would have been, centuries ago, the beginning of the Stone God's lands. Do their followers persist like the Storm Goddess's? Are there villages like the ones where I came from, sequestered up among those distant ridges? The lack of knowledge grows like an untreated sore, especially in the wake of the Renderers' grisly appearance. Nolan and I were entrusted by the Goddess to find the heretics, the stolen reliquary, but with only the barest understanding of the world we were being thrust into. What other crucial pieces of information are we lacking? What else is waiting to surprise us?

With every day that passes, those insecurities grow. Doubt isn't far behind. Even as I mentally chart my progress to Sethane, I imagine where the heretic on his way to Carsaire is. I wonder if I should turn around. I wonder if he's arrived by now, and whether he's already on the next leg of his journey, taking the best lead we—*I*—had to finding the reliquary with him. Prior Petronilla whispers in my ear, disappointed but not surprised I didn't stay on task.

I know the truth of it. Nolan would have been an acceptable loss, along with Jeziah, the other Potentiates who fell, the whole of the crowd in the Cathedral. Wars aren't won without sacrifices; I'm no Bellator, but that's basic strategy. It's the Renderers that have complicated the situation, creating an unexpected challenge. Maybe there's only a few of them, maybe a lot, maybe . . .

The maybes swirl during the long hours in pursuit of my prey. The questions. The fearful, visceral imaginings of what awaits in Sethane and the growing, bitter craving to be back in Lumeris. I picture the reliquary to drive the feeling away, imagine it in my hands as I confront Tempestra-Innara. Spin a mental tapestry of events that mirrors Emmaus's assassination attempt, only successful. I imagine staring over their remains emptied of humanity and divinity alike.

It helps.

# Twenty-one

The way is saved. And when the Stone God returns, their efforts will begin anew, reach higher and higher, until those starry heavens above are finally reached.

—FROM THE WRITINGS OF
THE HERETIC PLUTIS (RESTRICTED TEXT)

SETHANE IS BARELY LARGE enough to call itself a city. There's no grand wall surrounding it, no fine spires. It grows out of a morning fog like a cluster of mushrooms out of a rotting log, dark and unwelcoming. A haze of smoke rises from the cluster of large chimneys on its southern boundary; there's a metallic tinge to the air. Why anyone would want to live in such a dingy city escapes me, but then again, what better place for a trade as unpleasant and heretical as a Renderer's to call home? This is a fringed edge of the civilized part of the Devoted Lands. The Goddess is nearly as far away as they can be, a distance that must be as reassuring to the Renderers as it is unpleasant for me.

As the last of the fog burns away, something bright flickers in the distance, appearing on the mountain range. It's followed by another, and another. I pull my horse to a stop, unsure of what I am seeing. Spikes of faceted crystal rise out of the mountains, massive enough to make Belspire's towers look like toothpicks stood next to trees. There are dozens in view, more I suspect that aren't, all stunning and impossible ornamentations. A wonder, which begins to answer my questions about why anyone would bother to maintain a city in a place like this.

Entering Sethane feels as anonymous as my travels to it. Few of its denizens take notice of me as I enter the squat gathering of buildings, all of which are gray and uninviting. I pass through a lackluster market, where unenthusiastic vendors hawk their unappealing goods, and rotting bits of vegetables slick the road. The people here are drawn, tired, and there's a dark dusting of soot to everything from the chimneys. Smelting operations, I gather. But clearly not prosperous work. There are no fine smells to the air here, like in Belspire, no smiles, and the last thing I expect to come across is a festival. Still, as far from Lumeris as Sethane is, the Goddess is here. The flame insignia decorates stone facades or is painted on doors. Sure, the paint is chipped and the carvings worn down, but there seems to be no lack of outward piety.

I make my way through the streets, frustration growing as I fail to locate the Renderers' wagon. That's all I need: to have come this far in pursuit of them and Nolan, only to lose both at the very end. Nolan can't have much time; every moment the Renderers keep him alive is a moment he has to escape. If I were them, I'd want to get him drained, chopped, and stewed as soon as possible.

I'm going to need help to find him in this unfamiliar city, and there's only one place I can count on finding it.

A few minutes of searching is enough to bring me to a square with the Goddess's visage at the center, upturned palms flickering with small, oil-fed fires. A church sits nearby, dim within and smelling faintly of incense, wooden benches taking up most of the space before a small altar. The pews are empty, save for one shriveled old man who appears deep in prayer. He stirs as he hears my approach, takes me in, and then, clutching his reverie, rises shakily and makes his way to the exit with a hobbling gait.

Pious city or not, there's something about Sethane's brand of worship that already feels very different from Belspire's. Which is a relief—I've had my fill of enthusiastic executions.

"Hello?" Small as the space is, the word echoes. Seconds pass before a cleric appears in the doorway beside the altar. No traveling mud cleric like Avery, and yet, there's a shabby appearance to him, as if the road he's walked has been a long one.

"Hello," he says, with a touch of wariness. He must not get many visitors or strangers, or both. "May the Flame warm you."

"Oh"—I turn my palm upright, summoning the flicker that passes as my divine ability—"it does."

The cleric's eyes widen and he drops to his knees, averting his gaze. "Chosen of our Goddess . . . forgive me, I . . . I didn't realize . . ."

"Of course not, why would you?" I interject, annoyed and embarrassed. Maybe it wasn't a good idea to reveal myself so quickly, but I need information fast. "Get up, please. Kneeling is . . . unnecessary."

He obeys, gaze remaining downcast. "I'd begun to lose hope. Not faith of course," he clarifies quickly, stumbling over the words. "But it had been so many months, and we hadn't heard anything from Lumeris . . ."

"I'm sorry?" The way he's speaking, it's almost like he expected me. "I'm looking for your Prior. Or Cleric of the Blood. Whoever is in charge here."

Finally, the cleric raises his head, blinking. "I . . . Oh. Apologies, Chosen One. I assumed you were Prior Fedic's replacement."

Fedic. The name isn't familiar, but all that tells me is that they are old enough that we didn't share time at the Cloisters. "Prior Fedic is the Goddess's hand in Sethane?"

He nods. "But he departed some months ago. I thought perhaps you had come to take up his position."

"Departed? To where?"

"I'm afraid I don't know. He left quite abruptly, leaving no word on where he was going or when he might return." The cleric's eyes drop once more. "Of course, I would never question the comings and goings of the Chosen. It's only . . . at Prior Fedic's age . . . I had concerns, you understand."

*. . . no decrepit Prior . . .* The memory of what was said in the barn is less than heartening, and I suspect Prior Fedic isn't showing up again anytime soon. But if the Renderers got him, why hasn't the conclave in Lumeris sent a replacement yet? Or investigated the Prior's disappearance when reports stopped coming in?

"I would not presume to know your business, Chosen One," the cleric continues. "But if I can be of any assistance . . . ?"

"You can," I say, still mulling over the possibilities of Fedic's fate. It doesn't make sense. There is no greater asset to the Goddess than their Chosen . . . or so we've been told. I examine the humble surroundings plopped in the center of this distant smudge of a city. This isn't exactly a choice assignment. It wouldn't be given to anyone considered of high value among the Goddess's ranks. And the strength of our blessing fades, eventually. Maybe Fedic's had faded so much that he wouldn't be considered any great loss.

Prior Petronilla's threats rise in memory. I always thought she'd be doing me a favor, making sure I was stationed in some quiet, boring place. But if a city like Sethane is the reality of that? No . . . even Petronilla would never send me to a place filled with Renderers, not knowingly.

I turn my attention back to the waiting cleric. "I'd hoped to find the Chosen in charge, but it is not necessary. First, no one else needs to know I'm here, nor do you need my name, or any other identifying information other than what I've already communicated. Do you understand?"

The cleric nods emphatically.

"Good. I'm here to investigate some . . . disturbing rumors about heretical practices in the area."

The cleric blanches a little. "Heretics? Here? That's . . . unthinkable."

"Is it?" I crook an eyebrow.

"I mean, not unthinkable," he stammers, growing increasingly nervous. "Sethane is pious, of course. Dedicated entirely to Tempestra-Innara . . . and their Chosen."

"But . . . ?"

He twists his fingers. "You must understand . . . here, so far from Lumeris, beneath the crystal ziggurats . . ."

"The ziggurats? Those towers on the mountain?"

"Yes." The cleric seems surprised at my ignorance of them. "The former places of worship of . . . of . . ."

I stand straighter, summoning my feigned authority. "You may be frank with me, cleric. No punishment will come of it."

This seems to assuage him a little. "The Stone God," he gets out finally. "Prior Fedic was dedicated to smothering any questionable practices, but the ziggurats have always drawn those who cling to heretical beliefs, who feel they are a symbol that dead gods only sleep. Sethane used to be . . . more than what you see, but the number of penitents needed to work the mines at any meaningful level of production . . ." He pauses, hesitating again. "There were uprisings, aided by the heretics. Lumeris deemed support an inefficient use of resources, and so the majority of the mining enterprises were abandoned."

And a disposable Prior installed.

"The ziggurats," I say again. "Tell me what you know about them."

His head ducks. "Very little . . . and only what is common knowledge in the city," he adds quickly. "They were built by the Stone God's followers centuries ago—the materials quarried from the mountains—to be closer to the heavens, to the stars. They believed the Stone God's heresy that the answers to all would be found in the marriage of the stone to the heavens. But then . . . when the Stone God fell . . ." He trails off.

"Please." I keep my tone soft, encouraging. "You may continue."

"When the Stone God died, the ziggurats changed. It is said the earth quaked like it never had before, and a great wave of power washed through them, changing the normal stone to the crystal that remains today."

Crystal? "Interesting," I say aloud, yet again irritated that my extensive, Cloister-based education has so many gaps that a simple cleric in the middle of nowhere is better informed than I am. But I'm not here to learn about the Stone God. "The heretics who still worship the Stone God, are there any in the city?"

Again, the cleric hesitates. "We try to keep them out, drive them away, but . . ."

"Just tell me, cleric. I'm not here to report back on how well you are doing your job."

That doesn't seem to encourage him. "Most keep to the mountains, near the ziggurats. They come here for food, supplies. Every so often one of your honored Bellator brethren and their legion sweep the hills, but the heretics simply retreat deep into the mountains. And, of course,

Prior Fedic tried to find them when he could, but they are like rodents. No matter what is done they return."

"I am seeking some very specific heretics. I know they are here, though I don't know the city well enough to guess where they might be. Do you have any idea where they might congregate?"

The cleric shakes his head. "In the city they are very . . . discreet."

Not helpful. I try my next idea. "Would you have a map of the city I could consult?"

He brightens. "Yes, yes, of course. Please, follow me."

The cleric leads me deeper into the little church, into the rooms at the back. One appears to be an office, small but nicely appointed, though it's clearly been used by many as opposed to few. There's a door, half cracked, that opens up into a bedroom of a similar situation.

"These are Prior Fedic's chambers," the cleric explains. "I keep them dusted, but otherwise everything is as he left it." He goes to a bookcase filled with ledgers and scrolls, and chooses one. "It's a bit out of date, but—"

"This is fine." I unroll the map on a desk, using a pair of dried-out inkwells to weight it down. "Might I peruse it in privacy?"

The cleric blinks at me for a moment, unable to fathom that I've asked politely instead of barking an order. Maybe Fedic wasn't a pleasant boss. Then again, who would be, shoved off into this sad little corner of the Devoted Lands?

"Yes, of course," he says finally, with a final duck of his head before leaving me blessedly alone. I start to examine the map, but my attention is drawn to a stack of letters at the corner of the desk. There are dozens of them, tied into bundles, but it's their seals that pique my interest: the fiery-red wax of the Cathedral. Dispatches from the Priors and Clerics of the Blood who manage the more mundane affairs of the Devoted Lands bear that seal. I slip one letter out of its binding and open it. Inside is a message, short and direct.

*Your report has been received. Proceed as previously.*

I take out another letter, and another. All have some variation of that simple, dismissive message. They might as well have not written back at all, because what they are saying is clear enough: *You're no longer of use to the ranks of the Chosen; have fun trying to not die while being miserably far from the Goddess.* It's enough to almost make me feel sorry for Fedic.

But there's nothing I can do for him, so back to the map. It's a simple thing, black ink scratched on parchment, though better detailed than I expected. I trace a finger through the streets, starting at where the shrine and church sit, following the avenues through the same market squares and residences I'd expect to see in any town. As I do, I play a game: If I were going to dismember and render a human body, where would I do it? There's a nagging sensation in the back of my mind, since I know any building in the city might do, and that there's no way for me to search them all. But there's another thought too: one that says that if I didn't want to be caught doing the worst form of heresy, I wouldn't do it in the city at all. My finger travels around the outskirts of Sethane until I find something of interest.

"Cleric!"

It's almost amusing how quickly he reappears. Probably waiting no more than a step outside in case I needed something else. Which, now, I do. I tap my finger on the parchment, on an area filled with buildings and chimneys, though they have been scratched out. "What's this?"

He looks. "The remains of the old refineries, Chosen One. Only a few still operate, but when the mines were more active..."

"So, no one uses them?"

He shakes his head, pointing at a spot between them and the bounds of the city. "The city dumps its waste here. Beyond that... all ruins."

Ruins and trash. Not the sort of area anyone would frequent. Unless they had something to hide.

"Do you require anything else of me, Chosen One?"

I stare at him, summoning what I hope is something akin to the rock-hard, no-nonsense expression that Prior Petronilla used to affix me with. "Only your discretion. You are to speak to no one about why I was here, or what I asked you about. Do you understand?"

His chin drops to his chest in an instant. "Of course, Chosen One. I am only at your service, as representative of our most divine and holy Goddess, Tempestra-Innara."

With his head down, he doesn't see my eyes roll.

# Twenty-two

There is divinity in every bone, every pad of fatted flesh, every drop of blood. One must only know how to extract it.

—AUTHOR UNKNOWN

DESPITE THE PRESS OF time, I wait until evening falls to make my way to the outer edge of Sethane. A single rutted road winds down and away from the city, strewn with debris. Eventually, I catch a whiff of something foul in the air and reach a wide, rectangular pit. There's enough starlight to see shattered crockery, splintered furniture, and what appears to be a dead ox, ribs exposed by scavengers and rot. I trace a path around the dumping ground, having had my fill of pits lately. Of more interest are the remains of the buildings a short distance past it. Right away, I see that the cleric was telling the truth: There is little left here but broken walls tracing the shapes of what structures used to stand, along with the occasional intact chimney, cold and lifeless as tombs.

Which makes it an excellent place for privacy. I creep through the ruins, shadow silent, listening for any other signs of life. Unlike Novena, there are the usual skitters of rats, the call of an owl on its night hunt. But nothing else. Frustration begins to bloom, the aching fear that I'm wrong, that I've lost the Renderers, Nolan, and any chance of tracking down the heretics, when the wind suddenly shifts. I hear something:

a nicker, faint, but nearby. I follow it, making my way around the remains of some sort of outbuilding. It appears to be caved in, but I find a hole in the stone, catching the faint smell of horses from it. Cautious, I slip through into utter darkness, but a quiet whinny greets me. And it sounds familiar.

Risking the light, I call the flame, just enough of it to illuminate the chamber I've found myself in. The first thing I spot is a horse.

"Mortimer!" Buttons is there too, and a few other mounts, along with the Renderers' wagon. There's a section of wood roofing covering another gap beyond it. It's arranged well enough that I would never have thought to search within, if not for Mortimer's tip-off.

"Good horse," I whisper again, giving him a pat. But there's no time for a proper reunion. As cunning as this makeshift stable is, there's no sign of the Renderers, or Nolan.

But they must be close.

I make my way out and examine the nearby structures. The remains of more outbuildings, for the most part, but there's a larger structure too, what must be one of the old refineries given the wide, round chimney rising from it. I press myself into a shadowed juncture of walls and listen again. My sickles, in their bindings, press back with a heartening firmness. I unsheathe one, careful not to let the blade flash. There are no sounds of movement from within. Entering through the remains of a doorway, I find a floor half rotted away, but there's a series of stone stairs that lead down. At their bottom is a low-ceilinged cellar, strewn with the rotten piles of what might be ancient crates and a few lonely spiderwebs. As in the city, a thin layer of soot coats everything here.

Except the floor.

I examine the slate: nearly spotless, as if it has been swept lately. Which doesn't exactly make sense ... unless someone wants to ensure that there isn't anything incriminating like, oh, footprints left behind. It doesn't take me long to find the faint scratches on the floor, right near the sunken base of the chimney. I feel along it until one of the stones gives way beneath my fingers. There's a soft *thunk*, followed by a door swinging open on a hidden hinge, revealing a winding staircase leading down.

*Success.*

The passage is narrow enough that I'm forced to sheathe my sickle again. What little light there is filters up from below, and I keep a keen ear out for movement. Getting caught on these stairs would make for a tricky fight, one I don't need the challenge of. But I meet no one, and the stairs spill out into a wider tunnel that looks much older than the structure above. Part of the mines? Secret passages used by the followers of the Stone God? There's no ornament to tell me any stories, only a long stretch of tunnel reinforced with wood beams, and the occasional oil lamp.

I reach a split in the passage. Without a clue to what either branch holds, I choose left and follow it until I reach a dead end with three wooden doors. Again, not a single marking to indicate what might be behind them, but there are small portals with a sliding cover set into each. I go to the middle one and, quietly as I can, slide it open. Inside, there's nothing, only an empty stone room with a single, ominous iron ring set into the wall. Still curious, I try another.

This cell is not empty. A body is folded into a pitiable ball against the back wall, metal chain rising from it and fastened to the same iron ring I saw in the last cell. Immediately, I know what sort of person the Renderers might keep caged here. But the body is not Nolan's; it's too slight, and the sheen of skin darker complexioned than his.

"Prior Fedic?" I whisper. They stir. "Prior Fedic, wake up. I—"

A head snaps up suddenly, eyes wide and glassy, with a stare that hits me like a blow. Bruised, bloody . . . the person jumps up and lunges at the door with a snarl that no longer sounds human.

"Chooosssss—" The chain runs out and they snap back, seemingly having forgotten their binding. They lunge at me again and again with a low moaning sound that can't quite form into the judgement they're trying to make.

*Chosen.*

I snap the viewport shut, fearful of the noise. But the stone is thick and heavy here, and though I wait for a long minute, there are no sounds of anyone approaching to investigate. Only the faint sounds of the "hound" in their cell, scratching and scrabbling, but those, too, soon quiet.

I loosen, a sick feeling rising in my stomach. What did they do to these people to make them like this? I look at the doors. And how many do they have? A quick check finds the third cell equally occupied. The dead man near Novena must have called the empty one home. A shudder runs through me, though not from the chill of the earth. Nolan and I thought ourselves safe in our assumed identities when we first set out. But now? Knowing my divinity can be outed so easily doesn't exactly sit well. There's only one consolation: a marked difference between the man in the woods—who still sounded mostly human—and my new friend in the cell. Whatever is done to them to be able to pick Chosen out, it appears to degrade them over time. Just like Emmaus, if slower, and less extreme. Is it linked to divine power somehow? From what I've seen of both the pure methods of divine infusion and the tainted sort, it seems likely.

I retrace my steps and take the right fork. This branch continues for longer, but soon I come to another turn and another hall, at the end of which sits a large metal door with a barred window. Faint sounds drift from it. I creep down the passage, move to the window, and peek in. Immediately, I spot Nolan, gagged and lashed with chains to a table in the center of the room. The table is tipped up so that he's nearly upright, an ominous drain at its foot. At first, I think he's dead, but then the foolish thought disperses—who would gag a corpse?—and I see a steady rise and fall of his chest. He even appears to be awake, eyes open and filled with thoughtful intensity. Clearly still trying to figure a way out of a doomed situation—leave it to Nolan to never give up. Considering his surroundings, I'm pretty sure I would have.

Two things there are a lot of in the chamber: knives and jars. Knives with serrated edges, knives with smooth blades. Tiny blades for precision work. Cleavers. Jars full of strange liquids and jars full of . . . pieces. My stomach turns. I also recognize items a chemist might use, tools more likely found in a butcher's, and other things I cannot begin to place, only glean their grim use from context.

In the midst of all this horror is a tall woman, strong armed but fair featured, with her hair tied back and a heavy leather apron that's splattered with telling stains. She stands at a worktable that runs along the wall opposite the door, humming as she fiddles with some bubbling concoction, checking an open book at her side. As I watch, she adds a drop of something, then a healthy measure of something else. With each addition the humming swells. The cooks back at the Cloister kitchens used to do that—hum, sing, gossip among themselves as they worked. I suppose this Renderer is as much a cook as any of them.

I move to the other side of the window, making sure the woman is alone. I'll need to move fast to surprise her, which means I have to hope she's had no reason to lock the door. I unsheathe one of my sickles, keeping the other hand free. Open the door, throw a sickle, silence the cook. That's the plan. Inside, the woman has moved on to a vat bubbling on a brazier. She takes a handful of what looks like wet entrails and tosses them in. The mixture bubbles and burps, giving off a noxious odor that reaches me, strong enough that I flinch away from the window.

It saves my life.

Something flies by, small but intent, hitting the door barely a hairsbreadth away. It bounces off and falls to the ground—a bolt with a sinister metal tip. I spin as another one flies, barely avoiding it as I draw my second sickle. At the far end of the hall, a man leans around the corner, with what looks like a small crossbow pointed my way. He frowns and curses, and immediately, four more figures appear. I recognize Baldy and the woman from the barn and—with more surprise—the cleric from the chapel. *Unbelievable.* I guess I should have learned my lesson after Avery. Weapons drawn, they encroach on me. I move to meet them.

"Shoot her!" My traitorous cleric friend sounds nearly in a panic as the man with the crossbow contraption raises it again. I lunge, colliding with him before he can get the shot off, pushing him into the wall even as the point of my sickle drags across the cleric's midsection. A desperate move, but necessary. The man with the darts lets out a hollow gasp, wind knocked from his lungs as the cleric stumbles back, catching his spilling guts. No time to savor that little victory; I barely avoid the swing of Baldy's sword. It hits the wall with a metallic ring, nearly decapitating his friend, who lets out another choking wheeze. Pushing away, I back into the hall with the door, sickles raised. Not a lot of time to think. At my feet lies the weapon used to launch the bolts; its owner dropped it. At least I know now how they managed to get Nolan.

And if whatever poison is on those darts is enough to subdue one of *us*, I need to avoid even a scratch. I raise my foot and bring it down on the crossbow; it crunches beneath my heel.

"Get those blades off her!" the woman orders. She's got a nasty dagger in one hand, but it's the other that's more concerning. Empty, but reaching into her bag. I can guess what she's going for.

"Okay." I lob a sickle her way. She's fast enough to try to avoid it, not fast enough to actually manage. A scream sounds as it catches her above her elbow. Everything below it drops, including the crossbow she was reaching for. She backs into the wall and slides down it, blood pouring as she drops the dagger, but Baldy is unfazed, spotting the opening. He and the other uninjured Renderer surge toward me, blades swinging. I turn away Baldy's sword, twisting around him in time to avoid a wild swing by his friend. Even so, I know this is a bad situation. I'm down one sickle and these two know how to fight—I can see it in their movements—and the Renderer with the darts is near to catching his breath. I need room to maneuver. Time to think. Dodging another blow, I go for the door. I don't even need to break the lock; it opens easily, letting loose the foul smells within as I plunge into the room. Immediately, a line of fire scorches down my biceps. I drop to a knee, roll away before another one of the Cook's surprise swings ends the fight. The cut is deep, but I count my blessings once I see what did it: a massive cleaver that looks like it could behead a bull in one blow. The Cook wields it two-handed, serpent's gaze trained on me as the other Renderers push into the room.

"Leesh?" Nolan. Sadly, there's no time to savor the baffled surprise filling his eyes. "Lut ne oos."

*Let me loose.* A good blow from my sickle would probably snap the chains, but I have no interest in adding one more to the number of people trying to kill me. "Shush and stay put. I'll get to you in a bit." I assess the group again. "Hopefully."

Three people trying to kill me . . . no, four. Crossbow has recovered enough to join the others, sword drawn. I back further into the room, to where the horrid concoctions bubble. I regret not paying closer attention to the Cloister chemistry lessons, but it's not like I have time to take inventory anyway. I grab the most sinister-looking vial and launch it at Crossbow. He tries to move, but the doorway has gotten crowded, and my aim is good. The vial shatters, splattering his face and torso with something that, given his screams, is exactly the sort of brew I hoped it was. He stumbles back into the passage. But the Cook comes at me, moving around Nolan's table with a surprising speed. Baldy and the other remaining Renderer—a lanky man with a scar on one cheek—come around the other side in an attempt to squeeze me.

That's their first mistake. They may work as a pack, but skilled or not, they clearly haven't trained to fight as one. I duck a swing of the cleaver and slip between the two swords, Scar's blow sinking into the wooden worktable and sticking there. I put him between me, Baldy, and the Cook, using him as a shield as he attempts to free his weapon. Second mistake: Baldy attempts to attack around his companion, instead of through him, a sacrifice that might have actually achieved an advantage. But his angle is awkward, and he moves within my reach. I slice him across the chest and he falls back, blood pouring. By then, my shield has gotten his sword unstuck, and Cook is inching forward, searching for any opening. They're getting desperate, their eyes bright with it. And desperation leads to clumsiness.

They attack as a pair. I deflect one blow and dodge another, driving the point of my sickle into an unguarded chest. It finds Scar's heart; he's dead before he hits the ground.

But it's the chance Cook was looking for. Her cleaver comes crashing down—I never saw her raise it—and I barely twist away, its edge so close that I feel the painful kiss of it. I touch my ear; a small chunk is missing from the curve. Annoyed, I lunge, getting inside her reach as she raises the cleaver again. I strike, opening up her throat.

"Ack." The only word I ever hear from her. Drowning in her own blood, she falls, sprawling out across the workroom floor.

She's done. Which leaves Baldy. I turn to him. Impressively, he's still on his feet, an arm pressed to his wound and mad as hell.

He raises his sword and points, a mean grin spreading on his face. "Wicked abomination. When I'm done with you, there's not going to be enough left to bother making anything of—"

I raise my sickle and throw. The words cut off as its point embeds deep in his skull, and Baldy goes down like a dropped doll.

"Uh-huh." I go over and retrieve my weapon from his twitching corpse. "Sorry, but I win."

Well, almost.

Nolan, head lifted what little the chains will allow, strains against his bonds, muffled words caught behind his gag.

"I'll get to you in a minute." Returning to the corridor, I assess what remains of the situation. The cleric is on his back, still. The Renderer I hit with the liquid is also dead, with an unpleasant amount of his face melted away. But the woman is alive and attempting to crawl her way down the corridor. I retrieve my other sickle, then grab her by the collar, drag her back into the Renderers' workroom, and leave her slumped against the wall. She's as pale as a gravestone.

"I can stop that." I gesture with one sickle at her trickling stump. "You could live, walk away mostly intact. And all I'd ask in return is the answers to a few questions. Which I personally think is a pretty good deal for a bitch that would have boiled me for broth."

Her eyes find me, watery orbs in increasingly pallid skin. With every beat of her heart, a little more life spurts onto the floor.

"You were going to hunt Chosen if the Goddess fell. That part I know. So, what else are you up to, besides plying the grossest trade of all time? How many more of you are there?"

She glares. Says nothing.

"Okay, let's try something else. What do you know about reliquaries?"

This time, she looks surprised. And then angry. She spits at me weakly, teeth tinged red. "Monster. Lapdog of the Butcher Goddess. May you both drop dead tomorrow and usher in the return of the fallen divine." There's a distinctly pious flavor to her vehemence. And here I thought Renderers were all about the financial gains. Regardless, she has information I need.

I steel myself for the unpleasant task of getting it out of her.

"Mleesh!" Nolan's full mouth exclamation is louder this time. "Pees. Lut ne oos."

I sigh and turn. "Not *now*. Honestly, stop being so needy. I'm trying to work here!"

When I turn my attention back to the woman, it's just in time to catch her remaining hand drop from her mouth. She bites down.

"No!" I grab her, try to pry her jaw open, but it's too late; the poison goes to work immediately. Her face flushes as thick, cloudy drool seeps from the corners of her mouth. Within a minute, she's dead. "Fuck!" I spin toward Nolan, more annoyed than ever. "See what you did? She knew where the reliquary was. She—" I pause. Take a deep breath. Irritation bubbles like the liquids surrounding me, but there's no point being pissed off at a corpse.

I turn back to Nolan. "She knew where the reliquary was. And *your* distraction cost us that information. Remember that."

His eyes narrow.

"Yes, *us*," I repeat, picking my way through the carnage. I find a rag among the Renderers' supplies to clean the blood and gore from my sickles. I take my time. I need to think, and this next bit is going to be important.

Even if I hate every moment of it.

When I'm ready, I return to Nolan.

"Okay," I say, looking directly into the eyes that I can't believe I ever found gentle, or caring. "You and I are going to have a little talk."

# Twenty-three

> The path to victory is not always the clearest, easiest, or—and this is the most difficult to accept—smartest.
>
> —*WORDS OF WAR*, WRITTEN BY BELLATOR PRIME NAEVE, IN THE ERA OF TEMPESTRA-TERTIA

Nolan is very, very still as I raise one of my sickles and rest the point lightly on the ridge of his cheek.

"First off," I say, "fuck you for trying to kill me." To his credit, he doesn't flinch as the blade skims over his skin, then hooks into the gag, cutting it away. "I want to know why."

He doesn't respond right away, only flexes his jaw with an expression of irritatingly patient consideration. "You know why," he says finally, frowning. I flick my wrist, sickle kissing him again. This time, his head jerks away instinctively. The frown shifts into an amused smirk. "You survived."

"One of my better habits." I let my weapon drop. "You were planning to get rid of me from the start."

Nolan shrugs innocently. "We can't both be Executrix. I was doing what it took to ensure it would be me."

"What happened to you respecting the Goddess's wishes?"

"Don't be cross because you actually believed that."

"I'm not." But I am, as much as I try not to show it. Nolan sized me up right from the start, whipping up a sweetened, pious facade he knew I would think too well trained and obedient to be threatening. And I ate it up with a spoon. "Stupid not to wait until we actually found the reliquary, though."

"I saw an opportunity."

"And look where it got you." I put away my sickles and rifle through the workroom until I find a roll of bandages, then strip off my blood-soaked jacket. Despite the chamber now resembling an abattoir, the floor directly in front Nolan is clear. I sit before him, cross-legged, and begin bandaging my arm. "Unfortunately, you being an untrustworthy ass isn't my biggest problem right now. Or yours, for that matter." I gesture to the corpses surrounding us. "This is."

He crooks an eyebrow. "Seems to me like you made short work of the 'problem.'"

"Don't sound so impressed." I tip my chin at the dead woman. "You recognized her voice, yeah?"

He nods carefully.

"And I'm sure you've figured out by now why a pack of Renderers were teamed up with assassination-happy heretics."

A furrow appears in his brow. "Because it would have been open season on our brethren if the Goddess had fallen."

"A bit concerning, right?"

"Yes, but not quite as immediate a concern as figuring out a way to escape before they . . ." His voice falters. "Completed their work."

He's shaken. Good. "Sorry to interrupt what I'm sure would have been a spectacular getaway." Finished with the bandage, I put my hands behind me and lean back. "Well, while you were having fun with your new friends, I ran into one of the other heretics from Novena on the road. Mine was less . . . antagonistic."

"Where are they now?"

"Where all heretics should be," I reply. "Dead." Truth is a tool I need right now, but that doesn't mean I have to tell *all* of it. "I needed a horse, and he had one. But that's far from the most interesting part."

"And that is?"

"He was a cleric." I let the revelation sink in. "Not in disguise either. So is one of the dead Renderers out in the hall. *That* one I found in

Sethane. Thought he was helping me; instead he tipped his friends off. Which means that whatever this is, whatever plots are being hatched against Tempestra-Innara, it goes beyond a handful of unusually ambitious heretics. I think who we're after might have their fingers in more pies than we expect."

Nolan considers me for a long, cold moment. "You're saying they've infiltrated the Goddess's devoted?"

"Yup. And not recently. Probably been planning this for years."

Something flashes in his eyes. "And after killing the false cleric you didn't follow the heretic? Or send word to Lumeris? You came *here* instead?" His face flushes with true anger. "I knew you were a fool, Lys, but—"

"Oh, I'm sorry. I didn't realize you wanted to get carved up into pieces!"

"You *should* have gone after the reliquary!"

I jab a finger at the dead woman. "I did! *She* knew where it was. Until *someone* gave her the chance to take that very vital piece of information to the grave!" That chastens him. "They are *Renderers*. Do you not get that? Have you not figured out how they knew who—what—you were?"

His mouth thins. "One of them . . ."

"Yeah, met him. Good news is, he didn't survive. But that doesn't exactly offset the bad." I get to my feet again, gesture around the room. "All this? It isn't some enterprise they threw up overnight. These aren't vague, half-baked monsters meant to scare baby Potentiates. Or desperate scavengers on the fringes of the Devoted Lands scrounging up long-lost, dried-out skeletons." The book that Cook was consulting sits open on the table. I flip through the pages, each filled with tiny, cramped writing and illustrations that make my stomach turn. "They *know* stuff. Look at this. It's an actual recipe book on turning you and me into a really fun time. Purifying and concentrating Chosen blood, the best ways to dry and powder fresh bone versus old, rendering fat and brains into an oil that causes—"

"I don't need the details of their foul heresy," Nolan cuts in.

"Are you sure? Kinda think a lesson or two about all this back at the Cloisters might have come in handy." I spot something behind the book—a small red lacquer box, out of place among the tools and tinctures. Its contents turn my stomach: a trove of small jars and vials. I've never seen them, but know what they are in an instant. These are the culmination of the Renderers' work, vile concoctions that carry with them a temporary taste of divinity. A drop of blood tincture to bring on euphoria and strength; a balm to enhance the senses or even heal a wound. But one vial stands out. "Hello, what have we got here?" I pick it up. It's filled with a fine, crystalline dust. Nothing that would have been manufactured from human parts. And as soon as I touch it, it begins to glow. "Look familiar?" I ask Nolan.

"It's glowing like the reliquary did."

"Yup." I tip the vial slowly, letting the fine powder pour from one end to another. It sparkles with a brilliance that borders on unnatural. "Maybe Renderers like to mess with their eyesight as much as Arbiters. And maybe there's more than one use for a reliquary. That would have been helpful to know before we set out, right?"

Nolan doesn't speak again for a long minute. "It wasn't only his eyes. They had him on a chain. He was . . . there was something wrong with him."

"There are two more like him in the cells. This stuff must give them the ability to see or sense what we are in the same way the Arbiters' Judge's Sight lets them see within a person. But just like what happened with Emmaus, there must be side effects eventually." I twirl the vial between my fingers. "How many more do you think are out there? Renderers and their hounds, blending in with normal folks, who can take our measure in an instant?"

"Where exactly are you going with this, Lys?"

Here it is. The shitty part.

I place the vial on the table. "Tempestra-Innara wanted us to work together to find the reliquary. I can still do that, on my own, same as you were planning. But if the last couple of days have proved anything, it's that there are way too many things we don't know that we don't know. We can't even trust the clergy anymore. 'Alone' isn't the smartest option right now." I pause, letting him consider my words. "Divinely blessed or not, we still need sleep, food, all that human nonsense. We get tired. Sometimes we have to pull our pants down and take a shit.

And when it comes to those things, it's better to have someone watching your back than not."

Silence. Then: "Why in the world would you trust me after I tried to kill you? And, more importantly, why should I trust *you*?"

"Oh, I don't trust you in the least. But betrayal aside, if either of us had been somehow secretly in league with the heretics, we wouldn't be surrounded by this lovely mess." I cross my arms. "So, I propose this: We go back to our original agreement."

"And," Nolan says carefully, "after that . . ."

"After that . . . well, who knows if we will even get that far." I take a deep breath. "Listen, I get it. You want to be the Executrix. The truth? I don't. Too much responsibility, too much trouble." Nolan's eyes narrow ever so slightly. He thinks I'm full of shit. Good. Let him believe I'm lying, instead of egregiously omitting. "I'm perfectly happy to find the reliquary and use that goodwill currency to request a nice, posh posting somewhere that I can grow old without anyone trying to outdo me, kill me, or turn me into divine drugs. I'm not like you, I'm not like Caius. I simply want to serve . . . simply. But since you don't believe that, I'll offer this deal instead: If we get our hands on the reliquary, then we renegotiate. How does that sound?"

It sounds like a challenge. And in a way, it is. I've all but said we can fight to the death as soon as we have the reliquary in hand, but the fact is that there will be a lot of dangerous, unpredictable shit between now and then.

Nolan understands that too. "I can't express enough how much I dislike that I think you're right. This situation . . . I'll admit it's more than a little embarrassing."

"I won't tell if you won't. And you don't have to like it. Only agree to it."

"Fine." His tone is resigned, if not enthusiastic. "We find the reliquary, together. And after that . . ."

"After that," I say by way of agreement.

In an instant, our truce is struck. Like Nolan, I don't like the situation. But also like him, I know what I want, and I'm willing to get it any way I can.

And that means the Dawn and Dusk team-up is back on.

Nolan gives me a pointed look. "Unchain me now?"

I let him stew a little longer. Then I pick up the dead cook's cleaver. A couple of good whacks takes care of the chains and Nolan is free. He moves a cautious number of steps away from me, massaging his stiff arms and hands, moving less confidently than normal. Whatever drugs they gave him on his trip to Sethane are probably still lingering, not that he'd ever admit it. Able to finally observe his surroundings properly, he goes over to one of the jars lining the shelves, which is filled with alcohol or some other preservation fluid and several human fingers.

"This . . . this is . . ." The words stumble. "This was one of our brethren."

"Yup." I start picking through the various papers piled around. "Say hello to what I am assuming are the remains of Prior Fedic, the most recent Chosen stationed in Sethane."

Nolan's features go stony, an icy darkness filling his gaze. "It's unconscionable. Horrific."

"Sure is."

"This doesn't bother you?"

"Of course it does." Would Nolan care to know about the letters in Fedic's office? The ones that made it clear the Prior was all but forgotten? I could tell him; instead I nudge the nearby body of the Cook with one toe. "I already did what I could about the situation."

"Lumeris needs to be informed about this—"

"*This* is not our assignment. The reliquary is."

"If you'd followed the heretic to Carsaire, you might have actually found it."

"And you'd be dead."

"But the Goddess would be safe!"

The sincere, almost desperate worry in his voice makes me pause in my rifling.

He seems surprised himself, at the slip of his usual control. He takes a tight breath. "The heretics in Novena spoke of making a spectacle. Do you think they'll bother with that again? *No.* If they have agents embedded in the ranks of the clergy, we have no idea how close they can get to the Goddess without suspicion. We need to warn them."

"And how long do you think it will take the heretics to figure out we've sent warning if they do have spies in Lumeris?" I counter. "Best-case scenario, they go back into deep hiding and we lose the reliquary. Worst case, they're forced to strike again in any way they can. Maybe this time they get it right."

"Our blood brethren will protect the Goddess."

I snicker. "Even surprised, the Renderers managed to take you down. We don't know how many of them there are, how much help they might have, or whether they might start picking Chosen off any day now. The more of our blood brethren are gone, the clearer the path to the Goddess."

He considers this. At first, I almost expect him to accept those potential costs, embrace the same level of ruthlessness as Tempestra-Innara. But he seems to understand one important truth: that we have no real idea of what plans the heretics have in place. And there's another, more selfish consideration as well. Nolan desperately wants to be Executrix. Finding the reliquary is still the best way to ensure that.

"Maybe," he concedes finally. "But we have to assume the simplest scenario, that they'll retrieve more of the reliquary blood and try to strike again before the Goddess takes a new avatar."

This time, he's right. The window of opportunity is closing—for the heretics *and* for me.

"We need to get to Carsaire," he continues, "try to pick up the heretic's trail again."

"We don't know the reliquary is in Carsaire. It's a port. That heretic could have hopped on a ship going anywhere."

"That was the only lead we had. Unless you have a better suggestion," he adds tartly.

"Did you think I was looking for cooking tips?" Abandoning the fruitless papers, I go to the dead woman and begin searching her instead. There's something secreted in the lining of her coat: a folded letter. "Here we go."

Nolan leans over my shoulder. "What does it say?"

There are only a few lines written in neat script. "'Your wares will be more than welcome, your courier expected.'" Then a signature ... maybe. A series of symbols, but nothing that I recognize. "A code?"

Nolan snatches the letter away and peers at it. "If it is, I don't know it." He scowls, pressing one hand onto the wooden top of the worktable, as if needing to steady himself. "This is useless. We keep to the heretic's trail."

"Fine." I stand, the only useful source of information in the room growing cold at my feet. "Then there's just one more thing."

"And what's that?"

I draw a sickle, arcing it down so that the point skewers the back of Nolan's hand. He cries out, dropping the letter, then swallows the pained sound, features darkening again.

"I thought we had an agreement," he says through gritted teeth.

"We do." Which isn't to say I'm not still mad. I twist the blade, compounding the damage, hoping for another cry. He's tough, though. Barely grunts. I lean close, so that there's only a handbreadth between our faces. He smells of old sweat and blood, and this close, I can see flecks of gold in his hazel eyes. The eyes that fooled me, that veiled his true intentions. But I see through that now.

And I want to make sure he knows it. "This is only fair, though, considering. Right?"

He winces again as I wrench the point free, but a smirk appears on his lips. There's a new hint of respect in it. One that acknowledges who—and what—we both are.

Liars. Killers. Very, *very* reluctant allies.

"Sure," he concedes, though his gaze has closed off, hidden whatever true thoughts he might have on the matter. "Only fair."

I keep my distance as Nolan tersely bandages his injured hand. But he doesn't seem interested in retaliation—at least, not against me. Not yet. His face betrays nothing, but the longer he takes in the Renderers' workroom—the tools, the macabre concoctions, the fragmented remains of Prior Fedic—the more a grave air grows around him, simmering and sharp. He pauses in front of the table he was chained to, running a finger over the deep butcher-block markings scarring its surface.

Maybe I should be more bothered as well, but the deep personal offense that Nolan appears to take at the Renderers' existence . . . I can't summon it. A crawling disgust, yes, but more than that, I feel a growing anger at the concealment I continue to uncover. These secretive, expansive, crucial pieces of the world both within and beyond Tempestra-Innara's control. And here I thought they only kept us ignorant of the world beyond theirs.

"If there are other Renderers or their allies in the area"—Nolan's words pull me from my thoughts—"we can't give them the chance to rebuild elsewhere."

I watch as he starts rifling through the bottles and jars. "What are you thinking?"

He chooses a jar, something pale yellow and oily. "These heretics deserved to be judged. To suffer as much as they made our brethren suffer." Removing the stopper, he tips the jar and pours the contents over the bodies on the floor. "And Fedic deserved a proper interment in Cineris. But this will have to do."

Oh. *That's* what he's got in mind. As he repeats the process with another jar, a nagging sensation grows in my stomach.

While Nolan's back is turned, I slip the Cook's book into my jacket, next to Jogue's diary and the letter. After a brief hesitation, I add the lacquer box. I'm not sure why, but the Renderers risked the worst fates in the Devoted Lands to trade in these spoils. Maybe they can still be useful. Then, I pick up the Cook's cleaver and sweep it across the table, obscuring my theft, as well as shattering the vial of reliquary powder. *That* I definitely don't want in any other hands. Nolan startles at the sudden crash, but I only shrug in response, as if impatient with his more restrained level of destruction.

"That's enough," says Nolan. "Let's go." He calls the flame. It catches on the spilled substances, a line of blue fire racing across the worktable. Then, he turns and strides purposefully out of the room, leaving me to catch up as noxious smoke fills the air.

He doesn't get far. I find him standing over the cleric's body.

"Dead," I say, trying to draw him away from the sight of an enemy costumed as an ally, but as if to contradict me, the cleric coughs suddenly, body shuddering. "Or not."

The cleric's eyes open a crack. Not gone yet, maybe, but gutted as he is, it won't be long. Fear flashes in his face as Nolan kneels down beside him. I wait, unsure whether to intervene, not sure if there's any mercy I can offer now.

Or if I want to.

The cleric's mouth works desperately, forming soundless words. Begging, cursing . . . I can't tell their intention.

"When they whisper, we wake . . ." Nolan begins. "At their command, we follow. In their light, we are seen . . . we are *judged*."

At first, I think perhaps it is Nolan who is considering mercy as the smoke reaches us, the growing inferno not far behind. But instead, he stands, a chill entering his voice. "May their blessed flame find purity of faith, or else leave cinder and ash."

With that, he turns away. The cleric's gaze moves to me, pleading. If we were alone, the ache in my gut tells me I would be swayed. But we're not, and right now I need Nolan's trust more than a quiet conscience.

It's not until we reach the fork in the corridors that I hesitate again. "The hounds . . ."

Nolan doesn't slow. "Let them all burn."

Ice-cold and unflinching. Not the Nolan who seemed to accompany me to Belspire, who dispatched Magda quickly and painlessly. Not even the Nolan who shoved me into the pit. Whoever he is, I don't know him at all.

It's enough to make me wonder exactly who I've struck a bargain with.

The cool night air feels like a blessing when we emerge from the ruins. I take a deep breath, chasing away the lingering scents and acrid taste of smoke, then go to the structure housing the Renderers' wagon and pull down the false wall covering the entrance. Nolan shoves past me and reappears a few moments later with his sword and gear.

I go after something better.

"Mortimer!" I cradle the horse's head in my hands, then rub the bridge of his nose. "Oh, are you okay? Did those mean Renderers feed you enough?" Mortimer whinnies softly. Beside him, Buttons nickers. "It's okay, you two. You're back with us now. No one is going to steal you away again."

"Are you really coddling the horses?" Nolan straps his gear to Buttons's saddle.

"Jealous? Awww, do you need to be fawned over after that trying ordeal?"

A tight frown tells me he's not in the mood for teasing. The real Nolan's sense of humor seems to be about the same as the false one's, which gives me some measure of him at least. He mounts up, but I go to the Renderers' horses first and lead them out into the yard before I turn them free. Smoke is beginning to leak from the old refinery, and the makeshift stable is close enough that the fire would be a threat.

Nolan watches with irritated patience. "Your concern is touching."

*Sarcasm.* Good to know real Nolan wields that too.

"The horses didn't try to kill me. And you're awful cranky for someone who is still in one piece." I arrange an expression of mock horror. "You *do* still have all your parts, right? They didn't take anything before I arrived? Some toes perhaps, or maybe even your—"

"Everything is right where it should be. *Thanks.*" Now he sounds annoyed.

Good. We're back where we started.

"Hurry up," he orders, starting off in a direction that will circumvent the city and allow us to pick up the road toward Carsaire. Behind us, the ruins of the refinery continue to be engulfed, flames licking out of the brick chimney. It won't be long before someone from the city comes running to investigate. But by then it will be too late. Any evidence of the Renderers will be long gone, consumed by the justice that is the Goddess's divine flame.

# Twenty-four

*A fine smile has all the power of divinity,
when wielded smartly.*

—FROM THE PLAY *THE LADY'S WINDOW*

REAL NOLAN TURNS OUT to be about as chatty as the Nolan I set out with back in Lumeris. For two days, he speaks to me only when necessary, shutting off all insight into what might be going on in that traitorous noggin of his. Not that it takes much to guess what's going on—urgency has taken hold, driving us to be moving by first light and pushing travel late into the evening. He doesn't seem to sleep. I know I don't. We may have a truce, but that's not enough to put faith in that I'll awake each morning sans sword through heart. Add on the threat of Renderers around every corner, and the sweet dreams don't come easy.

And while we might not need much sleep, that's not to say it doesn't help. Our patience frays in tandem, resulting in snipes about where to stop at night, how to build the fire to keep it from being seen, who takes first watch. It's enough to make me wish we were still pretending.

Still days out from Carsaire, we are forced by a steady, stormy rain to stop early and take shelter beneath a rocky overhang off the road. Nolan's temperament leaks almost as much as the stone; I can tell the delay needles him by the way he stabs at the fire we cobble together. And the way he gets up every quarter hour to check the sky.

"Is this cursed rain ever going to let up?" he grumbles, taking his seat again.

I don't look up from Jogue's diary. Not my preferred choice of reading material, but I'm not going to explain to Nolan why I'd steal a book that outlines how to chop me up like a fatted hog. I've only managed a few minutes with the Renderers' tome here and there, during the bathroom breaks, which are my only chance at solitude, hoping to learn something helpful or decode the mystery signature. But though I find a number of strange, script-like markings—and a lot of descriptions that do wonders to keep my appetite at bay—they're nothing like the blocky, more geometric symbols on the letter. "Not before morning, I'd wager."

"Do the followers of the Storm have some special sense about the weather?"

A dozen snappy retorts spring to mind, along with the urge to toss back the sharpest one. Instead, I reply simply: "No."

Silence follows, and I sense the briefest hint of remorse. No, not that. More like a wonderment of where the comment came from to begin with. Fake Nolan didn't seem to take offense at my origins; I wonder whether that opinion is shared with Real Nolan. Either way, the jab clearly slipped out unbidden.

"I'm eager to get there too." It's a kinder concession than he deserves, but I'm tired, damp, and—for once—in no mood for an argument.

"We're days away still."

"That gives us time to figure out how we're going to find one man in a port home to thousands." Quiet follows. A suspicious amount of it. "Unless you have an idea already?"

At first, I don't think I'm going to get an answer. Nolan stares into the fire. The furrows in his brow deepen, then loosen a little. "I got a look at him." The admission is slow, reluctant. "The heretic, as he left Novena. It was from a distance, but close enough that I think I'd recognize him again. I didn't want to risk getting too close, meant to follow his trail . . ."

"But—*surprise*—Renderers put a stop to that plan?" Maybe I'm not above a jab too. "Care to share a description? I mean, just in case anything *tragic* were to happen to you along the way?"

He ignores that. Which, fine. He can keep one card hidden in his sleeve; I have my own stashed away.

"It doesn't matter," he grumbles. "The heretic will have probably moved along by the time we get there."

"Or not." I close the book, whose pages are endangered by the misty spray carried in by the wind. "Just because a score of ships come and go from the port everyday doesn't mean he won't be waiting for a particular one. Or that he's even leaving Carsaire. For all we know that's where they are hiding the reliquary. Or it's close."

"Sure," he says bitterly. "Maybe they've secreted it on one of the hundred little unoccupied islands that run along the coast nearby."

"Even better. I've never seen the ocean."

I don't bother to see what kind of response that incurs. Instead, I pull out the letter from the dead woman yet again. The symbols on the bottom are as confounding as ever, but there's a pull to them as well. Something I can't quite let go of. With a stick, I start sketching the symbols out in the dirt next to the fire.

"You're still trying to figure that out." Nolan says it flatly, in a way that doesn't tell me what he thinks of the endeavor.

"Gives me something to do."

"You studied the same codes and cyphers as the Dusk Cloister did. It doesn't bear a resemblance to any of them."

"Nope," I agree.

"So then how do you expect to unravel it?"

I finish copying the marks. "Stop trying to pick a fight because you need a distraction."

His mouth thins. "I wasn't."

"You were."

If his goal *was* to start an argument, he abandons it. I keep to the drawings, utterly clueless about what they might mean but happy to use the excuse of them as a focus for my attention. There's a brief flicker of longing—Fake Nolan and I might have passed the time sparring, which had actually been kinda fun—but it extinguishes as quickly as the sparks that stir from the fire. We made our deal and being friendly again certainly isn't part of it. I don't regret having someone to watch my back, but I also can't deny that Nolan's concerns are legitimate. The trail turned cold when I decided to pursue the Renderers instead of the lead heretic. Now it's practically frozen.

But there's no unspilling that blood. So I quietly trace the symbols, over and over with my stick, until I know them by heart. Then, I trace normal letters below them, searching for any hints in the shape, the pattern, the design—

My stick stops and I stare at what I've been doing. Not the symbols, but rather the stick.

Something cracks open and a memory slips out, wispy and diminutive. It takes a minute to get a tight grasp on it, but when I do, I drop the stick and the letter, and return to Jogue's diary, flipping to the sections near the front, where Jogue describes the deities' places of worship. There's nothing in the descriptions themselves, but the drawings he sketched in the margins of the page . . .

What I am looking for—that tiny pebble of recollection that's been stuck in the shoe of my mind for the last couple of days—practically jumps off the page.

Nolan notices my agitation. "What?" He stands and moves around the fire when I don't respond right away. "Did you find something?"

I pull the book to my chest. "Are you going to stop being a jerk if I show you?"

"*Lys.*"

"Fine. Here." I reveal Jogue's drawing. It depicts a street, or maybe an alley. He's captured the scene in great detail, right down to the graffiti on the walls, a mash of symbols that look like nonsense, or a child's scribblings.

Symbols that match the signature on the letter.

"Are there more?" There's an eager tightness to Nolan's words. "A translation of what they mean?"

"No. That's the only drawing with them. But one of Jogue's goals was to spot the nuances of his destinations, capturing the unique aspects of them." I turn a few pages back, to show him what section the rendering is part of.

"Cyprene?" Nolan takes the book and examines it closer. "We can't be sure."

"Makes sense, though, doesn't it?" The city of Cyprene lies on an island far from the mainland, in one of the most isolated areas in the Devoted Lands—the former territory of the Salt Goddess. And, most importantly, a place where no Chosen lasts long. It might technically owe fealty to Tempestra-Innara, but it hasn't been directly within their control for nearly half a century. "The heretic headed to a port city. And where better to keep something as important as a stolen reliquary than as far beyond the reach of the Goddess as it can get?"

He wrestles with the revelation. "We should follow the heretic. That's a solid lead."

"Unless he's already on a ship to Cyprene."

"Which we could find too."

"But would find faster if we detoured to a closer port."

Everything about Cyprene is logical. He just doesn't want to admit it. But I wait, and predictably, the desire to succeed wins out over the desire to prove me wrong. At least that hasn't changed.

So, when the rain finally breaks around dawn, we turn our intentions south, toward the port of Phrygis.

"You want to book passage," says the captain of the *Squid's Shadow*, "on *my* ship?" Captain Cleophas's voice is low and rich, her manner straight to the point. And a little bit suspicious, which it should be.

"I do." The haughtiness in the response makes me want to cringe. I do not like this new Nolan, who appeared upon our arrival in Phrygis. Bold. Confident. With the mannerisms of someone who expects to get his way. He slipped on this new skin as easily as he shed the old one the moment he shoved me in the pit, the moment we finally reached the port. The tension of the road, his clear anxiety to gain ground on our target . . . gone like they were never there. Maybe this is who he really is: a manipulative, slimy liar who knows how to shift himself in order to play whomever he comes across.

Or maybe it simply bothers me that it seems to be working.

"Passage for myself and my bodyguard, as well as our horses." A hand gestures vaguely my way, followed by a broad smile. "Your ship came highly recommended."

I stifle a snort. This ship was the *only* one recommended, after two careful days of picking around Phrygis's docks, making inquiries about reaching a destination that, strictly speaking, shouldn't be one any upstanding citizen should be asking about. The crawl of eyes trying to glean our intentions made things even edgier than they'd been while traveling. Exhausted and twitchy, we keep our hoods drawn when on the streets, taking special care to avoid clerics and city officials—anyone whose social stratum might be worth infiltrating. Any gaze that lingers a little too long is suspect, and I find myself searching for hints of the unnatural—a too-bright glaze, a reddening, the gleam of realization. In Lumeris, Belspire, even Sethane, I wouldn't have given these people a second glance. Common, weak, and meant to serve us. Now any of them could be a Renderer in disguise. Any one of them could be our undoing.

If this worry needles him as much as it does me, he hides it. "Let me do the talking," Nolan said at the start of our search, more an order than a request. "You wanted us to work together," he pressed when I objected. "So let's work together. There's no smashing through the door here, killing everyone to get what you want. And I've no interest in sneaking aboard and hiding in some musty corner of a hold. If we find a ship that goes to Cyprene, we need to make them think we are worth having aboard." He waited for me to argue this. I couldn't.

I have to admit that Nolan looks the part he's playing, that of an enterprising, ambitious young merchant, clad in new garb we acquired for him upon arrival. Unassuming enough to not draw attention, high-quality enough to hint at means. Still, a boat to Cyprene isn't as easy to find as a new jacket. But between that and his newly calibrated persona, the captain seems to be interested.

At least, she hasn't tossed us out on our butts yet.

"And where exactly do you wish to go?" The captain doesn't ask who recommended her ship, or why.

Which is interesting, though Nolan only smiles knowingly as he sips his tea. "To where your ship goes, and others don't."

Captain Cleophas refills his cup from an exquisitely patterned pot unlike anything I've ever seen before, then sits back, considering the request. She's tall, with a very dark complexion that tells me either she or her recent ancestors were born somewhere beyond the Devoted

Lands; bare, muscled arms; and what I suspect is real gold woven into her braided hair.

I like her almost immediately—her weird tea set, her cabin filled with exotic trinkets, but especially her maps pinned to the walls. For the first time, I am able to fill in the margins of Prior Petronilla's map. There's unfamiliar coastlines, inlets to foreign rivers, even an archipelago shaped like a sleeping cat. It sets off a deep ache in me, and a desire to contradict Nolan and pick out one of these other places instead. Except . . . I wouldn't make it that far. Which adds jealousy to my longing. Captain Cleophas is clearly untethered, able to go where she wants, when she wants.

Meanwhile, she stares at Nolan, who remains unfazed by the lingering examination. If pressed, his story is that he is from a modest but upcoming family, with a very particular business opportunity. Which of course he couldn't share, but is willing to pay handsomely to reach his desired destination. None of this has been spoken aloud, and yet he manages to exude the vague shape of it with unnerving ease.

"You'll have to be more specific, I'm afraid," she says. "This ship goes *many* places."

Wary. A good sign. Or bad, if we've made a poor choice. There's nothing in Cleophas that indicates she's thinking about picking us apart for a profit, but the wrong sort of request could get us reported to the local authorities, trouble we don't need.

"Cyprene." Nolan tosses the word out like a coin, telling me he doesn't read anything threatening in the captain either. Or he's eager enough not to care. "Though I'd rather keep my reasons for the destination to myself."

"A common enough sentiment." The unspoken finally spoken, the captain sits a little straighter. "The Goddess favors you. Cyprene is among the destinations we are headed to, and I have a cabin available. But this is not an inexpensive passage." She names an exorbitant figure.

Nolan's soft, satisfied smile doesn't falter. "That's robbery."

"This isn't a pleasure cruise."

"Good," says Nolan, "because I prefer business." His teacup clinks gently as he returns it to its saucer. "Your price is acceptable. As long as it comes with privacy."

Captain Cleophas's lips spread into a feline smile. "Guaranteed, so long as you observe the same for the rest of the *Squid*'s passengers."

"Of course. I would ask that we depart soon, though. My business is... pressing." An impatient note leaks into his tone, though I can't tell if it's affected or real. Time is not on our side. At least no one in Phrygis is buzzing about any new avatars... yet. Still, if the heretic headed to Carsaire is already on his way to Cyprene, we can only hope they will linger there, give us time to arrive and root them out.

"We sail on the evening tide," says Cleophas, "with stops along the coast before we reach your destination. My cabin boy Mishael will see your horses into the hold and your baggage to the cabin."

"Excellent," Nolan replies, though I can tell from the slight tightness of the word that, if he had his way, we'd be raising anchor immediately.

# Twenty-five

> There is nothing beyond the Unlit Seas that is not cold and dark compared to the Flame. I will not, cannot, ever call it home again.
>
> —WRITINGS OF THE PILGRIM EKKRU,
> IN THE ERA OF TEMPESTRA-ENOCH

WHEN CLEOPHAS SAID SHE had a cabin available, apparently she meant one cabin, singular.

And only one bunk, of course. As far as amenities are concerned, they're a bit lacking, consisting entirely of a small desk, one wobbly chair, and a salt-worn strip of rug. I awkwardly maneuver through the narrow doorway and dump our gear onto the floor, already growing tired of our little fiction.

Nolan leans against the doorframe, giving me a saucy smirk as he nods at the bed. "So . . . are we going to share?"

"You wish." I extract my bedroll and blanket from the pile. "I'll sleep in the hold with the horses. No offense, but Mortimer and Buttons smell better than you."

He steps in and closes the cabin door, keeping his body between me and it, still smiling. "You won't seem like a very good bodyguard."

"I'm not. You should probably keep that in mind, seeing as how easy it is for someone to accidently fall overboard."

"I thought we had a truce?"

"I said 'accidentally,' didn't I?"

He falls onto the bunk, shedding his new persona and the teasing tone in a heartbeat. "It will look strange if you don't keep to our story. We don't need anyone getting more than the normal level of suspicious about what we are doing here. As you said, it's easy enough for someone to disappear overboard."

"Fine." I drop my bedding. "Floor it is." I can't fault his logic, even if I don't like it. Even if there's as much potential danger within this cabin as without. Part of me doesn't even care; after our anxious, sleepless journey to Phrygis, a floor is as inviting as a feather bed.

"Don't worry." Nolan stretches out, throwing one arm behind his head. "I'm not going to cut your throat while you sleep."

"How reassuring. Especially given how truthful you've been so far."

The air around him cools. "You know, eventually we will have to trust each other enough to let our guards down. Or this isn't going to work."

I snort. Clearly, I'm not the only one who is exhausted. "Oh, does someone need a nap?"

He frowns. "Lys—"

"Take your own advice. You're the one with the history of betrayal."

"It wasn't personal."

"Hmm, I guess that makes it okay then."

"What I'm saying," he continues, more tartly, "is that I would have done the same to any other Dawn Cloister candidate. It was a means to an end. It wasn't as if I particularly *wanted* to kill you."

I stop what I'm doing. Look him in the eyes. Whatever truths lie behind them might as well be locked in the vault with the Goddess's reliquary. "I *know* it isn't personal. It hardly ever is with us Chosen, but that doesn't stop what we inflict on each other, does it?"

The ship creaks around us, more reaction than Nolan emits. For a moment, our truce feels as fragile as Cleophas's pretty teacups—one decent wave and it will be upended, shattered. But I won't be goaded again, or picked apart by Nolan's mind games. "If we're keeping up appearances, you'd best stay locked in the cabin when I'm not with you. And right now, I'm going to go make sure Mortimer and Buttons are nice and comfy."

Before he can say another word, I retreat from the cabin, back up onto the deck, where the sailors rush around in a flurry of final preparations for our departure. The horses don't need me—I just wanted away from Nolan—but that goal achieved, I find myself without a task or destination. The frown of a passing sailor tells me I'm in the way, so I retreat to the rail of the ship. Beyond it, Phrygis glows with the reds and oranges of the setting sun, like the whole port is aflame. It almost resembles Lumeris, a thought that's followed by an ache in the pit of my stomach. Fingers gripping the rail, I stare downriver instead, away from the mainland, to where the open ocean waits, and everything beyond it.

Cyprene.

The reliquary (maybe).

A hundred lands I've never even heard of.

Then I see Cleophas, leaning against the frame of her cabin door, still sipping tea as she watches her crew work. She spots me spotting her and a small, almost teasing smile appears on her lips. "Settled in?"

I take the question for an invitation to approach. "Uh . . . yes." The reply is stilted as I fumble for what *my* adopted persona would say. How does Nolan do this so easily? "My employer finds the cabin quite . . . cozy. He's resting after our travels."

There's a glint in her eye, as if she knows I'm spinning horseshit. "A little crowded for you, though."

"I haven't spent much time on ships." Or any. "Used to a bit more space to move around."

"First time off the mainland, isn't it? Or will be. I can always tell."

No point in denying it. "Is it that obvious?"

Her head tips. "The way you were eyeing my maps? A bit."

The captain is observant. But there's no harm in her catching me in curiosity. Or me in continuing it. "Would it be an insult to ask to take a closer look at them?"

She drains the remainder of the tea. "Not as far as I'm concerned." She turns back into the cabin, gesturing for me to follow. "So long as you handle them carefully. A good chart is worth more than a brick of gold out at sea, and only a little less than the last cask of fresh water."

Something ignites in me again, being back in her cabin, with its collected proof of a world beyond the Goddess's, wrought in ink and paper, carved out of wood and stone. A pile of maps now covers the table Cleophas and Nolan took tea at, weighted to keep them open. I recognize the coastline on top, and the little dot that represents Phrygis. Carefully, I remove one of the weights and lift the corner, revealing a chart beneath that shows a swath of islands that appear to lie to the south of us. Maps of our imminent voyage. And beyond that, the Unlit Seas, and a world not bound by Tempestra-Innara.

"Have you been to all these places?" I say, referring to the other charts tacked to the walls around us. It's not quite the question I want to ask. But *Where would you go, if you'd never been anywhere else?* catches in the back of my throat. An answer might become an aspiration, and for all that I crave exactly that, hope of escape is still too fragile to bear that sort of weight.

"Many," Captain Cleophas replies. "I've spent far more of my life on a ship than off, but it would take a dozen lifetimes to visit *all* of them."

I move closer to one, admiring the details not only rendered in black but washed with blues and greens, and limned in some places with gold. "You've always been a sailor then."

"I was born on a ship—my parents', to be precise. Plan to die on one too, gods willing, and let the waters swallow my remains as repayment for what I pray will be the many years I was given."

Not Goddess. *Gods.*

She notes my awareness of her wording. "A lot of beliefs out there. I prefer not to pile my hopes around the favor of any one deity. Who knows what god might lay claim to the particular patch of water I find myself traversing one day?"

Is that heretical, coming from someone whose bloodlines didn't begin flowing here? For all my education, I hardly know. The Salt Goddess was once favored by sailors, but did that include those that came from beyond their reach? And what else might a sailor like Cleophas have encountered in her time? Intrigue overpowers the good sense to keep my mouth shut. "There are other gods like Tempestra-Innara beyond the Devoted Lands?"

Cleophas shakes her head. "No living, breathing divinities. Not that I've seen anyway."

*Good.* Begs the question *Why only here?* though. "So these other lands believe in stories."

"Stories carry power." She sits down on a padded bench that lines a window at the end of the cabin. "Not power like the Flame Goddess, admittedly."

"Is that why you came here?"

She laughs—a deep, comfortable sound. "There are certainly those that hear the stories of the Devoted Lands and flock to them, make them their new home. It's been that way for centuries. My parents' ship must have ferried hundreds of expectant pilgrims so tempted by the Flame that they left the religions of their ancestors behind to see what its warmth had to offer."

"And they stayed when they experienced Tempestra-Innara's power?"

"Many, yes." Here she pauses, considers me again, this time for longer. It's not hesitation, exactly, but I can tell she's choosing her words carefully. I am a stranger. And we are still close enough to a cleric to lodge an accusation or two. "Others turned around. Called the Goddess a demon made flesh and fled back to the safety of their homelands." She shrugs. "Either way, my parents were paid. A sailor sails where there's wages to be earned. And here, there aren't many willing to trade with the . . . less reputable parts of the Devoted Lands, not when they can fall afoul of the Goddess's devoted so easily. Be labeled a criminal or heretic and be punished."

"But that doesn't bother you."

I can tell she hears the statement, not a question. "I have felt the Flame's warmth and know it to be a true thing." Not exactly a clear picture of her beliefs, or her loyalties. "I have also learned that those who hold the Goddess in their hearts can be persuaded to remain unbothered by my operations for the right price." She pauses. "It took a lot of winds and waves to earn that experience, though. Your employer, on the other hand, seems quite confident in his destination for someone so young. I do hope he hasn't taken a larger bite than he can chew."

"If he has, that's why I'm around for."

She considers me. "And what about your interests? Do they lie upon the waters?"

"I don't know." Only half a lie. "Do I come off as the seafaring sort?"

"Hmm," says Cleophas. "Too soon to tell. But you'll know soon enough." She winks before standing again. "I need to go see if preparations are complete for our departure. But please, stay. Indulge your interest. Certainly, I would never stifle the sea's call, if that's indeed what you're hearing."

It's not, but just like Nolan, I can pretend.

By the time I return to the cabin, blood buzzing with the names of new lands and countries, it's late enough that Nolan is curled in the bunk, face to the wall, sleeping. Or pretending to. I don't plan to follow suit, despite his assurances. But I've never been on a ship, and foolishly underestimate the gentle lull of the water combined with my own growing exhaustion. So, when I do wake—with a start, in the thick dark of the deepest part of night—I'm more than a little surprised to be alive. As my pounding heart slows, accepting that Nolan has kept his word, I realize what has roused me: a voice. I keep still. The sound is barely there, faint as a mouse's scratching, and it takes me nearly a minute to understand that what I'm hearing is Nolan.

He's praying. I hear the recitation of the words, too faint for me to truly make out, but familiar enough that I don't need to.

More surprise. I'd assumed Nolan's frequent prayers were part of the act he used to lull me into a false sense of confidence. That his deep piety was part of the costume. But the whispers continue, and I begin to feel embarrassed, as if I am intruding on something private. Which is stupid—prayers were never a secretive thing in the Cloisters. And Nolan was never shy about them before. Still, the feeling persists until, finally, the devotions cease. I tense again, waiting for movement. The shifting of a body. The drawing of a blade. But there is only the sound of Nolan's breathing, falling slowly into the rhythm of sleep.

Eventually, and more than a little reluctantly, I allow myself to follow.

# Twenty-six

> Our purpose is to serve. But secondary to that is to distinguish ourselves, in order that our opportunities to serve are the best they might be.
>
> —WRITINGS OF PRIOR JEVGENI, THIRD PRIOR OF THE DUSK CLOISTER, IN THE ERA OF TEMPESTRA-SESILIA

THE FIRST TIME I see land as a thin strip of grayish green far in the distance, it's a little disconcerting. No . . . a lot disconcerting. Ships, sailing, the ocean—all concepts I read about at the Cloisters, but the reality of being kept safe by nothing more than some bobbing bits of wood . . . there's an unnerving nature to it I can't ignore. The vastness of the water, heaving below us, stretching out to the horizon and beyond. There's excitement, but apprehension as well, just like back at Cineris. I can't deny the fear that comes from leaving the mainland behind, not all of which can be explained away by my divine tether.

Then I spot the dolphins. Another thing I've only ever seen in a book, they race alongside the *Squid's Shadow*, more graceful than I could have imagined, their slick skin catching bits of sunlight as they rise and fall in the frothy waves.

Mishael, the cabin boy, wanders by, toting a sack of something or other.

"Hey!" I call to him. "Do you ever see whales out here?"

His features narrow, as if I've just asked the stupidest question he's ever heard. "Sure, sometimes. You'll see the plumes they make when they surface, if they're about."

*Whales.* I spend the next hour with my eyes glued to the water, hoping to spot one of the giant sea beasts. I left Nolan still asleep in the cabin, and I'm so intent on my sightings that I jump when he appears at the rail beside me.

"What are you doing?"

He sounds awfully sour for someone I left alive, when the opposite was tempting. I'm about to scold him for leaving the cabin unaccompanied, when I see the pallor of his skin—paler than normal, with a distinctly unhealthy tinge. "Watching for pirates. You look like shit."

"I'm fine."

He is most certainly not fine. His knuckles whiten on the rail, as if he thinks he's going to tip over it at any moment. A thin pink scar remains where my sickle skewered him, and I'm briefly annoyed that we heal so fast, and that my little reminder will be soon forgotten. Even my injured arm is only a vague, occasional ache at this point. But Nolan appears so miserable that I'm not *too* bothered.

"Maybe you should go back to bed."

"I said I'm *fine*."

"Oh." I turn back to the ocean. "Okay, then. Well, just so you know, Mishael will be bringing your breakfast to the cabin shortly."

He grimaces. "I don't want it."

"Are you sure? The cook makes a mean breakfast porridge apparently. Looked a little slimy to me, but that's apparently from the fermented fish he uses to give it a salty, savory—"

With a lurch, Nolan pitches forward and vomits over the side of the ship. I take an automatic step back to avoid any wind-carried spray, smothering a smile. It's certainly not in character to relish my employer's suffering. But I'm enjoying it on the inside. And understanding what Cleophas meant about seeing whether I had a sailor's constitution. Nolan, for sure, does not.

"Oh, are you all right, sir?" One of the other passengers stops a few paces away, eyes wide with concern.

Nolan straightens to reply but only manages a weak, dismissive gesture before another heave takes him.

"He told me he's fine," I say. The man is of nondescript height and build, maybe a decade older than we are, with a receding hairline that ages him beyond that. He's also the only other passenger that's acknowledged us since boarding. I know there are more on the ship, but they've kept to themselves. "Been a while since my employer was last on a boat, that's all. C'mon." I take Nolan by the shoulders. "Let's get you back to the cabin so you can lie down."

Nolan doesn't resist. "Thank you for your concern, sir," he mumbles thickly as we pass.

"Ask the ship's cook for some of his special tea," he calls after us. "Settles things right down."

I wave thanks as Nolan and I make our way below deck. But as soon as no one is in sight, Nolan breaks away from me and stumbles to our cabin, where he collapses onto the bunk.

I consider the other passenger's suggestion, about fetching the tea, then return to my aquatic vigil instead.

We follow the coast for the first few days, making brief stops at smaller ports along the way to take on additional cargo. Nolan is scarce, only appearing when we are docked, as if needing to remind himself that solid land is still nearby. Then comes a morning when the land is completely gone, and we're surrounded by nothing but a dark, salty wetness. My wariness about leaving behind the known for the unknown grows, as does the ache for the Goddess's light. It is no longer a nagging discomfort, but a deepening, encompassing ache that leaves me tossing and turning, struggling to push past it into sleep.

It doesn't help that our cabin smells like vomit more often than not.

Driven below deck by a late-morning squall, I find Nolan exactly as I left him earlier, exactly where he's been for the majority of our time on the *Squid*: curled up in his bunk and miserable.

"You know, I have to wonder . . ." I take a seat at the desk, rubbing my tired eyes. "What would Prior Yiorgo say if he could see you now, felled by a rocking wooden tub?"

The angry glare I get is as strong as the sour smell of sick. "I'm not 'felled.' If I need to prove that to you—"

"You'll what, spit up on me like a toddler? No thank you, I'll take your word that you're fine and dandy."

He begins to retort, but the ship hits the roll of a wave, heaving up and down. Nolan's complexion pales further, mouth snapping shut.

I stifle a smile, affect a sigh. "If you're going to be laid up indefinitely, I guess it's on me to see what I can pick up about what awaits in Cyprene."

"I told you"—he starts to sit up, a movement that clearly costs him—"I'm perfectly well enough to—"

"Oh, shut up." I slump, annoyed at his pathetic defiance. "And stop pretending. It's *exhausting*. So our blessing doesn't protect against seasickness—what's the big deal? It's not like you're less of a Potentiate because you got a bit nauseated."

His face hardens further, pale lips thinning to near white.

I laugh, understanding. "Oh, that's exactly what you think, isn't it? You're reeeeally worrying you're less worthy to become Executrix because you get *seasick*?"

His mouth purses. "Weakness in an Executrix isn't—"

"Isn't what?" I roll my eyes. "How fanatical were they over in the Dusk Cloister? Do you really think any of us are perfect? That Andronica didn't have any weaknesses? Of course she did, or else she wouldn't have gotten torn to pieces and neither of us would be sitting here right now!"

"That was different. The reliquary blood . . . none of us could have been prepared for something like that."

The same way we weren't prepared for the Renderers. Which is what this is really about.

"No, none of us *were* prepared. Intentionally. Of course, if we *had* been, if we'd known about things like the reliquaries, the potential danger from them, then maybe we wouldn't have had to make such a big deposit at Cineris, huh? And maybe you wouldn't have gotten snared outside Novena?" As good as he is at hiding his thoughts, I can tell that question vexes him. But whether he thinks I'm being insolent or that I'm right or maybe a touch of both, I can't tell. "Relax. It's not like I'm going to run to Tempestra-Innara as soon as we get back to the Cathedral and cry 'Look, we found the reliquary even after Nolan nearly got butchered like a spring lamb, and oh, he started puking his guts out the moment we stepped off dry land.'"

Nolan turns over partway, so I can't see his face anymore. "Then you're foolish—to have an advantage and not use it."

"*You* just implied you could still kick my ass. So not much of an advantage, is it?"

He doesn't reply, and a heavy silence falls over the cabin, broken only by the creak of the heaving ship.

"Don't—" I bite the word off at first, but once the question starts, I can't stop it coming. "Don't you get tired of it? Being in competition all the time in order to get the best of a life we never had any real choice over anyway?"

Silence. Then: "The Goddess *chose* us. Blessed us. It's our honor to serve."

Of course it is. *Don't forget you're still the devoted Potentiate.*

"Service isn't the same as competition," I say, but inoffensively. "We all serve them in the end, and isn't that what really matters? That we do it, and do it well, no matter where or in what capacity?" More quiet follows, and I start to wonder if I've gone too far. But I suppose if he rats on me, I can play the seasick card after all.

"We should want to serve as well as we possibly can," he says finally. "Not simply adequately."

"Sure, fine. Look how well that turned out for Fedic."

"What do you mean?"

"I mean he got shuffled off to a half-rotten city where it was clear he was all but forgotten about. I saw the letters from Lumeris. However he served the Goddess, it wasn't enough to keep him close. And that's why the Renderers got him." Not to mention who knows how many others over the years, once their blessing had faded and they'd failed to cultivate the right anchors and alliances.

A few silent heartbeats pass. "Maybe he should have worked harder to ascend the Priors' ranks."

"You consider lack of ambition a weakness too?"

"I consider it a failure to serve to the best of one's abilities."

Frustration fills me again. "How many Potentiates died during your time at the Cloister?"

"What?"

"You heard me. How many of our blood brethren never even made it to serve, because they were pushed too hard, or presented too much of a threat to their fellow Potentiates?"

Another retreat into quiet.

"How many times did one of the other Potentiates try to sabotage or even kill you?" I press. "How many times did *you* try to kill someone?"

"None." The word comes quickly. Defensively. "I didn't need to resort to hindering anyone else in order to prove myself."

"Well, not until recently." I'm tired suddenly, of the conversation, of the years of vicious conditioning that led to it. It thickens the air, pushes the walls in even closer. I stand, keeping my eyes off Nolan's huddled form. "You've been sick long enough. I think it's time to go see if the ship's cook has any of that tea the other passenger mentioned."

"Tch. Doing something nice for me, Lys? After I tried to kill you?"

"I'm doing something to hopefully keep you from continuing to soil our very small cabin with the nasty contents of your stomach."

"If you were smart, you'd poison it." His tone carries a hint of teasing humor.

"Didn't say I wasn't going to."

There's a sensation of escape the instant I step out of the cabin. And not only because there's no vomit smell. I didn't mean for the conversation to happen, but it did, and now I feel like I've shown Nolan something that maybe I shouldn't have. Despite our truce, any honesty between us feels like a trap, set by our years in the Cloisters, ready to spring shut at the tiniest misstep. I can only hope to tread lightly long enough to find the reliquary.

After that, there will be no avoiding it.

# *Twenty-seven*

The fall of the Salt Goddess, while a great battle, was almost quiet compared to the deaths of their siblings. The waves did not rage, the tides kept their schedules. It was only after—once days, weeks, months had passed—that the mark they left became conspicuously, gruesomely clear.

—FROM *THE DIVINE DEFEATS*, BY THE
NOTED HISTORIAN ANAIS (RESTRICTED TEXT)

IN THE GALLEY, THE cook is chopping vegetables into a large pot. He's not alone—the balding passenger from the deck is there too, sitting quietly at one of the tables bolted to one wall, where the crew takes meals. He smiles widely when he spots me. "Special tea?"

"Special tea." I crook an eyebrow at the cook.

"Yeah, I can brew you up a pot." He's surprisingly skinny for someone who handles food all day, but as weathered as a sailor should be. "Have a seat, you can wait."

"Thank you." I head for the other passenger, who gestures for me to join him, and slide onto the opposite bench.

"You're an unfamiliar face on the *Squid*." The man cradles a mug of coffee. He's wearing at least a dozen rings, a mix of metals braided together. They glint and glitter as he taps his fingers on the pottery restlessly. Otherwise there is nothing notable about him, no clues to give away where he hails from from or what he's doing here. "First time on board?"

I nod warily and say nothing more. Captain Cleophas promised privacy. A man who asks questions is one to be careful about.

The message is received. "Of course, of course." He leans back, grinning. "I won't ask about your business, simply remarking that I hadn't seen you before."

By the way he speaks, it sounds as if he has made this passage many times. *Interesting.* "I wouldn't have much to say even if you did ask." I spread my hands innocently. "I'm a mere bodyguard, here to protect my employer on his travels."

"Ah yes, the sickly young man. A stranger as well, and one I'd surmise hasn't had much seafaring experience."

"I haven't been in his employ long enough to know."

"Oh?" The man turns serious. "You must be quite brave to take on a dangerous voyage like this. So many of the people I cross paths with on this ship . . . well, I see them once and never again."

I lean forward. "Really? What happened to them?"

The man's face darkens, then softens as he lets out a laugh. "Oh, don't mind me. I'm only playing with you." He's mistaken my interest for uneasiness. "The truth is Cyprene is rarely more harrowing than any other city within the Devoted Lands."

"It isn't?"

"Of course not. The Goddess may rule, but commerce has its share of worshippers no matter where you go. And anything that interrupts *that* doesn't last for long, including the sorts of dangers so often rumored to be found there. Ridiculous propaganda . . . well, most of it."

I'm hardly surprised. We were taught Cyprene was a city filled with heretics, pirates, and the lowest dregs humanity had to offer. A city that willingly turned away from the light and warmth of the Goddess and fed on itself, barely surviving. A place undeserving of the presence of Tempestra-Innara's Chosen. (That none seemed to be able to manage there was conveniently left out.)

"Where are my manners?" says the man suddenly. "My name is Tychus. And you are?"

"Lys," I reply automatically.

"It's nice to meet you, Lys. I do hope your employer recovers shortly. Seen it before, though—landlocked lads full of youthful ambition and the idea to make their fortune outside of the usual confines." One eyebrow rises in question. "At least, that's what I assume his plans are. Trade can be quite brisk in Cyprene . . . for jewels, rare dyes, all sorts of items closely regulated on the mainland."

For not asking about Nolan's business, Tychus is being quite curious. "Can't speak to it." I make a show of picking at my nails, as if the conversation is beginning to bore me. "All I'm concerned about is keeping him in once piece."

"Fair enough." Tychus knows better than to press for more details. He leans back in his seat, twists one of his many rings around and around. "At least he was smart enough to bring some level of protection. Cyprene rarely treats the foolish or unprepared well. There are plenty of . . . unpleasant elements happy to make a quick meal of the ignorant."

I hope he means figuratively, but after the Renderers, who knows? "I'll make sure to keep a close eye on him."

The cook comes over, delivering a tray with a pleasantly steaming teapot. "Thank you," I say to him, "and you too, sir" to Tychus. Then I stand, taking the tea quickly so I can report back to Nolan about what I've learned.

The special tea does not work. At least, not as much as Nolan—or I— would have liked. He puts in a solid effort at pretending he doesn't feel as sick as he does, but he barely manages a few hours on his feet each day. And there's the ever-present bucket of vomit. I do my best to ignore the retching sounds, but daylight hours find me above deck, leaving him with an adequate supply of cold tea and dry crackers to nibble. He's miserable, which was amusing to begin with but becomes very tedious, very quickly. Turns out that a questionable but capable partner is preferable to a ridiculously incapacitated one.

A slow week passes, during which I am left to ponder whether our mission still matters. Are the heretics already setting up a second strike? Has Tempestra-Innara taken a new avatar and locked themselves away beyond either of our reaches? I try to pass the time with Jogue's diary but glean little else from it. And I can't risk anyone catching me with the Renderers' book. So, to distract myself from the unanswerable anxieties, I watch: the waters, the creatures we share it with, the sailors at their tasks. I even enjoy it, if not as much as I'd like. As Lumeris grows farther and farther away, so does my ache for it. It's worse than on the mainland and triggers in me a new sort of irritation—that I can't take in any new wonders without *that* shadowing them.

"How far out are we?" I ask Mishael as he scurries by me one afternoon.

He peers up at the sails with a knowing eye. "No more than two days. Maybe closer, if this wind holds."

Back in the cabin, I give a fetal Nolan an almost-gentle kick in the backside. "Two days away. Time to get your shit together."

He makes a sound like a wounded cow. His mood hasn't improved any more than his constitution has. In fact, it's gotten worse; the more time has passed on the ship, the sourer and more irritable he's become. "As soon as we are off this godsforsaken ship . . ."

"Sooner than that." I am in no mood for whining. "We need to figure out what to do once we arrive. From what Tychus said, there will be folks trying to fleece us at every opportunity."

Nolan rolls himself into a sitting position. He's lost weight over the last the last few days, but not an ounce of stubbornness. "And you intend on letting them?"

"Of course not." I take one of the dry crackers from a plate on the desk and mindlessly break it into crumbs. "But given that tone, I'll take it you've thought of a sure way to find the heretics during all your long, solitary hours of careful contemplation?"

His mouth flattens. "Remember when I was just *pretending* to be continually annoyed by you?"

"Don't get mad at me for doing the hard work while you hide out in here."

"I'm not—"

"I knoooooowwww. Remember when you pretended to have a sense of humor?" I toss a cracker at him. "Eat. Drink. If it takes imagining Mommy Tempestra-Innara feeding you to get fit again, do it. I expect to see you on your feet before we reach Cyprene."

Nolan answers with a glare. But he picks the cracker up from his lap and takes a bite.

The city appears before Nolan does, a dark speck on the horizon that gradually grows bigger. At first, I'm a little disappointed at how unremarkable it is, this stretch of sea that garners such fear.

Then I glance into the water, and see a face staring back.

In a heartbeat, it's gone, carried away by the waves, and it takes me a moment to realize what it was—a ship's figurehead, floating free. More debris appears, bits of wood and sail, and other things I can't identify.

"We're entering the graveyard now." Captain Cleophas comes up to where I'm leaning on the rail. "I'd suggest heading below if you've got a weak stomach."

I snort. "Do I strike you as someone like that?"

The captain doesn't share my amusement. "No. But there are places in this world where fortitude fails even the most seasoned soul. This is one of them."

A whistle sounds.

"That will be for me," she says, heading for the ship's wheel.

I gaze back out over the water, chills running down my arms. It's not the captain's warning, though; the wind has changed, turned cooler. The debris increases. Masts poke from the water like sodden bones, whole boats appearing on either side of our path. There are hundreds of them, maybe thousands, all shapes and sizes, caught on the massive reef that surrounds the island. But not by accident. Centuries ago, the other gods came for the Salt Goddess, Astris. Like Novena, the battleground of their fall remains unnaturally intact, so much so that I can't pick out which ships might have come from the ancient battle and which were more recent. Captain Cleophas steers us carefully through the field, but even so, flotsam bounces off the hull.

Another figurehead appears in the water, pale skinned, empty eyed.

My breath catches. Not a body of wood. Flesh. Another appears, and another, all looking as if they've been dead maybe hours. But I quickly understand that's not the case.

*This* is what the captain was warning me about.

"Dear Goddess . . ." Nolan stands a little way down the rail. His fingers rise, searching for his reverie, though we discarded them when adopting our latest identities. "Their clothing . . . the insignia . . . those can't be . . ."

"Pretty sure they are."

Somehow, the sailors that died all those centuries ago, drowned in the battle between the Salt Goddess and their siblings, have been preserved. And been left eerily tethered to the reef we're passing through. They thump against the prow in ones and twos, bloated faces staring up at a sky they can't see, like the absolute worst version of the dolphins that joined our voyage earlier.

"Not even a nibble taken out of them." My breath is white in front of me now, and there's a heavy, sulfurous brine in the air. "It's almost like they've been pickled." Nolan makes a faint noise. He might be feeling better, but apparently not enough for me to talk about corpse-pickles. "Sorry."

He swallows hard. "First Novena, now this."

"Yeah."

"And the Storm . . . you've seen it . . ." He whispers the words, even though no one is nearby. "What else does the death of divinity leave in its wake?"

"Do you mean what else did no one bother to tell us about?" How many other secrets are we going to discover? Devoted as he is, after what we've encountered Nolan must be wondering the same. I tear my gaze away from the grim flotsam and plunk it on Cyprene instead. "How bad can the city be if it can put up with being surrounded by the floating dead? Not like the Priors said, I bet."

Nolan remains quiet, though I catch a hint of irritation at my vague blasphemy.

Soon we can make out the massive, sheer walls of the island, composed of a rock so pale gray that it's nearly white. A narrow passage cuts through it, leading into a large cove and the main reason the Salt Goddess and their followers were able to hold out for as long as they did. The reef took care of most of the invaders; the rest were forced to tighten formation and navigate themselves like thread through a needle, trying to avoid the island's defenses. That much I *do* know.

As we enter the passage, I feel a constricting beneath my ribs. My gaze shifts, pulled away from Cyprene, back in the direction we came from. The mainland is days behind, but for a moment, I expect to see it. Almost *want* to see it. Pushing that longing away, I let the memory of different waters rise, let the inky chill of that unforgiving river swell and smother my yearning, if only temporarily. I'll return to the Cathedral again, to that distant divine light, soon enough.

And, if I have my way, for the very last time.

That thought steadies me as, beyond the reef, the water turns a pleasant shade of blue, funneled by the high pale cliffs around us. I don't love how close they are to the ship—barely a stone's throw away, but it's clear we've left the hard part behind, thanks to Captain Cleophas. The cove is almost like a sea itself, large enough that a hundred ships could comfortably sail it without getting in each other's way. But there are only a few in sight, small as toys next to a pair of massive towers that rise from the waters. I count enough cannons to blanket the cove in cannonballs, turn any ship into scraps of timber. If an unwelcome visitor survived the reef and the walls, they would still need to contend with these. The *Squid's Shadow* runs up a series of flags. As we aren't sunk immediately after, I take it we are welcome.

Cyprene proper comes into view. I can't say it in front of Nolan, but I'm becoming decidedly less impressed with our home the longer our mission goes on. A fantasy resolves before us, the high white cliffs surrounding the city carved with dense, impossible intricacies—figures and ornaments, tunnels and balconies, flowing down from their tops all the way to where the foamy waves crash. There's a towering, repeated form that must represent the Salt Goddess (the smashed facial features give it away) but also sea creatures so realistic I expect them to slip into the brine at any second. The city itself is more conventional, spreading out in a half moon around the bay, but even at a distance it clearly rivals Lumeris in grandeur.

Nolan does a good job of hiding his awe, but I can see it, lurking in the depths of his careful expression. "Let it out."

"What?"

"You're supposed to be a young, green merchant seeing this place for the first time. Whatever you're thinking, don't hide it so well for once."

He must see my reason, because his expression changes almost immediately, turning into the bright excitement of a tourist.

Within a few hours, we are allowed to disembark into the bustle of Cyprene's docks. As soon as his feet touch dry land, Nolan lets out a sigh of relief, one I suspect is no performance. The horses follow, and then Tychus, as I am strapping our gear onto their saddles.

"You'll want to move away from the docks to find decent lodging. Go up the hill. I prefer the White Gull myself, though I'm afraid the owner doesn't let to strangers." He begins to depart, then pauses. "I'm headed that direction myself. If you don't object to a guide, I can bring you to where the better guesthouses are. You'd be surprised how many appear clean . . . until you find a plump cockroach swimming around your soup."

Immediately, suspicion fills me. New to town and with obvious resources, Nolan must read like an easy mark. Even if Tychus's intentions are no more than directing us to an overpriced guesthouse that feeds him a cut, it would be a poor start to appear like a pair of rubes. I give Nolan a little shrug, as if it's up to him. There's enough wariness in his face that I know he has the same misgivings.

Still, he smiles and says: "Incredibly kind of you, sir. That would be very welcome."

Tychus returns the expression. "Come. My baggage will be sent later."

I take one last look at the *Squid's Shadow*, hoping to see Cleophas. But the captain is busy with her own obligations, likely readying for wherever the winds and waves will bear her next. Which leaves me carrying a twinge of jealousy as Tychus leads us into the chaos of the docks with an easy familiarity. If only it could be so simple and relaxed for Nolan and me. We have no allies here. Anyone we pass may be one of the heretics we are searching for, or a Renderer searching for us. My only solace is that the Renderers have no reason to keep hounds in Cyprene; the Goddess's Chosen haven't had a foothold here for decades. Can't hunt where there's no prey.

Still, nothing is sure, and my attention is fractured as I fight the crowds to keep a few steps behind Tychus and Nolan while also taking in this new world. Phrygis, a bustling mainland port, is dull as dirt when set against Cyprene, which pulses with the brisk, vibrant energy of fruitful commerce. There are ships clearly from the mainland, and ships that clearly aren't, bearing goods and sailors from places I cannot begin to guess. We pass a gathering of dark-complexioned sailors clad in ochre and burgundy playing an elaborate dice game, elbow through a clutch of pale, heavily tattooed men dipping mugs of black beer directly from a barrel. I catch a whiff of spiced tobacco on one corner; on the next, the scent of something more potent suggests this as a likely origin for much of the Devoted Lands' black-market goods. But for everything I observe, it's what I don't that stands out.

"Odd to see no clerics in such a busy place . . ." Nolan puts a name to it. "And the Flame . . . it's nowhere to be seen."

He's right. Anywhere else, I'd see the Goddess's fingerprints in the forms of insignia and greetings, hear the calls of the clerics to prayer, reminders that Tempestra-Innara is near, even when they aren't. Here, the absence of them renders the city into an entirely different entity than any I've known. Here, the Goddess is wholly absent.

"Astute," Tychus replies. "It does surprise many of the newcomers, to not see the Goddess's presence. It is here, of course," he hedges, "merely in a quieter fashion than you're used to."

Though accepting Tychus's help is a ruse, I'm quickly thankful, as it's clear we won't find it anywhere else. The people of Cyprene appear to be especially adept at minding their own business, to the point that I have to force my attention straight ahead to make it appear as if I know where *my* business lies. Tychus may have tagged us as marks, but no need to draw any other bottom-feeders. The avenues turn from wide and open to winding and narrow and back, disorienting in a way I can't help but wonder is intentional. The best signposts are the cliffs that tower above the warehouses, shops, and dwellings.

"Those carvings," Nolan notes as we walk, sounding sufficiently awestruck by the ever-present views of them.

"Work of the Salt Goddess's followers," Tychus explains, "created over generations. An unparalleled show of devotion. The Salt Goddess used to reside in those tunnels and passages, when they weren't traveling the tides. Now they are mostly home to certain, uh, factions of the city. Some benign, some not. But regardless, I would strongly advise against entering them without knowing exactly where you need to be. They go deeper than you'd imagine, and many an unwary soul has gotten lost." He glances back at me and winks. "Or worse."

"Avoid the cliffs of no return," I say. "Gotcha."

We reach a cobbled plaza, where Tychus stops abruptly, drawing the hood of his cloak. Over his shoulder, I finally see a hint of the Goddess: the flame insignia—an antiquated version, at least—embroidered onto the sleeves of a blue uniform worn by two men loitering near a fountain. But the flame isn't the only sigil I spot. Graffiti is scrawled on the fountain, an array of unfamiliar symbols ... the same sorts as in the Renderers' letter.

Nolan clears his throat to tell me he's seen it too, then shifts impatiently. "Is there a problem?"

Tychus shakes his head. "No ... but wait a moment, if you would."

Across the plaza, the uniformed pair spot a third man, descending on him like wolves on prey. I can't quite hear what's being said, but the man—some common worker by the look of him—wears an expression of subservient fear. When one of uniformed men plucks a stray thread from his shoulder, the man flinches.

"Who are they?" asks Nolan.

"Caerula—sworn peacekeepers of the Goddess in Cyprene," Tychus replies. "At least, that's what they present themselves as."

"Then why avoid them? If they represent our Goddess ..."

"They do, but not like you're used to on the mainland." Caution enters Tychus's voice. "They claim to serve Tempestra-Innara, but they mostly serve themselves. Be warned, the last thing you want to do in Cyprene is fall afoul of them."

I'm more interested in the fact that Tychus wants to avoid them. It doesn't come as a shock that another passenger on the *Squid's Shadow* may engage in less-than-honest dealings in Cyprene, but as bland as Tychus struck me, I didn't expect anything of note.

By the fountains, money is handed over, an interaction that seems to be invisible to the people passing by. Then, the Caerula head down a different avenue without taking note of us, presumably onto their next shakedown. Once they are gone, Tychus's jovial attitude makes a speedy reappearance, leading us forward again. I take closer note of the graffiti as we pass, but it's not confined to the fountain; I spot it on walls and down alleys, along with the usual insults and raunchy renderings. But both fade the farther we get from the docks, until we are making our way up a gently sloping street lined with a mix of guesthouses and taverns.

"What about this one?" I can tell by the edge on his words that Nolan is tiring of this charade with Tychus. He indicates a plain but well-kept establishment as gray as salt, with a matching cat sunning itself in a window box.

Tychus looks appalled, waving a ringed hand dismissively. "Absolutely not. The rooms there smell like they're used to store old cheese. And that cat has never caught a mouse in its life. There are much nicer places farther up the avenue. Come, I'll show you."

Oh, I bet he will. We are clearly heading to whatever guesthouse Tychus has some useful connection with, passing by more places of lodging before a sunny, almost garish, yellow building appears at the broad intersection of streets. The sign is painted with the silhouette of a bird, and a man I take to be the proprietor leans beside the open door, clad in a stained apron and smoking a pipe.

"This will be more than adequate," Nolan says sharply, peeling away from Tychus. "Sir, do you have space available?"

The man removes the pipe from his mouth, a blank expression on his face as he considers. He's heavyset, with sleepy eyes and a coppery-brown complexion. Finally, he nods. "How many?"

Tychus's expression sours. "I'd recommend—"

"Two." I step forward. "Well, four. Two humans, two horses."

"The Petrel has clean beds and stables both," the man promises, also ignoring Tychus. "M'name's Hiram. Need anything, you ask me."

"If I may interject," says Tychus, appearing as if he just stepped in horse shit, "I truly think your tastes might be better served by—"

"This will do." Nolan oozes gratefulness, though. "Thank you so much for taking the time to guide us into the city. Your help has been invaluable."

Unable to protest further without added suspicion, Tychus can only nod. "I hope your business in Cyprene goes smoothly."

"And the same to you." Nolan smiles. "May the Flame warm you."

Tychus doesn't return the blessing.

Hiram, the innkeeper, eyes him as he departs, but with no more curiosity than someone watching a duck float by on a river. Then, he turns to us. "One room or two?"

"Two," we say in unison.

# Twenty-eight

Divinity cannot die. It can be weakened, it can be worn down to its nadir and kept there, but it cannot be killed. The storm rages. The blight remains. The tide bears its terrible spoils. And faith, if it persists, will one day be rewarded with their return.

—EXCERPT FROM CONFISCATED HERETICAL TRACTS

Soon, Mortimer and Buttons are set up in a dry, cozy stable, and I'm in a dry, cozy little room nestled in the eaves of the guesthouse. It's on the small side, but there's a convenient stair that leads directly to Nolan's room below. I utilize this immediately, tapping sharply on the door until he throws it open, looking vaguely annoyed. Undeterred, I push past him into the room. *Rooms.* Probably not as grand (or as expensive) as wherever Tychus had in mind for us, but there's a charming sitting area, adjacent bedroom, and, best of all, a private bathroom.

"You have a tub?" I jump into the empty porcelain basin. "I'm using this."

"Good," Nolan calls. "You smell like you've been on a ship for a week."

"I smell like I've been marinating in the scent of your puke for a week." I abandon the tub and return to the sitting room. "Are those lemon slices in your water pitcher? I barely got a clean blanket. Next time *I* get to play the rich merchant."

His expression hardens. He's got the letter I found on the Renderer out, apparently in the process of examining it again. "This isn't a game."

"I know that."

"Then act like it."

And here I thought his mood would improve being back on land. Silly me. "At least we know we're in the right place."

"That doesn't help us narrow down where to look for the heretics." He plunks himself down into an overstuffed chair and peers at the signature. "Are these letters in an alphabet? Glyphs that represent words or some instruction? For all we know, what these symbols mean drawn on the wall and in the context of that letter are two entirely different things."

It's true. "Well, it's clear they've been around since Jogue's time, so they must be familiar. We could just, y'know, *ask* someone."

"Without knowing what it says? Or what that reveals about us?"

"Fine." I snatch the letter away. "We'll figure it out on our own. But it's too late to start searching the city, or for your attitude. So, I vote for dinner." Nolan's mouth thins. "Oh, sorry, is your tummy still feeling icky?"

He doesn't move from the chair. "Have something sent up."

I want to protest—the common room downstairs seemed a lot more interesting than being stuck up here alone with Nolan—but the sour set of his demeanor keeps my mouth shut. Instead, I stomp downstairs, find Hiram behind the bar, and repress the urge to see if he has any jellied eel or fermented fish for my dear employer. "What's on the menu today?"

Hiram stops drying the mug he's holding and thinks, as if more than one task at a time is too much. He doesn't strike me as the swiftest sort, but there's a thoughtfulness to his countenance that tells me he's no fool either. "I've got stew now or roast chicken in a little while."

"We'll take both, upstairs. And wine."

Hiram hands me a bottle and two cups. "I'll bring up the rest shortly."

I rejoin Nolan and pour for us both. He accepts it, continuing to stare at the letter quietly, as if there's something there he hasn't found in all the hours of staring before. I wasn't expecting sparkling conversation, but I thought we'd gotten past the contemptuous silence. At the same time, trying to force him to pay attention to me feels like more of an act of desperation than I'm willing to concede. So I embrace the peace, leaning back into my chair and stretching my legs out, enjoying taking up space after so long on a cramped ship.

After a little while—and several refills to both our cups—Hiram delivers the food. I thank the man; Nolan ignores him.

"I don't think it would be amiss"—I drop the tray on the table with more force than strictly necessary—"to keep sprinkling on that false charm."

An unamused look is my reply.

"Fine. Be cranky and unfriendly." I claim a bowl of stew and dunk my spoon into it. "See how well that serves us here."

"I'm not cranky." But he pokes his food in a way that makes it clear there's something on his mind. I wait for him to say something, to air whatever concern has gotten its fangs in him, but instead, he takes a bite. And then another, and another. Hiram included a basket of bread and he takes a piece of that too, practically shoving it into his mouth between spoonfuls.

"Guess you do have your appetite back. Slow down. Wouldn't want you to *choke*." I have to admit, though, the stew is good—far better than anything we had on the *Squid's Shadow*. Nolan practically licks his bowl clean, then starts in on the roast chicken and braised vegetables. There's a second bottle of wine as well. Hiram may be a bit slow, but he clearly anticipates what his customers want.

Halfway through that, Nolan's cup drops abruptly to the table. I wait, the gesture catching my attention, but a long moment passes before he finally says: "You feel it too, don't you?"

I chew a mouthful thoughtfully, knowing what he means but wanting him to say it aloud. To *admit* it. "Feel what?"

His features pinch. "The distance ... from the Goddess's light. From their flame." There's the faintest slur to his words, a slight thickening. Whether he isn't used to so much wine or he's still weak after his seasickness, Nolan is a little drunk. Which is probably the only reason he's willing to call attention to what I'm sure he considers another weakness. "I thought time ... more prayer might ... It's worse than I expected."

I'm not surprised. Nolan was smothered in seasickness as we sailed farther and farther from Lumeris, a gradual incremental sensation for me that's now hitting him all at once.

"Of course I feel it. It's like . . ." I can't quite find the right description. "Like what we would have felt if we'd left the Cloisters for the Orders, only, y'know, worse." He doesn't seem any less perturbed. "And I get that you're impatient. I am too. We need to find the reliquary before the heretics strike again, and neither of us wants to be here any longer than necessary. But what did you say back in Phrygis? 'There's no smashing through the door here, killing everyone to get what you want.' Same goes for Cyprene, except you'll need to summon twice as much of that horseshit charisma here. Which means you have to play merchant for as long as it takes and keep anyone from getting suspicious of us."

He picks at a bit of bread.

"So are you going to keep up appearances or will I have to—"

"Do what?" he snarls, sharply enough to set me on guard. "*I'm* the one who's seen the heretic we're after. All you've got is a few symbols on a bit of paper."

My anger rises to meet his—*I've got more than the stupid letter*, I want to spit, resisting the urge to pull out the Renderers' foul wares and their book from where I've hidden them—but suddenly he appears remorseful. Even a little embarrassed.

"I'm . . . sorry. This feeling, it . . ." He doesn't finish.

"Yeah, you're also going to need to learn to hold your wine better than that if you want to blend in."

Nolan scowls. "I'm being serious, Lys. I . . . I had a lot of time on the ship to think." He takes another long sip of wine, as if bracing himself against his own honesty. "I want to be Executrix. But more than that—more than anything—I want to protect the Goddess in any way I can. And . . . maybe I haven't been as good at that as I should have been. Starting with how I've treated you. After what you said . . . about our time in the Cloisters, the competition . . . there's more than a little truth to it."

"Oh, you're definitely drunk, aren't you?" I manage not to sound flippant, surprisingly. "You'd think the Goddess would want their Chosen to work together to serve them."

He considers this. "They do . . . but they also want our loyalties to be to them, and only them."

And not to each other.

That part hangs in the air, unsaid.

"As a result, we are ill-suited to a shared task," Nolan finishes. "No matter how important it is."

I scoff. "I don't know, I don't think we're doing half bad. Really, we're at only one murder attempt and one maiming so far. That was, like, a typical day around Morgan."

Nolan chuckles. Then he laughs. Actually laughs, a sincere sound that would be at home in the Petrel's common room below.

A sound that could almost have been between friends, if not for secrets kept.

"We should assume we are being watched at all times," Nolan warns as we move through the crowded streets the next day.

"Yes," I reply, with a dramatic flair. "But by *whoooom*?"

He grimaces at me.

I roll my eyes, wondering how slow Nolan thinks I am. If there's one thing Cyprene would be wary about, it's newcomers. Maybe we aren't so interesting as to draw attention. Or maybe there are Renderers all about and they've already spotted us. There's no way of knowing. "If we don't take a few risks, we're not going to learn anything. The reliquary isn't going to drop in our laps while we're sitting in your fancy suite, is it?"

He's got no response to that.

But despite Nolan's worries, we don't particularly stand out. And excepting its beauty, distinctive stonework, and blatant heresy on full display, neither does Cyprene. It's full of normal-looking people, going about their normal-looking business. Nolan takes my advice; his easy charm reappears as we make our way through the city, taking in its layout. He exchanges friendly words with vendors as he inspects their wares in markets or peers in shop windows with a smile, all while I play protective shadow. There are fabrics on display, a street of glass merchants and a plaza of jewelers, a smelly little shop full of cosmetics and perfumes. We keep a sharp eye out for anyone who pays us more than passing attention, but none seem to. It comes as an unexpected thrill. If I were to wander Lumeris in the same manner, I'd be marked, revered, and catered to. In Cyprene, I am wonderfully, blissfully, no one.

The market streets turn to residential areas. Then into a fish market, rank with the smell of old guts, followed by a district of brightly adorned buildings where equally vibrant (and scantily clad) figures call out provocative offers to Nolan that I swear make him blush. And, finally, tranquil paths set along bluffs that drop directly into the sea before leading back down to the docks. As I drink it all in, thirsty for more, only one view remains constant—the white stone cliffs with their massive, faceless visages of the Salt Goddess. I can't help but imagine a time when they still reigned. Was Cyprene like Lumeris, constantly awash with pilgrims and penitents? Did their Chosen control the city, shaping it according to their divinity's will?

But, for all their absence, this is Tempestra-Innara's city now, and we find their shrine as the shadows begin their afternoon stretch. Its presence doesn't come as a surprise—my blood brethren *have* managed control of Cyprene from time to time—but the state of it is. There is a sense of obligation to it, of afterthought, the round plaza bordered on all sides by abandoned stone storehouses. The statue of the Goddess within is meager and worn, weathered harshly by the salt air. Clearly, the flames haven't burned in ages and what scant offerings there are lie at its foot, shriveled or rotted away. The worst of it is the graffiti: Curses and obscenities abound, along with a set of genitalia scrawled on the exterior of the Goddess's form, in the right places, but with exaggerated size and shape. Nolan says nothing as we enter, treading casually, as if just having a look. But the set of his shoulders tells a different story—he's tense, angry.

For a long minute, he stares at the statue, hands curling into fists at his side.

"Watched," I remind, when it goes on too long.

Still, another few heartbeats pass before he turns, displeasure expertly buried. "It's getting late. We should return to the Petrel."

He says nothing as we make our way back, but I imagine the thoughts stamping through his mind. The neglect and disrespect shown toward our blood mother's visage. The *heresy*.

At least he keeps it to himself so I don't have to pretend to agree.

I'm so focused on ignoring the dark cloud gathered about him that we almost collide when he stops abruptly.

"What is it?"

He waves me forward but doesn't reply. We've come to a junction of residential streets, one of the city's countless fountains bubbling away tranquilly in the center. A young boy is playing in it. As I watch, he carefully places a fleet of small wooden boats on the smooth water, as if acting out some ancient sea battle. At first, I don't understand what's caught Nolan's attention. Then the boy leans over, a white stone pendant swinging from a cord around his neck. A reverie. With the symbols from the letter carved in it.

Nolan saunters over, attention turned to the boats, as if invested in the outcome of their conflict. The boy glances up but doesn't pause in his efforts.

"Quite a battle," says Nolan, in a kindly way. "Is that entire fleet yours?"

The boy nods. "My older sister carves them for me. She works on real ships too, fixing them."

Nolan leans closer, as if examining the detail on the toys. "She's very talented. Did she make that reverie for you as well?"

"No. My father gave me that."

"Did he make it?"

The boy frowns, as if Nolan has just said something very stupid. "No."

"I'm sorry," says Nolan. "It's only that I am new to your city, and I keep seeing marks like that around. But I'm not familiar with them." He dips a finger in the fountain and writes out the signature from the Renderers' letter. The symbols dry quickly in the sea air, disappearing. "Do you know what that means?"

For the first time, the boy's eyes narrow in suspicion, but I can't tell if it's because Nolan admitted to not being from the city or because of what the marks spell out. But he shakes his head.

I catch a whiff of frustrated disappointment from Nolan. Then, the boy adds: "I can't read the Salt runes."

"Salt runes?"

"Used by the priests. Astris's."

Nolan stands straight again, glancing briefly my way.

Astris. The Salt Goddess.

"Are the priests nearby?"

"Yeah." An adult might have been fully suspicious of Nolan's inquiry by now—*should* have been suspicious—but the boy is losing interest, and returns to his boats. "In the salt baths."

"Thank you." Nolan starts to turn away, then pauses. He pulls out a few coins. "It's a fine pendant. Would you consider selling it?"

I'm not sure where he's going with this. Neither is the boy, but he's not so young as to not realize he's being offered a price well above the worth of the item. He eyes the money eagerly, then pulls the cord over his head. In an instant, the deal is struck, and Nolan and I are on our way again.

"Wow," I say. "One day in Cyprene and you're ready to join up with the Salt heretics?" The tightening of his jaw warns me this was the wrong joke to make so soon after the Goddess's desecrated shrine. "I thought it was foolish to go around showing off our ignorance?"

"We need to take a few risks if we are going to learn anything." Satisfied at throwing my own words back at me, he holds up the necklace. It's the same white stone of the cliffs. "Marks of the Salt Goddess, made by their priests. Now we have a good idea who was buying the Renderers' wares. And how far, on an island this size, do you think they are removed from the heretics who plotted against the Tempestra-Innara?"

"Not very," I admit.

"The salt baths." He palms the reverie and runs a thumb over the carved symbol. "This morning we had a clue. Now, we have a place to look."

# *Twenty-nine*

Within the waters, within the brine, their voice speaks, if one is quiet enough to listen, and hear.

—THE WORDS OF MARIS, PRIEST OF ASTRIS,
THE SALT GODDESS

THE BATHS WOULD DRAW no more attention than any other building in Cyprene, if not for the marks carved above the doorway. *Salt runes*, the boy had called them. There's a set of wavy lines that makes me think of water, but beyond that, they manage to keep their provincial significance to themselves. We spend almost an hour watching the entrance, tucked into a nearby alcove. A large building, it's as white as the surrounding cliffs, with an arched doorway that's opened a handful of times, including for a visit from one of the Caerula, who pocketed a fat purse. It's still hard to believe, the unchecked heresy that's as commonplace here as the worship of Tempestra-Innara is on the mainland. I suspect Nolan is thinking the same, the way he fiddles with the reverie he bought off the boy.

"What's the plan?" I whisper.

His hand tightens around the stone once more before he slips it into the pocket of his jacket. "To let me do all the talking."

"That can't always be the plan!"

He ignores this and heads for the door, leaving me to catch up. I do, but only because he doesn't give me the chance to argue before he starts knocking. It opens and a woman looks out.

"Welcome." She's older, hair white and bronze face weathered, but her voice holds a youthful lightness. "Have you come to commune with the waters, friends?"

Friends. Hah. Beside me, Nolan's features are loose—nervous—eyes wide with hopefulness.

"I . . ." He hesitates, as if fumbling with his words. "Yes. I mean, yes, I think so. May we come in?"

The woman opens the door further. "Please. Be welcome." There's a warm dampness to the air inside, tinged with the scent of salt. "I am Marzela."

Our host is dressed in a long, shapeless white robe, thin enough to give hints of a gaunt figure beneath, with a spiny choker of orange coral around her neck. As sparse as her uniform is, she has the air of a cleric. One of the Salt priests, without a doubt. "This way."

She leads us through the hall, then down a set of stairs that opens into a long chamber with a bedrock floor. There, dozens of shallow pools are cut right into the stone, lining a walkway that runs down their center. People float within the pools, eyes covered with strips of white fabric that briefly summon the memory of Jeziah and the other dead laid out in Lumeris. Only wetter. Each wears the same loose garment as Marzela, the fabric swimming around their forms in a way that gives them an appearance of giant jellyfish. The atmosphere is solemn, reserved. I catch the occasional snippet of a whisper in the humid air, each carrying the weighty tone of prayer.

Marzela halts us in a side chamber filled with privacy screens and more of the robes neatly folded on shelves.

"You may change here." The Salt priest begins to depart, but Nolan grabs her arm.

"Wait. Are you the priest here?"

Marzela gently extracts herself, a hint of suspicion appearing. "One of them, yes."

"My name is Nolan. I have to confess, I didn't come here to commune with the waters. This is my first time in Cyprene. Can we—is there somewhere more private we can talk?"

The anxious but hopeful eagerness is perfectly executed. Still, the priest's eyes narrow. "About what, if I might ask?"

"There are . . . practices in Cyprene that one can't find on the mainland." Nolan licks his lips and looks around nervously. "I have . . . questions."

The priest turns to me. "And you do as well?"

I shake my head. "I'm just here to make sure he stays in one piece."

Marzela considers before gesturing for us to follow once more. We pass through the salt pools, then down another stair into a smaller, more austere chamber, with a simple table surrounded by wood stools. Nolan and Marzela sit. I remain standing.

Before Marzela can say anything, Nolan blurts: "I come from the southern coast, near Aris. Devoted to Tempestra-Innara. Loyal." The priest's lips thin at the mention of the Goddess. "On the surface, I mean. But there have always been . . . whispers. Talk of the Flame being extinguished by waves."

Marzela tips her head noncommittally. "Despite the efforts of the Butcher Goddess and her spawn, there are those small corners where other faiths persist. That knowledge is common enough."

"But those corners aren't small here, are they?" Nolan is spreading it on thick, but even I have to admit he sounds legit. Keen, even, just the right amount of fumbling to his words. "My grandfather always spoke of the water and the waves, the call of it. He . . . he passed away a few months ago, leaving me his fortune . . . everything." Nolan makes a display of pulling the reverie from his pocket, letting it hang by the leather cord. "I found this among his possessions, hidden away."

It's a nice touch, mentioning the inheritance, and I start to understand where he's going with this. Whether Salt or Flame, a deity's blessing is never welcome more than in the form of hard currency.

It's enough to keep Marzela intrigued, at least. She reaches out, fingertips lightly brushing the carved stone. "Your grandfather was a devotee of the Salt Goddess. Is that what you came here for? Confirmation of his secret 'heresy'?"

Nolan pulls the pendant back. "No . . . I . . . It's only that . . ." He stops, hand wrapping around the reverie. "My parents are devoted to Tempestra-Innara, and raised me to follow that path, but . . . I always felt a call . . . to the water. To the sea."

I can't imagine the effort Nolan must be making, to speak so blasphemously, but there's not a hint of his true devotion to be seen. And I look.

The air around Marzela softens. "I understand. As do you, it seems. The Flame cannot quell the power of the ocean, not when it beckons, any more than a candle can stand against a wave." She folds her hands before him. "You've made the right decision, coming here. The waters welcome all those that seek their embrace."

"Thank you." A relieved smile appears on Nolan's face. Then, it falters. "My grandfather was devoted to the Salt Goddess, I know that much. Our ancestors too, I think, from what little I've been able to glean."

"And they never desired to return to Cyprene, where their faith has its home?"

I understand the trap Nolan has set right before he springs it. "They might have wanted to," he says. "But I believe they had their reasons to remain near the Flame Goddess . . . work that they felt needed to be done."

Marzela says nothing.

"That as long as Tempestra-Innara remained, returning to Cyprene would be turning away from the possibility of the Salt Goddess's return." A beat passes. "I inherited everything my grandfather amassed over the years. It is not . . . insignificant. I came to Cyprene not only to learn more about our faith but," Nolan finishes, "to try and continue his work with like-minded individuals."

I bite the inside of my mouth. I'm not sure what I expected, but it wasn't for Nolan to go this far, this quickly. It's too much, and nothing like the slow, careful snare he built around me. *Back off*, I want to hiss, but at the same time, I catch an encouraging glint of desire in Marzela's eyes.

Maybe Nolan does know what he's doing.

But instead of further inquiry, the priest turns apologetic. "We all have faith that, one day, the Salt Goddess's holy slumber will come to an end. That they will return to us in physical form and restore Cyprene as the heart of their worship. But I'm afraid that you'll find nothing more than simple reflection and prayer here."

Nolan's brow pinches with confusion. "But my grandfather . . . I know he—"

"His goals were noble, I'm sure," Marzela interrupts. "But here, the waters are patient. We know that waves work slowly, but eventually, they wear away the stone, extinguish the flame, and reclaim what has been lost." She stands, making it clear our audience has reached its end. "You are welcome to enjoy what the baths have to offer. The waters and the salt will always be welcoming. But more than that, the type of communion you seem to be searching for . . . I'm afraid it won't be found here."

"She's lying," Nolan spits as we leave the baths behind. "This was the Salt Goddess's territory. Still is, apparently. There's no way their followers don't know *something* about the plots being hatched on this damned island."

His tone is calm and measured, but manufactured. Something simmers below the surface.

"Maybe," I offer. "But I didn't get the sense she was hiding anything."

"Your senses aren't always the most attuned."

"Or *you* pushed too hard." I drop my voice an octave. "*Oh, let me do all the talking, Lys. I won't practically get on my knees and beg to become a violent heretic.*"

His head whips around, a retort threatening, but he exhales with frustration instead.

"C'mon . . ." I'm not used to keeping the peace, and unsure what to say. "It was clear she was interested, but you're a stranger. Let them get to know you. Build their trust."

"We don't have time for that."

The vinegar in his voice makes my blood rise, even if I suspect it's less for me than his own worries. "We don't have time to blow it on our first attempt either. Are you even sure she knows anything useful? Want to go back and try cutting it out of her? I'm not sure that's going to help maintain our cover *or* welcome on the island, but hey, all I'm good at is smashing through doors and murder, right?"

He softens. "No."

"Then keep trying to sell the aspiring heretic." We arrive back at the Petrel, whose common room is already half filled. Nolan moves for the stairs, but I hold him back. "Stay. Act like you *want* to be here. Have a cup of wine. Have three. It might improve your mood."

I expect a protest, but he sighs and takes a table in the corner, leaving me to fetch the recommended beverage. Hiram is behind the bar, which is empty save for one man quietly reading as he works his way through a bottle.

"Wine, please," I say to Hiram, who goes to fetch it. My eyes wander as I wait. They're drawn to the reading man's book nearby, which lies open on the bar before him. A pair of names catch my attention: *Tempestra-Innara. Serapia-Arne.*

A book about the gods? I lean onto the bar to get a better vantage, continuing to scan the lines without *looking* like I'm looking . . .

And barely swallow a squeak of surprise. I expected a historical text. Or a religious text. Or one of those historical texts written by the scholar clerics that's actually a religious text. Instead, I find an intensely graphic description of two gods engaged in a sordid, sweaty, and very naked interlude.

The man is reading divinity porn.

I can't look away, drawn into the absolute astonishment of it as Tempestra-Innara prepares to do something with two apples and a length of silk rope—

The man abruptly closes the book and slides it over. "Want to borrow it? I've already read it at least a dozen times."

I straighten, damn near on fire with embarrassment. "Nope." The word blurts out. "But thanks for the offer. I . . ."

An eyebrow crooks up. "Was just curious?"

"I'm . . . uh . . . surprised. Not exactly the sort of book I'm used to seeing."

The man nods sagely. He's neither young nor old, his dark hair peppered gray, and he exudes an air of comfort that tells me this isn't his first visit to the Petrel. "You're not from Cyprene."

"No, I . . . we just recently arrived."

"We?"

"My employer and I."

"Do you enjoy books?" he says. "I have many more in my shop, old and new. Perhaps you'd find something else better suited to your tastes?"

"Who says this one wasn't?" It's a joke to cover my mortification, but I hadn't even considered what I might find on Cyprene's shelves—here, where no one locks up or destroys texts that don't suit the Flame Goddess's agenda. There could be all sorts of books about the gods long wiped from the mainland. Even something about the reliquaries. "But perhaps I can find time for a visit."

"You'll find my door open." He holds out a hand. "Rion."

I take it and shake. "Lys."

"Welcome to Cyprene, Lys." Rion releases me, then opens the book again. "I hope you enjoy your time here."

He says it as Hiram returns with the wine, which I grab and retreat, feeling Rion's smile follow me. It's not unkind or mocking, but I'm still flush when I sit back down at the table and shove the bottle toward Nolan.

Furrows appear in his brow. "What's the matter with you now?"

"I just discovered something *very* important about Cyprene."

Nolan turns serious, leaning in. "Will it help us find the reliquary?"

"Not in the least." A giggle escapes. "You're not going to believe it, but they have dirty books about the gods here."

"What?"

"See that man at the bar? He's reading a book about the gods, y'know, *together*. About Tempestra-Innara and the Storm Goddess. *Fucking*."

Nolan scowls like I have lost my damn mind. Then he sighs. "Dammit, Lys."

"He even offered to lend it to me!"

"It's heresy."

I roll my eyes. "It's pornography. Don't tell me you've never heard of it." His mouth flops open and then closes again. "Ah, I see you have. And it *does* tell us something important. He isn't hiding it."

Nolan frowns again and yanks a cup over. "We already knew the city was full of heretics."

"But now we know their blasphemous interest extends beyond worship and attempted deicide. Who knows what else they might get away with here? There could be all sorts of things we aren't even considering..." I stop. Think for a moment. "Don't move."

I'm up before he can stop me and back at the bar. Rion looks up as I approach.

"I'm sorry to interrupt your reading again, but would you like to join us for a drink?" I add quickly: "My employer would enjoy the company, new as he is to the island."

Rion brightens. "I never say no to making a new acquaintance. Or a glass of wine." He follows me back to the table. "Thank you for the kind invitation, sir. I hear you've newly arrived."

"Yes." Nolan replays the introduction with him, thankfully going along with *my* idea this time.

"Have you come to Cyprene on business?"

"Of a sort," Nolan replies.

"Rion is a bookseller," I interject. "He has a shop near here... and some interesting stock, apparently."

Rion laughs. "Not all of it... at least, not in the way you mean. But I do carry a wide variety of writings."

"Old and new," I add.

Nolan catches on. "Ah, Lys recalls my interest in history. I will have to come browse sometime."

"Oh yes, I'm sure I'd have a few items that would interest you greatly." Rion takes a sip of wine. "How have you found the city so far?"

There's no suspicion in the question. "It's..." Nolan thinks. "Different."

"A fair assessment for someone from the mainland. Some visitors find it quite jarring." Rion gives Nolan a knowing expression. "Then again, very few come here without at least a little idea of what they are getting into."

"A fair assessment as well." Nolan leans back, relaxing somewhat. "I suppose I didn't expect so many things that would be unwelcome on the mainland to be out in the open here. The salt baths, for example."

"Oh? Did you pay a visit to one of them?"

"There's more than one?" Nolan says lightly. "I didn't realize."

"Several, in fact," says Rion. "Each run by a different sect. I don't share their dogma, but the baths are a sure thing when these old bones begin to ache."

Nolan's gaze catches mine for an instant, interest flickering in it. *Sects.* Our failure at the salt baths today might mean nothing more than we haven't visited the right heretics yet. *See?* I try to communicate silently, arching one eyebrow at him. *We simply need to be patient, and better informed.*

Of course, I'm as anxious as Nolan to find the reliquary. But Cyprene... already, it seems like a place that creates possibilities instead of limiting them. Such as making a living selling racy books. Back at the Cloister, I never would have even considered that an option. I want to ask more, *about* more, but I'm playing a role as much as Nolan is, and so I keep to myself, even after Rion excuses himself for the evening. When he's gone, Nolan tips his chin at me in the barest admission of approval and leans back in his chair, pensive. I do the same, content with observing the comings and goings as night settles. More folks wander in for a meal. A card game starts up in a corner. At one point, a young woman begins singing unprompted, a slow tune that eventually turns so raunchy it makes Rion's book seem as clean as a cleric's text.

It's so cozy—so *normal*—that I'm disappointed when Nolan stands, indicating it's time to return to our rooms. I dutifully follow and deposit him at his suite, tempted to sneak back down alone. But my hand touches my jacket, feeling the hard resistance of the lacquer box.

And the Renderers' book.

Right. I can't let myself lose sight of our goal, no matter this city's draw. I was too afraid to take the text out on the ship, where privacy was scarce, but that's not a problem anymore. The Salt runes have piqued my curiosity; maybe Rion's novel isn't the only book that can tell me something interesting tonight. I go to my room, lock the door, and begin to read, determined that, if there is any useful tidbit peppered among the ghastly formulas, I will find it.

# Thirty

The devoted have spent centuries developing methods to connect with the divine—prayer, fasting, meditation. But there's only one way to truly experience the power of the gods. And it's not cheap.

—THE HERETIC IBEN

THE SUN IS BARELY above the cliffs the next morning when we are back in the streets of Cyprene, making discreet inquiries about the locations of the other salt baths. Nolan starts the day with fresh optimism, but at each location, we are met with the same results: welcoming but wary priests, who turn their noses up at the bait Nolan lays. By the time the dusk turns Cyprene blush pink, clouds of irritated disappointment have gathered around him again, threatening a full-on storm. He tries to hide it, but the effects of being so far from the Goddess have left the intangible veils Nolan draws around himself more frayed than they used to be. Back in his suite, he slams the door so hard it makes me jump . . . as well as abandon the suggestion that we dine in the common room again. Instead, I simply watch as he throws himself into a chair, furrows dug deep in his brow.

"I don't understand."

"Understand what?" I remain standing, crossing my arms. "They're heretics. Even in Cyprene, they don't survive by inviting strangers into their inner circles an hour after meeting them."

"It doesn't bother you that we are getting nowhere?"

"Of course it does! But what does it solve to have *both* of us throwing a tantrum about it?"

I'm not even sure he heard me. "None of their plans are financed with faith. But when a fortune is dangled in front of their faces, they don't seem to care in the least."

"Maybe that's not what they want." It's a bad idea, the one that's been growing since last night, a little mushroom out of shit, but Nolan isn't the only one disappointed by the day's fruitless search. The thought sprouted as I picked through the Renderers' book, another endeavor that came to nothing. We are both right. We can't push too hard without risking our whole venture coming apart. But infinite patience isn't an option either . . . especially for me. "Or what they need."

"What do you mean?"

"Maybe," I continue, bracing myself, "they'll be more forthcoming if we can give them something useful. Something that we *know* they'd never turn down."

Nolan's eyes narrow. "And that is . . . ?"

Slowly, I remove the lacquer box from within my jacket and set it on the table between us. Surprise flickers on Nolan's face, but only briefly before it's replaced by an iron coldness as I remove the top, revealing the jars and vials within. "You *took* that?"

"Sure did. Thought it might come in handy."

Something new flashes at my glib explanation. Something dark. One hand reaches for the box, then stops, as if he can't bring himself to touch it. "You took *that*. Knowing what it was . . . *who* it was."

"Yes." I shift in my chair, feeling the weight of the cookbook move with me; *that* secret I'll be keeping to myself. "I saved it because it was what the heretics were willing to risk everything for. What's in that box is worth more than any fortune you could allude to. If we want the heretics to pay attention to us, well then, there you go." I let my proposal sink in. "Is it better that Prior Fedic died for nothing?"

Nolan stands suddenly, and for a moment, I think our truce has shattered. But instead of violence, he stalks to the other end of the room, not looking at me, or at what lies on the table. Fists balled, he takes a long breath, followed by another, and another.

My palms practically burn for a weapon; whatever version of Nolan this is, I don't like it. The room suddenly feels as if I'm sharing it with some unfamiliar beast.

"If you're praying on it, I bet I know what the Goddess would say."

And here I am, poking it.

"They'd say," I continue, as the muscles in his shoulders tighten further, "do what we need to in order to find the reliquary."

There's another taut stretch of silence. Then he turns back, features unreadable. "*That* should have been left in Sethane to be purified. To *burn*."

I expected vitriol. Even yelling. This—this flat, fortified absence of emotion—is somehow more threatening. Still, it says something that he hasn't lost his temper . . . yet. "But . . . ?"

His mouth thins. "But it wasn't. And as indescribably vile and unthinkable as it is, you may be right."

I lean back, letting a satisfied smile rise. "Say it again."

"What?"

"That I'm right."

It's a gamble, prodding him like this, in sensitive spots, but I don't know what's worse: Nolan turning his anger on me—in whatever form that takes—or him sensing that there's a part of him that genuinely scares me. One that I just summoned with the revelation of the Renderers' wares.

"It might not be enough," he continues, ignoring my teasing. "We're still strangers. They'll want this, but they won't trust us. We need someone they will."

A good point. But I've got a solution for that too. "Tychus."

"Tychus?" Nolan is skeptical. "He seemed more ambitious than accomplished."

"But he's known here. And it's clear he's had less-than-scrupulous dealings from time to time. Also, we don't know anyone else. So, unless you want to make friends with whatever random unsavory sorts we can find, Tychus is our man."

I wait for an argument, but Nolan has none.

The White Gull is small but tasteful, tucked into a district of Cyprene that boasts a spectacular view of the bay below. There, we find Tychus taking his dinner on the spacious patio that makes up the guesthouse's roof. The setting sun paints a long swath of warmth across the water below, speckled occasionally by birds drifting on the wind.

"And here I was"—Tychus offers a thin smile—"thinking our paths might not cross again."

Nolan sits across from him as I stand a few paces back, attention trading between them and the stairs leading up from the guesthouse below. If there's one thing this particular meeting requires, it's privacy. But between the look Tychus threw the proprietor when he delivered us and the surrounding trellises thickly woven with flowering vines, we've got the perfect setup for some seedy dealings.

Tychus pours a translucent liquid for Nolan, who accepts the glass graciously and sips. He grimaces. "Mm. Brinier than I expected."

"A Cyprene specialty." Tychus downs his in one gulp. "They say the salt cleanses the lies from one's lips. Though"—he tips his head conspiratorially—"I've never found it to be a hinderance."

Nolan gives an amused chuckle.

"How is your visit so far?" Tychus turns away to gaze over the water. It's a door deliberately opened; he's shrewd enough to know Nolan isn't here without good reason.

"Not as fruitful as I'd hoped." A frustrated sigh. "I expected the people here to be wary of newcomers but . . ." He pauses, as if considering. "Well, I thought that the promise of enough profit might overcome that particular barrier."

Tychus scoffs. "Cyprene is not wanting for riches; you must have gleaned that by now. Perhaps your business propositions don't quite tantalize here in the same way they might on the mainland."

"That's not the problem," Nolan says. "I know what I have to offer is desirable. But . . . only to the right parties. And finding those parties has been the challenge."

Tychus sits a little straighter. "Oh? And who exactly would that be?"

Nolan does a brilliant job of hesitating. A story winds its way over his face, frustration shifting to a new wariness, as if he's suddenly rethinking this meeting. "It's a delicate situation, one that normally

I would never breach with a near stranger, but . . . it's only that you seemed to be quite . . . well acquainted with the island. Though, maybe it was foolish—and unkind—to assume what sorts you might consort with."

Tychus laughs. "Oh, my young friend. On Cyprene, it's a poor businessperson who *doesn't* trade with both higher and lower elements. I can assure you, I do not discriminate. As long as my interests are served."

It's Nolan's turn to consider. All an act, tidbits laid out to tempt Tychus closer and closer. "I believe both our interests may be served, if you are so inclined. I'm in possession of some particular goods. Ones that are difficult to peddle, save to parties who are trying to reach a . . . different level of understanding in regards to the divine."

The delicate part. If Tychus doesn't have the sort of connections we need, then we've shown our hand for nothing. A miscalculation we might have to deal with in an unpleasant manner.

But he smiles knowingly. "Parties such as the Salt priests?"

I can't tell if the surprise that flashes on Nolan's face is genuine or not.

"Oh," Tychus continues, "I try to stay informed where I can. Which is to say, I hope I've shown I may be of use."

"You have indeed."

"Why not simply present your wares to the priests instead of trying to tempt them with resources of lesser interest?"

"Caution," Nolan says quickly. "Discretion. The consequences of trading in these sorts of goods are clear on the mainland. Here . . . ?" He shrugs. "I'd hoped to find a warmer welcome before I reached that level of . . . comfort."

"Hmm." Tychus takes a thoughtful sip. "Discretion is certainly not unwarranted. But I might be able to turn some of those cold attentions your way. First, though, I'd have to be sure you have what you allude you have."

Nolan gestures to me. I take the box from my pocket and place it on the table. Tychus does his best to appear unimpressed, but there's a tightening around his mouth, a glaze of greed in his eyes. He twists one of his braided rings nervously as I remove a vial of the blood tincture.

"It's what you think it is, yes," says Nolan.

Tychus seems to have forgotten how to blink. "Where did you get it?"

"I'll have to keep the specifics to myself, you understand. But there's more where this came from. Much more."

Finally, our new friend tears his gaze away. "I'm afraid I'll need more proof than this. The authenticity of something such as this must be beyond question." He smiles wider. "You understand."

"Of course." Nolan takes the vial and unstoppers it. If it pains him to do so, he hides it well. "Lys?"

I draw one sickle and carefully dip its point into the thick crimson ichor.

"Stick out your tongue," Nolan orders.

One drop. A tiny, almost minuscule dose of divinity—that's what falls from the tip of my sickle onto Tychus's tongue. I hold steady, forcing back memories of the Cathedral, of being on my knees, and the warm, searing sensation of the Goddess's blood flowing down my throat. This is not like that. My divine communion was a windstorm. This is barely a fart.

But divinity kicks, no matter the amount. Almost immediately, Tychus sucks in a gasping breath, pupils dilating, cheeks flushing like a pair of overripe tomatoes.

"By the Goddess," Tychus gasps.

"By way of the Goddess, you mean," says Nolan.

Tychus leaps to his feet, spinning so fast he nearly topples before catching the back of his chair, which splinters in his grasp. Pushing it away, he stumbles toward the sconces in the wall, blinking and grinning as if the flickering oil lamps are the most beautiful things in the world. "Unbelievable. *Unbelievable.*" He raises his hand, waggles his rings so that they glint and glitter. "The light . . . the colors . . ."

"The rush of divinity." Nolan smirks. "Strength and sensations like you've never experienced before."

I stifle a snort. We are clearly past the sell here—Tychus might as well be a fish writhing on a hook.

"Magnificent." Tychus stumbles back and collapses into the remains of his chair. "My heart . . . beating so fast . . ."

"It will wear off in a few hours."

Tychus looks as if he isn't sure that's what he wants. "How much can you get?"

"Like I said, more. But for the right sort of buyers. In Cyprene, well..."

"I understand." Tychus finishes his drink, which feels like his way of saying *We can deal.* "Even with my connections, it's a delicate endeavor."

"When?" demands Nolan.

For a moment, Tychus doesn't reply, and I'm afraid we've lost him to the seductive pull of divinity. Then he blinks rapidly, gaze filling with clear, voracious desire. "I'll need a few days. I expect you can enjoy the charms of Cyprene for that much longer?"

Nolan smiles, satisfaction limning his eyes as thickly as kohl. "I think we can manage that."

# Thirty-one

A lightning gasp cracked from their lips. "Tempestra..."

"Shhh... shhh..." they ordered as they ran their fingertips, warm as embers, over the smooth swell of skin, tracing promises and temptations as they moved down, down, to where a different sort of clouds gathered, ready to let loose a different sort of deluge...

—EXCERPT FROM *THE ASHES OF DESIRE*
(AUTHOR UNKNOWN)

Nolan's step is lighter on our return to the Petrel, and though I sense a hint of impatience at having to wait for Tychus to contact us, he is presently soothed by progress.

After that, all there is to do is wait. I pass the following morning with the Renderers' book, pouring over the pages and their strange markings, until visions of Prior Fedic's final hours begin to build themselves in gruesome detail within my mind. The rubbery slickness of fat being cut away. The papery sensation of skin peeling loose from muscle. The crack and pop that comes as a blade digs deep to split a joint.

There are no Chosen in Cyprene. No reason for the Renderers to have their hounds here. That is what I tell myself. And then, as a comfort, remind myself of the hundred other ways I could more easily die in this city.

But fantasizing about death only passes the time for so long. And Nolan isn't the only one being stretched thin by the Goddess's distance.

I may not be as cranky, but my body has begun to ache in a way I've only felt once before: when the effects of my divine baptism first set in. It leaves me restless, wishing for a task, a distraction, anything. I consider pushing Nolan to comb the city again, but I already know what he'll say: We need to wait for Tychus.

Well, it doesn't take two of us to do that. And while I may not be truly free of the Goddess in Cyprene, it's the closest I've ever been. Might as well take advantage.

Outside, I find Hiram sweeping the cobblestones. He dips his head in silent greeting.

"Hiram, can you point me toward Rion's bookshop?"

It's not far, but I let myself wander slowly, really taking in the details that make up the city: the people, its grand buildings, the peek of grander cliffs between them. I eavesdrop on gossip, listening for tidbits from the mainland. I buy a bag of sweets from a boy who scurries away at the sight of a Caerula, no doubt to avoid handing over free wares or paying a bribe. The candies are cloying and too chewy, with a flavor like licorice glazed, inexplicably, with salt. *Disgusting*. But I eat every one, simply because I have never had them before, while perched on a curve of cliff that overlooks the port below. I watch the ships as they sail in, sail out, as they raise and lower their many-colored sails. A breeze comes up and I take a deep breath, holding it, knowing this exact scent may never come again.

Eventually, I continue on to the bookshop, which is tucked into the curving crook of a narrow side street. A large paned window makes up the front, the tall shelves within filled to bursting, with more books piled on every surface. The afternoon light glazes some of their leather spines; others look so dull with age and worn down that I'd be afraid they'd fall to pieces in my hands.

A bell sings as I enter, summoning Rion from a curtained-off room at the back of the space. There's a hint of mint in the air. "Lys! A pleasant surprise."

"I had some time to kill. And how could I resist a visit, when you offer such tempting tomes?"

He chuckles. "I just brewed tea. Please, come join me."

Rion slides the curtain aside to reveal another room filled with even more books. There's a table in the center and I take a seat as he retrieves a porcelain pot and two cups.

"I hope your employer's business is going well," he says, pouring the steaming liquid.

"Better, now. With any luck, it may even be done with soon."

"Oh. I'm sorry."

"What?"

He sits. "It's only that you sounded a touch disappointed."

Had I? Did a sliver of emotion slip out unintended? Maybe Nolan isn't the only one who's not quite as in control as usual. "I suppose it would be a shame to leave behind Cyprene's charms so quickly."

"She is stunning. But your work must take you many interesting places."

"Actually..." I gaze into the amber drink, at a fragment of leaf drifting on its surface. "I haven't gotten to see as much of the world as I'd like...yet." Rion gives me a questioning look. "Bit of a strict upbringing."

"Ah."

Thankfully, he doesn't inquire further about that. "Have you always lived on the island?"

"Oh, no. I was born on the mainland. Been years since I was last there, though."

"What brought you to Cyprene?"

Rion's smile lessens a little. "Well, the freedom to broaden my wares, for one. I was...hmm, I suppose you might have called me a historian. More than texts, though, I collected information. Or tried to. Much of what I considered valuable, the Goddess's devoted deemed...inappropriate."

"I understand completely."

"That made me a few enemies over the years," he continues, "and I don't mind the healthy distance between me and them." Rion brightens. "But that's ancient history. I'm one who prefers to focus on the future."

Me too. I think of Cleophas, and the *Squid*. Wonder where they are now, whether they've returned to where we started or are making their way to one of the ports I saw on the captain's charts. "Have you ever traveled farther than Cyprene? Beyond the Devoted Lands?"

"Alas, only in books. Is that where you've got a mind to seek your fortune? Or does a financial motivation only appeal to your employer?"

I give a little shrug. "We're definitely not after the same thing."

"Hmm," he says carefully. "If you don't mind me prying, what *are* you seeking?"

"I . . . don't know." The honesty slips out before I can stop it. Freedom, yes, but as to what shape that takes exactly? A harder question to answer. Cleophas's maps were full of places I could go yet can't imagine myself in. Not because I can't picture them—chains of islands as lush as the green ink they are painted with, a land full of vast, sweeping plains, markings that tease cities unlike any in the Devoted Lands . . . No, it's the possibility I'll feed those dreams, fatten my desires, only to arrive at a moment where they become truly, entirely unreachable. The disappointment that would bear . . . I shy away from the thought. For all the progress made on our hunt, the reality of being no longer bound to the Goddess remains a shimmering, distant thing.

Rion's observations have been on the mark, though. Even as my tether to the Goddess continues to tighten, if we found the reliquary tomorrow, I'd hate the sight of Cyprene growing smaller in the distance. "At least, I'm not sure," I explain. "Not yet. But there's certainly a lot to offer in Cyprene. With less restrictions too."

"Enjoying the reprieve from the holy law of the land?"

Fear jolts me, as if my secrets have been spilled into the open. But new arrivals marveling at the looser, freer way of life here must be a common occurrence. "I can't deny it."

"Yet another reason I stick around."

"Who else is going to peddle the divine smut?"

Rion laughs, then quiets briefly. "People come to Cyprene for many reasons. Some they stay for, others they don't. But I have noticed that it offers a . . . a sort of clarity not found elsewhere in the Devoted Lands. Perhaps your stay here can help you to find what path you wish to follow."

"Maybe." I wish it were as easy as saying so.

"Tch." Rion sits straighter. "I'm keeping you from what you came for. You're welcome to browse the shelves. Or I can dive into the mess if there's a particular story or topic you have in mind."

I almost turn him down, enjoying the relaxed, almost cozy comradery (*this,* I think, *this* would be a welcome regularity), but he's right. I came here for a reason. A historian, he'd called himself. A collector of information. "Do you have anything old? Like really old, from when *all* the gods were still alive?"

His brow furrows. "A strange request."

"Nothing heretical." I don't know why I say it. Why would he care? "More like . . . books or stories about what life was like then. It's all curiosity," I add. "I've always wondered, but it's not something one should ask about back on the mainland, y'know?"

Rion gives me another examining look, then shakes his head. "I'm afraid all I have from that far back is a few volumes of poetry. Copies, nothing original. And, frankly, they're pretty terrible. I'm afraid most else has been destroyed over the years, by time or intention. Even before Tempestra-Innara stood alone, there was a tendency for the followers of the living gods to erase that which belonged to the defeated ones. Plus, paper burns or rots, ink fades . . ." He sighs. "What might have been copied and recopied over the years simply . . . wasn't. An inestimable amount of knowledge and art lost." He sounds genuinely forlorn at the thought.

"But not all of it, right?" I remember the blood offerings my birth mother released to the storm, the prayers spoken in the village. I don't know how old or original they might have been, but they certainly didn't become ritual overnight. "The followers of the dead gods still have their practices. Like the salt baths."

"True, though that particular activity has mainly endured thanks to Cyprene's relative isolation." He reaches for a shelf and removes a book, then flips through it until he finds a page. "And many others have faded despite the endurance of the Salt Sects."

He turns the tome my way. An illustration fills the spread, showing robed figures gathered within a sea cave, near the water's edge. A larger figure rendered in pure white stands in the water; their garments and hair swirl around them as if they are submerged.

"Those devoted to the Salt Goddess used to meditate to the sound of the waves on stone as they basked in their deity's presence. It's said that some fell so deeply under its spell that they were swallowed by the rising tide, pulled down into the depths."

"Astris didn't bother to save them? You'd think their Goddess would hold them in higher regard." But I know better. I remember that carpet of bodies strewn across the Cathedral floor. Followers were probably as disposable then as now.

"There may be no truth to the stories, but it does sound dramatic, doesn't it? In any case, communing with the waves is a mostly forgotten or discarded practice."

Forgotten or discarded. Or suppressed, turned into a crime, something to be done in hiding. I think, again, of the people floating in their salt pools, robes billowing. Imagine long ago secret gatherings in the cliffs of Cyprene, late-night prayers covered by the crash of waves. Shades of worship and devotion, wilted over centuries of subjugation, but still persisting. Still alive. "It's hard to understand sometimes, how folks can go on worshipping like that, with their gods long dead and gone."

"Well, that's just it, isn't it? Not everyone believes they are really gone."

Of course. The heretics are all betting on the old gods rising again the moment Tempestra-Innara is overthrown.

"But yes," he continues, "faith is an adaptable thing. A garment that can be tailored to fit any wearer."

"Or forced to." I can't keep the bitter note out of my voice.

Rion smiles knowingly. "Some people believe what they can see, hear, experience. Others need less corporeal evidence—they follow their heart, their gut, whatever you want to call it. And yes, still others have their following forced upon them." He pauses, his next words quieter. "I'm starting to wager you fall in that last group."

My jaw tightens. There I go again . . . as easily read as any book here.

Rion mistakes my silence for fear. "It's okay, there's no need to answer. I understand. You spend your whole life on your knees, it can feel strange to have the opportunity to stand up. Some folks come to Cyprene and take to it right away. Others, more slowly. And then there's a few that can't handle it in the end. They return to the mainland ashamed and appalled they ever step foot in such a horrible, heretical city in the first place."

"Interesting. But I'm one of those folks who believes what I've seen and felt. So, as far as I'm concerned, there is only one goddess—Tempestra-Innara." Loyal words. Loyal lies. "Anyone devoted to a dead god who's done nothing more verifiable than stay dead for centuries is a fool."

Rion closes the book. "*Devotion* is just another word for love. And love is a hard thing for anyone to give up, whether the object of that affection is living or dead."

*Love.* That's what Tempestra-Innara promises in trade for devotion, the drug peddled to keep us all in line. Love and favor mostly in the shape of power and wealth, doled out by their agents to whomever *they* think deserves it. The ache of absence rises, throbbing like a broken tooth as I think of the blissful warmth that radiates off them when they gaze down with affection in their eyes. I turn away, pretending to peruse a shelf to cover my discomfort. "So, what do you believe? In the Goddess? Or that the dead gods are in some kind of hibernation, just waiting for the chance for a triumphant return?"

He chuckles again. "Me? Oh, I believe the dead gods are dead. Bits and pieces of their divinity might linger here and there, but only because that kind of power doesn't exit this world without leaving a mark."

Bits and pieces of divinity. Exactly what I'm after.

Exactly what I am. "Do the people of Cyprene worry about Tempestra-Innara turning their eye here again? Sending their Chosen, accompanied by a well-armed fleet or two?"

"Of course. Every few decades they try to cement control anew, smother the faith of those who don't reserve it wholly for them. It won't stick, though. Never does."

"That what your history books say?"

He smiles warmly. "History books. Poetry books too. Even . . ." He picks up a familiar tome. "The smut. Faith, in whatever form it comes in, persists. Folks may believe the gods to be immortal, but the belief in them will outlive every single divine being that has ever walked this land."

"Unfortunate." I quickly add: "For their devoted. To have their faith be so empty and them unable to understand that."

Rion shrugs. "Perhaps I'm wrong. Maybe someday the dead gods will be nothing more than amusing stories to tell children."

His words bring forward a thought. I hesitate, then ask: "Do you have a bit of paper and a pencil?"

Intrigued, he hands the items over, and I sketch a few of the symbols from the margins of the Renderers' book, doing my best to re-create them from memory. "I know about the Salt runes used throughout the island. But have you ever seen any markings like this before?"

Rion takes the paper, the lines in his forehead deepening as he examines my scribblings. "Now where would you have seen these before, I dare wonder?"

"You recognize them?"

He nods slowly. "I couldn't tell you what they mean, though. I'm not sure anyone could. Those are old characters, even older than the Salt runes, from a language or cypher used by devoted followers of the Shadow God." He hands the paper back. "Lys, wherever did you come across the writings of the Shadow Cult?"

Too late I realize I should have prepared a nice, tidy lie. "The Shadow Cult?" I make a show of surprise to buy some time to think. "Oh . . . I . . . Where I grew up, there were . . . uh, some old ruins. Like, *really* old. We weren't supposed to go there. But I did . . . just once. Saw some of those symbols carved into the walls."

The fiction I spin seems adequate.

"Ah," says Rion. "There's so little left behind of the Shadow God, they fell so long ago. But as I said, the remnants of a deity have a way of persisting long after that deity is gone."

The words send a chill through me. It's an ill portent, a reminder that, even if I succeed in killing Tempestra-Innara, if *I* survive whatever that triggers, parts of them will remain. And who knows how those parts might be lifted, revered, twisted . . .

But that won't be my problem.

I shove the thought away as I return to the Petrel, instead pondering what the Shadow God's followers—long dead—might have to do with the Renderers. It's an intriguing revelation, if not one that seems as if it would be useful. I'm weighing the risks and benefits of showing Rion more, seeing if he can shed any further light, when I enter the common room. To my surprise, Nolan has deigned to leave his room and is waiting there. He flags me over.

"Where have you been?"

I hold up one of Rion's saucy novels, purchased from the shop. "I got bored."

He lets out an exasperated breath but doesn't scold me again. Instead, he pushes over an envelope and waits patiently as I remove the paper within. There's a brief scatter of words on it, written in neat script:

*Tomorrow. Be outside on horseback, at dusk.*

No signature, but also within the envelope, slipped in like a promise, is a braided metal ring.

# Thirty-two

After the Salt Goddess fell, their face was struck from the smallest shrine to the great, towering visages that watched over the city. But the rest of Cyprene's stonework was left untouched. It was said that even those who conspired to see divinity removed from our world could not stomach doing the same to such profound artistry.

—REFLECTIONS OF THE HISTORIAN XERSUS

MORTIMER DANCES BENEATH ME, as restless as I am to get moving. I pat his neck to calm him, half wishing I had someone to do the same.

"What do you think?" I ponder aloud. "Even odds that whoever Tychus is taking us to meet will try to kill us instead of dealing?"

Nolan tugs the hood of his cloak lower, as if we're not right outside the Petrel and already known to those within. "What would you put the odds at of them succeeding?"

"Oh, *I'll* be fine."

He tosses me an unamused look as I tap the hilt of one sickle. If he's unarmed, I'm the Salt Goddess reborn, but carrying his sword wasn't exactly an option. Before he can retort, Tychus appears. He, too, is cloaked and hooded, which tells its own story; clearly the less we are noticed tonight, the better.

"A fine night for a ride," I say.

Tychus dips his head in greeting, briefly drawing back his hood. "Oh, moonlight on the white cliffs is a sight no one forgets. Absolutely stunning. Breathtaking, even."

"Where are we heading?" Nolan prompts, clearly impatient.

Tychus replies with a cryptic smile, leaving Nolan and me no choice but to embrace our blind faith of him. Anonymous and unspeaking, we travel through the city neighborhoods, drawing closer and closer to the surrounding cliffs. The areas near their foot feel different—older, more private. Not a place for visitors. But we move past these sections too, leaving Cyprene behind, following a path that wanders along the island's bay. Through the clumpy trees to our left, I spot glimpses of sprawling beaches, the sand as light as snow in the rising moonlight. Always, the cliffs remain at our right, becoming no less dotted with statues as we move farther from Cyprene. There are tunnels and pathways into the stone here too, fewer in number but still easy to spot. And a few, I'm sure, that aren't.

After an hour or so, Tychus leads us into a small clearing at the base of a jagged cliff. "We'll have to leave the horses here."

"This seems like an odd place to do business." Nolan dismounts and hands his reins to me. "Even our kind."

I scan our surroundings warily as I secure Mortimer and Buttons to a tree. There are too many places to hide, too many shadows to swallow a threat. Mortimer seems to sense that too, shifting restlessly. I run a hand down the length of his nose then press my forehead to his to settle him. "I agree, buddy."

"Some transactions require extra privacy," says Tychus. "And even though the interested party is known to deal in the items you offer, they do so with a particular level of caution. Surely, you can't object to that?"

"No." I can just see an amiable smile beneath Nolan's shadowed hood. "Of course not."

He's nervous too. Of course, it's impossible to ignore our years of training. Every bit of me is screaming *Beware!* as we head for the cliffs on foot. Not to mention a good dose of common sense. I stay ready for anything, and the slight tenseness in Nolan's stride tells me he's doing the same.

We enter the cliffs through a natural crack in the stone, narrow enough that it's clear why we had to leave the horses behind. For a moment, an impenetrable darkness envelops us, too dense for even my sight. Then Tychus strikes a match and an oceanic wilderness bursts into existence. Some kind of natural petrified reef, I think at first. But it's more carved stone, impossibly intricate, putting every other carving I've seen so far to shame. As Tychus lights a lamp, I run a finger over a faux coral appendage, feeling its detail, barely touched by age. Hundreds—no thousands—of hours of work went into this. It is an expression of devotion, one that persists despite the Salt Goddess's death. It reminds me, suddenly, of what Rion said, about the marks the dead gods left behind. They go beyond the sepulchrae and their strange energies. Something like this carving may not evoke the same wonder, but it has a kind of power all the same. And as Tychus leads us deeper into the passage, I feel that power grow.

Dead or not, this is the territory of the Salt Goddess still.

The reefs turn to waves and foam, then to forests of seaweed. Finally, a bit of light teases in the distance. Nolan and I go on guard as we come to an arched doorway. He keeps his hood up, so I do the same.

But Tychus lowers his and moves lightly, almost jovial, as if we are meeting old friends for tea. "Here we are."

We enter a round chamber filled with pillars. Like the tunnels, they are carved in seemingly impossible ways, reaching up to a stalactite-studded ceiling. I smell salt and the minerally tang of damp stone. The space is large enough that the light from a handful of hanging lamps doesn't reach the outside walls, ringing us in deep, velvety shadows. But they do illuminate the stone table in the center of the space, at which a single man waits, hands folded, a patient but stern expression on his face.

Nolan slows his step ever so slightly. "Lys. It's him."

A whisper, barely. I search the man's squared, amber face, trying to tie it to one of the Salt priests Nolan tried to sway, when I realize what he means: This is the heretic from Novena, the one we would have followed to Carsaire.

The one who knows where the reliquary is.

My hood hides the *I told you so* smirk that hits my lips. But I can gloat later. And I will.

The heretic stands as we approach. "Right on time."

Tychus grins. "Machias, friend, when am I ever late to good business?"

Machias doesn't appear to share his enthusiasm for the transaction. "I would not call your usual fare 'good.'" He addresses Nolan and me. "The only reason I am here right now is because of what Tychus said you had to offer. Did you bring the product?"

I stifle a snort. *Product.* Sounds so much nicer than *jars of person.*

"Of course," says Nolan. In such a chamber, I expect the words to echo. Instead, they're blunted, barely carrying.

"Show me."

I wait for Nolan to nod, giving permission for me to reveal the Renderers' wares. Taking a few steps closer, I pull the lacquer box out from beneath my cloak. I slip the lid open and remove a single vial. In the low light, the tincture is nearly black. I tilt it so a hint of burgundy shows.

"It's real," chatters Tychus. "I sampled it . . . just to be sure. It's real and it is *quality*. Not something dug out of some ancient musty grave."

Machias clearly isn't sold by Tychus's endorsement alone. His eyes narrow as he moves around the stone table, hand rising as if to reach for the tincture. I pull back. "Eyes only for now, friend."

He stops. Stares silently at the box as I replace the vial, hand dropping back to his side. "I don't make it a habit to deal with strangers. Who are you?"

"Someone hoping to make a good deal," Nolan replies calmly.

"Show me your faces."

An order. Not a request.

"I would prefer to preserve some anonymity," Nolan counters as I return to his side. "At least, until we get to know each other a little better."

The heretic lifts his chin with resolve. "Suspicion is well warranted, given the circumstances. If only all parties present had been smart enough to do the same." He raises a hand. "Tychus, you utter fool. What have you brought here?"

Nolan and I trade an uneasy glance. But before we can do anything else, a new voice speaks.

"One thing I will never understand..."

Tychus tenses. Oh, something is wrong.

"... is how opportunities like this always fall into your slimy little lap."

*Very* wrong.

Dark figures appear from behind the pillars. Hope flares. If Machias brought more of his fellow heretics, the reliquary could be closer than we think, maybe within these very caves. But that optimism sputters out almost immediately; while the broad, bald man who steps into the circle of light is unfamiliar, his uniform isn't.

Caerula.

Paling, Tychus takes a fearful step back. "Ramiro, what are—"

"Shut up," says the man, Ramiro. "It real?"

Machias nods slowly. "I believe so. But—"

"Oh, Tychus," croons Ramiro, not waiting for Machias to finish. "Tch, tch, tch... you *should* know better. Should have come to me as soon as you found out what your new friend had. But instead... well, greed always gets the best of you, doesn't it?"

Tychus throws up his hands. "Ramiro, wait, this is different. He said he could get more... Once I'd confirmed with Machias that was the truth, the first thing I would have done was make sure you were cut in—"

"Shut," Ramiro snaps, "your mouth." Tychus obeys. "If I want your runny horseshit, I'll ask for it. It's bad enough you're back in the city at all, but this? Oh, I know. You think all your 'friends' here will keep your secrets no matter how often you exaggerate or fail to deliver. Maybe you've managed something worthwhile this time, but you've already long overspent that coin."

"Excuse me," Nolan interjects, entirely collected despite the unraveling situation. "We came here to conduct business. While I recognize you have your issues with Tychus, there's no reason they should extend to us. If your organization receives its due in transactions like this, I'm sure we can work something out."

Machias shakes his head. "He's lying."

Ramiro frowns. "You said it was real."

"It is. He's lying about where it came from." Machias's glare is so intense that it makes me itch, as if he can see through the fabric of my cloak. But there's worry beneath it, a concerned uncertainty. "That box—I know it. It's from our usual supplier. But these two are not their couriers. They're thieves . . . or worse."

*Shit.* There it is. Confirmation that this little meeting has gone fully tits up. I guess my fifty-fifty estimation of a murder attempt tonight was optimistic. My hands itch for my sickles, but I stay calm, giving Nolan a chance to charm our way out of this.

"Disappointing." He sounds as if he's been told they're out of his favorite pastry. "I came here to make a deal, not be accused of theft. Tychus assured me that despite not coming through known channels, these items would be in high demand."

"Oh, we'll definitely take them." Ramiro is obviously pleased. "That's a good payday there."

Machias bristles. "This is more serious than I expected. If they've stolen—"

"For fuck's sake, Machias," Ramiro groans. "What does it matter if your supplier wasn't as careful as they should have been? The Salt Sects will still get to suckle the teat of their Goddess; you'll still make your profit selling to them. But this time you'll pay that filth's value, not our usual cut to look the other way."

"Ramiro, listen to me. What if someone *sent* them here?" Okay, Machias is no fool.

This gives Ramiro pause, though Machias doesn't elaborate on who that "someone" might be. It's clear Ramiro and the Caerula are involved with what gets smuggled into Cyprene, but I'm starting to wonder if they have any idea of what else Machias is involved in. Nolan keeps stone-still, probably chewing on the same question, and our predicament. The path to the reliquary lies through Machias. But Ramiro currently stands in the way. And I doubt he plans to claim the Renderers' wares and let us take a walk.

This is going to be tricky. There are at least ten Caerula I see, probably more that I don't—too many for my liking, even if they have no idea what they are up against. They're closing in slowly, swords and knives glinting.

"You'd satisfy yourself with pocket change?" Nolan addresses the Caerula leader, shaking his head disapprovingly. "Because it sounds to me what Machias objects to is no longer having full control over supply. I'm offering you this and more ... much more. With my help, you—everyone here—could be richer than you ever imagined."

Machias frowns. "Another lie."

"Or not," Nolan challenges. "Because you suspect I can deliver what I promise. Which makes me wonder ... Ramiro, are you certain you always get your fair share of what Machias imports to Cyprene?"

It's a smart move, trying to cast doubt, spread temptation—to Ramiro and beyond—but a quick snort of laughter makes it clear the attempt is futile.

"Legitimate or not, you really don't understand how it works here, do you?" Ramiro says. "Unlike Tychus, I'm satisfied by a little bit of greed. Enough to keep my pockets full, not so much to draw attention from the mainland."

*Damn.* We wanted overly ambitious heretics. Instead, we get under-ambitious common criminals.

"Whoever you are ... if someone sent you ..." Ramiro shrugs. "People disappear in Cyprene all the time. Hand over the box," he instructs, flashing a cruel grin, "and we can finish this up, quick and easy. Promise you won't feel a thing."

Nolan doesn't move. Neither do I.

But the Caerula step closer, tightening the ring around us.

"I'll get it from her," Tychus squeaks, desperate to regain some small favor, save himself.

"No need." I step forward, holding the betraying, but not terribly sturdy, box high. "Don't come any closer, though. Or I'll smash your good payday here all over the cavern floor."

Everyone goes still. The encroaching Caerula wait for instruction from their leader.

"I thought so." A little bit of greed is still greed. "Now what?" I say to Nolan.

He sighs. "There's only one thing we're after." *Machias.* "Looks like we'll have to get it your way."

That's all I need. Nolan goes low the instant I toss the box high into the air, pulling a knife from his boot and arcing it at Ramiro. But the Caerula is quick. Not quick enough to avoid the blade entirely, but enough so that it only sinks into the meat of his arm. But Nolan's second blade finds a chest—

Just not Ramiro's, as the man jerks Machias in front of him at the last second.

"Shit!" The heretic crumples. I launch myself onto the stone table and draw my sickles as most of the Caerula scramble to catch the box. My blade takes one that doesn't across the eyes, blinding them. The next strike opens a man from gut to collarbone. But we are surrounded, and this is going to get real ugly, real fast.

Nolan darts around the front of the table, brandishing a sword claimed from one of the injured men.

"Machias?" he screams as he cuts down another Caerula.

I have a clear view of the heretic, if not a good one. "Very dead."

Rage flashes, Nolan's next strike so brutal that it parts head from body. That's enough to give the attacking Caerula pause, but only briefly. They've still got an advantage, especially if they can tighten ranks around us.

So we're not going to let them.

I jump down beside Nolan, slashing. He deflects a blow and kicks, sending a body tumbling, giving us a chance to break free of the deadly ring and run. The cave entrance isn't far, but not as close as I'd like. A slim figure suddenly appears alongside me. I almost strike before realizing it's Tychus. He's white as the salty walls around us, but miraculously unharmed. Apparently, no one considered him much of a threat.

"Help me!" he cries.

"Stay close!"

I say it even though I know he won't. He can't. Nolan and I are too quick. By the time we plunge back into the tunnels, Tychus is already falling behind.

"Wait, please!"

I ignore him.

And then I don't, my feet digging into stone. I spin in time to see him catching up, half a dozen Caerula on his heels. Not my favorite odds, but the tunnel is narrow enough that they'll bottleneck. I raise my sickles.

Tychus grins with relief. And then jerks forward, an arrow punching its way out of his throat.

"Fucking fuck." I'm moving again before his corpse hits the ground. "Nolan! Arrows!"

He's already well ahead of me and I don't expect him to stop, but he falters, glancing back as if he didn't realize I wasn't right behind him anymore. I push to close the distance. He disappears around a turn, then reappears when I take it, flawlessly retracing our steps. The Caerula fall behind, but not far. I can still hear their pursuit. At least in the winding tunnels it's hard to get a good shot at us.

Finally, I see night sky through the exit, framing Nolan. He waited, just long enough to make sure I was still there. It's damn near touching. By the time I'm out of the cliffs, he's mounted on Buttons. I bolt that final distance, sparing only a second to cut Tychus's horse free and give his rump a good slap so he can't be used for pursuit. Then I swing up onto Mortimer. The moment I'm seated a sharp line of pain pierces through my shoulder.

Nolan twists around as I cry out, then dodges as an arrow flies past his head.

Not from the tunnel. They're somewhere above us on the cliffs.

"Go!" I dig my heels into Mortimer's flanks.

Another arrow whistles by, kissing my cheek. I ignore it, ignore the pain, focus only on Nolan's back. I sense more than hear the bolts streaking around me, and every second, I expect another one to find a kidney, a lung, the back of my skull. Then, we are away from the cliffs, swallowed by the tree line. I look back. There's no one trailing yet, only the road, dappled in shadows. But they'll be coming. Nolan knows it too, and instead of following the path, he turns off into a break in the trees, taking us deeper into the foliage. We keep moving for the better part of an hour, changing our path frequently, making sure that we have lost any possible pursuit.

Only when we break onto an open beach, a thin line of sand curving around the water like the blade of my sickles, do I reach for the arrow in my shoulder. I wrench it free and toss it aside, grunting with the fresh pain. It hurts like hell. But it's nothing. Not to me. Not to the Chosen of Tempestra-Innara.

The wet, warm sensation of blood sheets down my side.

Well, maybe it's a little something.

Nolan turns back. "Are you okay?"

"Okay?" I laugh. No, I crow, ripping my hood back to release the sound. We'd walked into a trap—even if it wasn't the one we'd anticipated—and walked right out again. I am almost giddy, though Tychus is dead. And Machias. Doesn't matter, not right now.

*We're* alive.

I have a moment more to savor that feeling before Mortimer suddenly slows, stumbling once before he goes down, pitching me forward into the sand.

# Thirty-three

*The flame does not know devoted from heretical, just from unjust. That distinction belongs to the one who wields it.*

—PRIOR YIORGO, DUSK CLOISTER

I LAND ON MY WOUNDED shoulder. Pain flares, but it is distant, narrowed. So is the gritty sensation of sand pressing into my face. The airy near hysteria of triumph is gone, consumed like gas vapors by flame as I stare back at Mortimer, lying several lengths behind me.

An arrow sticks out at a sharp angle from his ribs.

"No." Whenever the shot landed, I didn't realize it, caught up in battle fury and the fervor of escape. And Mortimer . . . Mortimer must have felt it but carried on anyway, saving me. I crawl to him. Right away, I can see the arrow is deep. Thin rivulets of blood snake out, barely enough to reach the sand, but there's nothing heartening about that. Nor about Mortimer's breath—uneven, ragged.

*No.* My jaw tightens, unwilling to let another sound slip out as I gingerly touch the feathered shaft. Mortimer twists, trying—failing—to get back on his feet. I lurch back, dodging one flailing hoof, feeling every muscle tense with understanding.

"Shhhh . . ." I slide around his other side, away from his legs. "Shh, Mortimer, don't move. Don't move."

I'm telling an injured horse to stay still. The foolishness of it rings in my ears as Mortimer lets out another horrible, burbling screech, which pierces deeper than any arrow. A vinegar sting fills my eyes.

"Lys."

Nolan. On one knee beside me, taking in the situation. "Lys, get up. There's nothing you can do. The arrow is in his lungs. He's drowning in his own blood."

I shake him away. No. *No.* There's nothing I can—

Yes. *Blood.* Yes, there is.

I reach into my coat and pull out a vial of the Renderers' blood from where it's hidden in my jacket, along with the jars of salve—everything but the sample I showed off to Machias. Nolan's idea, just in case it was a trap. In case we needed leverage to ensure our dealings would go smoothly. So much for that.

I have it open before he grabs my wrist.

"What are you doing?" His fingers tighten as I try to pull back. "Are you crazy? It's a horse. You have no idea what that will do. If it will do anything."

"It could help him!"

"You don't know that."

"You don't NOT know that!" My voice rises, sharp and unchecked. But muted too, the way everything but Mortimer seems to be. His breathing is getting worse, blood leaking from his mouth. One glassy eye rolls up at me, devoid of anything but pure, animalistic pain.

I have to do something. I *have* to.

I struggle again. This time, Nolan lets go. He stands and moves away from me, frustrated. I lean over Mortimer, ignoring the panicked flaring of his nostrils, position myself, and pour . . .

A thick, dark stream disappears down Mortimer's throat. I back away, waiting. Hoping. I know what a drop of the Renderers' blood did to Tychus. What a torrent of pure, divine blood did to *me*. All I can do is pray for something in between.

But nothing happens. Nothing beyond the weakening wails of a dying creature.

My fist curls around the empty vial, trembling. I feel hot all over— my eyes, my cheeks, in the distant throbbing of my wound.

All except my free hand, which is cold as ice as I draw one sickle.

It's over quickly. No more cries. No more suffering.

No more Mortimer.

I bury my gaze in that silent, motionless form.

"Lys."

I ignore him.

"*Lys*," Nolan says again, more forcefully. "We don't have time for this."

I ignore him some more.

When he grabs my uninjured arm, hauling me up, I let him. I take in the irritated anger on his face, the hard line of his mouth.

And then I haul back and punch. Nolan tumbles backward and lands on his butt in the sand.

"We have time," I yell, not caring if there's anyone around to hear. If the Caerula are still nearby, I'd welcome them right now. Cut them down like weeds and be happy for it. "We have time because I say we have time."

Nolan is as pissed off as I've ever seen him, bloodied teeth bared as he rises. "Do you not get it? Do you not understand what just happened?"

"Oh, I do." It bursts up and out of me before enough sense gathers to stop it. "We had the heretic right there. And then, oops, *you* killed him."

"That wasn't my fault!" Everything that's been simmering in him since the Renderers' workshop suddenly rises to the surface. I saw a hint of it when I revealed what I'd saved. Now comes a surge of viciousness—twisting his features, blackening his gaze—frightening enough to make me retreat a few steps, put space between us. For the first time, I feel like I see the truth of Nolan: driven and devoted beyond anyone else I've ever known, and left dangerously wounded by failure. "That was our only lead," he snarls. "We are back to *nothing*. Nothing but new enemies and the vaguest notion that the reliquary is somewhere on this godsforsaken island. And your concern is for a godsdamned *dead horse*?"

"Fuck the reliquary!" Despite the threat of him, I throw the empty vial, angry at its uselessness. It bounces off Nolan and disappears into the sand. "Fuck the Caerula and the heretics." I barely stop short of adding Tempestra-Innara to that list too.

"The reliquary—"

"I don't care!" It hits all at once. The dragging, drowning, *empty* feeling. The inescapable *need* for the soothing balm of their light. I thought Nolan was the weak one, being so sensitive to the Goddess's absence, making him impulsive. But it's been rooted deep in me all along too, kept at a manageable distance by anger and the novelty of the unfamiliar. But this impure freedom was only a distraction. A makeshift bandage for a festering wound. "I don't care," I say again, but with less resolve. I want to sink into the sand at my feet, disappear like the vial.

"Of course you do. Even if you've lost your mind enough to not realize it." His voice thins, quiets, as if taken by the same tide that's washed over me. "We're . . . failing Tempestra-Innara. After we already failed to protect them in the Cathedral." He pauses, as if drained by speaking the words aloud. "But if we even consider giving up now and going back empty-handed, if they are forgiving, do you understand what we'll be?" He goes tense all over. "*Nothing*. Nothing in their eyes. In the eyes of our brethren. *I'm* not nothing. And I won't give up on showing *our* blood mother *my* potential just because your horse got killed!"

I damn near punch him again, with the plan to take out a few teeth this time. But my fist hangs at my side, stupidly limp, searing tears leaking over my cheeks. Nolan isn't simply mad. There's fear in his face, in his voice, glazing those hazel eyes. Fear of failure. Fear of loss.

*Innara is dying.*

I take a deep breath and understand. *Really* understand. His dread and distress about the Goddess's vulnerability, and his own. Of their avatar being weak and the need to find the reliquary quickly. Of failing to do so and, therefore, failing to show his strength and capability.

Of being nothing.

All the pieces, broken up and scattered in front of me so I couldn't see the whole picture.

"This isn't about becoming Executrix, is it?" It coalesces as I put it into words. "You want to prove you're as good as that and better. Tempestra needs a new avatar." A bitter laugh escapes. "You want it to be *you*, don't you?"

He doesn't answer. But he doesn't need to. There're some truths even Nolan's acting can't conceal.

Something in me turns brittle, the part that is always honed, always waiting to be challenged. This was never a competition, not really. We both had plans all along—big plans.

I can't even be mad. I kept my secrets and Nolan kept his. There's no escaping the games we play, the blades we keep hidden.

It's too much. I turn back to Mortimer and sink beside him in the sand. Place a hand on his chest. He's as warm as in life, but still. No rise and fall of breath. No thick, heavy beating of his horse heart. Just meat now, lying on a beach, waiting for the tide to come and claim it, add it to whatever else rots beneath the inky blue. I sit like that, hand on horse, stuck. Stranded. Distantly, I am aware of Nolan taking a few indecisive paces toward me, then away, then toward Buttons. I wait for the sound of him riding away. It would be the smart thing to do, to leave me behind, abandon me to our pursuers.

Instead, his footsteps approach once more.

"Lys," he says quietly. "Your shoulder."

I know it's bleeding. I don't care.

His hands fall onto my shoulders, remove my cloak, tug my jacket off. I don't fight, don't take my eyes from Mortimer and the dark patch of wet sand, not even when pain flares. There's a rustle of fabric, followed by the scrape of a lid being opened. Only then do I turn, see the small jar of Renderer salve in his hands.

"This isn't over," he says by way of explanation. "You need to be able to fight. And as horrific and frankly disgusting as this is, it will help. I . . . I think the Goddess—and Prior Fedic—would understand."

I want to protest—or laugh—at Nolan's pragmatism, so deeply ingrained that it manages to overcome revulsion. But I can't find the energy to do either, returning to my vigil as his fingers probe my broken skin. There's a tingling rush of warmth when the salve touches me. It's less concentrated than the blood tincture would be, but localized—focused—on the wound. Nolan dabs it so gently, so artfully, that I almost forget the salve's grisly origin, especially when the faint, distinctive sensation of healing flesh begins. It spreads like the bitterness I feel about the concoction's inability to save Mortimer.

When Nolan is done, he washes his hands in the ocean, scrubbing them vigorously with sand. Then, I hear him sit. Not near me, but not far either. Minutes tick by, and then hours. No one comes for us; either we outsmarted the Caerula in our retreat, or they didn't care enough to pursue us. The sky turns darker, waves lapping at the beach in a hypnotic rhythm. The air chills. Still, I sit, lifeless as the corpse beside me. I stare out at the water, beyond the pass, in the direction I know the mainland lies. To where Tempestra-Innara is. I suspect—no, I *know*—that if a line were drawn along my sight, it would lead directly to them. Every little piece of me leads right back to them.

And that's what Nolan wants more than anything.

We are a perfect pair. I want to break free of the Goddess; he wants to give himself over entirely, body and soul, mind and blood. The very thought hollows me out. Makes me want to slump forward into Mortimer's cooling form and close my eyes. There's something almost liberating about that dedication. It is who I could become, filing off all of my edges to become the blood-bound servant I was meant to be. But to do that, a part of me would have to die too, be left here on this beach with Mortimer. And as much as I wonder if that hole could ever be filled with the pure, sacrificing devotion that Nolan seems to feel, I know it won't.

If I cut out that part of myself to save myself, I'd be saving a broken thing.

Nolan waits. And waits, until the dark begins to recede, a thin blur of morning feathering along the stone cliffs that surround the bay. I hate the sight of it, knowing what it heralds. Knowing that I can't stay here forever, no matter how deeply I crave it in this moment. We have to go back to Cyprene.

Nolan is right. This isn't over yet.

I straighten and turn to him.

He sits with his knees out in front of him, arms resting on them, staring at me. Nothing readable on his face anymore. Only the slightest knit to his brow as he waits for me to speak.

"I won't leave him for the scavengers." My voice is thick, mouth dry. I can feel the tight lines left by salty tears on my cheeks. And despite the salve, my shoulder throbs a lively cadence. "He was a good horse. He didn't deserve to die like this." I remember Nolan, sick and wan on the ocean voyage, chained by the Renderers. His fear of weakness, the very thing that is spilling out of me now, through cracks I cannot be bothered to conceal. Let it be weakness. I don't care. "And he doesn't deserve to be left like this either. But I . . . I can't . . . It's going to take me too long."

The pinch of skin between Nolan's eyes deepens. I can't sense what's happening in his thoughts—anger, annoyance, confusion. So I turn back to Mortimer and hold my hands just above his flank, palms down.

Then, I call the divine flame.

The flickering pale light comes to life, jumping from me to Mortimer as if it were a creature with its own mind. I am reminded of Belspire, of Caius's execution. Our gift came so easily for him, consuming his victim. It comes for me too, but slower, a trickle spreading feebly over the still horse body. I redouble my efforts, trying to draw from deep within myself, harness the damnable divinity that I am supposed to be a creature of. But I am a candle compared to Caius, a firefly's flicker compared to Tempestra-Innara. And for the first time, I consider that it's *my* fault the flame comes so weakly, that its light is so faint in me. That this—the most extraordinary of my gifts—is weak because in my heart, I am as much a heretic as any to be found in Cyprene.

Which wouldn't matter any other time save now, the first time I truly want it to come. To burn.

Sand shifts behind me. Suddenly, Nolan is there, kneeling.

His flame is fierce. It entwines itself with mine, becoming one force that moves purposefully, spreading until the entirety of Mortimer is consumed. We remain like that, directing our divinity to a purpose that neither of us ever dreamed we'd use it for. Sweat pricks my brow and cheeks. Nolan flushes with the effort. But neither of us stops, not until some deep, shared instinct tells us that the fire has taken root.

Only then do we let go, standing back from the burning body of a very good horse, and watch until only bone and ash remain.

# *Thirty-four*

> Neigh.
>
> —MORTIMER

"I'M SORRY ABOUT YOUR horse." It stumbles out of Nolan as we leave the dawn-soaked beach behind.

"Thanks." I sit behind him on Buttons, trying not to let fatigue and emptiness drag me forward. I have never been so tired, not even when the Goddess's armies drove me through the mountains and the snow. Not even after I watched all those familiar faces go to their wet, icy deaths. "So how fucked do you think we are?"

He says nothing for a few heartbeats. "I don't know. The Caerula didn't get a good look at us, and Machias is dead, but we don't know how much Tychus told him. Names, where we are lodging . . . We need to get back to the guesthouse, see if we can get to our gear before they do."

"And after that?"

"We'll figure something out."

He doesn't intend to give up. Even now, when we have, by his own words, nothing. I should have expected it. Given the choice between staying here and completing our failure and retreating to Lumeris, Nolan's choice is obvious. But if we've added the Caerula to the list of people hunting us, it's gonna be a lot harder to accomplish anything in Cyprene.

"So . . ." I say. "You want to be the next avatar."

Nolan tenses—only a little, but our tight proximity makes it impossible to miss. At first, I think he's not going to reply. He didn't admit to it on the beach, no reason for him to do so now.

Then he takes a breath and holds it before letting go. "It's . . . it's not something I—or any of us—should desire. But a chance to be considered . . . that's all I want."

To be a puppet controlled by the Goddess. Slowly consumed by them, until only the barest hints of what was truly Nolan is left. No, he wouldn't see it like that. An honor—that's what being the Goddess's avatar is to him. Same as dying on a battlefield in their name. The sacrifice of the pure devoted. And all I want to do is make that dream impossible. The idea never bothered me much before, when I thought he was only angling for Executrix. I don't like that it does now. Something in me buckles, pushed past tolerance. I lean forward, pressing my forehead into Nolan's back. He tightens before relaxing again. Says nothing. I take a deep breath. He smells like sweat and blood and burning horse. So fleshy. So human. I wonder if that sticks around. Do avatars have body odor?

"Okay." Guilt wriggles in the pit of my stomach. "Good luck with that. Let me know if you need an Executrix. I know someone back at the Dawn Cloister who'd be interested in the job."

Despite it all, he laughs. I can feel the echo of it in his ribs, reverberating against my guilt. I grit my teeth and straighten, not wanting to hear it.

We ride a bit more before he speaks again.

"I really am sorry about Mortimer."

"Me too."

"Really," he presses. "I . . ."

"A horse," I interject. "That's all it was."

"Not to you."

I swallow. "Thank you for helping me cremate him."

"Please don't tell anyone we did that."

"Sorry. I added it on my snitch list already."

"Of course you did."

Cyprene's early risers are stirring by the time we make our way back. We keep a sharp eye out for Caerula as we navigate the streets. Or Nolan does. Fatigue—and probably the side effects of the balm—plays tricks on me. My vision swims, then sharpens, then creates impossible tableaux. I see Innara in a young woman bent over a fountain. Mortimer in the horse drawing a cart of water barrels. Even Avery, a hurried figure ducking into a doorway. Phantoms all, raised by . . . what? Guilt? Frustration? The narcotic effects of the divine? I can only hope it passes soon; I won't be much good against an enemy if I'm not sure they are even there. The Caerula may not have seen our faces, but they might recognize the cloak I'm wrapped in, which is still less conspicuous than clothing drenched in blood. Nolan, mostly unspoiled, discarded his cloak. The question now remains whether they know where we're staying.

The answer is clear the moment we get close enough to see the Petrel, from the vantage of a nearby alley. Half a dozen Caerula linger outside it, and judging by the number of horses, there are more inside.

I curse. Probably a bit more than necessary, but I was really hoping to lie down in bed, even briefly. "Now what?"

"I'm not sure." Nolan watches the gathering. "We could try to find somewhere else to hole up."

"Or," says a voice from just beyond the alley opening. "You could simply wait until they've gone."

I peek around the wall, already recognizing the speaker: Rion. I'm not seeing things; Nolan's reaction confirms he's actually there. The two of us must be really exhausted to have missed him. Rion leans against the building, book under one arm, mug of coffee in hand, appearing quite put out.

"They were making the common room unbearable." He doesn't turn our way as he speaks, giving away nothing. "Exciting night, was it?"

I snort, keeping to the shadows. "Not the word I'd use."

"I'd ask what you did to fall afoul of them," Rion says, "but plenty of folks manage the same, and besides, it's none of my business."

Nolan shifts nervously, and I realize it's intentional, that he's slipped back into his merchant character. "It wasn't so much us as a gentleman we'd become acquainted with," he lies smoothly. "Seems like the Caerula had reached the end of their patience with him."

"Ah. The *end* end?"

"Unfortunately." Nolan waits a respectful beat. "We can't stay here. If they are searching the Petrel, they must have been told we're staying here."

"They're searching *all* the guesthouses." Rion calmly sips his coffee. "Been working their way through them for hours, after two recently arrived strangers. There was a pair like that, but they returned sometime late last night, hastily packed before sneaking out, leaving their bill unpaid to boot. At least, that's what Hiram told them."

I'm amazed I still have the energy to be surprised. "And why would he do that?"

Rion gives an amused snort. "Ramiro and the Caerula have as many enemies as friends in this city. Most of the time they aren't smart enough to realize which it is they're talking to. Oh, sure, they'll make a show of interrogating folks, but by now they think you took the first boat out on the morning tide." He straightens. "Ah, here we are. Good riddance, you bothersome bastards."

I relax a little as Caerula appear from out of the Petrel. Even more so when they ride off, disappearing into the web of streets. Only then do we file out of the alley.

Rion takes us in. "An exciting night indeed. Are you injured?"

"It looks worse than it is." Only half a lie. Thanks to the salve, my shoulder will heal even faster than normal, though every movement brings a stab of pain. "Nothing some rest won't take care of."

"C'mon," says Rion. "We'll sneak you in through the back."

I am thankful even as the bone-deep weariness crests over me again. It's more than fatigue, more than grief—calling the flame left me drained. It used me like a fuel, which, in a way, I guess I am. I want to be back in my room. No, I want to kick Nolan out of his and take a long soak in his tub. Then I want to sleep.

"They tried to rob us. Killed one of our horses and injured Lys." Nolan sounds perfectly indignant as we make our way around the guesthouse, with a brief stop at the stables. The empty stall hits like a second arrow, though I'm too wrung out for more tears. "How can they call themselves the Goddess's justice when they comport themselves like common brigands?"

"Common brigands find themselves in positions of power more often than we'd all like to admit." Rion leads us into the kitchens.

Hiram is there. He nods at us.

Nolan pulls out his purse and hands over a frankly obscene amount of money. "To cover the bill we skipped out on. And whatever bill we run up from this point on."

Hiram simply nods again. Easy to buy silence from a man who tends toward it, I guess.

As soon as the door to Nolan's suite is closed and locked, I collapse into one of the overstuffed chairs. Nolan remains on his feet, though. He's back on edge, pacing from one end of the room to the other.

"The Caerula may be convinced we've fled, but we need to avoid them going forward. And find another way to the heretics. If Tychus was able to get to Machias, there must be other ways to connect with them."

"Sure, yeah." I close my eyes. "Can we figure that out after I have a little time to recover from major blood loss?"

His footsteps cease. I sense his considering gaze, which is laced with impatience again, now that we're somewhere safe. Or as safe as we'll get for now. I expect to be chastised, for him to tell me we need a new plan right here and now. I wait for the Nolan that showed himself on the beach to reappear.

Instead: "Yes. Okay. You should get cleaned up, and that arrow wound still needs to be stitched and bandaged."

I crack one eye. "Run me a bath in that fancy tub?"

Pushing my luck, for sure, but he heads into the bathroom. The sound of running water follows. First helping with Mortimer, now this. Two kindnesses—small ones, but more than I'm used to from a fellow Potentiate. A new sense of discomfort spreads, thick with suspicion and unease. Our truce has been a mutually beneficial thing. That I can manage.

What's harder to get comfortable with is the idea of Nolan being genuinely *nice* to me.

The next thing I know, it's morning . . . again.

I jolt back to consciousness, blinded by the light streaming through the window, and reach instinctively for the sickles that aren't there. Pain flares in my shoulder.

*Where—?*

Nolan's suite resolves as I blink away sleep, the room pale and quiet. I'm still in the chair, still in the clothes I had on yesterday, save my stained jacket, which has been folded and placed on the table. I spent all day and night here, passed out. Caked blood cracks as I shift, the sensation entwining with a deep, piercing ache. And a new tightness. With my good arm, I reach for the arrow puncture. It's been cleaned. Stitched.

A chill sensation pools in my stomach.

Hours, gone. And Nolan able to jab me repeatedly with a needle and thread without rousing me. The utter vulnerability of it sets off a sickening wave of distress. Not only because Nolan might have taken the chance for a fresh betrayal . . . but because he didn't. He probably didn't even consider it this time. Instead, he cleaned my wound, left me undisturbed.

*Of course he did. He still needs you.*

So why am I surprised?

*Everything* hurts as I get to my feet, a taste in my mouth like I've been licking the inside of someone else's boots. There's a water pitcher beside my jacket. I drink directly from it, draining half before my thirst is slaked. Then, I listen. It's early enough that I don't hear any telltale thumps below that Hiram is up and about, starting chores for the day. And Nolan . . . ?

The door to his bedroom is cracked a handspan. I approach lightly. From within, measured, even breaths sound, and I can just see the outline of his form curled in the bed. I wonder how long he watched me sleep before his own exhaustion overcame him. I consider waking him, then opt to return his kindness.

Which also means forgoing the noise of the bath I really, *really* want.

Making do with the basin of water in my room, I scrub off as much blood as I can, along with sweat, grime, and more than a little horse ash. It's a slow process, due to both my injury and a heaviness that refuses to dissipate.

Weakened and heartsick as I was yesterday, my dense, extended rest has left behind fresh clarity. And understanding. Nolan's outburst wasn't exactly unwarranted. Besides knowing the reliquary is—or was, recently—in Cyprene, we have, exactly, fuck all. Except the brand-new ire of Ramiro and the Caerula.

More complications. No leads. No allies.

Then again . . . Tychus may be dead, but he's not the only connection we—*I've* made in Cyprene. I use the single chair in my room to reach into a gap in the eaves, where I've taken to hiding Jogue's diary and the Renderers' cookbook. I was nervous leaving them behind, but now I'm glad they didn't end up as bloodied as I did. Flipping through the cookbook, I land on one of the pages with the Shadow sigils.

Rion knew what they were. Knows lots of things, about history, the gods . . . and Cyprene. Tychus managed to hold connections here even as a visitor. Who knows what sorts of acquaintances Rion has?

It's not a good idea. Local or not, Rion is only a bookseller, not whatever flavor of criminal Tychus was. And I can't pretend it's not born of growing desperation. Yet, no matter how I turn the situation over and around, it's the only idea I've got.

Cloaked, I sneak out of the Petrel's back door, eyes peeled for Caerula. It's still on the early side, but the streets are far from empty, which lends me added cover. I pass a window where the baker is putting out the first loaves of the day, so fresh that their warmth steams the glass. That earthy, malty scent wafts into the street, setting off a sudden, ravenous hunger. Since I apparently haven't eaten in over a day and a half, I pick out a large roll studded with dried fruit and citrus, then add a few extra—for Rion and one for Nolan too, as an explanation in case he wakes to find me gone.

There's a Salt priest standing across from the bakery as I leave. He gives me a languid, closed-mouth smile, then turns away as a young woman approaches him, hand folded and eyes lowered. Taking a pinch of salt from a pouch around his neck, he proceeds to sprinkle it on her tongue. I watch the ritual play out, then continue on my way. The blessing—which is what I assume it to be—seems strange, though it shouldn't be. On the mainland, Tempestra-Innara's clerics can be found on their cities' streets offering similar, sans seasoning. And yet, I'd somehow imagined the priests keeping entirely to their baths, hidden away, even if their practices are no more a secret than the baked goods I carry.

I eat as I walk, the fresh pastry divine in the way only good food can be, with a hint of something to it, a flavor I don't recognize. Some exotic spice, maybe. Leaves or seeds or roots preserved and dried, ground or powdered, all borne here on the tides, traveling more of the world than I ever have. All to add a pleasant, fragrant note to a bit of bread.

Something plunges in me, wondering if this small, paltry taste of existence beyond the Goddess is the most I'll ever achieve. We'd been close, so close. But now Machias is dead, an abrupt end to the trail we'd been following. I can only hope that Rion has some insight into who we are looking for, and that I can tease it out of him without revealing too much about what we're really after in Cyprene. But when I reach the bookshop, the windows are shuttered and the door locked. Knocking yields no response, and while I could wait for him to show up, there's no knowing how long that will be, or how Nolan might react if he wakes to find me gone.

As I ponder my options, a pale gray flicker reflects off the windowpane.

The Salt priest again, taken up on another corner. No smile this time, only an interest that makes me pull my hood lower and start moving. A few buildings away, I glance back. The priest is where I left him, still staring. I hasten my step. Head for the Petrel, but by a different route, weaving through the twists and turns of the city. Every so often I stop and wait, but there's no pursuit. Still, I keep to the busiest streets, then abruptly cut down a long, narrow alley. Not a desirable avenue—it's empty, save for rats and refuse—but if memory serves, it will dump me only a few streets from the relative safety of the guesthouse.

I'm nearly there when a figure cuts across the other end. The uniform is unmistakable: another Salt priest. But not the one I saw earlier.

No, that one is waiting when I retreat, blocking the only way out of the alley. In tandem, they approach, squeezing me in between them. I draw a sickle but keep it lowered.

"Can I help you gentlemen?" I keep it light. Smile wide. Because I don't know what's going on here. Two priests don't exactly scare me, but after the Renderers and their fancy little poison darts, safety is the last thing I should assume. "Just got my salty blessing yesterday, so I'm good right now."

The first priest, the one who followed me to the bookshop, smiles calmly. "We haven't come to deliver a blessing, rather a message: Marzela is very disappointed in your employer."

Marzela? The priest from the first salt baths we visited. "Oh? Huh, I know he seemed interested in partaking of your lovely pools, but he's been a bit busy. I'm sure he'll be along once he—"

"She would like him to know that if he'd been upfront about what he *really* had to offer, there would have been an opportunity to deal."

*Ah.* Well, well, well . . . someone's been talking to the Salt priests. Ramiro? Maybe, but the disdain in his voice when he mentioned them doesn't make him a likely collaborator. There was the Caerula taking the bribe the morning we met Marzela, though. I'd assumed it was to keep authority off their doorstep, but maybe it ensured information flowed over it too.

I shrug. "He could have been a bit less oblique, I'll give you that. Unfortunately, I can't speak for him. His business, his reasons to be careful around how he engages in it."

The other priest takes a step closer. "He lied to those he chose to deal with, left them with only a taste of what he had to offer. But there's more."

Not a question.

"Marzela would like to acquire it." The first priest again.

"What's not clear here, gentlemen? Bodyguard. Not proxy."

"You'll inform him of what we've communicated. He had the chance to flee Cyprene and didn't, which Marzela understands as a desire to not leave empty-handed. She will assist in that."

What had Ramiro said, about Machias profiting off the Salt Sects? So, Salt priests are trying to cut out the middleman. Makes sense, given their middleman is dead. "Sure. I'll do that. But you're going to have to let me out of this alley first."

The first man nods. "She looks forward to speaking with you again..." Both priests begin backing away. "*Soon.*"

And with that vaguely threatening farewell, I'm alone.

# Thirty-five

The waters welcome all those that seek their embrace. And some that don't.

—CYPRENE SAYING

I GO STRAIGHT TO NOLAN'S suite to wake him, but have barely managed a single knock when the door flies open.

"Are you mad, going out alone?"

Despite the question, there's less anger in it than I expected. "Being passed out for a whole day will leave you with an appetite." I step inside, toss him the roll. "Snuck out for some breakfast."

He catches it. Sets it on the table with barely a glance. "Did you see anyone when you went?"

Again, a distinct lack of chastising, which is suspicious to say the least. And there's a brightness to his eyes, a frantic energy about him that seems out of place in someone who was lamenting failure not long ago. I thought he'd regained some composure after the outburst on the beach. Maybe I was wrong. "As a matter of fact, I had a little run-in with a couple of Salt priests."

He blinks, then shakes his head. "No, not them. Anyone else?"

"Why?"

He grabs a fold of paper from where it sits beside the ignored pastry. "I found this slipped under my door."

"This wasn't there when I woke up." There's a short note written within.

*We regret the Caerula's involvement in our recent affair, and bear you no ill will around Machias's unfortunate end. Your business—which we would make ours—remains unfinished. Come at nightfall tomorrow, the Shrine of the Final Tide.*

I read it once, then again. No signature. Nothing else that might indicate who sent it. "You missed this being delivered?"

"You weren't the only one who was exhausted."

But the tight way he says it betrays him. Someone was sneaky enough to get into the Petrel, up to the landing outside the door, and then leave this note without a trace. Not exactly a comforting thought given the current circumstances.

"You think this is from the heretics Machias was with?"

"Who else?"

"This"—I hold up the paper—"is not exactly forthcoming, information-wise. And it sounds about as much like a trap as it can without a postscript that literally says *This is a trap*. Anyone could have left this. The Caerula. The Salt priests."

His mouth opens to retort, closes, then opens again. "The Salt priests?"

"Yup. Guess who is well informed enough to find out about what you were trying to sell? According to two of her errand boys—who cornered me in an alley, by the way; I'm fine, thanks for asking—Marzela is quite offended that she didn't get a chance to put in a bid."

Nolan mulls this over. "If she sent someone after you, also sending a note wouldn't make much sense."

"No. But it still could be the Caerula."

"Trying to trap us instead of just surrounding the Petrel and dragging us out?"

I throw up my hands. "I don't know, maybe they figured they'd inconvenienced Hiram enough."

"No," says Nolan. "This *has* to be from the heretics."

"Who," I remind him, "include Renderers. Trap. Trap trap trap."

"We don't know they know we're Chosen."

"We don't know they don't!"

He rips the note away. "We don't have any other leads!" Another flash of rage, another glimmer of the beach.

I hold my ground. "That doesn't give us a reason to do something stupid."

Nolan takes a breath, steadying himself. "I know. I *know*. But give me an option that isn't."

He's got me there. *Rion*, I almost blurt, but that was never really tangible. The note, on the other hand, is real. And if the heretics want us dead, there's no reason to send us an invitation to our deaths; they could have thrown that surprise party right here and now, easily taken us unaware, apparently.

Still . . .

Nolan isn't a fool. But desperation limns him, more than ever. *This isn't over.* No matter the setback, he won't . . . he *can't* fathom giving up the search for the reliquary any more than I can. Which means giving into that desperation, taking a chance that any other time, any other place, would be downright idiotic. But we both want what we want—him to become Tempestra's next avatar, me to kill them. And failure most likely means a lifetime of the aching distance from them that's picking us both apart, bit by bit.

It might be a trap. It's *probably* a trap.

But Nolan's already decided something I'm just coming around to: that we don't have a choice.

As a rule, it's wise to be early to a potential trap.

Better to have the chance to survey your meeting place and the best ways to escape it. So that's what we decide on. Neither of us remembers the appointed shrine from our explorations, and when we ask a street vendor hawking smoked fish about it, he gives us a confused, suspicious look before rattling off directions.

The Shrine of the Last Tide lies near the cliffs that overlook the docks, though turned away from them, out of view. A single, narrow footpath snakes down to it, barely wide enough for one person in spots, with a sheer wall of white stone on one side and exactly nothing to prevent a fall to the crashing waves on the other. A fine, salty spray anoints us as we finally reach a wider set of stairs that descends into a sort of open cavern, with an overhang of cliff acting as a ceiling. It reminds me of the drawing Rion showed me, but there are none of the Salt devotees' elaborate carvings here, a fact that catches in my throat like a swallowed rock, though I'm not sure why. The only decoration is tiered platforms of rock that circle a landing that slopes into the sea. Waves lap about halfway up it, around the tops of three stone posts.

"A strange sort of shrine." Damp shadows fall across Nolan as he methodically takes in our surroundings.

"I think that's because the only prayers said here were ones for mercy." I point. "Look at the tide lines. And the posts."

The sea is moving toward low tide, revealing rusted, pitted metal rings set into the stone pillars.

"Ah," says Nolan, understanding.

There's a tidy brutality to it. Tie the condemned up and wait for the water to rise. They'd endure hours of anticipation before the end came, torture that didn't spill a drop of blood. I've always thought Tempestra-Innara was ruthless. Turns out crossing the Salt Goddess wasn't a good idea either.

Nolan goes down to where the sloping stone begins. "Whoever sent that note has a sense of efficiency. One way down, one way up. An ideal setup if you're planning on an ambush."

I pick up a shard of shell and toss it into the water. "Disposing of the bodies would be a snap too."

Nolan sighs and stares back over the waves. "No, not bothered by the possible death trap," he mutters. "Why *would* you be?"

Oh, I am. Because I can't quite shake that this location is meant to convey a message. Somehow, I doubt the shrine has remained unused since the Salt Goddess's defeat, not with its remote locale and convenient, scream-muffling waves. "Do you want to leave? While we still can?"

No answer, but the expression on his face is enough.

I sit down to wait. Nolan, on the other hand, remains standing, pacing across the space, moving close to the posts to examine them, then pacing again.

"You're making me anxious," I snap. "Would you please relax?"

"And be caught off guard?"

"You aren't supposed to be worried about a threat, you're supposed to be trying to gain trust. Which you're not going to do walking around like a cat caught on a roof."

*That* he considers, chewing it over for a full minute before begrudgingly joining me on the lowest stone tier. The wind picks up a bit, chilly despite the warmth of the setting sun, which has finally dropped low enough to paint the cavern in lemony light. Long shadows sprout from the stone pillars, grim fixtures to pass the time with.

"Weird to picture, isn't it?" I lean onto my elbows. "Chain up the criminals—or blasphemers, or whoever the Salt Goddess found sufficiently irritating—and wait for the water to come back in. Do you think the crowds gathered to watch the whole thing, or only when it was almost drowning time?"

"I don't know," says Nolan. "It's barbaric to make someone wait so long to die. Cruel."

"Compared to immolation?"

"At least the flame is quick."

"Dead either way, in the end. I guess that's what matters." I wonder if we are being observed. Again, I picture the crowds that must have gathered here, once, watching as death rose inch by inch. "Do you ever think about what it was like back then?"

"Back when?"

"When more than one god was still alive. When *all* the gods were still alive."

Nolan shrugs noncommittally. "There is only the Goddess now."

"Yeah, but people used to be able to decide which deity to devote themselves to. If there'd been a choice . . . do you think you would have chosen Tempestra-Innara?"

I expect a rebuke of my near blasphemy. And it almost comes, Nolan's features pinching in the way they do when I've said something particularly offensive. Then, he stops himself, eyes falling.

"I'll admit it's been odd," he says finally, "seeing what goes on here. The devotions of the Salt priests. Cyprene's carvings and sculptures. Proof of how devoted the Salt Goddess's followers once were. I . . ." He stops himself again, considering his next words. "It's heresy to worship any other god but our blood mother. But in the past, if they weren't the only divinity I'd ever known . . . it would be ignorant to say I'd know for sure where my devotion would fall."

An acerbic truth, not easily admitted. And a marker. Before the incident with the Caerula, before the beach and my realization of his true motives, would he have answered the same? No. I'm sure of it. I wonder if it's a relief, sharing his aspiration with another, instead of staying curled around it, pushing it into the deepest part of himself.

A minute passes before I realize it's not curiosity I'm feeling, but jealousy. Maybe, like me, Nolan has lived with a secret for years. His desire to become an avatar could have been born long before the heretics tried to kill Tempestra-Innara, and their growing weakness made it an actual possibility. It's strange to think that the same seemingly impossible occurrence unlocked a new door for both of us. Now, even as desperation wears on him, having that part of himself revealed to another has seemed to soften something in Nolan. Made him more willing to mete out other pieces of himself too.

I can't do the same.

We fall silent, my thoughts anything but. They crash like the nearby waves, persistent and unrelenting, as the sun begins to set. Below them is the measured evenness of Nolan's breath, a calming rhythm I latch onto. Someday, maybe, I'll be able to sit with someone else like this, like I sat with Rion, in a time where secrets and threats aren't the keystones holding up my life. Still, this isn't the worst thing, watching the sun set with Nolan, its light warming the both of us until, almost suddenly, it is gone, leaving the shrine coated in a watery dark.

Only then do the footsteps come. We jump to our feet, turning toward the sound that had been muffled by the waves, which had permitted the sole cloaked figure on the stairs to get closer than our senses would have normally allowed. They are narrow and hooded, but there's a relaxed set to their stance that eases my wariness.

"I hope I didn't keep you waiting long."

In an instant, what relief I felt disappears. The voice is a familiar one. From the tensing of Nolan beside me, I know he recognizes it too.

On the stairs, the figure peels back its hood to reveal Avery, smiling down at us.

# *Thirty-six*

Prior Nils has not been heard from in over a month. The prudent course would be to claim an accident. A body will be found, an interment arranged. As to the disappearance, I will send some of my most discreet clerics to investigate in Cyprene. I fear, however, that any trail is long cold.

—FROM THE LETTERS OF HIGH CLERIC OF THE BLOOD SAMARA
TO PRIOR SUPERIOR JUNIAN, ERA OF TEMPESTRA-INNARA

I SENSE NOLAN'S SURPRISE IN the background of my own as the blood rises in my ears.

It *is* a trap . . . I just don't know what kind.

But as Avery calmly descends the stairs, he shows no sign of recognition. Curious and confused, I follow suit.

"Thank you for coming." Avery speaks as if he's invited us to a dinner party. No cleric garb below his cloak, of course. Not in Cyprene. Suddenly, I wonder if the vision I saw of him on the way back from the botched meeting wasn't a product of the salve. Has Avery been here, watching us? "We weren't sure you would."

"We?" says Nolan.

Avery doesn't expand on this, merely offers a patient, closed smile. "Especially after your recent involvement with the Caerula, and our . . . friend. I want to assure you that nothing like that will happen here, and that I've come alone."

Nolan stands taller. "And who *are* you, exactly?"

"My name is Avery," he replies, "though that is irrelevant. What isn't is you, the goods you are peddling, and how you came by them. And what inspired you to smuggle them here, instead of selling them on the mainland."

"A desire not to burn," Nolan says curtly. "As to how I came by them, do you care?"

Does Avery know that what we have came from the Renderers in Sethane? Machias didn't get a chance to tell them, but maybe he had other ways of finding out. Then again, if so, why this meeting? Something is off. I know it. I'm sure Nolan knows it. But if we want answers, Avery is the only one who can give them.

"If you *are* interested," Nolan continues, "rest assured that there's more. If you aren't . . . I have other buyers."

"Do you? Ones that won't cut your throat or turn you in to the Caerula?"

"How do I know *you* aren't planning to do exactly that? I know nothing about you, or who you represent. And one of your people is already dead, because he chose suspicion over a deal that benefitted us both."

"Well, first, I suspect she'd get in the way." Avery's gaze flicks to mine and holds it briefly. "And yes, Machias is dead. We mourn for him. But you need to understand that Cyprene is . . . complicated. He acted in a way he believed served our interests, when he expected a fragile peace with the Caerula to be upset by your association with Tychus. However, the collective that I represent wants what you have, more than anyone else in Cyprene. Enough to make us overlook what happened."

"Is that so?" Nolan sounds suitably intrigued.

"Some may wish to indulge in the blissful intoxication of the divine, others to use it to better commune with their chosen deities. But us?" Avery pauses meaningfully. "We have more specific uses for it."

Clever. He's all but told Nolan that they are the heretics who attacked Tempestra-Innara, who would use the Renderers' creations as a weapon against the very Chosen they were made from. The truth, technically.

"Frankly, I don't care what purpose you use it for. Not as long as I'm paid what it's worth." Words tinged with greed.

I get the sensation of watching a play, one where the audience knows more than the characters being played by the actors, though I don't quite get the plot. If Avery's heretics truly want the Renderers' wares—and maybe they do—why not simply kill us and take them? Why *this* instead?

"We'd need a sample first, of course," say Avery.

"You're welcome to try—"

"No," Avery interrupts. "I don't wish to test it. Not here. If we find it acceptable, though, we will, of course, compensate you."

Nolan appears to wrestle with the request, as any good seller would. "Even a small amount of my product is worth a fortune. And you want me to simply hand it over to you, a stranger?"

"You came here to find the best buyer for what you offer. And who I represent understands discretion. We stay informed." Avery pauses. "For example, about the Salt Sects' renewed interest in you." I fight to keep my surprise hidden. That was fast. "That knowledge doesn't run both ways. We can offer true secrecy, along with whatever price you ask."

Again, Nolan appears to deliberate. But Avery is good. If we were legitimate, this might be the beginning of a lucrative relationship. And all the while, not a hint of our prior familiarity seeps out, not a knowing expression or look that lingers too long.

Finally, Nolan nods at me. I take out a vial of blood tincture and approach Avery with what I hope is a sufficient amount of caution. *You're doing fine*, his eyes seem to say, a sentiment I'm not sure I agree with. I slip the vial into his waiting hand.

Avery pockets the profane treasure. "If my associates are satisfied that it is what you say it is, then we can discuss our partnership further."

"Of course," says Nolan.

Avery inclines his head. First at Nolan, then, markedly, at me. "We will be in contact."

When he's disappeared around a bend in the stone, Nolan lets out an aggrieved breath.

"You want to follow him." It's not a question.

"Of course I do. But if he notices, or has anyone keeping watch, we'll lose all chance of gaining their trust."

Right. After such a spectacular failure, another chance has presented itself, and it's clear Nolan will do anything to make his way into the heretics' confidence. Even be patient.

Unfortunately, I get the sense it's not him they're really interested in.

I watch from the window of my room. Near midnight, my persistence is rewarded, a slim figure appearing in the shadowed alley below. It gazes up at my room, and when I make no move to conceal myself, a hand beckons. While I might be able to sneak by Nolan's room without alerting him, I don't want to risk Hiram or any late-night customers seeing me leave, so I open the window and climb out. It's easy enough to make my way down the slope of roof, then scale the ragged stonework (though my still-healing shoulder doesn't skimp on the complaints). By the time I land lightly on the cobblestones, the figure is gone, but I follow the direction it must have come from. I spot it again on the next street. It lets me pursue, giving no indication of our destination, but never letting me lose sight of them either. With every step I question my sanity, calculate the odds of this being the last foolish decision I make in a lifetime not lacking in them, but not once do I consider turning back.

Finally, we arrive at a familiar location: the shrine of Tempestra-Innara. It's as empty at night as during the day, gloomy and forlorn. The figure—Avery, as expected—waits for me at the base of the statue. He smiles as if we are old friends; meanwhile, my senses strain for any sound, any movement, anything that might indicate we aren't on our lonesome. But there is nothing. Only the neglected monument and its sad, rotten offerings.

I stop a few paces away and wait for him to speak. Because I have no idea how to start this.

"Hello, Lys," he says, not giving me much to work with.

"I see you cut yourself free."

"Only because I was alive enough to do so." He tips his head in acknowledgment of my small mercy. "I thought you might want to catch up somewhere we can speak a little more freely."

Again, I search the area, wondering if we are being observed. But there's no more itch of eyes here than at the shrine. "And what exactly is it that we have to speak about? Oh, is it about how you showed up out of nowhere and didn't bother to tell Nolan that you were the cleric I'd met outside Novena?"

"I thought *you* would have done that by now. Or maybe you have?"

I wait before responding, still trying to pick out his intentions. "No. Have you told your friends here about me?"

He considers me briefly in turn. "I've said enough. They know you're both Chosen, that you're hunting us. And that you didn't kill me when you had the chance ... which is the reason they agreed to let me contact you. That, and your actions in Cyprene were beginning to draw unwanted notice."

So, not revealing our prior interlude to Nolan was calculated to show me I could trust him. But this isn't coming together. "You knew who we were, that we were here, and what we were up to. Meanwhile, we knew nothing about you ... until now. I have to be honest, I'm a little surprised we are still alive. Because if I had that unquestionable advantage over someone tracking me, I'd take it." I pause. "Or were you waiting for your Renderer friends from Sethane to arrive and deal with us?"

"I take it there's no chance of that?"

I shake my head.

"Ah," says Avery. "Not the avenue we would have taken, regardless. Just so you know. There are no Renderers here."

"Comforting." If it's the truth. "Did you come here immediately after I left you in the woods?"

"I had planned to remain on the mainland, but after our encounter, it seemed the wisest course of action."

"And how long have you been watching us in Cyprene?"

"Since soon after your arrival."

"So why haven't you killed us?"

"Well..." Avery's chin lifts, a questioning look in his eyes. "Because then I wouldn't have an explanation for why I'm alive."

"The Goddess is merciful. Maybe I can be too."

"We both know the Goddess's mercy would never stretch so far as to spare a known heretic, especially one masquerading as their cleric."

Can't argue that. "You're right. Maybe it was a mistake."

I draw a sickle and move toward Avery, forcing him to step back. But with the statue of Tempestra-Innara behind him, there's nowhere to go. I see a flicker of fear on his face; he's wondering if he's miscalculated. Only for a moment, though; after it passes, he simply waits, as if resigned to his fate.

Good. If his resolve had broken, if he'd broken down and begged for his life, I probably wouldn't have been able to get the next part out.

Nolan isn't the only one beginning to get desperate.

"You want to know why you are alive?" I say. "Because I know what you are trying to do." His fear turns to uncertainty as I resheath my weapon and take a breath. "There are two key parts to this situation. The first is that you and your heretical friends tried to kill Tempestra-Innara, and that you plan to try again. The second . . ." Here we are, the crux of the matter. The part that's likely to get me killed, one way or another. "The second—and far more important one—is . . . is that I want to help."

I give him a minute with that. A generous one. After all, it's not every day that one of the Goddess's Chosen professes to wanting to take them out. And I need it too; finally speaking that truth aloud feels like an unexpected blow to my solar plexus.

Like skin flayed back, revealing innards below.

Like the emptied aftermath of a particularly bad case of food poisoning.

I cross my arms over my quivering gut, willing my heart to slow. To not give away my own apprehension. This seemed like a good idea a minute ago. And maybe it is. But I don't have Nolan's silver tongue, his calculating subtlety that might have navigated this game with intricate caution. I'm showing Avery my whole hand and hoping I haven't fucked up completely.

I expect more fear from him, confusion, maybe even an accusation of mistruth, but he merely nods his understanding.

Which needles. "You *believe* me?"

"Are you lying?"

"No," I say. "It's only that . . . well, I expected to be challenged a bit more on that particular revelation. I've only been keeping it secreted away for most of my life."

A smile touches his lips. "It's certainly a first in regards to confessions

I've heard. And yes, hard to believe. I had my suspicions but . . . I never really imagined that any of the Goddess's Chosen would—*could*—turn on them."

"What can I say?" I shrug. "I'm not like other Chosen."

"After what you said to me in the woods, about the Goddess's mercy . . . when you didn't kill me even though you must have known who I was . . ." He trails off. "You've been a mystery, Lys, ever since we met. I'm glad to finally have some answers, even if I still don't understand why."

"Why what?"

"Why you would betray such a coveted life."

Suddenly, I feel like the vulnerable one. As if my revelation were a blade I handled, only to have Avery turn it back on me. "I shouldn't have to explain myself to a heretic."

"So-called heretic," Avery counters. "I know the power of the gods. What I don't believe is that we were meant to be ruled by only one."

"And I believe that when the Goddess is dead, I'll be free for the first time in my life. That *everyone* will be liberated from an era of divine rule that's obviously run its course. Actually, no, I really only care about me. The rest of the world can take up worshipping frogs and fiddleheads for all I care. So long as I don't have to be a part of it."

Another patient smile.

"Here's the deal," I continue, done with that subject. "We know about the reliquary." No reaction; he must have known—or at least expected—we'd been informed about the particular *hows* surrounding the assassination attempt. "Emmaus failed because he was too weak to handle the effects of the dead god's blood. But I'm already chock-full of divinity; I've been blessed by it, and survived that blessing. Which means the chances are much, *much* higher that I'll be able to control it. I came here to find it, take it from you. But we can make this easy: Hand the reliquary over, I'll take my shot at my dear blood mother. Hopefully, I'll win. And then we all get what we're after, yay!"

"Lys . . ." Despite the unparalleled offer, Avery has the *audacity* to shake his head. "It's not that simple."

"It sure can be. You have the reliquary. I have the capability. What else do we need?" Besides a whole lot of good luck.

My enthusiasm doesn't sway him. "Okay, say I believe you. It isn't my decision alone. The others will want to be certain that you're serious. What if I lead you to them and this is a trick? I was willing to risk my life, Lys, but not my friends'. I'd rather you killed me here."

"It's not a trick!"

"I need proof," he says.

"Um, you work with *Renderers*. The fact that I'm willing to ignore that should say something."

"All that says is that you'd gamble your life to get close to the only thing that can destroy the Goddess. I bet most of the other Chosen would happily do that too."

My mouth drops open, but of course I've got nothing. Avery is right to be cautious, and there isn't exactly anything I can do or say to make him trust me implicitly. "Fine. I can't prove what I'm saying is true. But what exactly was your backup plan for if Emmaus failed? And is it anything better than what I'm offering?"

He's quiet before conceding: "No."

"So how do we make this work?"

His eyes narrow pensively as he chews something over, suspicion and fear intermixing with temptation. "After this, what you've said . . . I need to talk to the others."

"You should know that my"—I fumble the word a bit—"*partner* is squarely on the Goddess's side. The time you bought with him today won't last. How long?"

"A few days. And any impatience on his part will be fruitless. He won't find us if we don't want to be found." Avery turns grave, trotting out the placating cleric voice. "Lys, I want to believe you. I really do. Give me time to work. Go back to your partner and keep him in check as much as you can. What you are offering is . . . well, it's a chance none of us would have ever imagined. But I don't know if that means they'll be willing to hand over the reliquary."

My cheeks warm with frustration. His reasoning is sound. But the minute I let Avery out of my sight, I run the risk of losing him—and my chance at freedom—forever. This isn't Nolan and me inching our way toward the reliquary. It's right *here*, dangling just beyond my reach, on the other side of a deal with Avery. I don't want to let him go. But if I don't, the only thing I'll ensure is failure.

"I take a chance on you," I say, "so that you can take a chance on me."

"Yes. Let this be a beginning. Or kill me now, if you can't trust me. But even if you make it seem an accident, I guarantee the others will know what happened, go to ground even deeper than they are now."

As is happening too frequently lately, I don't have much of a choice. "Okay. We have a deal."

Avery nods. "I'll contact you when I can."

He starts to leave.

I grab his arm. Fear reappears on his face. "This is the part where I threaten you. Swear to find you if you don't come through, and make you pay." I release him instead. "But the reality is that we want the same thing."

"If that's true," he replies, diminutive smile reappearing, "then all you need to do is have a little faith."

# Thirty-seven

> If only Cyprene were not so far. Heretical rot such as thrives there would not, could not, grow in the Goddess's light.
>
> —WRITINGS OF PRIOR ESDEN

*FAITH.*

I wake, still exhausted, from turbulent dreams, the word still ringing in my ears. Of all the weapons I know, faith is one of the sharpest. And the most brittle. Faith didn't spare my birth family or our village, it didn't save the devoted in the Cathedral, it didn't carry Emmaus through the assassination or free Magda from her cell. Now Avery wants me to put what frail version of it I carry into believing he can convince the other heretics that our goal is the same. All based on the fact that they know who we are, why we're here, and that they've left us untouched so far.

Then again, I've seen conviction balanced on less.

A few hours of restless sleep. It's all I've managed, shoulder wound aching like a reminder as I make my way downstairs. No surprises left at my door, or Nolan's. It's too soon for a message from Avery, but part of me hopes Hiram might have one waiting. Or, at the very least, coffee. But when I reach the common room, it's deserted, save for Rion, who is sitting at the bar. No drink, no book, only a small, rough-hewn wooden box sitting on the counter before him.

"Morning."

He looks up at the greeting, worry etched on his face.

I don't smell coffee. Or bread or bacon, or anything else that has greeted each morning at the Petrel so far. "Where's Hiram?"

Rion turns back to the box. "He wasn't here when I arrived. This was, though."

"What is it?"

"I don't know."

There's less uncertainty than the words convey. He might not know what's in the box, but from his tone and demeanor, he knows it's nothing good. I make a cursory search of the kitchen and the yard out back, but the proprietor is nowhere to be found. I return to the common room, draw one sickle.

"Why don't you stand back?"

Rion follows my instruction as I use the point to gingerly lift the lid. A bed of gray crystals lies within.

"Salt?" I take a pinch, feeling the grit of it between my fingers.

"It appears so," says Rion.

No, not only salt. There's a spot of pink. I brush some of the crystals to the side and the pink turns to red. Then, something else appears, grayish brown and blotched purple.

"Is that—?"

"Yup, a finger." A man's little finger from the size of it, severed roughly, jagged ends of flesh left behind. "And whatever was used to chop it off could use a sharpening."

Rion's mouth thins into a grim cut. "They would have used the edge of a shell."

"A shell?" Cold understanding forms. After all, it's not exactly subtle. "The Salt priests did this?"

"Appears so. Your employer's business in Cyprene seems to be making him more than a few enemies."

"He's still working on how to negotiate effectively." My gut twists. Apparently, Marzela doesn't appreciate being ignored. "Why Hiram?"

"To send a message, I expect," says Rion. "To you. To anyone helping you."

My hand tightens around my sickle. "Is he still alive?"

"I think if he wasn't, the box would be bigger. No, this looks like an . . . invitation." Rion closes the box, a storminess in his eyes. But by the time he turns to me again, they've softened with concern. "What should we do?"

"You should go make coffee." Angry heat gathers in my chest, along with the unwise desire to let it loose on the Salt priests. And if not for Avery . . . No. I cannot—*will* not—lose control now. Gotta do this smart. "And wake up Nolan. I need to run a quick errand. But after that . . . we're going to go get Hiram."

Rion insists on coming as far as the baths with us. "The Salt Sects aren't usually violent," he explains as we make our way there. "But sometimes they can be rather . . . determined."

"Clearly." Nolan stops us a few streets away. "Please, let me deal with this from here. It's my fault Hiram has been harmed. I need to find a way to resolve it."

Rion starts to protest, but I take his arm, turning him toward me. "If he can't resolve it with words, I have my little ways too."

The bookseller smirks with dark amusement. "If I could be of assistance . . ."

"This isn't your fight. Is there somewhere you can go that's safe for a while? In case they decide you've been too friendly to us as well?"

"I . . ." He nods. "Yes."

"Then go. We'll stop by the shop and leave something to let you know when it's safe."

He raises one eyebrow. "Not a finger, I hope?"

I wink. "Not unless the Salt priests make me deal with this the hard way."

When Rion is gone, we continue to Marzela's salt baths, where Nolan knocks on the door. The old woman herself is revealed when it opens. "Please, enter."

Nolan obeys, leaving me to follow. Within, Marzela closes the door behind us, hands disappearing beneath the arms of her diaphanous robe. She smiles as blandly as at our first visit, but the welcoming air is gone. Now, there's the sense of a facade, of what's on the surface not matching what lies beneath. Maybe we should have expected it. As innocuous as the Salt Sects had seemed initially, nothing in Cyprene would persist without some measure of cunning.

"Where's Hiram?" I snap.

"Below." Marzela is calm, unperturbed.

"Alive?" Nolan speaks tranquilly as well, but there's an edge to his voice.

"Alive," Marzela confirms. "And there's no reason for that to change. He's settled his part in this for now. You, on the other hand . . ."

"Tell me what you want," Nolan says, "and be done with it."

But Marzela only moves deeper into the baths, leaving Nolan and me no choice but to follow. The pools are empty—no communing bathers, though more Salt priests line the walls, watching us as we make our way down the center path. I find no malice in their faces, but there isn't on Marzela's either, and she worked in a dismemberment before breakfast.

"Cyprene is strong." Marzela stops in the midst of the pools, turning back to us. "As strong as the stone that surrounds it. But, like anything, it has its vulnerable spots. Its systems and rules that must be followed in order for its . . . conflicting forces to remain harmonious." She pauses. "Such were our agreements with the Caerula."

Nolan's chin tips up, a little haughty. "If you have a point, I'd ask you to skip directly to it."

There's a brief flash of amusement on Marzela's features. "Even if you'd been upfront about what you had to offer, going behind Ramiro's back on such significant trade would have upset our particular balance. But now, he and his Caerula think you have fled the island."

"A notion that you haven't enlightened them about."

"No. And which now frees us up to deal more openly. Ramiro doesn't understand, of course. He does not know what it is to taste the divine, to reach out to Astris and truly feel their touch."

Nolan scoffs. "But you do. And you want to keep that going, even though Machias, your usual supplier, is now dead. Frankly, sounds as if you need me more than I need you. There are buyers on the mainland, though, and I'm beginning to wonder how wise it is to bother with Cyprene any further."

Marzela looks around at the Salt priests watching us. *Surrounding* us. "Forgive me, I didn't mean to imply this was optional. It is not. But I did hope we might be able to put aside the past; after all, Cyprene is Cyprene. We will happily buy what you've brought here, now and in the future. But if you refuse, well ... then we will simply take what you have and count it as a generous gift from the Salt Goddess."

"Take what we have, you mean," Nolan echoes, "and dispose of us."

Marzela tips her head graciously. "The waves welcome all."

A few heartbeats pass, during which I very much wish to turn those clear pools red, but I wait for some direction from Nolan.

"I dislike being pressured into a deal," he says with a sigh, "but I understand your position. Cyprene is Cyprene, as you said. I suppose I have to respect its customs."

Marzela grins.

"But after that unfortunate encounter in the cliffs, and the circumstances of this invitation, I didn't think it prudent to bring my wares along."

The Salt priest's gaze jumps to me.

I raise my hands. "Go on, search. Nothing, I promise. And you won't find it at the Petrel either."

"Everything has been hidden away to allow *me* to deal more freely," Nolan continues. "You could be rid of us, but that would leave you to have to search every inch of Cyprene. An inconvenience, to say the least." He waits a beat. "And might even draw unwanted attention from the Caerula."

Finally, Marzela's calm demeanor ripples, giving way to displeasure.

"But I think we'd both be happier getting what we're after," Nolan continues. "Violence may have quick results, but rarely benefits long-term. Do you agree?"

Marzela clearly isn't pleased, but she nods. "It does seem that the most beneficial thing for both of us would be to come to an agreement."

"I will certainly take it under consideration," Nolan counters, "but you aren't the only interested party, you understand. There are other sects, other buyers."

The Salt priest's features cloud further. "You place a deal before me, then pull it away?"

"Not in the least. I will trade with whoever makes me the best offer. Whether that is you or one of your counterparts." He smiles pleasantly. "Or all of you, if you choose to combine efforts. As you said, we are now able to deal more freely. But until I've had the time to reach back out to the other sects, all paths to the divine will remain safely hidden away. Oh, and I would ask that Hiram be released now. As you said, he's settled with you."

At first, I think Nolan's tongue has failed to sway Marzela. He's called her bluff, dared her to make threats again and risk losing her desired prize entirely. And maybe she's tempted to do so. Certainly, the old woman looks as if she's taken a sip of seawater when she expected fresh. Then, her jaw loosens and I see the desperate desire beneath the intimidation and posturing—the hungry need for the Renderers' wares, to get closer to the deity she believes is waiting, just out of reach. One hand snaps up. More Salt priests appear, Hiram walking between them. His hand is bandaged, spots of dark red soaking through the fabric.

"Safe and sound," Marzela says, "as promised."

"Not sound." I meet Hiram halfway, flanking him as he joins Nolan and me. He has a touch of pallor but otherwise appears as usual. Even somewhat bored, as if the events of the morning are commonplace, bordering on tedious. "Are you okay?"

He nods. "S'only the little finger. Won't slow me down too much."

His blunt, serene acceptance of it sets off my anger again. I turn around, scanning every face of every priest, meeting every set of eyes. "I'd just like to make one thing clear." I speak slowly, making sure I am heard. "If this were my decision—if I had even a sliver of a choice in the matter—I'd leave every single one of you in the exact same condition as Hiram." *Or worse.* I let that remain unspoken.

"Lucky for all of you," says Nolan, "it is *not* her decision. Now. I'll be taking my leave."

Marzela's stare could melt ice. "Do *not* leave us waiting long . . . again."

Nolan only grins placidly at the veiled hostility. "Once I've reached out to the other Salt Sects, I'll entertain all offers, including yours. Which I'll expect to be delivered in a more conventional manner than your last correspondence."

I don't relax fully until we are out of the baths and well away from their zealous, salty miasma.

"I am very sorry," Nolan says to Hiram. It's his place to say it, true, but I'm surprised to hear genuine emotion in his voice. "They harmed you for helping us, when you had no real reason to. If there was some way to undo the damage done, I would make it happen."

Hiram's head hangs a bit as we travel. "Never did like the Salt priests any more than the Caerula," he mutters.

"We should return to the Petrel," I say. "I can clean and bandage that wound." And see if Avery has left any messages. It's only been a few hours, but now that Hiram is safe, I'm anxious to hear from my heretic friend again.

Suddenly, Hiram stops. We've reached an avenue that curves along a cliff, one that overlooks the harbor. Noise filters up from below, a buzz of voices, far more than the typical level of daily activity. It's indistinct, but the wind carries a clear note of apprehension. As much as I want to get back, I don't object when we shift our path to investigate. We reach the outskirts of the docks, where a crowd has gathered around a large frigate that appears freshly arrived. There's a pile of crates beside us; I climb onto one for a better vantage. The name of the ship—the *Golden Glory*—doesn't answer any questions. Neither does the appearance of Ramiro on its deck.

"What is it?" Nolan strains to see over the crowd.

"I'm not sure." The last thing that should come as a surprise is a ship arriving. Even a particularly large, affluent-looking ship. But when another figure appears beside the Caerula leader, a sensation like a punch catches me below the ribs. "Fuck."

It's Caius.

Standing tall and straight, stark as snow in his Arbiter's cassock, he gazes out serenely over the gathered citizens of Cyprene.

"Huh," Hiram grunts from below. "Figures this day would only get worse."

# Thirty-eight

This city is a remote, aching hell. And I have my doubts as to how deep the devotion of its local militia runs. In my opinion, the Goddess's Chosen have little purpose and less solace here. Which would make it the perfect posting for a rival one desired to see ensconced well out of the way.

—FROM THE PRIVATE CORRESPONDENCE OF CLERIC DELO TO HIGH CLERIC OF THE BLOOD SULLIVAS

AN ARBITER. IN CYPRENE.
When that might have last occurred, I have no idea. But given the jeers from the docks that followed Caius's appearance, it's been a while.

On the mainland, it would be blasphemy for an Arbiter to be treated with such disrespect; penance would be swift, severe, and put on display. But Caius seemed to eat up the indignation like a sumptuous dessert, a satisfied smile spreading on his lips as he raised a hand in greeting, even after some brave soul lobbed a gutted fish at the hull of the ship. The reason for that quickly became clear; dozens of Belspire's Thorn Guard appeared on deck behind him, fully armored, oozing the same discipline that I remember from our visit.

"They've taken the towers," someone near us growled, "closed the port."

That triggered new anger, the simmering sense of animosity spreading through the crowd. And understandably. After years of tolerated defiance, the authority of the Goddess had abruptly returned to Cyprene.

The question was: Why?

"If there was anything we needed less right now . . ." With Hiram bandaged up, Nolan and I have retreated to his suite. " . . . it's him."

"Agreed." Nolan slumps in his chair. "The timing is . . . less than ideal."

"Why is he even here?" I pace one end of the room to the other. "Lumeris wouldn't have sent him. The Goddess hasn't sent anyone here in—"

"I sent him a letter."

The words take a moment to sink in. "You *what*?"

Nolan sits up straighter, scowling. "A letter. From one of the ports the *Squid* docked at."

"I'm sorry . . ." Frustrated disbelief rises. "Please explain this to me like *I'm* the idiot here. After how he treated us, you decided to invite him along to Cyprene for . . . for fun?"

"I didn't invite him anywhere. But after . . . after the Renderers . . . after you told me about the cleric you encountered . . ." He exhales defeatedly. "Lumeris *needed* to be informed. The local clergy couldn't be trusted, but Caius is Chosen. I had no question where his loyalty lay."

Of course not.

"I sent him a coded letter with the instructions to go to Lumeris himself and inform Prior Yiorgo about Prior Fedic and the Renderers in Sethane. And that we were on a ship named the *Squid's Shadow*, continuing on our mission."

"Great. So, instead of going to Lumeris, he came here," I snap. "You remember this was a *secret* mission, right?"

"Caius was already suspicious."

"Exactly. Enough to track down the *Squid*, figure out its destination, and pack enough muscle to practically shut the city down." It was clever, I have to give him that. Caius didn't need an army to take Cyprene, just enough soldiers to take the cannon towers, giving them the power to sink any boat that might try to make a run for it.

"I thought he'd jump at the chance to make the report, distinguish himself. I . . . I underestimated his ambition."

"And his ego, and his obedience . . ." I throw my hands up. "Me, you read like a book, but Caius is impossible to predict?"

Nolan's frown deepens. "He still doesn't know where we are, or what we're doing. Right now, I'm more concerned about Marzela and her Salt Sect. You're sure they won't find the Renderers' abominations?"

"Not this year, or next, most likely." It took a little convincing for Nolan to accept I've hidden our best leverage away. Even more to keep him ignorant of where it is. But not as much as I would have expected a few days ago.

"Then we'll have to rely on their desire for that to overcome any further interest in harming us. And stall long enough for Avery to convince the heretics to deal."

Right. Avery. Vexation squeezes tighter. There was nothing waiting for us upon returning. How long will a response take? A day? A week? Having removed my jacket to tend to Hiram (my own blood barely rinsed out), I slip it back on and grab my sickles.

Nolan eyes me. "Going somewhere?"

"To let Rion know it's safe. Better than sitting around here twiddling my thumbs."

"You shouldn't go alone."

I begin to protest, but he's right about that too. Surprises have been in abundant supply lately.

Even with the Salt priests held temporarily at bay, we take care as we make our way through the streets. We're not the only ones. In a matter of hours, Cyprene has shifted into an entirely different place. There are fewer people out, and those that are huddle in tight groups or in doorways, glancing around with faces full of suspicion, anger . . . and fear. All because of one Arbiter.

Then again, after seeing the show Caius put on in Belspire, I can't blame them. This city might be filled with heretics, but they're also normal people, simply trying to *live*.

We reach the shop, which is dark and locked, as expected. No sign of Rion—also expected—but some part of me wanted him to be here, so I could reassure myself the Salt priests hadn't nabbed him after he left us at the baths. But he's not, which means all I've got is the hope that wherever he's gone to hole up, it's safe. Thrown by Caius's arrival, I didn't think to write a note, but there's a mud puddle in front of the shop. I think, then dip a finger in and draw one of the Shadow Cult symbols near the base of the door.

Nolan watches. "What, exactly, is that?"

"Rion will understand." I straighten.

Nolan grabs my arm.

When I turn, I find we're no longer alone. Avery stands in an arched doorway, waiting for our attention to turn his way.

He waves us over. "We need to speak."

"Are your associates satisfied with the sample?" Nolan pours the eagerness on, only some of which is affected.

"Yes." Avery frowns. "But there won't be any deal."

"What?" says Nolan. "Why?"

"The Arbiter." Avery practically whispers the word, as if afraid to summon Caius by speaking it aloud. "He's closed the port, with no explanation as to why he's here. But Cyprene has a long memory. When the Chosen come to the city, nothing good follows. We can't take any unnecessary risks." He looks directly at me. "Or make any deals."

"One Arbiter shouldn't stand in our way." Nolan's disappointment rivals even my own. "Please, you must get them to reconsider. He's barely arrived. If we move fast, we can settle this before—"

"I'm sorry," Avery cuts in. Though he's speaking to Nolan, I know the message is for me. "It's too dangerous."

My hands ball into fists. But as much as I want to argue the decision too, I bite my tongue.

"We don't know his reasons for coming here." Nolan isn't ready to give up. "They may be brief. If he were no longer an issue, would you . . . ?"

Avery contemplates this. "We might reconsider," he says finally. "But for now . . . I'm sorry." He steps clear of the alley and disappears.

Nolan slumps against the wall. "Shit."

*Glad you sent that letter now?* I resist the urge to speak aloud.

"Go on, say it," he mutters.

"Say what?"

"Whatever biting condemnation is caught in the back of your throat."

"Don't know what you could possibly mean."

He snickers bitterly.

I claim a bit of wall beside him, tense with defeat. Every inch of me wants to chase after Avery, but nothing I can say will change anything. The question now: Is there anything I . . . *we* can do? "So not only is Caius sniffing around, but the heretics we want have cut us off, and there's no telling how long before the heretics we *don't* want are up our butts again. Ideas?"

Nolan stares at the ground, gaze distant as he thinks. Finally, he sighs. "Caius is the obstacle. I don't think there's any way around it."

"Oh, please don't say it."

"We need to pay our blood brother a visit."

The least surprising thing about Caius's arrival is where he takes up residence: the Silvered Pearl, Cyprene's most luxurious guesthouse. Even at night, it glows with finery, six stories of the island's alabaster marble peppered with arched windows and pillowy clamshells carved into the stone. Most of the windows are dark, their occupants driven away, and Thorn Guard are posted at every doorway, smudging the guesthouse's pristine appearance.

"Do you think he's actually paying?" The narrow alley we've crept down is cleaner than any other in the city, nary a bit of refuse or opportunistic rodent in sight. Only shadows. Good cover for a bad idea. "Or did he use his toy soldiers to get what he wanted, like with us?"

"Shhhh." Between Avery and the Salt priests, and now having to deal with Caius, Nolan is more focused than I've seen since Novena. The distance from the Goddess still grips, I'm certain, but clarity of purpose has sharpened him again. "C'mon."

We climb, dark spiders in a darker night, scaling the guesthouse exterior, making liberal use of the abundant ornamentation. Four stories up, the ocean wind begins to tug at my hair and clothes. At five, I make the mistake of glancing down. My stomach lurches. It's not that a fall from this height would kill me, but I'm not keen to test out how it would feel.

"Given that everyone was kicked out"—I dig the toe of my boot deeper into a gap—"we really could have taken the stairs."

Nolan ignores me.

The top floor is composed of a single suite. Our target is a balcony there, its edges scalloped and trimmed with silver paint. We slither onto it like a pair of cautious lizards and creep over to the glass-paned doors. Warm light spills from the interior, a room that easily rivals anything Belspire would have had to offer. Caius is within, ensconced at a table scattered with the remains of a fine meal, calmly sipping a glass of wine. Heat pricks my cheeks at the sight of him; screams echo in memory. If anyone deserves to take an assisted dive off this balcony, it's him. Wouldn't kill him either, but at least it would hurt.

Surprise, surprise, he's not alone. Ramiro sits across from him with his own glass and a smarmy smile that makes it clear he thinks the *Golden Glory* was *his* ship coming in. There's also several Thorn Guard standing sentinel. Nolan and I lock eyes. Our plan, admittedly, is not much of a plan. And it's not going to get any better the longer we wait.

So, I stand up in front of the glass door and knock.

The Thorn Guard have their swords out before I finish. Ramiro, dulled by wine, moves a bit slower, though not by much. Caius barely reacts. He peers at me in the window, then takes another sip before putting his glass down—entirely unbothered, as if he fully expected Nolan and me to show up on his balcony.

"Everyone, relax." He comes over and opens the door. "Good evening, Lys. Nolan. You know, you could have simply taken the stairs."

"That's what I said." I shove past him. The Thorn Guard follow Caius's order, but Ramiro's sword remains out, his brow knit with confusion.

"So glad to see you." Caius drips with false warmth. "Saves me the bother of tracking you down."

"Well," Nolan drawls, "we didn't want to put you through any trouble."

"Trouble?" Ramiro finally catches on. He may not have seen our faces clearly, but he's not a total fool. "Wait—I know these two! They're the smugglers I told you about."

"I suspected as much," Caius says. "Though your choice of wares is . . . interesting." He turns calmly to Ramiro. "I assure you, as troublesome as this pair might be, they are here on the Goddess's authority. Whatever they've done, it's with a good reason."

Oh, *now* we get the benefit of the doubt. "Yeah and that good reason was that ass and his ass-kissers attacked *us*."

Ramiro goes tomato red. "I'm going to cut that tongue right out of your smart mouth."

"You will do nothing of the sort." Caius's words harden with Arbiter authority. "Not unless I say so." He pauses. "I understand the sentiment, though."

"Don't we all," Nolan mutters.

I shoot him a sour look.

"They *killed* my men!" The Caerula leader isn't giving up. "And they were peddling vile, forbidden contraband, made from *your* kin."

I roll my eyes. "Goddess, you are slow. *Our* kin too." I sidle over to him and use one finger to push aside his sword, cocking my head questioningly as his eyes widen with surprise. "And as I recall, we left a vial of that contraband behind. Did you happen to mention where that ended up? Or who tipped you off to what we were up to in the first place?"

"Hmm," says Caius. "He did not."

A frown drags Ramiro's mouth down so much that he looks like a very put-out frog. "At times, we are forced to deal with . . . low—but inconsequential—sorts in order to maintain order in Cyprene."

"Maintain your pocket money," I slip in.

Ramiro keeps going. "And I didn't want to concern you with the vile substance. We destroyed it, of course."

I snort. "Sure you did."

"I—"

"Enough." Caius cuts off his new ally, returning to his seat at the table. "We can discuss any impious liberties that might have been taken *after* I sort out some more pressing issues with my brethren here."

"Caius . . ." Nolan says, the one word carrying enough meaning that the Arbiter nods.

"Yes, okay. Everyone out." When Ramiro hesitates, Caius glares at him. "Out, Ramiro. I appreciate your cooperation so far, and your devotion to our Goddess in such a blasphemous place, but this particular discussion is not for your ears."

For a moment, it seems like Ramiro is seriously reconsidering his "cooperation." But he sheathes his sword and exits the suite, the Thorn Guard following. They won't go far, of course, but when the door closes, it's just Caius, Nolan, and me.

"Nice little family reunion," I say.

Caius smiles dryly, picking up his glass again.

"What are you doing here?" Bless Nolan, he gets right to the point. "That letter wasn't an invitation."

"No. But it was very interesting. Especially in the wake of your visit."

Nolan's mouth thins. "Why did you follow us?"

Caius scoffs, as if the answer is obvious. "I'm hunting heretics, same as you. I admit, curiosity got the best of me, especially after I discovered the destination of your ship. And Ramiro's report about recent happenings here was . . . intriguing. What *are* you two up to?"

"You shouldn't be here," says Nolan. "The Goddess didn't send you. No one in Lumeris did."

Caius's eyes narrow at the thinly veiled accusation of disobedience. "I serve them, even when they don't know it."

"Oh," I interject. "So, what you're saying is that you're butting in where you know you're not wanted."

Caius scowls. "Why the Goddess thought *you* were worthy for their favor, I will never understand."

I shrug dramatically. "They work in mysterious ways."

"Stop," commands Nolan. "Fighting doesn't serve any of us. Caius, you don't understand what you've done by coming here. An Arbiter? In Cyprene? You're drawing attention that we don't need."

"I'm not concerned with what attention I draw from this blasphemous rabble. They could all use a reminder that this vile city continues to exist only by the grace of Tempestra-Innara."

"Then be concerned with what *they'll* think," Nolan snaps. "We are close to locating the heretics that attacked. Or we were, until you arrived. How do you think our blood mother will react if they learned about that?"

Caius glares. "Better, I imagine, then finding out that two of their Chosen are peddling the wares of Renderers."

A laugh escapes me. "How do you think we got their attention in the first place?"

*That* perks him up. "So you've actually found them?"

"We've made contact," I concede. Caius still thinks we're only after the heretics. He doesn't know anything about the reliquary. And if we can get him to back off, he won't find out.

The Arbiter turns sly. "Then let me help. We are all children of the Goddess. We should be working together, instead of apart."

And sharing equal parts in the glory, no doubt. I can't help but wonder if Caius might have the same ambitions toward becoming avatar as Nolan does. But no. He'd have no desire to give himself over, not like that. I roll my eyes at Nolan. "Pfft. He wants to leave behind Belspire for Osturan. No, wait . . . Lumeris, right? Right to the top. All of this is him angling for a promotion." My attention shifts back to Caius. "Hey, even better—maybe the Goddess will appreciate your initiative and reassign you to Cyprene."

The scowl returns. "You're not funny. Ever. And I don't know why you'd even joke about that. The Goddess . . . to be so far from their light. It was trial enough when I departed the Cloister, but this?" He trails off.

"Eh." I shrug. "Some of us manage it better than others."

Nolan clears his throat pointedly. "Enough. We don't have time to argue. We've come here on a specific mission and you've endangered our success. You need to depart the island. Carry word back to Lumeris, tell them we are getting close—but *leave*."

Caius leans back in his chair, a clear signal he isn't going anywhere. "I'm sure my Thorn Guard and I can find *some* way to assist you."

So much for appealing to his pious obedience. Though neither of us really expected him to fold. "He's right." Time to try a different tack. "Okay. You *can* help us. Let it leak that you're here hunting smugglers suspected to be Renderer associates. If an Arbiter has come all the way from the mainland, it will lend us credence, show the heretics that we are who we say we are. That we can deliver what we promise. Make a show of it, search a guesthouse or two." I pause. "But reopen the port.

Make it clear you aren't here for long. If they feel threatened—trapped—we'll never hear from them again. If they don't, then we'll have an actual chance to root them out."

The room goes quiet.

"That," Caius says at last, "is not the worst idea I've ever heard."

"I'm known to have a few good ones now and again."

But he shakes his head. "I didn't come here to play games. Or look incompetent, for that matter. I came to deal with the heretics."

I tense, open my mouth to force the point, but Nolan beats me to it.

"Then do that," he says.

"What?" Caius considers. "What do you mean?"

I'd like to know that too. Whatever Nolan is getting at, it wasn't part of our plan.

"I mean . . ." He wanders over to where Caius sits and lifts a crock of salt sitting among the platters and plates. He takes a pinch, then lets the grains rain back down. "That if there's one thing this island doesn't lack for, it's heretics."

# Thirty-nine

Please . . . please, I cannot fathom another day in this godsforsaken place. An hour. A minute. Please!

—FROM THE PRIVATE CORRESPONDENCE OF CLERIC OF THE
BLOOD THIAGO TO HIGH CLERIC OF THE BLOOD SULLIVAS

G**RAY CLOUDS HANG LOW** the following afternoon as Caius stands on a raised stone dais at one end of the city's largest plaza. The gathered crowd fills it to overflowing, thick and impatient, and fraught with uneasy interest. Scowls outnumber smiles a hundred to one, but between the Caerula and the Thorn Guard, Caius is unworried as the gathering builds, until it seems as if every person in Cyprene is on hand. Nolan and I have taken up a spot near one of the scattered fountains, close enough to have a good view, not so close that Caius can easily pick us out. Any slip, any hint of his attention our way, is something we can't risk. Or at least as far as Nolan believes. We both expect that Avery, or at least his compatriots, are somewhere in this horde.

A murmur ripples through the citizens of the city as Caius finally rises and goes to the front of the dais. He scans the scene like a farmer taking in a growing crop, then clears his throat.

"When they whisper, we wake . . ."

I nearly groan. Caius might have agreed to play nicely (or as nice as he can manage), but he couldn't pass up a chance to remind Cyprene who is in charge. The crowd picks up the prayer in fits and starts, and I see a lot of hands move to reveries that clearly aren't the Goddess's. Nolan and I recite as dutifully as if we were in the Cloister, but even for him, there's a feeling of it being performative. As Caius concludes the prayer, a wary silence settles in its wake.

"May the Flame warm you all." It's so quiet that his words carry easily. "Let me first thank you for welcoming my guard and me to your beautiful city."

More grumbles.

"He could get on with it." Nolan's words are pitched only for my ears.

"Sure, but where's the fun for him in that?"

"I understand that Cyprene hasn't enjoyed the presence of one of Tempestra-Innara's Chosen in quite some time," Caius continues. "And I regret the disruption my arrival has caused, to both your lives and your trade." His lies come nearly as smoothly as Nolan's. "I'm afraid I come only out of necessity, as a heinous crime—murder—has been perpetrated against one of my Chosen brethren."

"Good riddance!" someone calls, and I suppress a snicker at the look that flashes across Caius's face. This is not Belspire, a fact he's forced to both taste and swallow. Instead of having the heckler clamped in irons before they made it out of the plaza, Caius is stuck practicing some very reluctant mercy.

"I have traced those involved to your island, a place several of their coconspirators called home, and engaged the assistance of your exemplary Caerula—who have endeavored so well in service to Tempestra-Innara . . ." At this, Caius waves a summoning hand to Ramiro, who comes up beside the Arbiter.

I hate the show. But I have to admit that Caius knows how to put it on. The crowd may loathe him down to the littlest bone in his body, but he has their attention. And here's where the edge lies: Too aggressive, and Caius risks revolt. Not aggressive enough, and the seeds of suspicion about his reasons for being here will take root, and then our goal will be no more possible than the deicidal daydreams I used to pass the time with. I take in the faces and postures of the crowd. They overwhelmingly hold a feeling of disdain, but also clear underlying fear. Caius is a threat; so are the Caerula, in their own, more familiar way.

And putting their alliance on display has fomented enough curiosity to make way for a certain cautious patience. *Get to the point*, expressions seem to say. *Give us back our acceptable, tolerated blasphemy.*

Except in a few faces.

I elbow Nolan, directing his attention nearby: a Salt priest. The one from the alley. His gaze is locked—not on Caius, like the rest of Cyprene, but on Nolan and me.

"Another," hisses Nolan.

This one stands opposite the first, a head above the crowd. And there's a third, to our left.

"Caius's arrival appears to have spooked Marzela too," Nolan whispers.

"Hmm." I count six priests in total. At least, that I can see. We are surrounded.

On the dais, Caius lays a hand on Ramiro's shoulder. "There is no higher calling than routing out the enemies of the Goddess. They will know of your fine work here, my new friend."

Ramiro dips his head in appreciation. Meanwhile, the Salt priests are drawing closer. The crowd is thick, near teeming, but the priests are respected here. It parts for them in a way they do not for Nolan and me; we are essentially trapped by a sea of bodies, unless we want to make a scene. Which wouldn't help—right now, we need everyone focused on Caius.

"But this"—Caius addresses the crowd directly again—"is not a responsibility that lies only with the Caerula. Cyprene may lie far from the light of Tempestra-Innara, but that does not mean it does not feel its warmth. The Goddess loves all of their followers. *All* of their subjects."

Oh, not what Cyprene wants to hear. A low roar of voices builds and I catch so many loud, enthusiastic curses that I'm able to add a few new ones to my repertoire. Caius smiles blandly, unbothered.

Suddenly, the crowd near us shifts, revealing a glimpse of Marzela before tightening up again. But it's enough. Though Nolan managed to leave our last encounter with what felt like an upper, if temporary, hand in the matter, I see none of that patient deference now. Unlike Avery and his friends, discretion and retreat doesn't appear to be the path she prefers. No, her intentions unfold clearly: With the thickness of the crowd, and Caius as a distraction, it wouldn't be difficult to spirit a person or two away unseen. A day ago, she might have been willing to play nice with Nolan in hopes of regular deliveries, but now I suspect she'd be happy with what we brought with us . . . one way or another.

The Salt priests continue to advance, tightening around Nolan and me like a noose. I wait for his signal to make a move. But a little shake of his head says *We stay where we are.*

"Heresy is a sin." Caius's well-practiced voice manages to carry above the still-smoldering onlookers. "But mercy is a virtue. The Goddess loves all of their subjects and, in their infinite wisdom, is willing to grant it to even those who have not fully embraced their warmth."

The Salt priests, only paces away now, are ignored entirely by the rest of Cyprene's citizens. Marzela reappears, a small, venomous smile spreading on her lips.

"But not"—Caius's words boom throughout the plaza—"to those who harm their Chosen."

Suddenly, a wave of blue breaks over the Salt priests' gray. Caerula appear, dozens of them, throwing aside cloaks to reveal themselves. Marzela's eyes widen in surprise, but she has time for only an indignant squawk before two grab her by the arms. Another jams a gag between her teeth. Around us, the same scene plays out with the rest of her priests, until every one of them is bound and being herded toward the dais.

On it, Caius exudes a triumphant, dominant satisfaction.

"We've become entangled"—that's what Nolan said to him, back in his suite—"with the priests who still worship the Salt Goddess. They're customers for the Renderers, goods, using them to reach what they believe to be a communion with their dead Salt Goddess." And even as my blood ran cold, understanding where Nolan was about to go, I could see the eager heat rise in Caius's cheeks.

"What," Caius said, "are you proposing, exactly?"

"Make an example of them." Nolan's temptation continued. "Come down too hard on the Salt priests and it doesn't matter how many Thorn Guard you've brought with you, they won't be able to put down a citywide uprising. But there are multiple sects in the city. Clear one out as a warning, leave the others. For now, of course."

"And I imagine you have a recommendation on which one to use as an example?"

"We do," said Nolan.

*We.* I nearly choked on the bitterness of the word. Oh, I knew I should agree with Nolan's solution to the problem of Marzela. The Salt priests had threatened us. They'd maimed Hiram. They were *heretics*. And yet, when Nolan offered them up as a sacrifice to Caius's ego, like they were nothing...

He gave me a pointed look as Caius considered. *Two birds, one stone*, it seemed to say.

I shrugged, as if in agreement, all the while envisioning the woman in Belspire. The hiss and crackle of her split skin. The smell of her in the air. Her screams.

Marzela and her priests aren't even afforded that outlet as they are dragged through the crowd. There is less protest than I expected from the gathered citizens; the Caerula may not be universally beloved, but they are as of Cyprene as the Salt priests are, and its population seems unsure of how to resolve this inner conflict. An eerie silence falls, broken only by the struggles of the priests and the cries of seabirds milling overhead.

Caius takes advantage of this. "To partake in the murder of the Goddess's holy Chosen, even peripherally, and make trade of their blood and bone is a crime nearly unspeakable in its dreadfulness. And it is one that will be swiftly punished. Tomorrow, these transgressors will be judged"—he lifts the bottle of Judge's Sight, chained around his neck, in a little flourish—"and, if found guilty, know the touch of the Flame. Of Tempestra-Innara, the true and *only* goddess of the Devoted Lands. On the day after that, only once justice has been served, the port will reopen." He pauses, as if allowing a chance for dissent.

By then, the priests are up on the dais, Marzela front and center. She stares at Ramiro, gaze pleading, but despite the prior dealings they must have had, the Caerula leader ignores her completely.

"I have no desire to be a hindrance in Cyprene," Caius continues, "nor remain longer than it takes to do my sworn duty." Despite my distaste, something unknots in my chest. When Caius is gone, Avery will come back. He *has* to. "But I also implore every good citizen to turn away from heresy and association with those that would harm any of the Goddess's devoted, from their Chosen right down to the very least of their followers. Cyprene is far from Lumeris, but it is not forgotten. And I would bring them word that it is still worthy of the Flame's warmth."

*Right after I take my unwelcome ass out of your city.* That's the underlying message, the one we want the crowd to pick up and spread to every corner of Cyprene. *The Arbiter has found who he's after, and as soon as they are dealt with, everything goes back to normal.*

From what I can see, it seems to have the desired effect. Oh, there's still plenty of angry scowls, whispers hidden behind hands, but no one is in open opposition. No one makes a move to stand up for Marzela and the other priests. Between the Caerula and an Arbiter, the crowd seems to have accepted what's been dished out to them, for what they've gotten in trade. It's disappointing, somehow. In a city of heretics, I thought there might be more fight, more willingness to rebel against the tyranny of the so-called Butcher Goddess.

But maybe that's why the city has survived as long as it has: a willingness to know when to fight rough waters, and when to ride them out until they smooth again.

"I'm not going."

Nolan didn't seem particularly surprised to hear I had no interest in attending the execution, which was set promptly for the following morning. No, the surprise was mine, when he didn't argue or try to order me otherwise, when he didn't give some speech about piety or a duty to bear witness to the sins of Cyprene.

"I've seen heretics burn," I pressed, into the space where his lecture should have been. "It's the same every time."

Only an understanding nod, whatever he might have wanted to say hidden away. I held his gaze, challenging him to criticize my decision— *wanting* the fight—but he didn't. Was that his version of remorse, pale and minuscule as it was? Sacrificing the Salt priests was his idea, and while there's no doubt about how Nolan feels about the heretics, how much of it was based on fraying nerves and a need to bring Avery's heretics back by any means possible?

How much of my own desperation was the reason I didn't even try to stop it?

I am so tired, trying to unravel what our desires—and our weaknesses—have made of us.

Nolan leaves for the burning; I stay at the Petrel, solo occupant of the common room. The windows are open, letting in a pleasant breeze. If this were Belspire, I might have heard the crowd, their cheers carried by the wind, echoing off the stone cliffs. Blessedly, it is not. Cyprene takes no pleasure in a burning. But try as I might to avoid it, the scene plays in my mind: The Salt priests on their pyres, Caius with his Judge's Sight, making his way down the line as he declares one after another in violation of Tempestra-Innara's holy doctrines. The crowd watching quietly, with nothing more than a low rumble of disapproval, like a distant storm that passes quickly. Then: the flames, small at first, licking at feet and calves, blackening flesh as they work their way upward.

The wind shifts and I smell it, suddenly. Not imagination—the acrid sting of smoke is faint but there, carried up the hill on the ocean breeze. If I were to go out into the yard, I might see the haze of it in the sky above. But I don't, staring silently at the dark, twisting wood grain of the table until a shadow falls across it. Hiram, I think, who'd also shown no interest in the ghastly proceedings. Or—I hope—Rion, presumably still making himself scarce with an Arbiter in town. But when I look up, it's Avery.

"I wasn't sure I'd find you here," he says.

I scoff. "Already seen this performance."

"Was this your doing?"

"No. Well, yes," I admit as he takes a seat. "It wasn't my idea. But I didn't do anything to stop it either."

Avery nods thoughtfully. Not in an approving way, but there's no judgement in it either. Somehow, that make me feel worse.

"And tomorrow, the port will reopen?"

"Yup, at dawn. And the Arbiter will be gone soon too. Back to business as usual."

"Good." His hand appears above the table, slides something over to me.

It's a fold of paper. I open it; a rough map is sketched within. "What's this?"

"They want to meet you," he says simply.

"When?"

Avery smiles apologetically. "Tonight." Then he glances over his shoulder, as if something is coming. He stands. "Come late, when the city is settled."

That's it. No other instruction or explanation. Within moments, he's gone and I'm alone. The paper itches between my fingers, but for a long minute, all I can hear are Avery's words.

*They want to meet you.*

The heretics. The true ones, not the ineffectual priests slowly roasting down by the bay. The ones that hold the chance to free myself from Tempestra-Innara. From things like *this*. I sit with that hopefulness so long that Nolan is through the door of the Petrel before I realize I'm still holding the map. I stuff it into my pocket right before he spots me and takes the seat occupied by Avery only minutes before.

"Is it over?" I don't let him speak first, share some detail I'd rather not hear.

"Yes." He sounds . . . tired.

"And Caius, is he satisfied?"

*Did he enjoy himself?* Nolan's eyes flicker up, understanding my real question. "For the moment. The other Salt Sects have probably made some connections, though. They should keep their distance. But wherever you've hidden the Renderers' wares, best leave them a little longer."

"Sure."

A tense minute passes, during which faces file through my thoughts. Magda. The woman who served out her sentence. Tychus. Marzela and the Salt priests. Every one of them offered up, by us, in order to reach our singular goal. I wonder if Nolan carries any guilt at all. It's a question I can't ask, not knowing what answer I'd want to hear.

So, a different one: "Do you think it will be enough?" Whether I'm talking about for the heretics or for Caius, I'm not sure, and Nolan doesn't ask for clarification.

"I don't know . . . but it will have to be. Either the heretics make a move, or Caius does. Because I've made all the ones I can think of."

The admission sounds more like a confession, one that crawls over me and climbs into the pocket of my jacket right next to the map, heavy as an iron ingot.

*They want to meet you. Tonight.*

Nolan may not know it, but the next move has already been made.

# *Forty*

> The Salt tunnels are both temple and tomb.
>
> —CYPRENE SAYING

Evening falls with a syrupy slowness. I listen carefully until the sounds of the common room fade away, then wait another hour. By then, a dark calm has fallen on Cyprene, and I can't bear to wait any longer. I spin lies as I make my escape from the Petrel, just in case Nolan decides to check in on me again—I needed a walk, to clear my head, get some air that doesn't smell like grilled priest. I can't help but pause and watch the dark window of his room, but with any luck, he's fast asleep. I don't know what kinds of dreams Nolan has—better than mine hopefully—but I wish him a good one. Something to cover the fact that his partner is going behind his back with the intention to destroy his *real* dreams.

*Partner.* When did that word start sounding real? I hate it. Hate that for over a decade, I didn't feel a lick of remorse for fantasizing about tearing the whole of Tempestra-Innara's empire down to nothing. About watching every one of my blood brethren cut from their divine mooring and set free to sink or swim as they could. And now, after a few weeks working with a backstabbing, overly ambitious Dusk Potentiate whom I should have been pitted against and not teamed up with?

I still want the Goddess dead. But it feels less fun now.

Nolan offering up the Salt priests may have sat poorly, but I have no doubt: That's the reason the heretics are willing to meet with me now. It's an opportunity bought in blood, settled with ash. I'm not going to waste it.

Get to the heretics.

Get the reliquary.

Get back to Lumeris and kill a goddess.

That's the plan.

I spot the first marker on the map—one of the massive statues of the Salt Goddess carved into a cliff, distinctive by the stone octopus clinging to her breast like a feeding child. It takes me nearly an hour to reach its base, the buildings giving way to a strip of ancient ruins. From this vantage, the Salt Goddess is a colossus looming over me, ghostly pale in the moonlight. I examine the note again. The drawing of the statue is distinct, but I can see dozens of entrances into the cliffs around it—simple ones with no more decoration than a curved top to elaborately carved portals with heavy, steel-studded doors. Like Tychus warned, the cliff dwellings don't come with much by way of directions. And going in the wrong one means I might never come out again.

If only the heretics didn't need to be so fucking cryptic. I examine the drawing again, specifically the bottom of the statue, where there's a heavier press of ink, a bit of scratching near the Salt Goddess's feet. Or maybe it's a fold of their robe. I can't tell.

The breeze picks up suddenly, ripping the paper from my fingers.

"Shit."

I give chase as it twists in the air and catch the paper near a chipped lump that used to be one of the statue's toes. There, I smell it—a dampness that's not entirely ocean. The minerally scent of cold stone. Crouching down, I find a fissure beneath the carved garment, barely there, but wide enough for a person to fit through. *That's* what the drawing was indicating. I say a little prayer before I enter. Not to Tempestra-Innara, but rather to the Salt Goddess, for daring to do something so scandalous as go under their robes without first asking permission.

But sometimes you gotta do what you gotta do.

I slip in, somewhat less than gracefully, trying to keep my guard up. On one hand, Avery and the other heretics could have made short work of me already, if their invitation had been anything other than sincere. On the other, nothing has gone as hoped lately. Inside the statue there's a dense darkness, broken only by a large candle on a metal holder. Someone has lit it for me. I am expected.

Map in one hand, candle in the other, I follow the first passage as it arcs gently through the rock, a curve reminiscent of my sickle's blade. The usual carvings are here, but worn more than others I've seen, a weighty feeling of age pressing down. It's cold too; the chill of the ocean is leaching its way through the rocks. The air tastes of salt as I reach a juncture with three paths. Following the instructions, I take the left tunnel, go down a series of roughly carved stairs, then take another left at the bottom. Silence practically smothers me. I move quietly on purpose, but even the minuscule sounds of my existence seem muted, my heartbeat as distant as if I'd left it waiting on the rocks outside. The shadows stuff my ears until they are full and dissipate my breath in an instant.

It is, I have to admit to myself, a little creepy. The ghost of Tychus whispers warnings as other passages branch off, leading who knows where, but I stick to my instructions. I take the next turn indicated, only to suddenly come face-to-face with a rock wall. Which doesn't make sense. I know how to read a map. But I must have taken a wrong turn, or else I wouldn't be staring at nothing. I backtrack to the last place I turned, another juncture where there were two passages.

Except when I get there, I find three.

"Fuck." My curse is a wan, deadened sound.

I search the note, desperate to figure out where I went wrong. But there's no getting around it: I'm lost. Which means I have two choices. Stay where I am and hope for a friendly heretic to stumble across me—bad. Or keep going, and hope I end up where I need to be or find a way out. Also bad, but at least I'm doing something.

My attempts at backtracking do not improve. Passages that seem familiar become unrecognizable within minutes, and I'm no longer sure if I've been any of the places I thought I had. It's not exactly panic that sets in, but rather a simmering irritation. A contemplation of what will happen when Nolan wakes to find me gone, never finds me again, my stupid ass lost forever in the cliffs of Cyprene.

Another turn, find another dead end.

"Ughhh." The simmer turns into a boil. I want to scream, but I don't know who might overhear. Something is wrong here, the walls seeming to grow increasingly tight, the air thicker than before.

It's not panic. I do *not* panic.

Moving faster, I take turn after turn, all sense of direction gone. Have I gone deeper into the stone cliffs, or is Cyprene just beyond the wall in front of me? Am I above the city or deep below it?

Suddenly, a glow appears at the end of a long, narrow passage. Sweat beads my brow as I move toward it, ears straining for any bit of sound. I reach a doorway and step through it into a bright, round chamber with a domed ceiling.

In the center, on a pedestal, is a reliquary.

I know it as soon as I see it, though it bears only a passing resemblance to what Tempestra-Innara showed us beneath the Cathedral. This one is more bulbous, with an emerald-studded base and a silver stopper. Blood fills it less than halfway, dark and viscous.

Oh, this has got to be a trap. I scan the chamber, but there's nothing else, no one. No instruction as to what I should do now.

But maybe I don't need it. Maybe this *is* the instruction. Is this the heretics' way of telling me they trust me? Giving me the reliquary without giving away their identities? Even if I fail, or if I'm caught, the only thing I can betray is their location, and that barely.

Cautious, I approach the pedestal, expecting each step to bring an attack, a warning. But there's nothing. No ambush, no traps, and suddenly the reliquary is only inches away.

I reach for it.

"Oh, Lys..."

The voice comes from all around, freezing the blood in my veins with surprise.

With recognition.

Across the chamber, the stone begins to ripple. A familiar figure appears, stepping forward with an expression of disappointment that slips between my ribs like a blade.

Tempestra-Innara, my blood mother.

Here in Cyprene.

Their mouth hangs down at the corners, eyes brimming with heartbreak. "Oh, daughter. I never thought it possible."

The world shifts, its edges turning soft. Spots flicker at the boundary of my vision as panic drives the breath from my lungs.

Tempestra-Innara's features turn angry. No, *furious*, teeth baring like a rabid dog as they take another step toward me. "I never thought that one of my own children could betray me like this."

There's no choice now, no lies that will get me out of this mess. Only commitment. I drop the candle and grab the reliquary, then tear the stopper free as I raise it to my lips to drink.

The blood does not sing.

It doesn't even pour.

And in the moment when I try to sort out that mystery, I realize something pretty darn important: I felt nothing when Tempestra-Innara appeared. No limb-trembling rush of divinity. No warmth from the light I crave nearly as much right now as my freedom.

Nothing.

When I look again, the Goddess is gone. Instead, in their place, is Avery.

And Rion.

They both smile, as if pleased.

I look down. The reliquary is gone, replaced by an empty, utterly normal bottle that slips from my fingers and clunks against the stone floor before rolling away.

*No...*

A minute ago, I saw a reliquary. And a goddess, clear as anything before me right now.

"Godsdamned it, did you *drug* me?" I yank the note from my jacket and toss it away before wiping my fingers on my pants. I learned about things like that, potions that could be soaked into paper before—

"No one drugged you, Lys."

Rion is calm. Too calm.

"Then what the hell did I just see?" I step back as they approach, drawing my sickles. "No. You stay over there."

"Lys, please." Avery stops, holds his hands up in a placating gesture. "I know that was upsetting, but . . ."

"We needed to be sure," Rion finishes.

*We.* "You're with the heretics."

"Oh yes." Rion laughs at some joke I'm clearly not party to. "Very much so."

I'm beginning to have regrets about this meeting. Unfortunately, the stony labyrinth prevents any storming out.

"Please," Rion implores. "Follow me and we'll have a chat. Just like at my shop. We even have tea."

Every extremely confused fiber of my being wants to refuse. But . . . "Given the chances of me finding my way out of here alone, I don't have much of a choice, do I?" Rion says nothing, though he glances meaningfully at my weapons. I sheathe them.

Appeased, Rion turns, presses the stone I saw ripple like muddy water only minutes ago. A door depresses and slides to one side, a clever bit of engineering. Avery goes first, then Rion, beckoning me. Hesitantly, I follow. We enter another chamber, with a mosaic floor and carved walls, oil lamps in cerulean glass hanging from the ceiling. More than just another piece of the Salt Goddess's old stomping grounds, this chamber has the feel of being regularly utilized. That sensation deepens thanks to the figures lining the walls. I nearly mistake them for statues, until I see one of them shift. They are robed in gray, faces veiled, offering absolutely nothing about their identities.

"Well, this is creepy as fuck." My hands itch to draw my sickles again. "Are we having a party?"

"They all wanted to see you," says Avery.

"To see proof that you are who we say you are. Please," says Rion. "Show them."

"Are you kidding me?" *Proof.* The heretics who still have faith in gods who have been dead for centuries aren't willing to extend me the same belief. I scowl. Rion and Avery wait. So, I give in, calling the flame. "Will this do?" I brandish the pathetic flicker, turning so no one misses out.

A sense of wonder and relief—of hope—suddenly fills the chamber. One of the heretics lets out a joyous laugh, which deepens my annoyance. I close my hand, smothering what I've summoned.

"Thank you," says Rion.

There's a table in the center of the chamber, a more recent addition than the rest of the décor, with the promised tea and cups. Rion and Avery sit, gesturing for me to do the same.

I obey but wave away the drink. Maybe they haven't drugged me yet, but no sense giving them any new chances.

"Okay, I followed. Proved who I was. Now, what the hell just happened?"

"You were given a test." Rion, placid to a level that is increasingly maddening, traces the whorl of a knot in the wooden table with a finger. "One you passed."

"We couldn't take you on your word." Avery is apologetic. "We needed to know that, given the chance, you would truly stand against Tempestra-Innara."

Can't exactly fault that, as much as I want to. "That doesn't explain how or why I just saw them."

"You are a unique opportunity, Lys." Rion ignores my inquiry and stares—a searching, probing gaze that makes me want to squirm. "As far as I know—and I know quite a bit—the divinely Chosen have only ever turned against each other, never their masters."

"Maybe they're all smarter than I am."

"Maybe," Rion concedes. "Or perhaps everything occurs, even the seemingly impossible, given enough passage of time. At the bookshop, you told me you believed Tempestra-Innara was the only goddess."

"That's right. And no one better get the silly idea that I believe in your cause. I may be a traitor, but it's for one reason: freedom. Specifically, mine. I know better than to believe the old gods are gonna come roaring back because *you* kept the faith and got rid of the competition."

Avery's eyes take on a fervent brightness, a grin spreading on his lips. "We don't need to believe," he says. "We know the dead gods are dead. But they're still here."

This is making less sense by the minute. "I don't understand."

"*They're* still here." Avery smiles even wider. "Another divinity. The Whisperer."

The—?

*Fuck.* I have made a very bad decision. Not only have I surrounded myself with heretics, but I have willingly walked into a cave full of lunatics. I'm on my feet immediately.

"Okay, that's it. I knew you all had to be mad to take on the Goddess, but at least I could relate. This? The Whisperer fell eons ago. They're *dead.*"

"With all due respect," says Rion in a new tone, one that sends a familiar shiver through me, "I'll have to disagree. Because I feel very much alive."

# Forty-one

Weakest of the gods, the Whisperer tried to manipulate their siblings, turn them against each other. Instead, they came together in unity, a force against which the Whisperer could not hope to stand. They were destroyed, their power so insignificant, their followers so few, that unlike all future divine deaths, they left no trace upon this land...

—*THE DIVINE HISTORIES*, VOL. II (RESTRICTED TEXT)

O**SIRON... THE FIRST GOD** to die.

A lie. A delusion. A game. This must be one of those things, or all of them, since there's no possible way the Whisperer has survived for as long as this in secret.

And yet...

No, it can't be possible. I am clearly in the eye of some storm of unchecked heretical madness. I consider fleeing—fighting my way out, if necessary. Wandering in the labyrinthine cliffs for as long as it takes to escape.

Instead, all I can manage is to echo what was asked of me: "Prove it."

Rion tips his head. "Haven't I already?"

"What—oh." The changing passages, the vision of Tempestra-Innara... "Not enough. You could be trying to pass off some druggy hallucinations as divine."

"Fair enough," he says. "Please sit, though."

"I'll stand, thanks."

The stone beneath my feet suddenly shifts. The mosaic floor churns briefly before lurching up, encircling my wrists. I am yanked downward, back into my seat, the liquid stone solidifying again. Then comes the hiss, a nearly imperceivable reverberation whose source seems to be everywhere. The two faces before me ripple, change. Across the table suddenly sit Morgan and Prior Petronilla.

The sound stops. I blink.

Rion and Avery are back.

And I am still trapped, but sufficiently convinced. Rion is a godsdamned god.

He . . . they . . . smile patiently. "Will that do? I'll admit my most significant abilities lean more toward perception than such tangibles as fire and lightning, but the world bends to my will as much as it does for any other divinity."

I don't fight. Strong as I am, I won't break free. And the grim absurdity of the situation is rising, as if the world is filling with some invisible, vicious liquid, threatening to float me like a pickle in a jar. I can barely breathe. Moments ago, there was a singular truth that burned at the center of my universe: that Tempestra-Innara was the only living divinity. Now, Rion's demonstration has extinguished that flame, leaving behind a befuddling dark.

A god . . . another deity . . .

A sour taste rises in the back of my throat, my fingers tingling distantly.

If he . . . they . . . *whatever* senses my growing panic, he is polite enough not to mention it. Which makes me wonder if I am handling this gut punch of knowledge better or worse than folks usually do.

"So, uh, Rion . . . Osiron. Whisperer?" I seriously might puke. "I . . . I'm gonna be honest. I don't quite know how to address you."

An amused sigh. "I have lived so long as a man that the designations of the divine feel overly formal. If continuing to know me as Rion makes this easier for you, then . . . please."

"Okay." I flex my hands into fists. Release. "Now what?"

"I imagine you have questions."

"Oh, a few."

"Then let's make you comfortable." Rion drums his fingers.

My bonds release, the stone and mosaic pieces snapping back into place like a loosed bowstring, no sign that they were ever disturbed at all.

Rion notes my bewildered examinations of the floor. "As I said, the world bends to divine will. But temporarily, and it much prefers its mundane state." He folds his hands on the table. "So . . . questions?"

About a hundred flutter fitfully through my thoughts, but one—one rises above the others. And it's a doozy. "If you're a high and mighty god, then what the hell do you need *me* for?"

He laughs. "A question with many answers. But you already know why: to help kill my dear sister."

"That answers exactly fuck all—"

Rion holds up a hand. "It will make more sense if I start at the beginning, when Avery arrived with his strange story about a young woman he met in the woods. One who was Chosen but didn't speak or behave like it. Later, I sensed you almost as soon as you and Nolan stepped foot in the city. Tempestra's children—here, for the first time in decades. But, oddly, in secret. An intriguing situation, to say the least. Even more so when I began to speak with you, got to know you." There's an uncomfortable, quiet moment where it feels as if Rion can see through my flesh and bones, into some buried part of me that even I haven't uncovered yet. "A pair with a mission, that much was obvious, as well as what it was. But some of the things you said to me . . . and when you helped Hiram . . ." He stops. "I started to understand what Avery had conveyed."

"That you knew who Nolan and I were doesn't answer my question."

"Doesn't it? To me, your divinity radiates like the heat of a hearth, wafts through the air like a perfume. Especially here, where there is a marked absence of it."

I glance at Avery, and the masked followers. "You're saying Tempestra-Innara can do the same?"

He nods.

Okay, that explains why Emmaus, despite being under the orders of a god, was not blessed by one. If the gods could sense the divinely gifted children of their siblings, Osiron sending one as an assassin would have been as good as sashaying into the Cathedral and announcing they were still alive.

"Avery... your buddies in the cloaks... are any of them your Chosen?"

This time he shakes his head. "I've never 'blessed' followers in the way my siblings did. You couldn't know this, of course, but that was the core of our initial falling out. The stories say I tried to steal their power. In truth, I tried to stop them spreading it around." A scowl appears. "They became so enamored of their Chosen's affection, so glutted with the devotion that a bit of their blood bought, that they surrounded themselves with armies of their blessed. Then someone realized that divinity trickled down. Blood and flesh became commodities. There were even periods where a ritual was made of it. Try to imagine it: dozens, sometimes hundreds of a god's devotees gathered to set upon a corpse. Tearing it apart by hand, consuming that divinely infused flesh, reveling in the temporary elation of it."

Honestly not something I wanted to picture. "Gross."

Rion gives me a look of agreement. "Weird times, let me tell you. I was 'dead' by then, of course. Turned on by my siblings for counseling restraint. They learned eventually, of course. When they built empires around themselves—great, grand things that grew and grew until they were all pressed up against each other... when those armies of the blessed turned on each other, devasting the land and giving rise to such horrors as the Renderers... they learned."

I scoff. "You don't seem to have qualms about working with those 'horrors.'"

He shrugs. "They have their uses. And they only knew what they needed to."

For the first time in a while, I feel as if I understand something—the Renderers knew they were dealing with heretics, but not a hidden god. I scan the room again, at how few followers are present. "How many of the folks involved with your plans know who they are really working for?"

"A special few. My Chosen, in a way, I suppose."

"And you're keeping the rest ignorant, leveraging their belief that the old gods will return if Tempestra-Innara falls, taking advantage of their faith."

"Of course," says Rion, smirking. "Why do you think I started that little rumor in the first place?"

*Oh.* "The other gods are really dead then."

"Very. Not by my hand, of course. I kept myself hidden over the years, watched them turn on each other one by one. I'd already learned my lesson. I was the oldest of the gods, but never the most powerful. And six against one . . . it was never going to be a fair fight. But I knew things, understood mysteries of our world that my siblings never did. Do you know why they call me the Whisperer, Lys?"

"Because of your whispered lies, your manipulations."

"No." That single word carries an ancient weightiness that reminds me who I am speaking to. "Because *I'm* the one who called them into being in the first place."

"When they whisper, we wake . . ."

Around us, the prayer begins, then stops just as quickly. Something cold settles in my bones, born of a growing comprehension. *When* they *whisper* . . . Not Tempestra.

Osiron.

"Old words," Rion says lightly. "Made good use of over the years. Nothing like familiar incantations and rituals to cement the stones of belief together, whatever those beliefs may be."

"You created the other gods?"

"Called more than created," says Rion. "From a place I can barely remember, somewhere outside the world of touch and taste and smell. I found my way here, the first of us to become flesh. The first of us to *trade* that flesh, when it began to fail. And even when my siblings destroyed that, when they overwhelmed me with the brute force of their combined power, well . . . they always understood destruction better than what they were trying to destroy. Lucky for me, though they were always able to sense each other, and their Chosen, I myself have always been a blind spot. A quirk, I suppose, of my part in their making. I was able to shift myself, find a new body, disappear. Which brings me to where I am now."

"Eons later?" Each answer spawns more questions. "What have you been doing all this time? Hanging around guesthouses and peddling naughty books?"

Rion laughs. "Not the *whole* time. Your incredulity is understandable, and so very, very mortal." He pauses. "But I am not. I saw what was coming when my siblings turned on me. Peace never holds between spoiled children. I might have been their first conflict, but I also knew that—eventually—they'd turn on each other. That someday, only one would be left." A sly smile rises to his lips. "I have the luxury of time. And as you can see, I can be very, very patient."

"And yet you still need me to do your dirty work."

That erases Rion's smile. "Unfortunately, yes. Tempestra, even with a failing avatar, is still stronger than I am. Which is why I turned to alternative avenues of attack."

"The reliquary. And the blood of a dead god."

"Not the most eloquent solution, I'll admit."

"Or successful."

"No," he concedes. "Honestly, it took even me ages to conceive of the plot. It was the Stone God who made the reliquaries, as a gift to his siblings. None of them considered that the vessels might preserve their blood indefinitely, or how that preservation following their deaths would change it. I certainly didn't. Thousands of years and there are intricacies about this world—about divinity itself—that even I haven't fully unraveled." His nose wrinkles, as if smelling something unpleasant. "Did you know the Arbiters are entirely Tempestra's creatures? They didn't exist until after Arcadius fell, and I've never sorted out exactly how they create the potion that gives them their particular ability. I suspect they drew some inspiration from the Renderers' 'hounds,' but . . ." He shakes his head. "Someday, there will be time for learning and research unhampered by secrecy. Now is the time to strike, while my sister is in decline, before they take a new avatar."

"What if you're already too late?"

He shakes his head. "I'd know, feel that shunt of power."

Well, that's something at least. "And after Tempestra-Innara . . . then what? You take their place ruling the Devoted Lands?"

"Do you care what happens after? You'll be free."

There it is—the bait dangling at the end of the stick, my dream come true. Except I'd always imagined it to be in a world devoid of divinities. *All* of them. Now the landscape of that world is becoming something very, very different. Again, I feel a touch of winter, a sensation like ice cracking beneath my feet.

"*Then* what?" I press.

Rion seems to understand, reluctance filling the air between us before he speaks again. "Mistakes were made, I'll be the first to admit that. But it's not too late to try again."

"What do you mean?"

"The old gods are dead. Gone forever." A fresh intensity ignites behind Rion's eyes. "But that doesn't mean we can't make a few new ones."

# Forty-two

It was only when the gods arrived, vivid in their potency, did the Devoted Lands truly understand what had always been there, just beyond knowing, ripe to ascend. The gods are of this land; divinity is its blood.

—FRAGMENT UNEARTHED NEAR THE SHADOWED VALLEY, TITLE AND AUTHOR UNKNOWN (RESTRICTED TEXT)

CREATING GODS. AS IF it were as common as baking a loaf of bread.

"You want to *make* new gods."

"Hmm." Rion tips his head pensively. "*Make*, in this regard, would be one of those words scholars and philosophers would fall over themselves to endlessly debate. But essentially, yes." His gaze moves up, around. "I sense them, almost always. They are never far. Beyond some veil, in that space between what is and what isn't . . . there are more. Given an opportunity for flesh, some will listen. Some will come."

I flick a finger toward Avery and the other heretics. "Is that what you offer them then? The chance to become an avatar for a newly minted divinity?"

"Absolutely not." Rion sounds insulted by the suggestion. "Unlike my siblings, I don't use divinity as a bribe to buy—or force—loyalty, or pluck children like flowers to use them to control the rest of their devoted." He gestures. "Everyone here is present because they *want* to be. Ask them, if you like. Over the years we have planned and spied, spread rumors, fanned the smoldering embers of dissent . . . even infiltrated, as you've already learned. We have cultivated beliefs like the return of the old gods because it serves our purpose. And every single one of my followers has contributed in their own way. But not for the promise of reward. Because they believe in a world beyond the fallen, failed divinities."

Belief. *Faith*. That whole fucking thing again. Faith that the Whisperer will bring about something better than what is, or what used to be. I don't have to ask Avery if he agrees. He practically glows with conviction, reminding me of Tempestra-Innara's most fervent devoted.

Of Nolan.

Oh, to have the slightest clue of how he'd react to this.

"New gods," I say again. The words taste like madness in my mouth.

"New gods," Rion echoes. "To serve humanity instead of rule; to help advance, instead of keep intentionally ignorant and subservient. And no more innocents"—he locks eyes with me—"forced or manipulated into the service of faith."

A promise of unfathomable depth. A promise brimming with choice. My mouth opens to speak, hangs there for several seconds before I know what I want to say. "How do I know you're not lying? That you don't want to—I don't know—enslave the Devoted Lands once the way is clear?"

"Because if I'd wanted to do that, I would have millennia ago, alongside my siblings." Rion's answer is simple, unadorned. "Fear is its own kind of devotion, just like love. My siblings understood that, used whichever served them best. But that's not what I envision." He shifts in his seat. "Lys, no pantheon is built in an hour, a day, even a century. The process is . . . draining, to say the least. And when I called out before, I did not take the time to consider who answered. What kind of divinity they might become. I have since shed that youthful ignorance. What I want to do, the world I want to build, will be careful. Meticulous. And measured out over time."

Which means I won't be around to see most of it. That's what Rion's saying. That I'll be rotted away long before his vision comes to full fruition. Freedom in this life, all for the low, low cost of not worrying about any future consequences of my actions.

It's a deal that sounds better than I want to admit.

Rion stands. "Let's take a little walk, Lys. Have a private chat. You can see some more of the tunnels."

I've seen enough of them to last a god's lifetime. But when Rion moves, so do I, following him out of the chamber into another dimly lit passage. And then—

I am alone with the Whisperer. Somehow, this is worse than having the veiled heretics hovering around. The lack of divine sensation—a feeling I am so used to while being in Tempestra-Innara's presence—is like a void between us. An unnerving dead space opened up by knowledge. How did I never sense this before, in all the hours I spent with Rion? How stupid am I to have completely missed that I was drinking tea and browsing books with a *god*?

I smirk to hide my thoughts. "Now comes the part where you try to bribe me, right? Offer me power? Riches?"

Rion chuckles. "No power, no riches. I only ever offer anyone what they actually want. You were partially right back there, though—some of my followers *do* desire to become an avatar, when and if the time comes. They don't fully understand what that means, of course, but that is why I must be as careful in choosing them as I am in choosing the power I call into this world. Of course, if any of them were to find the experience disagreeable, we would simply find the divinity another host."

At first, I'm revolted that Rion would spend his followers lives so callously. Then I understand what he is *really* saying. "Wait . . . avatars aren't permanent?"

Rion gives me a patient, knowing smile, one that makes it clear that he purposefully led me into the question. "They don't have to be. But that bit of truth never served my siblings, most of whom preferred to choose their avatar, tempt or force themselves into the skin of their choice. The Shadow God was an exception; they moved from avatar to avatar quite often, only occasionally settling in one for an extended period. Of course, none of the gods lacked for volunteers, but you've read the texts. The allowed ones, at least. Even they speak about how the gods typically went into seclusion after taking a new avatar."

"The scholars said it was so the deity could commune with their new form. Find balance."

"More like to confirm it didn't fade too quickly, and cement their control over it," says Rion. "Oh, for sure, the divinity will always triumph if it's a struggle between the two. But for a period of time, it is still possible for the god to separate from the avatar without lasting effects to either."

An almost giddy shiver races through me at this new information. At the understanding that so much more than I ever imagined has been kept secret. I'm so deep in my thoughts that I don't realize, at first, that Rion has stopped in front of a massive wall deeply carved with sea creatures. But there's a difference between it and the others I've seen. Here the creatures are only bones, a tangle of ribs and spines.

"Dramatic, isn't it?" Rion pokes beneath the backbone of some huge fish. There's a click, and a door opens, expertly disguised within the motif. It seems like a terrible idea to go into some unknown room hidden behind skeletons, but I'm beyond fear at this point. Or even curiosity. I've gone so far past any expectations that I doubt I would blink an eye even if I found the Princess of Belspire within the chamber, leading a troupe of performing rats while naked.

But there are no rats or royalty. What there is, is a corpse.

Or parts of one. Old, desiccated limbs stretched out on a stone table within a chamber shaped like a beehive, with a series of niches cut into the wall. A mortar and pestle, knives, and various other implements are scattered across the platform. There's no head on the body, or pelvis, and only about two-thirds of a rib cage. As far as I can tell.

"Okay, so no bribes." My mouth suddenly tastes like I've been sucking iron. "Threats, instead?"

Rion chuckles. "Oh, I didn't kill them. They've been dead for centuries." He waves at the niches. "All of them have been. Perfectly natural deaths as far as we know."

The contents of the mortar answers another question. "Bone? Are these bodies of the Salt Goddess's Chosen?" My hand goes to the Renderers' book in my coat pocket, still secreted away. "Have you been supplying the Renderers with blessed bodies when they can't manage any on their own?"

Rion nods, unbothered by the macabre nature of it all. "Mostly old ones."

"Mostly? And what about the powder that gives their 'hounds' the ability to see us? You supply that too?"

"Yes, once I figured out its curious little effect." He goes to a niche and pulls out a box. Within are dozens of crystal shards, large chunks down to tiny slivers. "Most of the reliquaries have been destroyed over the years. But I was able to put the remains I found to good use."

"Putting remains to good use," I say flatly. "How economical."

"I know. It's all a little distasteful. Especially considering the unintentional inspiration possibly given to the Arbiters. I'm showing you this because I wanted to be transparent. Staying unknown all these years, inserting spies into the followings of the living gods, building my network . . . none of that came easy. Or inexpensively. I followed paths that you might find disagreeable, I understand that. But are you at peace about everything you've done to survive while in servitude to the Goddess?"

He's got me there. I cross my arms and say nothing.

"Divinity is scarce these days. But remnants of it, no matter how well hidden, sometimes call out. They pulse at the edges of my senses like fireflies in the night. And by feeding the continued demand for those remnants, Tempestra's Chosen are reminded that even they are not protected from every threat. That their 'blood mother' is not all-powerful." He pauses. "But you don't want *more* divinity. No, what *you* want is what I'm offering in return for your help—freedom. Nothing more, nothing less. And in the end, what is more valuable than that?"

*Freedom.* The word quivers in my throat.

"All you need to do is say yes."

Such a small thing. But decisiveness feels as far away as Tempestra-Innara right now. Staring at the ancient remains on the table, at the shards of reliquaries I can't shake a sensation like when I was falling in

Novena—drowning in the dark, grabbing blindly for whatever salvation I could find. The idea of more gods is stifling. But at the same time, *I* wouldn't be bound to any of them. They wouldn't be *my* problem.

"If this happens"—my tongue is heavy, forming the words with tacky slowness—"if I agree to work with you . . . how? How does it play out?"

"As simple as this." Rion walks over to another one of the niches. It opens, not to a body, but to something that I recognize instantly. Mostly because I saw it only minutes ago. Crystal, emerald, and silver. The Whisperer's illusion was faithful save for one detail.

The reliquary is nearly empty.

When he places it in front of me, it's clear there's no more than a few swallows' worth. More than Emmaus had squirreled away in his reverie, but not by much.

He taps the silver stopper with one finger. "This is all that is left of Arcadius, the Green God. I spent centuries searching for any remaining reliquaries, understanding that there was no better weapon against my brethren, even if I would have to wait to wield it. Most of the ones I found were empty or, more often, reduced to shards. I could never risk sending a follower divinely gifted with my blood against Tempestra—I would be revealed before they got close enough to strike. So, I waited until I judged that their current avatar would be close to being spent before sending Emmaus." He shrugs in defeat. "It was a gamble that failed. And now my only choice is another gamble: to give you the last of Arcadius and hope what Tempestra did to you will result in *their* undoing."

"You'll just . . . *give* me the reliquary."

"If you agree to help us, yes."

Dead gods. Dead blood. New gods. New . . . I don't know. I don't know what to do. My own blood beats thickly in my ears, making my cheeks feel like overplump ticks. Thoughts stumble over themselves, trying to make sense. And even more frustrating, they keep casting back to the Petrel. To Nolan, ignorant of the absolutely shattering truths I've been gifted tonight. What would he think if he knew what I know now? What would he *believe* after learning it?

And why do I even care?

"You need time." My indecision is as clear to Rion as the reliquary crystal. "I do not know how much of that there is. We have a ship waiting, ready for when the Arbiter reopens the port. But there's no telling if that will last."

"I need to think . . . to consider." Hesitance isn't the only problem right now. But, for once, I may have a solution. "Nolan, my . . . partner. And Caius. They believe we've gotten close to your heretics. That you're almost willing to work with us."

"And you're suggesting . . . ?"

"Continue letting them think that. The closer they think we are to your inner workings, the further we'll be able to back Caius off."

"You believe that is the best way to deal with them?"

Everything tightens, my eyes going to the table. And the body parts.

"I wasn't implying another avenue," Rion says, as if reading something he doesn't like on my face. "Enough attention has been drawn to Cyprene as it is. We can spin a fiction instead, give you time. But not much."

My chest loosens, though only a little. "And . . . what happens if I say no?"

Rion knows what I'm really asking—if refusing will lead to *me* becoming the heretics' next source of illicit income.

"I told you, Lys. I don't force anyone into service." His eyes are forgiving as they meet mine, but hard. "If you say no, that's your choice. You've proved that you know how to keep a secret. But"—his words take on an sharp note—"this offer only comes once. Decline and you'll never see the reliquary, or me, ever again. I've been patient this long, I can be patient a little longer. The rise and fall of another of Tempestra's avatars is the blink of an eye to a god."

But not for me. That part hangs in the air, thick as incense.

Avery escorts me out of the cliffs, through walls and passages that stay where they should be this time. Not that I would have noticed—there's a lot on my mind as we make our way through the maze. New gods and old, truths and deceptions, enough to keep me pensively silent until we reach the crevasse that leads back out to the city.

There, I pause. "How long have you been a part of this?"

My question seems expected. "Since shortly after a kind man took me off the streets and offered me a purpose."

Offered. Not "gifted." Not forced.

"Why bother with Nolan at all? Why not just give me the reliquary when I asked for it and cross your fingers?"

"There are only so many chances we can spend. If our next fails..." He takes in a breath and holds it before freeing it again. "You are our best chance to destroy Tempestra-Innara, by far. But if you fail, so do we. Only divinity can destroy divinity, and what might be used to stand against the Goddess didn't work in the way we'd hoped. We wanted you to know the real stakes, and how important your decision was. Which means you needed the truth."

No pressure. "You're really on board with all of this?"

"I would have been in Emmaus's place, if I could have."

It's an unpleasant image, Avery's gentle features contorting into the monstrous. The same thing might happen to me if I agree to Rion's terms. Of course, there are other kinds of monsters I might become. Might already be.

"When you've made a decision," he says, "light a candle and put it in your window. Then, go to Tempestra-Innara's shrine."

"Got it."

"Lys... I know this is a lot to consider. But you could help us rebuild the entire world."

Not my goal, or my concern. But Avery looks so damn imploring. "You know, since I learned about the one thing that might help me kill a goddess, I thought I'd have to tear it from the grip of some zealot's corpse. It wasn't until you showed up that I considered you might hand it over willingly."

He gives me a fragile smile. "There's more places to put faith than in the divine, Lys. You trusted me enough to bring you to where we stand now. Why is it still so hard to believe we'd put our faith in you too?"

Avery's sentiment catches me like a bludgeon—foolish, unfounded sentiment that it is—the weight of it pressing heavy on my chest. Confidence in my skills as a killer is one thing, but he actually seems to believe that I'm the crucial missing piece in their crusade. And maybe I am.

Or I might be another failure waiting to happen.

We slip back out into the night, climb down to the base of the statue. I scan the area quickly, training and habit taking command, but it's as shadowed and deserted as when I arrived. "I can find my way back from here."

"Are you sure?"

"Are you going to protect me if I'm ambushed?"

Avery smiles at my joke, but what do I know? Maybe the favor of a god means he could, somehow. But he doesn't argue, only gives me a hopeful nod and returns to the tunnel entrance.

Good. I need some time alone, to think. Because I have no godsdamned idea what to do. I don't. And it leaves a slimy pull in my stomach, tightens the muscles in my shoulders so much that my shoulder wound begins to ache again. My plan made sense when one fact sat as a cornerstone: that Tempestra-Innara was the most powerful force in existence. But now? That must be technically still true, if Osiron desires my help. They *want* me. I *need* the reliquary.

Except . . . new gods. I've known the Flame. What is left of the Storm, Green, Salt, Stone . . . ? What new forms might these new deities take? What, like Osiron seems to think, could they offer?

What could they take away?

Fragments of possibilities roil, some hopeful, others fearsome, too many impossible to label. For all the deaths of a god I have imagined, I can't seem to picture the new life of one, no matter how important it is to the choice I've been given. Maybe if I had weeks, months to consider . . .

But I do not have the luxury of endless time. Or even enough of the human sort.

And if I say no to one god now, I belong to another forever.

# Forty-three

There are those followers that are fickle, moving from Storm to Shadow to Stone, with only one desire driving their choices: to bask in the presence of the divine.

—*JOGUE'S DIARY OF A SUPPLICANT'S TRAVELS* (RESTRICTED TEXT)

New gods. I don't think I'll sleep, gripped by the idea of them, but I'm startled out of twisted dreams by a pounding knock at my door a few hours after dawn.

It's Nolan, looking probably as rested as I do. Which is to say, not at all. Mind and body, I feel like one big, living bruise as he pushes into the room, all tense energy. "Good, you're dressed already."

After last night's outing, I never even managed to get my boots off. "Are we going somewhere?"

"We need to go see Caius. Another message"—he holds up a folded piece of paper—"was slipped beneath my door last night."

Rion works fast. The mysterious appearing notes, Avery's well-timed comings and goings . . . it all makes more sense now.

At the Silvered Pearl, Caius eyes the paper skeptically, Ramiro so close he might as well be curled up at the Arbiter's feet. He glares. I give him a smirk that sends his hand to his sword.

Caius refolds the paper and flicks a hand at the Caerula leader. "Out." Curt as the command is, Ramiro has apparently been well trained (or well bought) enough to obey promptly, though not without a last edged look for me. "You're *sure* this is from the heretics who attacked our blood mother?"

"Yes." Earnestness clings to Nolan in a way that unsettles my conscience. It isn't as easy as I'd like, seeing him set upon on this fool's errand while still believing what he desires is within reach. Even if I was always going to take the reliquary and run.

Of course, maybe he's not the only one being played. I pick through the memory of Osiron's offer, looking for traps or snags, for whatever it is they're keeping close. It seemed sincere, the chance at freedom being offered . . . but then again, so does this note.

*Dusk, the day of the Arbiter's departure. Same location.* —A

Clean and simple, with only a single requirement yet to be fulfilled: for Caius to get the hell out of Cyprene.

"They *want* to deal with us," Nolan continues. "When you're gone—"

"When I'm gone," Caius echoes sourly. He tosses the note onto the table and leans back in his chair, letting out a sigh. He looks tired. There are dark circles under his eyes, consort to a growing air of irritation. Apparently, the distance from the Goddess is hitting him even faster than it did Nolan and me. Or maybe his fancy feather bed simply isn't as comfortable as he expected. "One note. One line. And I'm supposed to believe that this is what you've been waiting for."

I scoff. "You expected a gilded invitation delivered on a silk pillow?"

Caius blinks at me with red-limned eyes, unamused. "I expected something more."

"It's a where," says Nolan. "A when. And if you—"

"I have no intention of going anywhere."

Nolan stiffens. "We had a plan. An agreement. The heretics—"

"Yes," Caius cuts in. "The heretics." He sits a little straighter. "Those particular, special heretics, not the common ones you laid at my feet to placate me. Do you think I'm a fool? That I'd been pushed away that easily?"

"I knew it." Exhaustion and vexation turn my words acid. "We never should have tried to work with *him*."

Caius frowns. "Don't test me, Lys. The port may be reopened, but my guard still holds the towers. *I* am still the authority in Cyprene right now."

"Exactly," says Nolan. "Do you not understand what you're doing by being here? It's more than the heretics. Cyprene is placated for the moment, but only because they believe you are leaving soon. How long do you think it will be patient? Before the people decide to push back?" His words tighten, come faster. "The longer you remain in the city, the more likely it is something will go wrong. Something neither you nor we can control."

The Arbiter merely stares, waiting for him to finish. "Or this foul, cowardly city will do nothing. Because they know the Flame will come for them if they do. A tempting thought—burning Cyprene to the ground would certainly take care of the heretics you seem so determined to handle like porcelain dolls."

A chill silence falls. Then:

"Caius," Nolan implores. "Please."

The sound of that word, the desperation in it . . . My hand almost moves. Almost deals with the problem of Caius in a definitive, conclusive way. As revolted as I am by Nolan's casual damning of the Salt priests, even worse is Caius taking away what brutal, but strategic, justification there was for it, making their deaths pointless.

"Let me clarify," Caius continues. "I understand my power here . . . and my part. I *am* willing to leave Cyprene . . . in exchange for one thing." He speaks to us both, but locks those cold Arbiter eyes with mine. "Tell me what you're really after."

*Shit.*

Nolan and I trade a startled look, one that tells me he's thinking the same thing I am: that Caius is more perceptive than either of us gave him credit for.

"It's not just a few heretics," he continues, "even capable ones. Those, the Goddess's forces could have flushed out, given the time and resources. But they didn't send Bellators and their legions, or even Arbiters. They sent *you*."

Nolan shakes his head. "Ambition is making you see riddles and machinations where there are none. You're imagining—"

"A weapon," I say. Nolan turns sharply, but we've had enough delays. "A weapon that's able to kill the Goddess. One that almost *did*."

Caius's arrogant facade finally wavers, a glimmer of alarm appearing. Self-centered ass that he is, I almost forgot that his devotion likely runs as deep as any of Tempestra-Innara's children. "Impossible."

"It's not," Nolan says flatly. "We saw it, saw what it was capable of during the attack at the Cathedral."

"But," I add, "we're sworn to secrecy about the details, so that's all you get. At least until we find it."

"And what..." The Arbiter exhales. "What if you don't?" He's rattled by this new information. *Good.* "If I knew what it was—"

"Why?" I interrupt. "How many guards did you bring with you? A hundred? Two? You could close the port again, set every one of them to tearing the city apart, and yes, likely come up with more heretics. Or, like you said, burn it to the ground. But while you did, that weapon would disappear. And if that happens, none of us are gonna be rewarded." As this logic seeps in, it's clear he understands, if begrudgingly. "You ever try chasing a rat? Not nearly as easy as baiting them to come to you. Which is what we were doing until *you* showed up and ruined the trap."

Caius is silent for a long minute. The debate on his face is clear, weighing the indiscriminate thrashing of his approach against the targeted cuts of ours. His eyes search mine, a gaze I hold, forcing expectant impatience into them.

"Three days," he says finally. "That's as much as I'm willing to give you. If you don't manage to find this weapon by then, well..." His folds his hands. "Then I decide how to proceed."

"That's not enough." Nolan paces to the other side of the room, agitated. "We may need more to truly earn their trust, figure out where they are keeping—"

"Three days." Caius isn't about to budge. "The Goddess has confidence in you"—his mouth flattens into a cheerless, mocking smile, the Arbiter we know returning—"and so do I."

The *Golden Glory* sails the next morning on the early tide. Nolan and I watch as it slides from the docks, through the relinquished canon towers, and disappears into the passage that leads to open waters. A crowd has gathered for this too, as if the whole of the city wanted to see the Arbiter gone with their own eyes. If only they knew how short their reprieve will be.

Three days. We got what we wanted from Caius, just not enough of it. At least as far as Nolan believes. As for me . . . I already have what I came here for. All I need to do is accept the terms tied to it.

A god's terms.

My skin itches as we wait for dusk to arrive, wandering the streets of Cyprene, almost aimlessly. There's an unmistakable air of relief, a sense of release that seems to highlight the little holy moments that play out all around. The clasping of a reverie. The sprinkling of salt on a threshold. A bottle of the briny liquor Tychus drank being shared among friends. They captivate my attention. There is nowhere else I might see so many gestures of fidelity not directed toward Tempestra-Innara. Is this what the world was like when the gods were young, their followers spoiled for choice about whom to pledge their devotion to? Is Cyprene a glimpse of the world that Osiron would make again? And would that world—could that world—ever hold?

I'm so deep in thought that I don't register the plaza we're passing through until I spot the stakes, pitted and blackened by fire. An acrid tang of smoke still hangs in the air, touched by a hint of roasted meat. But, thankfully, whatever remained of Marzela and her Salt priests has been cleared away. And, at the base of the posts, little piles have appeared. Shells, braids of seaweed, but mostly tiny piles of salt, starkly pale against the dark scars left by the flames. I glance at Nolan, no hint in his face about whether there are any lingering feelings about having sent the priests to their deaths. But he knows the world he wants.

*They learned eventually, of course. When they built empires around themselves—great, grand things that grew and grew until they were all pressed up against each other . . . when those armies of the blessed turned on each other . . . they learned.*

The death of Tempestra-Innara would fracture the Devoted Lands either way, but free of the gods, it would settle into something new—something wholly human, if not entirely peaceful. But if new ones rose to power . . . I can't help but picture a cycle started anew, playing out over and over.

*Faith, in whatever form it comes in, persists . . . will outlive every single divine being that has ever walked this land.*

And so, some deep part of me knows, will the sins of their devout. New gods or old, there's no knowing where the reality of either will land. I refused to walk across the ice because I thought death would come regardless. Instead, I was made a thrall to the Goddess. To this day, I don't know which was the worse outcome. And here I am again, with a decision that feels as if it will end in some similar, damning result.

This should be an easy choice. And yet . . .

When we finally make our way to the shrine, the tide is rising instead of falling, the stone pillars fully exposed, waves slipping their way closer as dusk falls. The sun sinks behind a low sky of clouds, muting what little color there is in the shrine, making it feel even more ancient. And heavy too, as if the ghosts of who knows how many executions have seeped into the stone ceiling above us and are trying to bring it down. Like at our last visit, we wait on the lowest tier, where the water will submerge our words, drown them like offerings. Or would, if we were talking. Instead, Nolan stares quietly out across the bay, gaze hard but unfocused, toward . . . well, *that* I can guess. The light. The *Flame*.

"You've barely said a word since Caius set sail."

"I know."

"Well, there's two."

He sighs. A moment stretches with careful consideration. "You know Caius is going to try to kill us, right? If we find the reliquary?"

"You're sure?"

"You're not? It was all there, beneath the conceit. The way he looked at us . . ." He pauses. "You were right."

"Ooh, I do love it when you say that, but about what?"

"About the competition we're forced into with one another . . . the consequences of it." He gazes back out at the water. "I thought Caius served the Goddess above all else, and maybe he believes he does, but he wasted no time in trying to serve himself by coming here. And he has no interest in sharing success. He'll turn his Thorn Guard on us at some point. If we find the reliquary, he'll present it as *his* prize. And if we don't . . . well, maybe he lets us live and lays the blame at our feet." When I don't respond, he continues. "No 'I told you so'?"

Oh, if only I felt like teasing. My chest tightens. Tempestra-Innara. Osiron. Caius. Nolan . . . I feel like a needle spinning around a compass, unable to orient.

"Not to draw unfair comparisons, but . . . weren't you still planning something similar?" His silence returns, a sudden, brooding stillness. "We'd set terms in our deal," I hurry to add. "Find the reliquary, then . . ."

"Yes . . . then we renegotiate." The way he says it, I almost wish he *were* Caius, all ambitious transparency. A minute passes. "Were *you*?" The question creeps out. "Planning to turn on me once we got the reliquary, I mean? Or . . ." he continues, with even more caution, "is that particular part of our agreement no longer beneficial to either of us?"

My stomach manages to find a new way to twist, wringing out what little resolve had pooled there. I turn away, as if considering it, afraid Nolan will spot the newly discovered truths in the purse of my mouth, the tightness of my eyes. "I'd . . . like to think we've both learned it's better to have someone watching your back than not."

"You're not just saying that to keep me off guard?"

"Of course I am." Keeping my voice light feels like trying to lift a dead cow. "In truth, I'm conspiring *with* Caius against you. We've fallen for each other, you see, and plan to live in Belspire's castle together, with a pet drooling princess and ancient Arbiter to keep us company."

Nolan's features soften. "Are you sure you wouldn't rather be dumped overboard at sea?"

Humor. My innards twinge again.

"A toss-up, really," I say. "Okay, no renegotiation. Getting the reliquary back to Lumeris . . . that was always the job, and we were given it together." A lump grows in my throat. "Tempestra-Innara can sort out who deserves what after that."

Relief. He doesn't even hide it.

"How do we handle Caius?" I say, before he can say anything that might further stir up what's roiling in me.

"He's handled... for now. But we need to find the reliquary and get off the island before he returns... if we even can at this point."

His doubt hits me off guard. The way he'd pushed Caius, bought us time... I might know tonight's meeting is futile, but from his bleak tone, it's almost as if he does too.

"If there's no hope, what are we even doing here?"

Nolan's mouth turns up in a frail, amused smile. "Giving up isn't an option, Lys. Failure might be, but not giving up."

I don't like the new note in his voice, one that sounds less like defeat and more like honesty. It echoes, sinking into the depths of me, mingles there with the guilt growing like mold. I've never been truthful with Nolan. But after everything, somehow, there's a part of me that wants to be. We both started this endeavor so determined, so sure of our direction.

And now?

Now I have the chance to upend the world, just not in the way I thought. And Nolan seems more and more like a sword left in the dirt, growing dulled and pitted. He hasn't had a chance at success since we first stepped onto this island.

"It's not failure." A half truth. A tainted one. "Sometimes... sometimes you can do everything as right as you possibly can and it still doesn't turn out the way you want."

Finding the reliquary. Becoming Executrix... or avatar. I don't need to specify what I mean. All must seem nearly impossible to him now. Nolan might not be giving up, but there's a part of him that's giving in.

"Okay, new plan: If we make it back, we blame Caius for *everything*. It's what he deserves for butting in where he wasn't wanted."

A laugh. Quick, but true. "I guess there's that. And..." He takes a deep breath. "And the Goddess's favor isn't necessary to serve them, no matter where one might end up."

It certainly helps, though. "Look on the bright side: If anyone is going to get shipped off to waste away in some forgotten corner of the Lands, it will be me." I lean back. "Hey, maybe I'll even get tossed back to Cyprene."

"Maybe both of us will be sent here."

"Would that be so bad?" I mean for it to lighten the mood, but as soon as it leaves my lips, I want to take it back. Not because of any lie.

Because there's a taste of truth.

And maybe Nolan senses that too. He turns fully toward me, almost luminescent in the low, dusty light of evening.

"I mean, I know it would be bad," I say quickly. "The Goddess's light—"

"Still reaches here, as faint as it is." A flash of longing crosses his face, there and gone, replaced by something else. Understanding. Acceptance. "Low service is still service. A service that is a punishment is still service."

With anyone else in the world I'd be calling bullshit. But not Nolan. For all his lies and manipulations, there's one truth about him that has remained immutable—Nolan wants to serve. Whether as avatar in Lumeris or pariah in Cyprene, his dedication to Tempestra-Innara is pure, absolute. So absolute that jealousy rises in me suddenly. It steals the moisture from my mouth, puts a lump in my throat, simply from the ease of it.

Nolan hasn't spent his life filled with hate, fueled and burned by it at the same time. He hasn't felt the cold touch of hope followed by the discovery that success would be an entirely different—and unimaginable—creature than expected. Nolan aspired, yes, but the fall from that attempted climb has always been cushioned by the simple comfort that to serve Tempestra-Innara is enough for him.

"And maybe," he continues, face turning away. "Maybe it wouldn't be so bad with some company."

The lump grows. What if this *was* enough?

Cyprene isn't freedom, but it's freer than anything else I've ever known. Would suffering here, so far from the Goddess's light, be any worse than suffering closer to it? Would I end up as desperate as Fedic, or could I make peace with the longing? Is there somewhere between accepting I can't escape what the Goddess made me and destroying them and the whole of their world?

*Low service is still service.* Can an undesirable life still be a fulfilling one?

My gaze creeps back to Nolan.

And what circumstances could bridge those two things?

We don't need to do this. *I* don't need to do this. Osiron's battle with Tempestra-Innara may be inevitable, but it doesn't have to be mine. I've been seeing my choice as two extremes: suffer beneath the Goddess or serve Osiron by helping usher in their new-world vision. But Cyprene is proof that there could be another option. That I could find a corner of existence where I might find less than I dreamed of, but more than I've ever had.

The idea is like picking at a wound, peeling away at skin and scab, unsure whether infection lies below. But I don't get a chance to find out. Nolan starts suddenly, turning toward the figure that has appeared on the steps above us. Dark has fully fallen, and Avery, fully cloaked, has the appearance of a misplaced shadow. Before we join him, Nolan and I share a silent acknowledgment that whatever is going to happen, it happens now.

No more delays.

No more chances.

We turn back to Avery, Nolan raising a hand in greeting.

But before either of them can say anything, Avery bucks forward, as if punched from behind. He catches himself at the top step. Then, he looks down, cloak shifting aside just enough to reveal the point of the arrow sticking through his chest.

# *Forty-four*

As the sea rose, so did the fear on the faces of the condemned. They began to beg, to plea for mercy as they strained against the stone pillars. Little good it did. Perhaps the followers of the Salt Goddess would have once been moved, but this was no exercise of justice. This was as much an offering as an execution. A hope that the Salt Goddess might know their devoted still believe, still wait for them to wake from the watery depths and rise to power once more.

—EXCERPT FROM THE OBSERVATIONAL NOTES
OF THE HISTORIAN THEAN

F<small>OR A LONG, LIQUID</small> moment, Avery stares down at the dark shaft of the arrow. Then, he crumples, pitching forward, momentum tumbling him down the stairs until he lands with a meaty thump at our feet.

I cannot breathe. My lungs harden, solid as the stone around us, air refusing to move through them. Then I fall too, to his side, tearing at his hood. When I pull it back, dead eyes stare up at me.

But they are the eyes of a stranger.

Relief—crass and callous—floods through me. I do not know this young man, his hair darker than Avery's, skin paler, a slight build the only feature they share. But I don't get a chance to unravel the mystery of Avery's absence. Footsteps sound—lots of them. I look up at figures that now surround us: the Caerula, dozens of them, encircling us like an audience anticipating a show. Which maybe they are. A handful carry lanterns, which cut through the dark and leave sharp shadows on the men's faces. Some are armed with blades, some with long spears like the fishermen on the docks, and the rest, crossbows, all of which are trained on us.

I feel Ramiro's mean-as-hell grin before I see it. He stands at the back of the pack, filling in the space the unknown heretic occupied only seconds before.

Nolan's fists tighten. "What have you done?"

Ramiro shrugs, unbothered. "Taken care of a pest."

"You've destroyed our chance at finding the heretics!"

"You're a fool to believe that. The Arbiter too. Neither of you understands Cyprene. He and his fancy soldiers can tear apart the city, search the cliffs. They won't find what they are after, unless it's an untimely death."

I get to my feet, hands aching to reach for my sickles, though I keep them carefully at my side. "So why didn't you share that information with him?"

"Because whatever you want, it doesn't matter a rotten fish head to me," he spits. "And I don't care whether you're Tempestra-Innara's prize puppies. You came to *my* city, killed *my* men, and crossed *me*." His face darkens. "None of you understand where you are. These 'heretics' you're after? They always come back. Same way you Chosen always run back to Mommy when you can't stand it anymore. You have no place here, and the Goddess belongs exactly where they are—far away."

Nolan tightens, his jaw clenching. "Cyprene is under the rule of Tempestra-Innara."

Ramiro laughs. "Devoted or heretic, Cyprene belongs to Cyprene. And with Arbiter Caius gone, well . . . Alas, your meeting tragically went wrong, the heretics turning on you. Oh, after he's done mourning"—he says it sarcastically—"he may try to flush out the heretics, but once he loses a few men to the tunnels, I suspect he'll cut his losses." He gestures. Chains appear. "You have my thanks for making this so easy, though. It's fitting that your clandestine meeting would take place where the heretics could punish you in the old way."

Nolan and I draw our weapons. But the Caerula have the high ground. And a dozen crossbows, ready to make short work of us.

"None of that," Ramiro grumbles. "Drop them."

"Lys..." Nolan hisses.

I hear the question. But I already know the answer. "Not much of a choice here." Slowly, I lower my sickles to the stone. Even slower, Nolan follows suit. There's an ominous, almost musical slink of chains as the Caerula move in on us, more cautiously than in the cave. Clearly, they've learned something. The ones with chains keep behind the ones with spears, who prod Nolan and me, herding us like animals. I feel the chill mass of the stone pillars before my back hits one, waves already licking at their base with hungry impatience, as if they know how long it's been since they were last fed.

"And here I thought immolation was the worst way to go." I smirk at Nolan even as the pair of Caerula begin looping chains around us. "At least that would be quick."

"Much quicker," Nolan tosses back, which is how I know he's caught on.

Flames explode from his palms, leaping onto the Caerula binding him, engulfing his cloak in an instant. He screams and Nolan's chains drop. Mine stay where they are, but the distraction is sufficient. I jerk forward, yanking the Caerula with me. She slams face-first into the stone and crumples. Then I'm free too. I twist, barely avoid getting spitted by a spear, and grab its shaft. One yank and its mine; I jam the butt end into the wielder's face, feel bone crunch. But I don't need weapons, I need cover. I throw an arm around the man's throat and pull him close as I brandish the spear in my other hand.

When I risk a glance over, Nolan has his own human shield, hands twisted in the man's cloak. "Fight me and you'll end up burning like your friend." The "friend" was smart enough to break for the water. Not smart enough to know it wouldn't smother the divine flame quickly enough. His screams sound for a few more agonizing seconds before the waves swallow him, cries and all. "Same goes for you," I whisper in my Caerula's ear.

*Now* it's a fight. The Caerula may have learned something from our last encounter, but it wasn't enough. Nolan and I slowly walk our shields forward. Their companions, whey faced and unsure what to do, retreat.

Ramiro's curses echo throughout the shrine. "What are you doing? Kill them!"

I laugh. Loudly, so Ramiro can hear it. "Should have told your archers to put a few bolts in us first. Well, live and learn. Or not. We'll see how it goes."

No one moves. It was a gamble, wagering that the Caerula actually gave a damn about their own, but like Ramiro said, Cyprene belongs to Cyprene. These people are compatriots. Neighbors. Friends.

At least, I hope.

We gain more ground. Nolan scoops up his sword, and I speedily discard my spear for a sickle, then slip it into its holder before grabbing the other. Our meat-shields whimper but know better than to resist.

"Not willing to make sacrifices, Ramiro?" It sounds like a taunt, but Nolan is stalling, giving us time to press our way up the steps. The Caerula tighten as they recede, making it even harder for the archers to risk a shot.

"You're prolonging this. There's nowhere to go but through us." Ramiro is right, but at least he sounds *pissed* about it.

"Lys." Nolan speaks low as we reach the last, highest tier of the shrine, where the crowd of Caerula block any further advance. "We're probably not going to get out of this."

"I know." I lock eyes with him. Wink. "But it will be fun to try."

In unison, we shove our shields into their companions and attack. There are shouts, a clatter of footsteps, the *thwap* of crossbows loosing their arrows. Nolan and I go for the lantern carriers first. I duck a sword swing as my first target panics, dropping his light in a scrambling attempt to draw his weapon. It shatters. He goes tumbling as I barrel into him, arcing my blade at the next-closest light bearer. This one is more steadfast, and catches my sickle across her throat for that bravery.

Blood flows.

Darkness descends.

For the Caerula, at least. I can still see well enough. Some of the Caerula try to attack as chaos erupts, others to flee, but Nolan takes out another lantern, and what little light is left creates more confusion than clarity. Shadows flutter like oversized bats as I disembowel one, take three fingers off another. Nolan sends someone flying off the end of a stone tier—not a fatal fall, but the landing should take the fight out of them. Moments later, the last of the lanterns winks out. Beneath the shadowed overhang, the Caerula can't tell friend from foe.

"Kill them!" I don't see Ramiro but I hear him. "Kill anything that comes at you!"

His panic makes me smile. Makes me seethe, calling to those dark depths within. What answers grows like a flame—an inferno. And for the first time, I sense it in Nolan too. Blood singing to blood. Our divinity, as strong as it will ever be, rising to meet this trial and not giving it a single fucking inch. When we move, our training mirrors itself. Our techniques, our strikes, all born from the same place, following the same rhythm. There are dozens of Caerula, the whole of Ramiro's forces for sure. I don't care. He could have brought a hundred. A thousand. I don't even flinch when a line of pain scrapes up my back, or when something pierces the meat of my arm. We fight on, the salty spray of the waves now deliciously bloody, wolves cutting through a foolish flock.

Then, suddenly, I have a chance to breathe. A hand clamps down on my arm. I raise my sickle to strike—

*Nolan.*

He points.

The cliff path is open, clear.

We run.

The way is narrow, and Nolan falls in behind me, stone to one side of us, air and a long fall on the other. There's no telling if the Caerula know we're gone, but they'll figure it out soon enough, relight their lanterns, be on our heels. The unevenness of the path slows us, but we have a head start. We'll be able to lose them in the city.

The path curves, and a figure appears. Before I can react, it hurls something with a force that knocks me off my feet. I collide with the stone cliff and fall to the ground, tangled in netting; its thin, tight strands slice into my skin. I twist, getting a glimpse of the attacker as

Nolan leaps over me to confront them: Ramiro, not looking so scared now. No, there's a bright sheen of desperation in his eyes, in the flush of his cheeks. One hand holds the other end of the net that has ensnared me.

The other, an empty vial.

The Renderer blood tincture we left behind in the caves. He's downed the whole lot, pupils practically bursting with the flood of temporary divinity racing through his veins. In the instant it takes me to realize what he's done, Ramiro drops the vial and draws a slick, curved sword. I anticipate a swing of that weapon. So, apparently, does Nolan. Instead, Ramiro jerks on his end of the net . . . the net that Nolan is half on top of. We both go flying, Ramiro's strength augmented in a way that makes us like weak children in comparison. The breath slams from my lungs as I hit the ground again. Gasping, I manage to twist one wrist, feel my bindings loosen as my sickle cuts through the netting.

Nearby, metal screams against metal. Nolan is down on one knee, blocking Ramiro's blade with his own, muscles of his neck taut as he struggles to regain his footing. When Ramiro takes a half step back to steady himself, Nolan manages to do so, but an instant later the Caerula is swinging again, over and over, driving Nolan back toward the shrine.

I saw at the net, seemingly endless strands tangled around my legs. Finally, it falls away. I scramble up, yanking my sickles free. Ramiro is behind me now, down the path, fixated entirely on Nolan. Good sense screams to get away, escape. Then, the Caerula leader strikes a beastly blow that sends Nolan's sword flying over the cliff. Ramiro crows, a brutal, primitive sound—viciously human, but honed to an edge by the divine. He raises his blade again. Under that murderous arm, something comes over Nolan, neither fear nor anticipation, but from the space between them. His eyes lock with mine, mouth forming one word.

*Run.*

But I don't. I can't. I strike, arcing my sickle at Ramiro's exposed back, feeling the connection of the cut, the split of flesh. It might as well be a scratch. Ramiro heaves himself to one side and kicks, boot catching me in the chest. A rib, maybe two, cracks and I'm on my back again. Coppery blood coats my tongue. But the dark flame inside me flares again. I'm not dying here, like this, felled by some cut-rate divinity-laced bully. And neither is Nolan.

I push into the pain, gather it to me, making it to my knees in time to see Nolan pull a dagger from who knows where and lunge at Ramiro. It sinks into the Caerula's side but doesn't slow him at all. With a force like an oak tree felled by a storm, his arm whips out.

Time slows—creaking, fracturing—as Nolan goes airborne.

Then, it breaks as he arcs through the night, and over the side of the cliff.

# Forty-five

*This* is your responsibility. *This* is the Goddess's will. There is no other.

—PRIOR PETRONILLA

The cry that catches in my throat is nearly freed by Ramiro's blade, which wastes no time in seeking me out. I push back out of reach, blood pounding, but ice-cold.

*Nolan . . .*

Another attack, a hairsbreadth from opening me shoulder to hip. I keep close to the path wall, but Ramiro is fast, too damn fast. Sloppy, though, no finesse to his strikes. Except who needs skill when they've got enough stolen divinity to make a raging bull seem as gentle as a kitten? It's all I can do to dodge, or turn his blows aside. No trying to block or overpower him. Both are a death sentence. I can only keep moving. Survive. And I barely manage that, every strike putting me a little more off balance.

Then, my foot catches a rock. I drop straight onto my backside like a clumsy toddler.

The only thing that saves me is Ramiro himself, wasting a moment on a manic, crackling laugh before his sword falls again. I throw myself to one side, kick out, heel catching the side of his knee. Something snaps, tears. But Ramiro's pain is a thousand leagues away right now.

With a frustrated cry, he sinks his sword into the meat of my thigh. I scream, reflexively dropping a sickle and reaching for the wound, the reckless need to pull out the blade overcoming all reason. I needn't have bothered. Ramiro yanks it free, triumph spreading on his face as quickly as the dark stain around Nolan's dagger, which is still planted in his side. He straightens—*looms*—bloodlust glinting in his blown-out gaze as he raises his arm again.

It's a bad angle. And I have to wait until the very last, riskiest second, when Ramiro drops that final strike, one that looks aimed to remove my head from the rest of me. I whip my sickle around and release, then jerk back as far as I can as a line of fire lights up across my chest, just below my collarbone. A well-aimed strike.

But not as good as mine. Ramiro stumbles, sickle sunk deep into his sternum, before his knees buckle. The sound he makes is doomed enough that I scramble to the edge of the cliff, bracing myself for the sight. Nolan's body broken on the rocks below. Him sinking beneath waves, too injured to swim. Nothing at all, the waves having already claimed their meal.

What I see is Nolan, balanced precariously on a narrow, jagged ridge just below my vantage, clinging to the stone.

A breathy, thankful laugh escapes.

Nolan grimaces. "Be relieved later, please."

I reach down and hold tight as he pulls himself back up over the ridge, then spots Ramiro, slumped over and gasping. Heaving, really. But a few inches of steel in your lungs will do that. I don't feel in better shape. I get back on my feet, ribs feeling like they're likely to take a stab at *my* lungs, leg red and wet and screaming.

"You want to finish him off?"

"No time." Nolan grabs Ramiro's sword.

Oh, but there is. Enraged fury radiates from Ramiro's gaze as I sweep by, retrieving my sickle with a yank. He bucks once, mouth filling with blood. It spills from his lips, dribbles down his chin, oily black beneath the cloak of night.

"That"—I lean close—"was for Mortimer."

The rage in his eyes flickers, turns to utter confusion. Then they go dark. Almost as dark as the satisfied smile that dances onto my lips.

"Lys?"

I catch the pleading note in Nolan's tone, along with something else. Fear? But he's right; it's time to run.

The Caerula may still be in pursuit, but our way forward is clear. We reach the city and dive into the maze of it. When Nolan turns, I follow. When I bolt down an alley, Nolan is on my heels. We are a pack of two, moving as one, running until even our lungs begin to burn. And then, finally, we stop, in the shadowed courtyard of an empty, crumbling warehouse, moon peeking over its ragged roof. For several minutes, we listen, backs pressed to the cold brick. But there are no sounds of pursuit, nor anything else. We are alone.

Nolan turns to me, streaks of drying blood across his pale skin, eyes alight with the glow of battle. I want to laugh again, or howl, a primal sensation tearing through me. But I can barely catch my breath. My gaze locks with Nolan's, both of us still treading the consuming, velvet darkness.

Then, in a wordless, mutual agreement, we drop to the ground.

I press my forehead to my knees as victory recedes and the pain comes crashing back. "Ghmmmm."

Nolan shifts closer. "You're hurt."

"S'nothing. Scratches, a rib or two that's been better. Back there, I—" *I thought you were dead.* "You almost died."

"Almost but didn't. You're *hurt*." More insistent this time. Hands unfold me, straightening my wounded leg.

"I'm—OW!"

"No, you're not." Methodically, he examines the cuts, then slips off his belt and removes the scabbard from it before tightening it around my thigh. "We need to take care of this."

"Sure." The night air is cool, but I'm hot all over. Burning, even. Simmering in my own blood loss. "Just need a minute."

I expect an argument. Instead, Nolan takes a deep breath and sits back, drawing his own knees up. For a moment, he looks strange. Looks . . .

Small.

"It's over," he says quietly. "The reliquary . . . we'll never get to it now."

Small . . . and broken.

Something settles around us, weightier than our bare survival, yet gossamer thin. Nolan stares at me over his knees with a piercing, brittle intensity. It sinks deeper as my breath slows, heartbeat returning to normal, flesh redoubling its efforts to remind me that *divinely gifted* does not mean *totally invincible*. But those corporeal discomforts slip into the background, pushed back by Nolan's words and the recollection of those few torn-apart heartbeats where a hole had suddenly opened up in the world, in the place where he had been. They'd passed quickly, that empty space refilled, but left something behind. A truth, deep as the wound inflicted by Ramiro and twice as dangerous. A truth I can't find a name for.

Nolan and I aren't family. We aren't friends. We're—

"It should be you." The words rupture out of him, blunt as a confession.

"What?"

"It should be you," he says again, and this time, it sounds *exactly* like a confession. Like a secret that can't be kept anymore. "Executrix. The Goddess's hand. If there is anyone in the Devoted Lands that can carry that honor . . . Lys, it's you."

I try to laugh, but my busted ribs don't get the joke. "I told you, I'm not—"

"You could have escaped Ramiro. Retreated to safety. Instead you stayed. Saved me."

"*Barely*."

"But you did, though you didn't need to. Like you did at the Cathedral, when Emmaus attacked, and when the Renderers . . ." He looks away suddenly, as if embarrassed by that memory. "You play the fool, but you're not. You were willing to partner with me even after I tried to kill you, because it meant a better chance at finding the reliquary and that mattered more. You're one of the finest fighters I've ever seen, even if you don't need a blade to get under someone's skin. You improvise. You cross lines when you need to. I . . . I thought I was in control in Lumeris, Belspire, Novena. That there was no challenge I couldn't conquer." He takes a deep breath. "But I've failed, over and over. Made every wrong decision. And since coming here . . . all I've felt is the constant cracking, as if . . . as if I'm flaking away bit by bit. I . . . I don't trust my own instincts anymore."

"I've felt it too—"

"Not like I have." He tenses further, shrinking into himself. Withering. "We both know that. Even if you are only staying afloat, it's better than drowning. The Executrix needs to be ready for anything. You bend. You flex. You're unbridled and unconventional, and . . ." He pauses, still staring at the worn-down cobblestones. "And that is exactly what our blood mother needs more than anything right now."

Too warm a minute ago, now a perplexed chilliness trickles over my skin.

His eyes find mine again. "That's what I'm going to tell Tempestra-Innara, if we make it back to Lumeris. If . . . if they'll hear me. That even though we failed to find the reliquary, *you* should be Executrix, and that it would be an honor to see you at the Goddess's side."

And just like that, I win.

Nolan is conceding. But not surrendering. *Competitor*, *adversary*, *rival* . . . those words no longer matter, held up against whatever we are now. Nolan is not Jeziah, a companion of convenience and necessity. And he's not my blood brethren, that forced distinction that has always been as much challenge as collective.

I don't know what he is.

Only that there is too little space between us now. Cyprene turns into a diaphanous thing, a mirage shimmering at a distance a Nolan stands, a ghost threading through the fractured, faded world. And maybe that's what we are—ghosts of two doomed children resurrected by a merciless baptism. He offers a hand, sticky with the blood that is our shared lot, and I accept it, letting him help me to my feet. For a few heartbeats, we stand like that, silent, dressed by the night, by death, by the divine chain that links us to one another.

I drop my hand first. "The Petrel."

We move like shadows through the city, and by the time we sneak in through the back of the guesthouse, we hardly need to. The windows of the common room are dark; the stairs, dark; the interior of Nolan's room, dark. Within, he lights a lamp and goes to work immediately, sitting me in a chair, cutting away my ruined clothing to get at my wounds. He cleans them as best he can, binds my ribs with lengths of torn sheets, stitches the puncture in my thigh. With every touch of cloth, every snug stitch, the ruthless years of our Cloister training shine, infused now with something more—an unfamiliar conviction. A lacy, unsure devotion. Bitterness grows in my mouth as Nolan draws a bath and leaves me alone to cleanse the rest of the night's grim leavings. It spreads through me like the blood staining the lukewarm water, but refuses to drain away. Minutes pass thickly, congealing around me until, finally, I towel off and re-dress enough for basic modesty.

I return to the sitting room. Nolan is there, face filled with questions, though he waits for me to speak. To *decide* what comes next.

My chest tightens in a way that has nothing to do with the bindings. "Giving up isn't an option." His words, my conclusion. "We need Caius, to get him and his Thorn Guard back and . . . tell him everything."

He nods, once. "About the reliquary."

The words are heavy with resignation. But this search of ours has gone on too long, become too frayed. Borne too many unintentional consequences.

"Yes. The reliquary." I lean on the table, borrow its sturdiness.

Nolan takes a concerned step forward, misreading the gesture. "You need to rest."

I do. I need . . . "We'll find a ride to the *Golden Glory* in the morning." I can't help the smirk that tugs the corner of my lip. "Just need a little beauty rest first."

"Tomorrow," Nolan says.

"Tomorrow." And then, before either of us can say anything else, I retreat to my room.

Inside, I lock the door. Discard my bloodied garments and go to the basin of water, splash it on my face. It's blessedly cold as hell, tempering the persisting heat in my cheeks. Head hanging, letting the water drip, I watch the ripples grow, fold over each other, and disappear as they meet the relentless confines of the basin. There, half naked in the square of light streaming through the room's single window, I let myself understand. The indecision gripping me, the hesitation . . . it isn't about what I wanted. I've known what that is since the moment a goddess's blood trickled over my lips, binding me, emptying my life of everything but *them*.

Except now, there's something else that matters. Someone else.

I make my decision... a decision I've already made countless times since Nolan spoke those four little words.

*It should be you.*

This cannot go on.

*I* cannot go on, like this.

I open the window and place a candle in it. Light it. Then, I put on fresh clothes and clean my sickles. All while marking the time in my head, the count keeping my heartbeat steady, my thoughts manageable. After half an hour has passed, when I'm sure Nolan has succumbed to the fatigue left by our battle and my message has had a chance to be spotted, I make my way down the side of the building and drop gracelessly to the street.

*Tomorrow.*

Tomorrow, bodies will be found. Caius will be told the truth. Cyprene will be torn apart.

But I will be gone, on my way to Tempestra-Innara, and the death of one of us.

# Forty-six

Oh, my darling. Affection is neither a poison nor a cure, though to those touched by it, it can often feel like either. Or both.

—IDALINE, *THE MERCHANT OF LUMERIS*

I*T'S OVER.*
But it's not. Not for me, not yet.

The darkness seems heavier in the deserted desolation that is the shrine of Tempestra-Innara, stone walls surrounding it like the ragged edge of a grave. The night bleeds into my skin, chills running over it, save where my wounds throb with aching heat. But even that fades behind a deeper pain, and the tight grip of fear.

That Osiron is gone. That the attack on the shrine has driven them away, along with the reliquary. By now, they must know their follower is dead. Or did they expect this, and that's why they didn't send Avery? I don't know. I cannot fathom the expectations or motivations of a deity that's been planning—manipulating—for centuries. I only know that they offered me a chance, and now, despite my prior hesitations, all I want is to take it. To leave Cyprene behind and stand before my Goddess one final time.

As minutes tick by, each more impatient than the last, the statue at the center of the shrine tugs at my attention. It's only stone, and defaced rudely, but the blank stare of that holy visage still manages to stir up memories.

Of Tempestra-Innara, looming above, gaze piercing into the depths of me.

Of divine blood dripping over my lips, its searing warmth trickling down my chin.

Of a deity watching on as I fight, kill, fight, all in their name.

"Lys?"

I know the voice before I turn, the figure before I take in its lines, the cloak wrapping it not fooling me this time. Avery pulls back the hood, letting the little moonlight that reaches into the shrine wash over him.

"I'm in," I say, before he can speak. Before anything else can poison my resolve. "But I have to go *now*. Caius is waiting nearby in his ship. Tomorrow, Nolan will go to him when he finds me gone, tell him everything about the reliquary."

A smile twitches onto Avery's lips, as if he knew that my full defection was never in doubt. That it was an inevitability.

And maybe it was.

"Thank you." I've never heard more true gratitude in those words. "I always believed you would help us."

Something twists in my gut. "I'm helping myself. Not you, not Rion, not whatever mad scheme he has to reshape the world or whatever. Getting rid of Tempestra-Innara is, above all else, *for me*."

"Even a selfish choice can serve the greater good."

*Good*. I swallow a snicker. Do any of us deserve that distinction, after everything that's happened? "When this is done—*if* it gets done—I'm gone after. Forever. No one comes after me, or tries to sell me on any new faiths, got it?"

Avery nods, more solemn now. "No debts, Lys. Not to us."

No debts to pay. No chains to keep me down. No ties at all. The night air is nowhere near as refreshing as the simple thought of it. "I'm sorry about your friend, at the shrine. The Caerula . . . we didn't know."

Avery's hopefulness diminishes a little. "It should have been me. But Osiron . . . they were so sure you'd agree to help us . . ." He swallows. "If you did—*when* you did, they wanted me close, knew you wouldn't trust anyone else to deliver the reliquary." A moment passes. "The ship is waiting. *Splendid Rumor*, east end of the docks. As soon as you're on board, they'll cast off."

"*Splendid Rumor*, got it." The ache to be gone from Cyprene is suddenly so deep, it's as if I've been stabbed again. "Fair warning, when Caius returns, things are going to get messy here."

Something like sorrow touches his eyes. "We never expected to win this battle without losses. But now the tide has truly turned."

"Let's not plan the victory party yet. But . . . maybe."

Avery stares at me as if I am salvation made flesh. Like I am a deity and he is my devoted. Which is something I've had more than enough of tonight. "Do you have it?"

He reaches into his coat and draws out a wooden box—an unremarkable thing, unadorned, boring. Until he opens it. Inside, on a bed of silk, lies the reliquary. The emeralds and silver catch what little light there is, the crystal taking on an otherworldly glow that attests to its divinity. But I've fallen for that before. The bottle lights up as I remove it from its casket and pull the stopper.

Blood sings, a song both divine and damned.

I close it up again.

"Can't wait to find out what it tastes like." I slip the box into my jacket. "Time to go."

Avery nods. "Thank you again, Lys."

"Thank me when Tempestra-Innara is dead. But from a distance." I start toward the shrine entrance, then stop and turn instead toward the far wall, loosening a brick there. Behind it is the Renderers' remaining blood tinctures and balms, stashed away safely since Marzela's threats. I add the Renderers' book and Jogue's diary, hand the lot to Avery. "These might come in handy . . . one way or another."

He examines the contents and nods, understanding.

"And tell Rion . . . tell him . . . I don't know. That I felt like I should say something but ran out of cleverness. Or just a farewell. Frankly, whether I end up dead or free, I'll be happy if I never come across any of you ever again. Do me a favor and sort things out so that's what happens, okay?"

Avery smiles again. "We will do our best. If you promise to survive. And then, to live."

No. I won't promise something I can't hold to. "I'll do my best too." Without another word, I plunge back into the streets. Avery does the same, in the opposite direction. One hand in my pocket, my fingers grip the reliquary box so tightly they go numb, a sensation that spreads through the rest of me. Everything narrows, tightens around me like a shroud. By the time I get close to the docks, dawn is teasing its arrival. There are more stirrings of humanity, the smell of morning fires being lit in stoves, the occasional crow of a rooster. On a city bridge, I pause, the harbor barely visible below through the early-morning fog. I can see movement, sailors on rigging, cargo being loaded and unloaded. There, the *Splendid Rumor* waits for me, its traitorous assassin, and my most precious of cargo.

The bridge empties me into a plaza. Here the fog lies thicker, but in a comforting sort of way. A soothing blanket of anonymity.

Except.

Halfway across the plaza, a figure appears, planted with deliberate stillness. Waiting. I freeze, skin tingling as the silhouette calmly, damn near casually, strolls to where I stand.

Caius.

The Arbiter's eyes blaze with a stormy blend of fury and triumph. "Good morning, Lys."

Boots hit stone, and suddenly the plaza is littered with Thorn Guard. Reflexively, I reach for my sickles, then stop. I don't know what this is. What it means. What I do know is that these are elite soldiers, not Caerula. And that I'm already injured. If I start a fight, I'm going to lose.

"You . . . you're back."

He doesn't reply, only glares, and I understand suddenly: Caius never left.

The Arbiter takes a few steps closer. "I always thought there was something off about you. Something wrong. But not until now did I truly understand how deep the rot ran."

I straighten, doing my best to seem annoyed. "It's too early for mind games, Caius."

His mouth twitches up. "We both know who is playing games here. I know you didn't want to believe me, but here we are, aren't we?"

It takes a moment to realize that he's not talking to me. Suddenly, the blood ripping through my veins seems to stop entirely.

All because of the look on Nolan's face as he steps out of the fog.

Not the one that Caius, and the rest of the world, sees. No, Nolan is as expressionless as he was on that morning at the Cathedral, as we were preparing for the funeral procession. Calm. Considering. A mask that doesn't fool me anymore, now that I've seen what's underneath. And the bewildered disappointment I perceive pierces my chest like a blade.

"Boys"—somehow, I keep my voice steady—"I'm not sure what's going on here, but—"

"Shut up." Caius's words crack like ice. "Nolan didn't want to believe. I didn't want to either. But it appears there's a good reason you've yet to root out the heretics—because you've been working alongside them."

I laugh, despite being the least amused I have ever been in my whole cursed life. I turn to Nolan. "And just when you thought you were the one whose brain was getting the most scrambled by being away from the Goddess. Caius here—"

"Knows where you go at night." The Arbiter takes another step closer, hands folding behind him, the dark circles under his eyes even deeper than before. "And who you meet with, just now in a place where you should be on your traitor knees, praying for mercy."

*Oh.* Oh, *godsdamn it.* In a heartbeat, I am back in the library, startled into attention by Caius. By the only person who has been able to sneak up on me in as long as I can remember. *We all have our little talents.*

"Do you think I believed either of you would tell me the full truth?" says Caius. "That I wouldn't keep an eye on you?"

The air goes out of my lungs. I did it again. For the second time I didn't question my own perceptions about one of my blood brethren, or the story being sold to me by them. Caius may be a spoiled, arrogant bastard, but he's also Cloister trained. And when Nolan and I both thought he was indulging his Belspire-pampered backside at the fancy guesthouse he'd shacked up in, he was doing the exact opposite. And I revealed myself almost right away.

A pleased-as-punch expression spreads on Caius's face as he watches me figure out how well and truly I've fucked up. "I gave you time. Then I watched you use that time to sneak out, go into the Salt cliffs; watched you emerge with the heretic. I thought you'd merely found some way to manipulate them, outside of Nolan's knowledge, wanting the rewards for success all to yourself. Honestly, I even respected that. I've never had the forces to really sift through this city's filth, in that maze or otherwise. But I didn't need to. All I needed to do was wait for you to finish your treachery, and then intercept." He scowls. "That idiot Ramiro almost ruined everything, of course. It's very lucky that you're at least competent. And then, when you put out your obvious little signal—well, I knew it was time. And given how, hmm, aligned the two of you seemed to be, I decided to rouse Nolan, so he could witness your betrayal with his own eyes." The scowl recedes, replaced by something much worse. Much . . . darker. "But even I didn't suspect your true intention."

As much as I want to curse, or yell, or lob some clever quip at Caius, I say nothing. I have nothing *to* say.

"Is it true?" When Nolan speaks for the first time, I hate it. The searing accusation in his voice makes Caius's sound gentle. He's not asking because he wants to know. He knows. He's just working on the acceptance part.

I keep quiet.

"Search her," orders Caius. "Let's see this weapon. This . . . reliquary."

The number of Thorn Guard who descend on me makes fighting back both pointless and foolish. Caius isn't Ramiro—he knows our limits, our skills, and has prepared his soldiers for any resistance I might put up. So, I don't bother. They push me to my knees, rip away my sickles, and rifle through my coat. They find the box. Give it to Caius, who opens it.

His eyes brighten with uneasy reverence as he touches the reliquary . . . within. It glows faintly in response. "This is it, what you were after."

"Yes." Nolan just looks tired. "A power unlike any other in the world."

I grasp, desperate. "A prize. You're right. I didn't feel like sharing the glory with anyone else. Sorry, Nolan, but you should understand the lengths any of us would go to in order to be chosen Executrix. Even playing the heretics for the chumps they are."

I can see right away that the ruse is not going to fly.

"We heard what you said, Lys." For the first time, a hint of anger breaks through Nolan's carefully arranged mask. "About consuming the blood, killing the Goddess. Being *free*. Don't deny it. No matter what you think, you tell the truth far better than you lie."

My own fury rises to meet his. "Fine." In an instant, the deceptions fall away, as liberating as the reality is damning. "Fuck Tempestra-Innara. Fuck what they did to us, what they turned us into. Yes, I agreed to help the heretics and do my own encore to Emmaus's attack. All so I could be freed from their manipulative, horseshit 'love.'" I snicker. "And you would have been too, even if you assholes wouldn't be smart enough to realize it."

Caius strides forward and backhands me so hard I taste blood.

I laugh, loudly and for real this time, and spit red onto his boot. "Keep that. It'll fetch a good price around here."

He raises his hand again, then lets it fall. "I never believed such a foul thing as you could even exist. Divinely gifted—*Chosen*—and a traitor." He takes a deep breath, composing himself. "You and the heretics will be punished. But them first, so you can watch what happens to your new friends." He summons one of the Thorn Guard over. "The heretic she met with, have you found where he was going yet?"

The guard shakes his head awkwardly. "Arbiter Caius, we . . . we lost him."

Caius reddens. "What?"

"We trailed him." The guard delivers the report in a flat, detached tone. "Closely. But he . . . he turned down an alley. We were only a few steps behind, but when we entered it, he was gone. Disappeared."

"Disappeared?" spits Caius. "A person doesn't simply disappear."

They do if they have a god on their side. I smile to myself, even though I won't be getting the same assistance. "Tch, tch. You really think you're gonna outsmart my 'friends' in their own city?"

Caius simmers. "The Goddess will send their legions. They might escape for now, but eventually they *will* be flushed out."

No, they won't, but that's not an argument worth having.

"The heretics are roaches. It's only a matter of time before they are crushed." Caius's eyes narrow. "But you . . . *you* will pay a much higher price."

I'm dead. The knowledge doesn't sting quite as much as I expect. Not nearly as much as Nolan's glare, which I can feel despite keeping my gaze firmly locked on the Arbiter. But maybe I've been dead since that morning in my village, that day on the ice, the moment a goddess's blood passed my lips. Who I've been since is simply a puppet of Tempestra-Innara, as much as any of their avatars.

"You will be executed," says Caius. "By the Goddess's hand."

"Yup," I sigh. "The usual. Got it."

"But first, your heresy must be found to be incontrovertible, here and now. You will be *judged*."

*No.* I jump to my feet, moving before I realize what I'm doing, but the guards are ready. Chains appear, weaving around me, driving me back to the ground as I struggle.

I can die. I can bear the thought of the divine flame consuming me, turning me to ash. But Caius, his Arbiter's power, forcing its way into my mind?

No. *No.*

I kick, feel a bone break. Bite and taste blood that isn't my own. It comes to nothing. There are too many Thorn Guard. Manacles lock around my arms, my wrists, my ankles. I am dragged onto my knees, subdued. Caius has handed the reliquary box to Nolan, whose expression is even emptier than before, lips pressed into a thin line. And in the Arbiter's hand the blue bottle appears. A reliquary in its own way. Two drops, one in each eye. The last of the morning fog swirls around Caius as he steps forward, eyes alight with power. He reaches for me. There's a heartbeat right before his fingers find my face, before his thumbs dig into my cheeks, that I think to fight back again. But then his flesh touches mine.

And I—

# Forty-seven

Please . . . I will go quietly. To be purified by the flame cannot be worse than the judgement that condemned me to it.

—LAST WORDS OF THE HERETIC MIKOLAUS,
IN THE ERA OF TEMPESTRA-INNARA

E<small>NGULFING . . . SEARING . . . AGONY . . .</small>
Descriptors that are too small. Decimation begins behind my eyes, flooding my throat, threading through my veins to the soles of my feet. Divinity turned violation, a torrent that shoves reality aside and sends me careening into some incomprehensible realm of semiconsciousness. I still sense the fleshy parts of me—knees aching against the hard stone, scream locked behind my teeth—even as my inner self is flayed open and turned out by the caustic invasion that is Caius. I can feel him, his mind throwing itself against mine, bruising wherever it lands. There's no resisting; I might as well be a sheet of paper trying to stop the thrust of a sword. He breaks through, a lumbering, unyielding force that ruptures into uncountable icy shards, shredding its way through memory.

*They are mine.*

Through it all, that tiny clarity: An Arbiter cannot read thoughts. Only feelings. Intentions.

*Mine. My secrets are safe.*

But I am breaking.

Visions begin to rise, blood screaming to blood, of *them*—Tempestra-Innara. The Goddess whom I have betrayed. The mother who gifted me with their divinity. I taste salt and copper, in memory and in flesh, mine and theirs. Blood swirls, entwines itself with agony, and begins to pulse. Heartbeats. *Mine.* A great, distant drum as the Goddess's light begins to shine. So bright, so warm. It burns, turning the edges of my agony into blackened cinders. Then, the gripping chill recedes, and with it, the pain.

I am small. A tiny, worthless thing staring at the stone floor trod for centuries by offerings to the Goddess. Shivering, I lick the last of their gift from my lips as their divinity spreads with wildfire hunger, filling me with heat, rewriting those weak, human parts of me. *I am nothing.* The vessel that is my flesh tenses with the sheer ecstasy of it, appalled by the understanding of how frail and empty I was before. *Nothing . . . made something . . .*

And when I finally raise my eyes, my blood mother stands above, gazing down with an emotion I have never truly experienced before this moment: *love*. The intensity of it buries the heretic I used to be even as, deep in some shadowed part, a seed takes root. Later, anger and resentment will sustain it, but now, it, too, feeds on the holy light.

*I stand, achingly proud, over my first kill . . . watch blood flow under the pleased gaze of Tempestra-Innara.*

*I bear witness to their consuming justice, basking in their invigorating light as ash swirls like snow in the Cathedral air.*

*I desire, desperately, their love and approval as they entrust me with the most important task of my lifetime, and hate myself for it.*

Caius's gift rifles through me, picking me apart by pieces, by memory, by every shameful lust and longing.

*I kneel before Tempestra-Innara, gazing into their eyes, drinking the whole of them in and soaking every fiber of myself in their divine light. More . . . I want more . . . I want to drown in them.*

In their love.

And mine.

The world tears again. No, it stitches back together, resolving into filthy cobblestones spotted with blood and spit. My muscles tremble as if I have a deep fever. I want to cry—with relief, with joy, with defeat . . . I don't know.

I don't know.

"I don't understand." Caius's voice, above me.

His feet come into focus. A hand tangles in my hair, jerks my head up. The Arbiter's face is red with exertion and anger, and tight with confusion.

"It's not possible," he says, as if by spitting that observance at me, I will *make* it make sense.

As if I could.

"You betray our blood mother. And yet, you . . . your love . . ." He cannot finish.

The morning fog has begun to clear. Around us, faces fill windows, roused from sleep by the commotion. By my screams.

"I don't understand," Caius says again, and throws me back to the stones, where my elbows skid against the rock. But the physical pain is nothing, blunt. Welcome compared to the Arbiter's touch. I push myself up, force myself to meet his gaze.

"That . . . was . . ." I gasp, still trying to catch my breath. "A rude way . . . to wake the neighborhood."

And then I begin to laugh. And sob, a hemorrhage of emotion, borne by the mirror Caius held up, and its truth. *The* truth. That I am a traitor to my Goddess, my blood mother.

Just not the traitor I want to be.

Caius, eyes hollowed by anger, draws a dagger. Raises it. I see the strike coming.

And then.

Nothing.

I wake with one hell of a headache, in a dark little chamber that smells like salt and wet burlap left to mold. Nausea jostles my gut, almost pleasant compared to the splitting sensation pushing at the seams of my skull, especially in one spot near my temple. But when I try to raise my hands to examine that pain, I encounter resistance. My hands are manacled. So are my feet. The chains are bolted into the floor and wall, reinforced by more iron. What slack there is barely allows me to sit up. The chamber is empty, save for a door, one filthy porthole, and a darkness heavy with abandonment.

After a few minutes, I realize that the faint rocking sensation isn't a side effect of my head wound. I'm on a ship.

*Great.* If I had the energy to give a damn, I would. Because being on a ship can only mean one thing: We are going back. To the Cathedral of the Enduring Flame and Tempestra-Innara.

To the end of me.

Which would be more bothersome if I didn't feel like week-old shit soup. My tongue is tacky, lips sour, as if I threw up at some point. I hope it was on Caius, but that's probably wishful thinking. I'm cold too, flesh stiff. My coat is gone; I've been stripped down to a shirt and pants, both heavily stained with blood and filth.

What a huge fucking mess this has turned into.

I drop my head to my hands, a terrible move. Hot pain stabs at my temples, taking some immeasurable amount of time to recede again. When Caius hit me, he was aiming for real damage. If only he'd managed to kill me outright, because I am well and truly fucked now. I pick through muddy memories, find a better thought: Avery got away. And if Avery got away, so did Osiron and the rest of the heretics, probably cursing themselves up and down for putting their trust—their faith—in a fool like me. They handed over their best and only weapon against the power of the Goddess, and I didn't even make it to the *Splendid Rumor*.

So much for being the only one who could stand against Tempestra-Innara. I couldn't even stand against Caius and his goons.

Hours pass. The dirty light of the porthole fades to dark, then brightens again. No one brings me water, or food, or a bucket to piss in, which leads to some very unpleasant contorting. Occasionally, I hear voices beyond the door, or footsteps, but more than a day passes before I hear a faint clunk of metal.

A key turning.

I sit up, attempting to look at least a little less cowed than I feel, but when the door opens, my muscles loosen and slump.

Nolan.

His expression is that familiar unreadable page. A tome written in an inscrutable hand. Though as he lingers in the doorway, the veil over his eyes seems to waver slightly. There are hints of emotion, though not enough to betray any thoughts. Maybe he's simply nauseated; he's pale, a thin line of sweat along his brow betraying his old friend, seasickness.

He steps inside and closes the door. Still says nothing.

The silence rates about as enjoyable as the pounding in my skull.

"Miss sharing a tiny cabin with me?" I barely recognize my own voice, a sound that stumbles and scrapes over the dry tissues of my throat.

Nothing. Not a hint of reaction. Only a probing, searching look.

"I don't understand." When he finally does speak, the tone is as inscrutable as the rest of him.

"Hearing that a lot lately."

"This isn't a joke." Now there's irritation. "You were going to help the heretics. Try to kill Tempestra-Innara."

"That was the plan." I drop my gaze, head pounding even harder as my heartbeat thuds against my damaged ribs. This line of questioning isn't one I'm fond of, but Nolan is undeterred.

"Caius says you love them. That your devotion runs deep as any Chosen's should and yet . . ." He tightens, seems to curl into himself before softening. "I *want* to understand, Lys. What you did . . . why you did it."

"Does it matter now?"

He ignores this. "Caius thinks maybe it's because of our gift. Confusing his Arbiter senses, making it unclear whether your devotion is real or not."

"Yes! Exactly!" I bark, heedless of the resulting pain. "Don't you get it? That's what the godsdamned problem is—I don't even know my own mind! I hate them, what they've done to me, to so many others, and yet, I . . ." I swallow, bile rising in my throat. Explanation isn't something I owe Nolan, or anyone. But I can't stop it. "The tiniest glimpse of them makes me ache with devotion. When they appear, I want to fall to my knees. When they smile at me, I want nothing more than to please them again and again, to be close to them, always . . . forever . . . I . . ."

I shut up.

"It doesn't make any sense."

"Doesn't it?" My eyes flicker up again, pinning us both in place. "Are we only what Tempestra-Innara made us? Or what we've been made to do, in their name?"

Silence.

"Or am I a traitor and nothing else? No one else? Not the person you schemed with, fought with, *killed* beside?" Moonlight. Blood. Victory. "*It should be you.* How long ago did you say those words?" His jaw tightens. The whole chamber seems to contract at the mention of that resigned moment. "Do *any* fragments of that conclusion remain? Can none of the respect I've earned be applied to who I am—who I could have been—beyond the Goddess? What are you thinking right now, Nolan? About me and what I am?"

He doesn't answer.

Or maybe, in a way, he does.

I force a smirk I don't feel. "I hate Tempestra-Innara. But it would be a lie to say I don't love them too. So deeply that I loathe it." I turn away from him. "It's a wound I've learned to live with."

Always there. Always festering, in its own devoted way. I ignored it as best I could, focusing on anger instead. That ecstasy of their presence, that craving for their approval... for years, I wanted to believe it a side effect of their gift. But I knew better. I knew more. That love was born as soon as I saw them, before they chose me. The same way my hate was fed by the actions of their devoted Chosen, branches from the trunk of their divine tree. All of it—connected. Entangled in a way that can never be undone. Maybe not even after their death.

But that was a risk I was willing to take.

"What happened to Buttons?"

"Left behind," he replies, "with Hiram."

"Good."

Then: "You were going to leave me behind in Cyprene."

"Yup."

"You knew where to find the reliquary all along."

"No, but I found out eventually." I wonder if there is any point to these answers. If they are helping at all. "Avery was the heretic masquerading as a mud cleric. I lied about killing him." I pause. "Sorry."

He gives me another confused look. Why I'm apologizing for *that* and not every other way I've betrayed him . . . I don't know. Maybe I just want to apologize for something. Even if I don't regret it.

"I can't live like this." I can't give him all the truth, but now, when it doesn't matter anymore, I can give a little. "Be this person. Follow this path. It doesn't matter what I feel. Love. Hate. I . . ." I sink, pressing my forehead against my knees. Close my eyes. "I want to be free of this. One way or another."

And soon, I will be.

A few seconds pass. "You were given a gift." His voice simmers, anger finally making its grand entrance. "The greatest gift anyone can possibly be given. You were *chosen* by the Goddess, made divine."

"I was a *child*," I spit, ignoring the vicious stab of pain as my head snaps up again. "A child whose whole world was razed before she was forced to become something she never really had a choice about." My teeth clench. "How could I have said no, awash in the Goddess's power? *Of course* I wanted it. I wanted it and I hated it and I craved it and even now, the thought of it makes me sick. The Goddess's divinity is as much a drug as the Renderers peddle. And they know that. They know how badly we all want their 'gift,' their favor, and what we'll do in order to get it. That's the power of the gods." Oh, Osiron. Oh, that wretched truth. "It's what it's always been."

Nolan says nothing.

"How far to the mainland?"

"A few days."

A few more days to the Goddess. To the end.

"Here." He pulls out a flask, pours the contents into a cup. "It's only water."

Nolan hands it over and I drink. Sips at first, then greedily. It's empty long before my thirst is slaked but at least my mouth tastes less like something took its time dying in it. "Thanks. You sneak that in for me? Better not let Caius find out. He know about the seasickness?"

"We haven't exactly been socializing." Nolan takes the cup back. "I've kept to my cabin."

I manage a cracked smile. "Don't worry, your secret weakness is safe with me. Just do one thing?"

"What?" he says, wary.

"Don't let him take the credit for all of this. Don't let him spin some tale to Tempestra-Innara where he's the hero and shove you to the side. I don't mind being the villain so long as they know the truth—that Caius got lucky and not much more. *We* were the ones that tracked the reliquary to Cyprene. Make sure the Goddess knows that. You still deserve to be Executrix. Or avatar, if that's what you really want. More than Caius deserves whatever he's after. And a hell of a lot more than I ever did."

I wait for a response, but nothing comes. The only sounds are the creaking of the ship bearing me toward my doom, and the faint rhythms of our breath as we stare at one another.

Eventually, Nolan gets up and exits, and I'm alone again.

# Forty-eight

> Whatever you may think or believe, Tempestra-Innara is merciful.
>
> —SOMEONE WHO SHOULD KNOW BETTER

I WOULDN'T RECOMMEND DELIRIUM, BUT it does help pass the time. Days go by with little water and less food. Nolan doesn't return. No Caius, either. At least, not that I'm aware of. Consciousness becomes an unreliable thing. The swaying of the sea turns into the rattling of a windowless wagon. I don't know when it happens. I don't know where I am. I am cargo again, like the first time I was ferried to the Cathedral, and somehow even more doomed this time around.

Mother visits me in fevered, broken dreams. First my birth mother, and then my blood mother. Their voices sing, back and forth, tunes I never quite remember or hear the words to. When I'm awake, sometimes I can't tell if its day or night. Dusk or dawn. And before I figure it out, the dreams come again, pulling me into a different fractured state.

Until.

I wake, clearheaded, enveloped in the softness of what can only be a proper bed. Briefly, I think I am already dead. Dead, laid out, and waiting for—well, whatever a traitor's death gets me. But why make a corpse so comfortable? I test my appendages slowly—fingers, toes, arms, legs. Move my neck around a bit. Everything seems to be in working order. I'm thirsty. And hungry. But even those sensations have regained a certain normalcy.

Gingerly, I roll over, find a table beside the bed bearing a jug of water and a bowl of soup. I drink the water in one go, then start in on the soup. They are the same temperature, left at my side for an indeterminate amount of time. The broth tastes wonderful, though, and vaguely familiar, as if my body already knows its flavor. Given that I'm no longer in the throes of dehydration and starvation, it probably does.

But who, exactly, has been tending to me?

The chamber I'm in now is small and neat, with plastered stone walls and—markedly—a line of iron bars bisecting it. I am on one side, the exit from the room is on the other. A jail, certainly, but for a certain kind of prisoner. Whatever kind of prisoner I am, apparently.

There's a thin slit of a window above the bed, almost hidden behind the draping of its canopy. I get to my feet, wavering a little with dizziness. But as deprived as my body was, it recovers quickly. The window is high enough that I have to strain to see through it, but when I do . . .

It takes a minute. Countless times, I've gazed up at the Cathedral's pointed tower. But I've never looked down at the delicate buttresses, at the roof scaled with slate, lightly touched by the glow of the eternal flame that burns above. A tremble starts in my gut and spreads outward. A cell I would understand, somewhere deep in some dungeon below the Cathedral. Not . . . whatever this is. Again: Why make a corpse comfortable?

I pace to one end of the room and then the other, searching for a way to escape. There's a heavy lock on the cell door but nothing to pick it with, and the hinges are solid enough that no meddling of mine would damage them. Abandoning that idea, I stop and listen, letting minutes pass in pure silence, but there's no new answers to be gleaned there either. Exhausted by the effort, there's nothing for me to do but sit down on the bed and wait, with only thoughts of what is coming to keep me company.

Hours pass before something in me stirs. Something all too familiar. My heart pounds, ticking off the seconds before the door opens, and the full power of Tempestra-Innara's divine light washes over me. The Goddess pauses as they enter, as if surprised to see me awake.

They carry a bowl of soup.

"Daughter." Their voice is a caress, flower petals trailing lightly across my skin. I shudder. "Finally."

Still as prey, I watch as the Goddess approaches the cell door. They move carefully, as if afraid to spill a single drop. One touch, and the lock clicks open.

"You ate. I'm sorry, it was probably cold. Here, this is fresh. Hot."

They hand me the bowl. I take it because I have no damn idea what else to do. If this is an execution, it's by far the strangest one I've ever experienced. I glance down into the steaming broth. Is that what it is? Mercy? Maybe the food is poisoned. Maybe I eat this and drift off into an endless sleep, forgiven by my blood mother for all my sins against them.

Or maybe it's just soup.

Either way, I eat.

They stand nearby as I do, watching. Pleased. Despite the familiar aura of divinity, I take note of little things that weren't there before: a webbing of wrinkles on their face; a slight fade of color, as if their skin is thinning; dark circles beneath their eyes. The wilting of their avatar, continuing even now, when the reliquary is no longer a threat. I can't see the wounds inflicted during the assassination attempt, but I suspect they're still there.

"How do you feel?" they ask, when I am done with my meal.

A single answer comes to mind. "Confused."

The Goddess smiles. "Yes. My poor girl, my poor little Lys. You were in terrible shape when you arrived. But you are growing strong again."

*Because executing someone already half dead isn't any fun?* I resist asking that particular question, fingers clenching the bed linens as the Goddess glides over and places a hand on the side of my face. I can't help it; I lean into that warm touch, pour myself into it, a desperate, aching shiver running through me. Shame floods my veins; sorrow sends tears to my eyes. I want to tell them how sorry I am, to throw myself at their feet—not to beg forgiveness, but to apologize, over and over and over.

And, broken as I am, I might have. If not for the last secret left to me: Osiron.

"May I ask you a question?" says Tempestra-Innara.

"Uh . . ." The unexpected inquiry thickens my tongue. "Sure."

The Goddess's gaze locks onto mine. Not a hard look, or angry. Soft. Smothering. Inescapable. "Why?"

Again, I freeze up. Not because I don't know what to say. But because I didn't think they'd care. What is a traitor's motivation to the most powerful deity in existence? The shame deepens. But it is mine—for myself, for my failure.

"Because"—the word slips out, thin as a final breath—"I never wanted to be what I am. Who you *forced* me to be. Because I . . . I *hate* the bloody deeds soaked into my skin and how much it pleases me that they please you." I let years of repressed hate pour into the explanation, and yet cannot pull away from their touch. "Because I want nothing more than to be free of this riven existence, and of *you*."

A moment passes before the Goddess speaks again. "Ah."

No hint of meaning behind that sound, no anger or hurt in their features. Only an understanding I don't like. It's too passive, too cryptic. The desire to beg them for their thoughts rises like an ember escaping a fireplace, only to extinguish as their fingers lightly trail down my cheek again. I am lulled.

"Rest, daughter," the Goddess says, still ignorant of the one thing I hold back. Of that crucial sliver of knowledge anchoring my sanity. I begin to feel warm. "We want you strong. Sleep and rest, and later we will talk again."

The warmth grows, turns into a soft, silky darkness. A blanket that spreads over me and pushes me down, down, into a dreamless sleep.

The next time I wake, I have a larger, but less divine, audience: the Goddess's senior Chosen, as ghoulish as when I last saw them; Caius, sour as anyone can be; Prior Petronilla, stoic in a way that I definitely, absolutely do not like.

And Nolan.

The only one not watching me like the caged animal I am.

I sit up. "Good morning." I'm probably a sight, hair messy from sleep, still a little shaky from my deprived deliverance back to the Cathedral. "Or good afternoon? Evening? Whichever applies."

Prior Petronilla's stoicism wavers, and she sighs. Guess she hasn't missed me.

"Potentiate Lystrata." The Senior Arbiter speaks first, voice raised and measured, as if this is a very official occasion. The designation throws me at first. I didn't think I warranted being called a Potentiate anymore. "You have been accused of heresy, blasphemy, and treason."

Ah, a trial. Or as much of one as I'll probably get. That explains the formality.

"I'll save you some time." I go to the bars, wrap my hands around the cold iron. "Guilty of all charges. Super guilty, even."

The Arbiter's lips thin with annoyance. Caius makes a small sound of disgust. Nolan still doesn't look at me.

"No one asked for a plea," the Senior Arbiter continues. "Your guilt has already been confirmed by Arbiter Caius and Potentiate Nolan. You assisted the heretics in their plots to assassinate Tempestra-Innara, actions that are unfounded. *Unprecedented.*"

"So why the party?"

"Lystrata..." Prior Petronilla's voice is strangely pleading. "For the love of all that is... Please stay quiet for once."

I scoff. "Don't worry, I'll be quiet forever pretty soon. So how about it? When's my execution?"

The atmosphere in the room shifts to even more uncomfortable, impressive given the level it started at. Caius goes so rigid that if I were able to land a punch, I wager he'd shatter like glass.

The High Cleric of the Blood steps forward. "You are not to be executed."

Prior Petronilla gets her wish. I am silent.

"As I said, we have spoken with Arbiter Caius," the Senior Arbiter continues. "He has told us about his judgement of you, and that your love for the Goddess runs as deep as your..." He falters, as if unable to comprehend the next part. "As your hate."

My fingers tighten around the bars. "Moot point."

"Not to our blood mother," says the High Cleric of the Blood. "In their justice, mercy, and unfathomable wisdom, they have passed sentence on you."

I feel the familiar prickle of divinity again. The Bellator Prime moves quickly to open the chamber door, admitting Tempestra-Innara. Sans soup this time.

Everyone bows their head in deference. I don't bother, not anymore. "Finally, the bitch in charge. What's this about me not being executed?"

It's pure spite at this point, but I puff a little at the ripple of utter horror that goes through the room in response to my brazen address. Tempestra-Innara doesn't react, though. My blood brethren part obediently to let them pass, a patient smile on their face. I don't shrink under it, but it's harder than I'd like to keep my muscles from trembling.

"Such fire," they say. "You've always had it, of course."

I bite the inside of my lip. Not to silence myself. To steady.

"You *all* have a fire in you," the Goddess continues gently. "A flame that must be cultivated, guided, shaped. But not all flames are as easily molded as others. Isn't that right, daughter?"

"You can't mold flames," I spit, confused and impatient. If I'm not to be executed, then what, exactly, is going on?

"Lys," says the Goddess. "You have betrayed me. But I forgive you, because I know your love, your devotion, is true."

*It's not*, I want to say. To *scream*.

But I would be lying.

"And you have many gifts," they continue. "To which I will add one more: the gift of mercy, so that you may repay what you've done, and serve your blood brethren and me as you were always meant to do." Tempestra-Innara reaches out with one slim finger and pushes my chin up, so that they can peer into my eyes. As much as I crave their touch, this time it feels like a shiv held to my throat. But I can't move away.

"Your strength, cunning, and persistence are undeniable. And these will serve us well, when you become my new avatar."

# Forty-nine

> There is glory in the choosing of an avatar. The awakening of a new era. And, for the chosen vessel, another, greater gift than they have ever been given: the gift of eternity.
>
> —WRITINGS OF PRIOR SUPERIOR RADHICK

**WHAT.**
*The fuck.*

That's what I *want* to say, but speech is gone, strangled by disbelief, as tight and draining as a mortal wound. Only the smallest sound escapes. "No."

The Goddess's patient expression doesn't flicker.

"No," I say again. "*No.*"

*Innara is dying.* I hear Nolan's voice as if he's spoken aloud. I look to him, his attention finally on me, only to see a knowing, tired expression. He knew. They *all* knew. Even though I'm suddenly the Goddess's most favored, I'm also the last to be told that my body, my mind, is to be co-opted, invaded, and stolen away. And that not only am I *not* being executed, but I will likely live another century or more.

Except not me, not really. I'll be absorbed by Tempestra, a slowly devoured meal.

I jerk away from the Goddess's touch, skin crawling. "Burn me, gut me, string me up in front of the Cathedral as a message. But I won't be your cursed puppet."

"It's what you'd deserve," the Prior Superior snaps, speaking for most of the room, myself included. "You are being given a gift you don't even begin to—"

"Shh." The command slips softly between Tempestra-Innara's lips. The Prior Superior obeys. "You aren't going to die, Lys. Not for a very long time."

I grip the bars again, pulling myself close. "Please . . . Mother . . ." A plea, a sad, pathetic prayer that grinds what little pride I have left beneath its heel. "Please, if you love me in the way you claim you do, you won't do this."

A delicate chuckle. "Of *course* I love you. I have loved you from when I looked into your eyes, saw what lay there, in the very depths of you. For all your disobedience, your defiance, the kernel of what I search for in my children was always there. And as I had hoped, it grew. Oh Lys . . ." They are as patient with me as with a fussy child. "I promise that you will not feel this way after. When we are bonded, entwined, and our thoughts become one, you will understand."

*Thoughts* . . .

*Fuck fuck FUCK.* When Tempestra takes up residence in my brain, they will know me . . . *all* of me. Disregarding the particularly long list of fantasies about murdering them, there's one other very choice tidbit that they will find interesting.

And that will be bad. Very, *very* bad.

I struggle to keep calm, measured, though it already feels as if I am losing pieces of myself, even before the Goddess gets their divine claws into me.

But before I am fully gone, my betrayals will be complete.

Tempestra-Innara.

Nolan.

And finally, Osiron.

A traitor to all. What follows then, when Tempestra learns about the Whisperer? Another war? Something worse?

I knew killing the Goddess would bring chaos. I didn't expect failing to do so would too.

I have to stop what's coming. For me. For everything. I can fight... but I will lose. That's what Osiron said, wasn't it? That the avatar possession need not be permanent, but also that the divinity gets who they want, when they want it. Whatever chances I had to win this game are already long spent.

My knees give out, the world around me retreating to some distant horizon.

"We will hold the ritual in a few days," the Goddess announces, in complete disregard of my breakdown. "And then..." Their hand falls to the crown of my head, a damnable blessing. "Innara's service will be done, and yours will truly begin."

I stare at the place where their feet meet the floor, cold as ice.

"Come," says Tempestra-Innara. "It would be unfair to Lys to have her anything other than her full self in front of her blood brethren. We must let her finish regaining her strength."

The others shuffle toward the door obediently. Prior Petronilla eyes me as she passes. She appears as if she wants to say something. I feel like *I* should say something. Like *You were always right about me*. Or maybe *You were completely wrong* instead. But I say nothing, the weight of her disappointment barely a pebble on the mountain I've built.

Only Nolan remains where he is. "May I speak with her?" He addresses the Goddess, a young boy asking Mother for a sweet. "Alone?"

The departing parade falters momentarily, scandalized yet again in this absolute clusterfuck of events, but the Goddess nods.

"Of course." It is as if the request is nothing at all. They run a hand lightly over Nolan's hair—affectionate. Loving. "The two of you... I have never been so reminded of the differences between my children. And of their similarities. We will all work well together, I think."

My eyes meet Nolan's. I'm not sure what that means, but I can guess. I'm not the only one who expected punishment and got rewarded instead.

Everyone, including Tempestra-Innara, leaves the chamber; I am left alone with Nolan.

And we're back to awkward silences.

"Sorry." I speak first, another apology. "It should be you."

"I know." He doesn't specify what part of what I said those words apply to. "But I accept the Goddess's will."

"I don't want this."

"I know."

"Executrix, then?"

"Yes."

"Congratulations."

We go back to quiet, during which everything in the room, in the whole world, seems to still. Then Nolan sits, bringing himself down to my level. Very considerate.

"Lys," he says. "Being chosen as avatar . . . it's an unimaginable honor."

"No," I spit. "It's a life sentence. Now not only will my life not be my own, but my body won't be either." A laugh escapes, only a little hysterical. "The Goddess really got it right. *This* is the worst possible punishment they could have given me."

Conflict rolls off Nolan like a heavy perfume. Within it, I scent a way out.

"It *should* be you." I grab the bars again, pull myself closer to him. "Maybe it still can be."

His brow knits with concern.

"Give me a blade." A desperate grin splits my face. "And go. Couldn't be any easier."

Shock flashes in his eyes as his face turns hard. Then, sadness—a flood of it. More emotion than I've ever seen from him. "No."

"*Please.* You *must* hate me for all of this."

"I know. I should. And I *was* angry with you, so much so that I wanted more than anything to see you pay for betraying the Goddess . . . for betraying me. And then, when they said they'd chosen you to be their avatar, I . . . I knew I should be even more angry. But I wasn't. I . . ." He stops, the struggle within him bared. Exposed. Is this what our blood mother's unwelcome mercy has bought me? The full truth of Nolan's thoughts? Two frustrated tears—honest to goodness *tears*—escape, leaving glittering tracks over his pale cheeks. Everything makes even less sense now with him broken open, silently spilling like a damaged dam. "I don't hate you at all. You were an obstacle ... a means to an end ... and then ..."

He can't finish. For all our training, our education, our experience, he doesn't have the words for this. To be fair, neither do I. "Everything was a lot easier back when you were just quietly planning to kill me, huh?"

Silence, again.

"It was a bad idea, making us work together. Always was. Should have kept us at each other's throat." I reach through the bars, fingertips just able to brush the back of his hand. I'm not sure why I do it; any past contact was out of necessity. Or maybe that's exactly why. Outside of the Cathedral, the people in your life come with pats on the back, an arm around a shoulder, a hand on yours when the world has gone dark. Not that we'd know. Nolan looks down at the touch. He doesn't engage with it. But he doesn't pull away either. "Nolan, if I mean anything to you ..." I suck in a breath. "No, fuck that. Mercy—that's what I'm after. The kind I need, not the kind the Goddess wants to give. And that mercy is sharp."

Nolan stares at me. The air around us stretches, goes taut.

"*Please* ..."

His hand twitches, moving closer to his belt.

Then freezes.

Horror spreads on his face as my weak hope shatters. He starts shaking his head. I don't even know if he realizes it at first, but the motion increases.

"No," he says. "I won't. I'm not going to help you hurt yourself." He leans closer. "Lys, you have to live."

I pull my hand back, grip the bars again. "What's going to happen to me isn't living."

"Yes, it is!" The words are strained. "Why must you be so damn stubborn? You will be alive, together with the Goddess, part of the greatest thing left in this world. And ..." He falters. "And you'll still be here ..." His voice fades, going so quiet I can barely hear. Then, his hands find mine, wrapping around them. "Please, Lys." The words plead. *Beg*. "Let me serve you *both*."

His fingers tighten. Mine grip cold iron. I stare at him, the weak spots in my resistance becoming clear, threatening to give way the way his almost did moments ago. I can almost imagine it—it's not really losing, for either of us, if I become the avatar. The bond we've formed remains, after a fashion. And maybe I won't lose myself to the Goddess too quickly. Maybe there is some way to trade on my knowledge of Osiron, bargain some kind of peace between the two deities. There's an undeniable appeal to the fantasy of it.

But that's all it is, one more fantasy.

Osiron wants the last of their siblings gone. I won't be a skin worn by Tempestra. And Nolan . . . there's no changing him. There never was. For whatever grew between us, the soil is the same as it was when we started this misadventure. Always the same obedient, devout, *loyal* Nolan. No matter what edge I ended up on, he was always going to push me over.

I extract my fingers from Nolan's, gut aching as his touch falls away, the hope in his eyes fading to disappointment.

"It's a nice thought," I say simply, and turn away.

I focus on the hollow thump of my heart until he speaks again.

"They'll come for you no matter what. You *will* be the next avatar."

"Then it won't be much different from when we were kids. Except this time, I know I have a choice. And this time I choose to not be part of my own corruption."

I close my eyes, saying nothing more as a hot frustration builds in them. And keep them closed until, eventually, Nolan stands, makes his way over to the door.

And leaves me behind.

# *Fifty*

> The hour grows near. The devoted gather. There is no greater hour in their lives than that which will be witnessed here, today.
>
> —WRITINGS OF PRIOR RAOLF, FROM THE FINAL
> HOURS OF THE ERA OF TEMPESTRA-ENOCH

I AM WATCHED. ALL DAY, all hours. Two Cathedral Guard and a Prior keep an eye on little old me while I eat, sleep, pace, piss—all to make sure I don't try to do anything drastic. Maybe Nolan ratted me out to Tempestra-Innara. Maybe they were simply smart enough to know that I'd find any escape I could. I still give it a go, spending hours scheming, picking apart my surroundings as I search for some way to end it all before the Goddess gets to see the last card up my sleeve. Starvation or refusing water is out; can't wait that long. Which leaves scouring the meager contents of my cell instead, for anything that might choke or puncture or cut.

But I've got nothing. Where's a giant bottomless hole in the ground when you need one?

Three days later I am irritatingly still alive. But well rested. Which is a strange sensation when mixed with hopelessness. On this morning, I decide to pray. Pointless, but Tempestra-Innara's followers believe they hear their devotions, or at least get the gist of them. Maybe it's true and Osiron is the same. Maybe if I pray hard enough, they'll be tipped off and get as far away as possible before Tempestra-Inna—before Tempestra-*Me* starts hunting them and their followers down. I do it soundlessly, lying in my prison bed, without clasped hands or lowered head or anything else that might draw attention.

But I do pray.

*You probably can't hear this* . . . I try to picture Osiron as the divine being they are, but in my thoughts, they shift to Rion, with an easy smile and a dirty book. *But I'm sorry for what's about to happen. To me, and then to you. To Avery. I hope you all got out of the city okay. I hope that you've gotten somewhere safe. And I hope*—this is the part I wish for more than anything else—*that I won't have to look into your eyes as the Goddess uses my muscle and bone to kill you.*

It's a shit prayer. But I'm a shit devotee, so it is what it is.

On the fourth morning, I hear the sound of footsteps. More than the normal shift change, at least half a dozen people approaching. But when the door opens, only Caius enters. He is wearing an Arbiter's formal cassock, extra clean and pressed, not a speck of dust marring the stark white. He dismisses the Prior and guards on duty but doesn't close the door after them.

I go cold, mustering a lazy smile regardless. "Time already?" He'd clearly rather gut me than escort me anywhere. Which would be preferable for the both of us, but I don't bother to point it out. "I don't get a fancy outfit or anything?"

Caius's mouth thins to near disappearance. "Within the hour, you will become avatar for the most powerful divinity to ever walk this land. Show the occasion the respect it deserves."

I move to the bars, grinning even wider. "And then you'll have to take orders from me. Won't that be fun?"

"I'll take orders from the Goddess."

"Uh-huh, of course, sure. But we both know there will always be a piece of me in there too." I let the smile spread. "And if that piece has even a crumb of control, you'll know . . . by the hell I try to make your life into, you cruel, self-absorbed ass."

Caius goes red in the face. Oh, he wants to retort; I can practically see the shape of the words caught in his throat. But he's right. Soon I'll be little more than a marionette controlled by divine strings. And even if there's not a damn thing I can do about it, I'm happy that one of my last acts can be to make this day as miserable as possible for Caius.

"We will take you to the Goddess now." His tone is pleasingly bitter as a clutch of Cathedral Guard enter. "Please do not resist."

I could. No one will *want* to hurt me—not me, their next blessed avatar. But I have a distinct feeling that the guards have been prepped to know exactly how much incapacitation would be allowable without risking punishment, or worse, delaying the ritual. And I don't fancy being dragged through the Cathedral because of a few sliced tendons. If I'm going to my fate, I'm going to do it on my own two feet.

We move in a somber procession, Caius in the lead, me surrounded. For some reason, I am reminded anyway of that original trek to the reliquary chamber, back when Nolan and I were first roped into this.

*Nolan.*

I hate the feeling that surfaces when I think of him, and the last time we spoke.

Anger, because he could have spared me from this, and didn't.

Anger, because he refuses to accept that whatever remains of me after this will be only scraps and shards.

And anger because soon nothing so trivial as the patched-together friendship that passed between us will matter at all.

When we reach the Cathedral's main hall, it's a godsdamned party. Dozens of my blood brethren are gathered, lining the second- and third-story galleries, familiar faces staring down at me with a plethora of expressions. Some are definitely not too happy about the current developments, but others gaze at me with a wide-eyed reverence, no doubt thinking how lucky they are to witness this less-than-once-in-a-lifetime occurrence. Tucked in the back corner of the Cathedral, masks hiding any indication of their thoughts, are six attendants of Cineris. An escort, waiting quietly to perform their duty of bearing Innara's ashes to interment in the necropolis.

The remaining, older Potentiates are also present, done up in full ceremonial armor and on the floor this time, like an honor guard. Peeking through the gaps between them are clerics—eyes wide, reveries clutched in their fingers—so many that they must have come from all over, as fast as they could. I'd expected this to be a family affair, especially given the events of Emmaus's execution, but it makes sense that the Goddess would want witnesses, mouths that could spread the joyous words of the new avatar to the farthest edges of the Devoted Lands.

They gape at me, awestruck, even though they must know—or at least wonder—why I am surrounded by guards. It's tempting to scream the truth, tell them about the reliquary, that divine weak spot. But I remember what happened to the gathered devoted the last time they learned something they weren't meant to. Instead, I seek out Morgan, a little surprised the fury pouring off her doesn't immediately set me aflame. Our eyes lock, and I give her a wink, just on the off chance she's mad enough to lose her temper and put a spear through me.

I am not so lucky.

I don't see Prior Petronilla, though, which is a bit of a relief. Maybe she's already been demoted. Or, martyr that she is, demoted herself in shame. It would be like her to skip witnessing this as a personal punishment. But I don't have time to wonder. Caius clears his throat, wordlessly telling me it's time to make our way forward. I obey, though every step forward feels like a failure. The Goddess waits ahead, framed by all of their golden, conquered dead. Their hands are folded before them, a patient, eager expression on their face—Innara's face. But their light feels more wan than usual. Maybe that's part of it, the divinity already separating from the flesh, the beginning of the fade. Or maybe they've simply been hiding how weak they are until there was no longer a reason to do so.

Nolan stands beside them in the Executrix's place of honor, holding the reliquary. His expression is so neutral he might as well be wax, but it doesn't fool me in the least. He watches me approach. I keep my gaze off him. If I don't, I'll see something I don't like, even if I'm not entirely sure what that will be.

My blood brethren are silent as we approach the apse, but the onlooking devoted can't contain themselves. Hands begin to reach for me—despite my guards—pawing at my arms, my shoulders, my hair. My name is spoken like a prayer. One cleric even has tears streaking down her face. All of it its own sort of insult, but there is no stopping it, this unwanted reverence, with its undercurrent of hysteria. Ahead of me, Caius holds his head high until we reach the steps. Pissed as he is, he's still puffed like a peacock about this ceremonial place of honor. He stops before the Goddess, squaring his shoulders.

"Mother," he says, in a voice loud enough for the whole Cathedral to hear him, "I have brought you your daughter, betrayer, and"—he doesn't even falter—"chosen vessel, known to us as Lystrata of the Dawn Cloister."

"Lys." I make sure I'm heard too. "My mother called me Lys. My *real* mother."

The crowd murmurs, shocked, and Caius's head snaps around before he can stop himself. "May your joining with her be infinitely blessed," he finishes, with a bitterness that makes it clear I've ruined his moment.

Here we go.

My eyes drop to the shiny, burnished stone at my feet. The spot I know so well it's almost as if all my years in the Cloisters never happened. I am a child again, doomed to another unwanted baptism. A numbness spreads over my skin, but I bite the inside of my lip until I taste blood, using the pain to focus. My faint reflection wavers in the stone as I take a deep, steadying breath. I am surrounded by those to whom weakness is one of the worst things I could show. Not that I care what any of these assholes think, not now. But the only way I can stick it to them is to try to maintain as much dignity as possible. I'm probably not as successful in that as I'd like, given the pity I read on Nolan's face when I succumb to the urge to glance his way. Oh well. It's not as if it will matter for much longer.

Caius steps to one side, giving me an unobstructed view of Tempestra-Innara. Cool serenity paints their tired countenance. No defiance of mine will throw them off now. This is their time. The elevation, execution, absorption—all simply a set of rituals for the hundreds of eyes boring into my back. Another bit of theater playing itself out.

"My daughter," the Goddess begins. I loathe the love in their voice, the forgiveness I don't want or deserve. "A short time ago, you were entrusted with a secret, crucial task: to find a dangerous weapon acquired by the heretics and used against us. You were to retrieve it from them and return it here to me." A calculated pause. Or maybe a test, to see if I'll challenge that weak fiction with the truth, damn a few more of their devoted. I'm sure there are plenty more beyond the doors of the Cathedral who would elatedly take their place. "Instead, you conspired to join with the heretics, to try to use this foul, murderous concoction against your own."

"No," I interject. "Not against my own. Just you."

Caius steps forward, as if about to strike, but the Goddess gestures. He stops.

"Such anger," the Goddess continues, "hiding such love."

I begin to tremble.

"Daughter"—Tempestra-Innara's voice pours into me like warm, honeyed milk—"I am so sorry. I failed to see the war within you, how it has poisoned your soul with such suffering, for so long." They look around at the audience, to my blood brethren surrounding me and those watching from above. "Lys needed not suffer in silence. None of you do. You all have my love. And if I have not fully earned yours, then it is I who have failed, not you."

For the briefest instant, regret pricks me, needle sharp. Then, I feel the sting of winter, hear the cracking of ice. I see blood at my feet, feel it warm and sticky between my fingers. My jaw tightens. "Horseshit." A broken whisper. Then again, louder. "Horseshit. I can tell you where those who've died in the name of your path would tell you to shove your love, your *mercy*. You want our adoration—crave it. But underneath it all, you're nothing more than a monster with a kind smile and a gentle touch, who forces us to be your claws and teeth."

I expect anger. Maybe even a blow or two. But the Goddess only smiles so sweetly, so patiently, that I want to scream.

They say nothing, only turn to Nolan and gesture for the reliquary. He doesn't hesitate in handing it over, his eyes snagging briefly on me.

The Goddess considers the crystal vessel, blazing beneath their touch, with an almost respectful gaze. "There is malevolent, blasphemous power here, created with ancient knowledge not meant to remain in this world. The creators of this horror are long gone, dead." They raise the bottle up for everyone to see. "Which is how it is meant to be."

In a blink of movement, the Goddess's fingers release the reliquary. It plunges to the stone floor and shatters. And as the dark ichor that is the last vestige of Arcadius, the Green God, becomes a pathetic trickle on the Cathedral stairs, something in me breaks as well, giving rise to the mad desire to lunge forward, to lick that power from stones that already know spilled blood so very well—

The Goddess points a finger. In an instant, the flame appears, running over the blood as if it were lamp oil. It burns away, leaving only a dark stain in its wake.

Another piece of me crumbles. I slump to my knees, chin hanging to my chest.

"The weapon is destroyed," announces the Goddess. "Taking its darkness with it. Soon, daughter, yours will be gone as well. Stand."

I ignore the order. I am not a puppet yet.

But the guards are listening. Two of them get their hands under my arms and pull me up. I expect to be dragged to the Goddess, but instead they come to me, gliding down the steps, hands held out as if to embrace me. And—even now, I can't fucking help it—I lean toward that gesture. Long, thin fingers rise, reach for my face. But instead of the soft touch I expect, I flinch as thin lines of pain scratch their way over my cheeks. The hands recede, blood—*my* blood—painting their tips. Tempestra-Innara anoints their lips with it, an inversion of my blessing years ago. Or maybe simply a representation of the consumption that is about to take place. Then, they slice a line across each of their palms with the same pointed nails.

It doesn't make sense for a goddess to bleed, but they do. This time by choice.

When they come for me again, I can't help it—I struggle. The Cathedral Guard shouldn't be enough to hold me, but under the Goddess's engulfing gaze, I am half frozen, at the mercy of the waters rising around me. Yet in that moment—that last, desperate moment of me being only myself—my craving for their touch suddenly splinters, broken as swiftly as the reliquary. Muscles tense, warm defiance flooding my veins as I shift my eyes away, to the person who could have stopped this, to Nolan. Because I need to; because I want him to see the difference between me right now and whatever it is I'm about to become.

And remember it.

Then Tempestra-Innara's flesh skims mine and it begins. A trickle at first, but rising like a swollen river. Tempestra's light... their warmth... their searing, ravaging divinity begins its inescapable feast. Nolan is gone. The Goddess's gaze bores into mine, eyes like mirrors, reflecting the consuming light enveloping me.

Mingled together, our blood sings.

*No... it burns.*

But there is still resistance, deep within. In a place where the light has not reached yet, far down where I hid those countless fantasies of deicide. Of escape to freedom. It is there for me to tap, to draw strength from as I try to push back the light, the flame, disentangling it from what is *me*.

I won't simply give in. *Can't.*

*Shhhhhh...*

A sense of irritated tolerance spreads, reaching across the bridge building between us. I shove it back, push it away...

*Lys... shhhhh... soon it will be...*

Stop. Please.

Already, the borders between me and them feel as if they are weakening, crumbling. And behind those walls...

Innara's face shimmers in front of me and I see the separation, that schism between the divinity and the flesh, driven by Tempestra's fire. Skin darkens, begins to peel and flake, bits rapidly turning to ash as the Goddess shrugs off their former avatar in favor of their new...

Oh. *No.*

Something in me thins beyond tolerance, a membrane tearing apart, opening me in full to the Goddess's divine source. Every thought, every fear...

Every secret.

Surprise, Tempestra.

The recoiling that follows their discovery is borne on that surprise, like a rush of fresh air into my lungs as the searing light recedes. Distantly, I feel one of my guards tighten their grip on me, though I'm not struggling, relieved as I am to still be myself. The world clears slightly, Innara's singed features tightening with Tempestra's bewilderment.

Again, I feel the grip of the guard, fingers digging into my flesh meaningfully. *Insistently.* It takes every ounce of will I possess to turn my head, toward that helmed head, through whose slits I find Avery's familiar eyes gazing back at me.

*How—?*

I don't have time to understand more than that he's here, and that if he's here, the only reason must be to rescue me. To keep me and my crucial knowledge from Tempestra-Innara.

And that he's too late.

I try to tell Avery this, to form the words, but only see his lips spread in an apologetic smile a heartbeat before I feel the knife slide between my ribs.

# Fifty-one

> When you strike, strike true. An enemy is never more dangerous than when in the desperate haze of survival.
>
> —PRIOR PETRONILLA

**THERE ARE GOOD WAYS** to be stabbed, at least in terms of survival. Ways that are the least likely to result in damage that can't be repaired, missing those vital organs and arteries.

That's not how Avery stabs me.

The divine light breaks away fully, releasing me, the comparative darkness of reality so thick it might as well be night.

Or maybe it's simply shock.

Either way, I fall. I simply . . . slip, plunging away from Tempestra-Innara's reach to the ever-welcoming stone floor.

Strangely, my immediate concern is for Avery. Forget how he got here—who knows what tricks his boss has managed to learn over the centuries. But crossing the Goddess in their own Cathedral is not, historically, a survivable action. *Run*, I want to cry, before the flame takes him too, but I can't move, can't speak. Briefly, I wonder if he struck so true that I'm already dead.

But then the pain comes crashing in.

Oh yeah, I'm still alive.

"Lys!" Nolan calls my name, somewhere beyond my field of vision.

All I see now is Tempestra-Innara, face twisted with unimaginable fury. And it's aimed at Avery. He drops the knife, takes a step back.

He's dead. Worse, if this was some desperate act to keep my awareness of Osiron secret, he's too late. Not to mention that, while the Goddess was kind in allowing me not to show up to my own party a battered mess, all they have to do is complete the ritual and I'll—well, my body—will be as good as new.

But Avery isn't afraid, or disappointed. Instead he appears . . . expectant?

Three loud knocks sound on the Cathedral doors.

The Goddess's face changes again, disbelief mixing with the prior anger. They aren't looking at Avery anymore. They are looking at nothing. And then, slowly, their gaze drags toward the doors.

Beyond them, Nolan moves toward us. He shoves Avery out of the way and drops to his knees. Arms wrap around me, lift me up. "Lys—"

"All of you, stop!" Tempestra-Innara throws up one singed hand. "Be still. Be *silent*."

Their will is obeyed.

Except by me, who coughs quite painfully, though I can't exactly help it.

I manage to twist around a little. The doors. Everyone's attention is on the doors to the Cathedral, now open, one man standing beneath their pointed arch.

Rion is gone. Whatever they'd been holding back radiates now, and there is no mistaking the deity who stands before us.

The Whisperer has come to Lumeris.

"*You*." One word falls from the Goddess's lips, flutters over us, and spreads through the Cathedral like sorcery. People shift uncomfortably, but no one understands what is happening, not yet. Especially Nolan, who is staring at the person he knew as a bookseller with damn near comedic confusion.

Osiron smirks placidly. "Miss me, little sister?"

If I weren't bleeding out, I would have almost enjoyed the deepening bewilderment on Tempestra-Innara's face.

"This is impossible. We killed you. Centuries ago, we destroyed you."

"You certainly tried. And while I was never as powerful as you and the others, I called you into existence. I was capable of making you believe you'd removed me from it too."

Despite that explanation, the perplexed air in the Cathedral persists. At least until Avery's voice cuts in, crowing with reverence: "Osiron returns!"

That does it. The spell over the spectators breaks. There are cries of surprise. Of disbelief.

I feel Nolan go as still as death. There's fresh betrayal in his eyes as he realizes that I knew. His mouth opens, but before he can say anything, the Cathedral doors slam shut again.

"You thought you destroyed me," the Whisperer says. "I sent an assassin after you. Now, I can no longer hide, and neither can you. No more feints, no more games, Tempestra. This time, one of us is going to get it right." Something begins to flow from Osiron—water, I think at first, until it reaches the arches and begins to rise. And spread. Within seconds, stone webbing covers every archway, closing off the galleries above—with my blood brethren behind it—as well as every avenue for retreat.

It's impressive, but against Tempestra's consuming fire? I almost expect the Goddess to laugh. But they have not moved, and I sense, in whatever lingering connection we still have, unease. *Fear.*

I understand. Avery wasn't too late; he intentionally interrupted the ritual. Already fading, Innara's flesh has been weakened further by their own power's destruction of it during its transition to me. Now is the time to strike a fatal blow.

Nolan understands too, lowering me to the ground and reaching for his sword.

Though it hurts like hell, I grab his arm. "Don't." I say it quietly, as if anyone is paying attention to us. "You don't have to."

The furrows in his brow deepen. "You're wrong." Good old dependable Nolan. Loyal to the end. Then his expression softens. "Stay alive, Lys."

Then he's gone, and I'm staring up at the damn ceiling, nearly crippled while the most epic showdown in well over a century is about to begin.

Figures.

Suddenly, Avery appears. His hands hook under my arms and lift, dragging me away from the growing commotion. If Osiron got Avery into the Cathedral, there must be other heretics here too, ready to fight, as absolutely futile as that seems. Nolan could cut a dozen of them down on his own. And yet... Osiron didn't come off like a deity about to fight a losing battle...

*Dammit.* This is no time to be on my back. I push past the pain, rising into a sitting position. Avery helps me with the rest; a moment later, I am on my feet, even if it feels like I've left half my blood on the floor. But I'm standing, ready, and—

Face-to-face with the blank red masks of the Cineri.

"I'm not dead yet," I blurt. Ridiculous, but the only reason I can think of for them to have made their way to the front of the Cathedral, to me, instead of rushing to the Goddess's aid.

"No, you're not," says Avery. Then: "Now, quickly!"

He's not speaking to me. The Cineri tear off their masks, revealing faces filled with resolve. With purpose. But it's not until I see the vials in their hands that I see where Osiron's blow is really coming from.

That lying bastard. The Green God's blood was supposed to be all that was left, the last of the... No, wait. It was the last of Arcadius's blood. *That's* what Osiron said. They never specified further.

One by one the heretics drink, blood darkening their lips before they rush past Avery and me, the change already coming over them.

Avery leans me against the wall. We are still closer to the apse than I like, the boundary of golden bones only a few arm lengths away, but partially sheltered by a thick column.

"Your boss could have been a little clearer about how many intact reliquaries he found over the years," I say bitterly. Exactly how many more exist is a question I'm rather curious about, but survival first, details later. I can't see clearly past the column, to whatever is happening between the devoted and their deities. The Goddess is weakened, yes, but... "It's not enough... What if they aren't enough?"

"Then *you* will be." Avery's palm opens to reveal another vial. "With a little help from the Storm Goddess."

At first, I can only blink. Then, a laugh, cracking up out of my throat, bringing with it the taste of blood and bile. "Vengeance has a sense of humor, I guess."

"Did you really think we'd let you die for no reason?"

I recall Emmaus's wounds, and how they healed so quickly. "Same plan, different execution?"

"Not the word I'd use, given the circumstances." Avery presses the vial into my hands. "Now, quickly, before—"

A brutal thud cuts off the rest and Avery drops to the ground, a white-robed figure looming behind him.

Caius.

He grips a spine of blood-spattered stone, a bit of Osiron's handiwork turned impromptu club, chest heaving up and down with the exertion of the fight. For one blisteringly frigid instant, we lock eyes. Then the moment cracks, and his gaze drops to the vial.

I close my fingers around it. Turn. And *run*, fueled entirely by a new rage.

*Avery...*

I don't know if he's alive or dead. I don't even consider where I'm going. All I can do is move, slipping between the pillar and the wall, darting around the threshold of golden bones, doing my best to ignore the growing gray haze at the edge of my vision as I struggle to pull the stopper from the vial—

Something hits me in the small of the back with the force of a cannonball. At least, that's what it feels like as I go sprawling, colliding with the wall of the apse. I gasp, lungs emptied, bits of gold flashing in my ruptured vision that eventually resolve into femurs and ribs scattered across dark stone. And then into a pair of feet, crushing smaller pieces of bone beneath their heels as they approach.

*Shit.* My hands. They're empty.

Which is the reason Caius doesn't bother with me, passing by where I wheeze thickly, being pulled under a tide of my own blood. Because that's worthless compared to what sloshes around in the vessel he plucks from the field of gilded debris.

He examines it, and then me. "This is your weapon?"

I don't respond.

"Nothing clever left to say?"

I open my mouth but can't quite make *Not while choking on my own fluids, you fuckwit* come out. What I manage is a feeble "Don't."

"This was what you were going to use to murder our blood mother?" Caius leans over me and grabs my hair, snapping my head up.

I look out upon chaos. The heretics have managed no more control over their stolen power than Emmaus, now only vaguely human forms composed of sickly green miasmas, like the sky before a tornado. Some rage at Tempestra-Innara, who is still standing and surprisingly vigorous, half engulfed by the power of their divine flame. Others, fully feral beings now, tear through the gathered clerics. A few of my blood brethren have broken Osiron's barriers and are confronting the deity, who is making an impressive show of fending off both the Chosens' blades and their sibling's power. I can't tell who is winning, only that this is a battle on the edge, ready to tip in either direction.

Caius's grip tightens. "If this is enough to defeat the Goddess"—he hisses each word into my ear—"then it is enough to save them too."

He releases me, and I remain upright just long enough to watch him unstop the vial and drink.

# Fifty-two

Blood sings to blood.

Honestly, I'm surprised. I never thought of Caius as anything other than self-serving. Not like Nolan and his tedious, selfless devotion. Or even Morgan, dedicated to a fault. But here he is, trying to play the hero.

The change comes over him as quickly as the others, though immediately, it's clear something is different. Power radiates off him like heat from a hearth, an aura not quite like Tempestra's or Osiron's, but unmistakably divine in origin. Caius swells with it, inhaling deeply before tossing the empty vial aside. Then, with one final, gleaming look of triumph over me, he plunges into the fight.

I can't let him. Desperate, I grab a nearby femur, use it to push myself up ...

The world grays.

Then brightens again, some indeterminant amount of time later. As it comes back into focus, I find myself staring at a familiar golden skull. Missing teeth, daggers in the eyes.

"Alastair." The name croaks out. "Good to see you, buddy."

I must not have passed out for long, because when I turn my head, the battle is still raging. Caius is taking on two of the altered heretics himself, lightning crackling off him. Storm Goddess. Makes sense.

"That would have been neat," I say to Alastair. "Bet it tingles."

Then Caius throws a punch that lands with a massive bolt, obliterating one of the heretics.

*Shit.* I blink back the spots of light and search for help, for a weapon, for . . . for . . .

I stop. The realization comes, quiet and whole, epochal despite its simplicity. I gaze again over the frenzied sprawl of the Cathedral. To the blood and the bodies. To the devoted and the divine.

None of this began with me.

And it doesn't need to end with me either.

I slump back into the wall of bones, letting out a deep, aching breath. There's no reason to fight, not anymore. Not if I don't want to. Gingerly, my fingers creep to the wound in my side, which is leaking slower now. I wanted freedom. Here it is. Freedom from the Goddess, from the constant rending of my contrary feelings for them. Maybe this isn't the way I'd fantasized, but severing that divine leash, making it beyond the boundaries of the map—it was always a bit of a longshot. And this was never my game. No, this contest between divinities began long ago, ebbing and flowing in its consequence, chewing through players dedicated and ignorant alike.

This was never my game, and I was never going to win it.

"But that's life, right?"

Alastair doesn't respond.

Just beyond the boundary of the apse, Tempestra-Innara succeeds in immolating another of the heretics, the heat of it reaching me like a caress. On the other end of the Cathedral, Osiron has partially encased Caius in stone. It spreads over the Arbiter like a film, though he breaks it away nearly as quickly as the divinity can replace it. I can't find Nolan. Between the flames and the storm creatures, smoke—or maybe fog—fills the Cathedral, turning the scene before me into something out of a fever dream.

What a godsdamned mess.

Tempestra. Osiron. Their conflict is nearly over. And now, as the end approaches at a reckless pace, it turns out I don't really give a fuck which one wins. Numbness begins to encroach, a welcome sensation as I settle against the gilded ossuary, only one question still quietly itching at me, and that's whether I'll hang on long enough to see who comes out on top.

Across the Cathedral, Osiron manages to fully envelope Caius in the webbing, while closer by, Tempestra-Innara battles the last two remaining heretic storm-monsters. Despite their earlier successes, something has shifted. Their flame has withered, still burning, but no longer blazing with the same strength as before. I thought I was past caring, but when they falter, knees hitting the very spot where they once claimed me as their own, a smile rises. My fantasy, or some small sliver of it, played out, if not fulfilled.

A trembling begins, barely noticeable beneath my growing lack of feeling. But it doesn't dampen my contentment.

Let it come. I'm satisfied.

I'm ready.

But the low vibration isn't death. An explosion thunders through the Cathedral, filling the air with glass, with stone, with screams. When these clear enough to see what has happened, Osiron is no longer on their feet. The deity has been thrown into the Cathedral doors, which are now cracked and splintered. The Whisperer tries to rise once, twice, then falls, bleeding from countless wounds.

And Caius . . . he's freed himself from Osiron's stony enclosure, energy crackling off him in a way that eclipses both true divinities. From my vantage, I can see his eyes, hostile and dark as a hurricane, and just as unforgiving. Storm crossed with Flame and fully unleashed . . . Caius bears downs on Osiron's remaining heretics like a feral bear, tearing them away from Tempestra-Innara and ripping through them with an anger that is nothing short of ravenous. Bit by bit, piece by horrific piece, I watch as the tide of battle turns against the first god in favor of the last. Osiron's heretics are dead or dying, and what's left of the Goddess's devoted begin to appear out of the devastation, including—curse the relief of it—Nolan, absolutely painted in gore.

Just like Tempestra-Innara, who rises shakily, a smile of triumph spreading on their face.

"My Chosen." Their voice is weak but clear, cutting through the death cries of the final heretic-creature. "My son, you have done—"

Caius whips their way with a flash, sharp and bright, a lucent blade that seems to pierce as deeply as Avery's knife.

But not nearly as deep as my blood mother's scream. It rips through what's left of me, shredding what is already in pieces, turning existence blank for what feels like eternity. Until it isn't, and my vision resolves to find Tempestra-Innara sprawled on the stairs to the nave, fully half of their body charred black. Caius stands above them, a foggy miasma pouring from his eyes, skin charred and cracking with the power roiling just below it. Some kind of fluid—I'd rather not know what—pours from the corners of his mouth, sizzling as it hits the stone below. Then it—because whatever I'm looking at clearly isn't Caius anymore— begins to growl, a rumbling, savage sound utterly devoid of humanity.

"Alastair, I'm beginning . . . to think that messing around with the blood of dead gods . . . is a universally bad idea." And I laugh, a sound that comes out half sob, because Tempestra-Innara is dying. I know it like I know my own death is creeping closer.

So does everyone else left in the Cathedral. There's the thick beat of realization, followed by the plummet, that shattering of pure devotion to what can no longer be saved. An opening of an endless, heart-rent chasm. The cry that tears from Nolan is a sound I could have lived— died—without hearing. *Anguish* falls short as a description; what emits from him is the cry of someone who's entire existence has been undone. He lunges at Caius, raising his battle-stained sword with both hands . . .

*That foolish, godsdamned idiot—*

. . . and plunges it directly into Caius's heart.

Futile horror floods me, but I can't look away. Not even though I know what's coming . . . and that Nolan's end will be much, much worse than anything I've witnessed so far.

Caius coughs once, thickly, staring down at the weapon skewering him. Then the growl returns—the low, impending thunder of reprisal— at the same moment the divine flame ignites around the hilt of Nolan's sword. An inferno bursting to life, it races up the blade to Caius, engulfing him. There isn't even an attempt at resistance—Nolan's strike is so swift that there is barely time for a single, abruptly strangled screech.

Then only the flame, followed by ash, which crumbles to the stone floor, swirling in the air like bits of snow.

But whatever Nolan has done, it comes at a cost. No longer held fast by flesh, his sword falls free, and he collapses. Not dead—I can still see the rise and fall of his chest—but pushed well passed his conceivable limit.

Silence falls on the Cathedral, a stillness tinged by smoke and blood.

Then: footsteps.

Osiron's, as they make their way down the center of the Cathedral, past what few devoted are left. "Go," they order as the mangled doors of the Cathedral fly open.

The survivors waste no time obeying. Except for one: Avery. I feel a trickle of relief seeing him stagger out of the destruction, one hand pressed to the back of his head, battered but alive.

"This isn't exactly how I saw this going." The Whisperer limps over to Tempestra-Innara. "But what would endless life be without a surprise now and then?" They sigh. "Not endless for you, though. Not anymore."

Tempestra-Innara tries to speak, but only a faint creak passes over charred lips. Their unburned hand lifts as if to point, to call the flame, then falls.

Osiron shakes his head. "This is the end, Tempestra. And even now, I'm a little sad for it. If only you and the others hadn't been so . . . childish. But rest assured that valuable lessons have been learned. I won't make the same mistakes again."

"No . . ." Slowly, agonizingly, the Goddess takes a deep breath. Their head tilts up, teeth baring. "You . . . will make . . . all new ones."

Forgotten along with the rest of the dead, I chuckle quietly. Defiant until the end. Maybe I take after my blood mother more than I thought.

The insolence doesn't sit well with Osiron, who frowns. "Someday, far sooner than you think, Tempestra, you will be nothing but a memory. Your power is spent, save that of your death and whatever stain it leaves on this world. It bleeds out of you even now." The Whisperer leans in closer. "I feel it, spreading across the very fabric of existence, and so do *they*, just beyond the veil that separates here from there. The ones like us, who we used to be. They come closer and closer, drawn by the scraps of you, scavengers to an old corpse." Then, Osiron straightens, flush with purpose. "I have had so much time to think, to wonder. What the others left in the wake of their deaths, those unfading, obscene scars . . . are they inevitable? Or could that expression of power be, hmm, countered, I suppose one might say? Consumed? When those beyond sense the fall of one of their own, do they come out of curiosity . . . or desire?" He smiles. "Why don't we find out?"

Wait . . . what?

"Fitting, don't you think, to have a new god born from the fade of another? But we need a vessel." Avery takes a hopeful step forward, eyes brightening, but Osiron shakes their head. "Not you. Not yet. It's been eons since I last called a divinity into flesh, and I won't risk wasting you if, say, I'm a bit out of practice."

I flinch as Osiron's eyes find me. But there is no intention in them, only pity. It's not as surprising as it could be. After all, I bargained with the Whisperer for freedom. They are simply giving it to me. "I am sorry, Lys. You wouldn't survive," they say, as if reading my thoughts. "A newly born deity can be quite . . . rough." Instead, they reach for Nolan and lift his unconscious form like he's nothing more than a doll.

*No.*

"You chose well with this one, little sister."

*No.*

"Find solace in the fact that he will continue to serve the divine, long after you are gone."

*Fucking NO.*

"Rion, please, don't—" I move too sharply, nearly losing to the gray again. "He wouldn't . . ."

I can't get the rest of the words out. *He wouldn't want this.* Nolan might have aspired to be Tempestra's avatar, but some random newborn god—?

It doesn't matter. Osiron ignores me completely, and it's crystal clear that our dealings are done. I am just another piece now, sacrificed, like the rest of their fallen followers, to the game too large for our tiny selves to fully understand. Or at least I'm sure that's how Osiron sees it. It's why they kept the secret of the Storm Goddess's blood, just in case something went wrong with me, which of course it did. And why they don't give a damn about using Nolan, now, to stick it to Tempestra in their final moments. Very patient, indeed.

But still petty as hell.

Osiron carries Nolan to one of the pillars, leans him gently against it. I can only watch, as useless as an empty reliquary. But maybe . . . maybe this is not the worst ending. Our divinity was a gift; that's what Nolan, Caius, and every other one of my blood brethren tried to drill into me, from the day I was chosen. And he *wanted* to become an avatar, was wholly willing to give over everything that he is to Tempestra's continued existence. Maybe he would like this, even choose it if the offer were presented to him . . .

Except Osiron isn't making an offer. This isn't Nolan's choice, any more than my divine damnation was. This is the will of a god, being forced upon him.

And I will *not* let that happen.

Resolve floods through me, a burst of strength that feeds my increasingly heavy limbs. I reach up and grab one of the daggers in Alastair's eyes, wrench it free, and begin to crawl.

As soon as I do, it begins. A faint thrum, a change in the air.

A whispered call.

Osiron looms over Nolan's unconscious form, lips moving silently. And yet I can feel that soundless invocation buzzing over my skin, thickening the air around me. I push through it, ignoring the protests of my failing flesh as I scrape across the stone of the apse. Death can wait a little longer; Nolan needs me now.

The Whisperer pays no attention, wrapped up entirely in their new ritual. The call continues to rise, a quiet cacophony, making the whole Cathedral vibrate with it.

A fresh shudder of pain bursts from somewhere deep beneath my ribs. I crumple, muscles mutinying, unable to go any farther. Though Nolan is only a few dozen paces away, he might as well be in Cyprene.

*Fuck.* Tears of frustration spill over my cheeks. What was I going to do anyway, against a god?

I don't know. I don't know.

But I wanted to try.

*Lys.*

My name comes beneath the whispers, from everywhere and nowhere, leaving me questioning whether I heard it at all.

*Lys.*

Barely, I manage to turn toward the ephemeral call. Lying nearby is what is left of Tempestra-Innara.

They do not glow anymore. They appear, in a word, dead, Innara's flesh nearly colorless, except where it's burned crisp. Only one eye remains, no longer bright, but most definitely fixed on me.

*Lys, please hear me.* Their bloodless lips don't move. They don't need to. The Goddess reaches across whatever thin, sinuous bond they managed before Avery stabbed me. *While Osiron is engrossed.*

I listen, but only because I don't have much choice.

*Daughter.* Tempestra speaks again—and it is *only* Tempestra, I understand, Innara's dead flesh still housing the last of their power like a wine barrel with a leak. *It is not too late. Open yourself to me. Save us both.*

If I could still laugh, I would. Even now, when they no longer have the strength to force their way in, the Goddess is trying to get me to be their avatar.

Not a chance.

*You can still save him.*

I go stiff. Swear to myself. Or maybe the Goddess hears it, because there's the slightest flutter of hope from them.

*The binding is not immediately final. Not for him. And . . .* There's a pause. *Not for you.*

"Fuck." This time I manage it aloud. It would be an easy lie to fall for, if Osiron hadn't already told me the very same thing. And . . . it feels right. Like truth. Like neither of us can keep secrets anymore.

*Let me in.*

The world ripples gray once more. Turns cold . . . so cold. I don't think even divine healing is going to make much of a difference now.

*Probably not.* There's that truth again. *But either take this chance now, or we both die. We don't have a choice.*

They're wrong. We do. *I* do. And I know exactly what I'd choose, except for one thing.

Osiron's power has coalesced fully around Nolan now, and there's... something new in the air. A feeling. A presence.

A *hunger*.

*Lys*... Tempestra's call grows weaker. *Please*...

I choose.

In my mind, it isn't easy. For my flesh, even less so. Hand tightening around the dagger, I use the absolute dregs of my strength to slink closer to them. Innara's arm is outstretched, fingers broken and stained red. I raise the blade with one hand and draw it across the other, then let that limb fall. Barely—barely—my failing flesh reaches theirs and—

Desperately mingling, our blood does not sing.

It *screams*.

# Fifty-three

When they whisper, I hear.
When they whisper, I come.
When they whisper, I *wake*.

—PRAYER (ORIGINAL)

A NEW PLACE. HEAVY AND *jagged. Thick with the unfamiliar—shapes, sounds, feelings. Words that come later. I know only that I was called, and that I came.*

*And I am not alone. More like me, waiting, welcoming. I am not alone.*

I am not alone. The emergence from beyond—that's where it begins. I see and feel Osiron's petition, feel the dense anchor that drags me down (flesh), the aching turbulence of my birth (pain)...

But these are Tempestra's memories. Not mine. Those remain intact. I remember kneeling on the floor of the Cathedral, looking up

*looking down into the eyes of a child, and seeing death staring back—*

No.

I careen through two sets of memories, images mashing together, voices a syrupy, fervent buzz and . . . beneath it all, a heat. A raging firestorm that threatens to consume me.

I won't let it.

*Stop resisting.*

Tempestra.

*We'll both be lost.*

Right . . . yes. I remember that now. The memory of a face comes together, the reason to not fight this tearing and reweaving of thought, of my very soul.

Nolan. Nolan needs help.

*save us we can save him*

but it hurts . . . it hurts so much . . .

I do not want this feeling. The Goddess pours into me—a torrent of power and yet . . . a weak, fluttering thing. A moth with shredded wings. A heart, struggling to beat . . .

*Osiron takes me by the—the word what's the word—hand. A hand, a foot, vein and bone. Fleshy things, fragile but I can fix them, make them stronger, infuse them with . . .*

Stop. Please stop.

*Think of Nolan*

I stop. Stop fighting.

*My siblings surround me. Their faces change, skin tiring. Needing replacement. So does mine, but within we are the same, we are the power this world needs . . .*

Tempestra is a spreading fever. I give in, let it take me. Their memory, their light, their power—the full onslaught of divinity soars like a firebird ascending higher and higher above the leaden deficiencies of my primeval humanity . . .

Too high. I feel control slip away because Tempestra does. Their power has already been pushed so far . . . bent . . . no, broken.

*Broken . . .*

They are too weak. I am too, the battered casing of my flesh—the one thing they actually need that I can offer—overfilled and failing, splitting along its corporeal seams.

*Lys . . .*

Too many memories, too fast, too fractured. And the light, flickering without focus or control. Tempestra fades, a candle about to be snuffed out, taking me with them.

No. NO.

I did not make a deal with one god, and then another, for them *both* to go to shit. Maybe I'm dying, but I am *not* weak. I wasn't before the Goddess claimed me, and I'm not now.

I call the Flame.

At first, there's no answer, the divine power that has infused me since I was a child a distant, papery thing, tied to a near corpse lying on a cold stone floor. I reach for it, straining into that growing ashen darkness without letting it take me. My own memories rise—that first rush of divinity, the slice of a blade through my skin, the feeling of sinking sickles into flesh.

A taste of a gifted pastry. The loss of a very good horse.

The first time Nolan laughed and meant it.

I stop calling the flame and *demand* it. This time, it answers, an ocean wave of burning blue, orange, and red. The blaze envelopes me, wraps around me like a new flesh, bringing Tempestra with it. Dragged from whatever place a dead goddess goes to, their existence folds back into mine, their divine light infusing the entity of us. I let it happen. I *make* it happen. Because out in the world I'd so wished to leave behind, there is someone that needs me.

And all it costs me is my freedom.

Now, finally, Tempestra gets the full measure of my hate, my desire to be rid of them and embrace what little bit of independence I had during my time with Nolan. There is no judgement; as we merge, they understand. They disagree, but understand.

*I have always loved you. All of you.*

And we loved you. But only because we had no choice.

*You* still. Not *us*. I feel our minds weave together, but the threads remain their own colors.

*Not forever. Eventually we will be one.*

But not now. I have time.

I have time. And I have myself.

Now shut the hell up and heal us, "Mother."

It is already happening. In that faint feeling that is my . . . *our* body, blood begins to pump again; skin stretches and knits itself back together. The gray cold recedes behind the warmth of the Flame, which drives death back to a place more distant than ever before.

And oh, oh, there's more . . . The world feels like a garment around me, tight in some spots and loose in others, itchy and rough, silken and fine, and when I press back against the discomforting spots I feel it answer, try to obey my will. Such awareness of the stone, and the bone, and the dead things I—*they* once called children. And life too . . . little flickers of it . . . still fighting to remain.

Nolan is there, blood singing, but so quietly now.

And something else.

*Lys, daughter, it is almost . . .*

I know. I sit up, body again in full working order, and stronger in ways there's no chance to contemplate.

Because something else is here. Someone new.

And they are looking at me through Nolan's eyes.

# Fifty-four

*Some will listen. Some will come.*

—OSIRON

---

**WE ARE TOO LATE.** Tempestra and I succeed in our joining, but not before Osiron finished his work: A new divinity has been born into the Devoted Lands.

Desperate, I search familiar eyes for the recognition they *should* hold, but find nothing, and though I know Nolan is still in there, the deity is in control now.

*It's weak. He belongs to me. It can be forced out of him.*

I can feel Nolan. Blood sings to blood. And he was part of me—of Tempestra—first. Osiron might have called in a new tenant, but they couldn't get rid of that claimed territory. And now that I have a goddess inside my head, I understand.

That is how I get Nolan back.

Osiron collapses, weakened by the strain of the calling. Good. I get to my feet, then still as my movement draws the new deity's attention again. They mimic me, pushing up against the column Nolan had been leaning against, then falter, catching themselves.

*A newborn. A colt that needs to find its legs.*

I'm not giving it that chance. I am not newborn, and right now I am absolutely bursting with divine power.

*Osiron is weak as well.*

Picking the sword off a guard's corpse, I advance. I want my sickles, want to feel that familiar weight in my hands as I slice through Osiron, see whether they can pull their little survival trick again, but oh well. Any blade will do. I will flay and I will burn and I will not be stopped. This rage is not my own, not entirely. The memories, the anger . . . this was a betrayal. Same as when Osiron tried to hobble us, make me less than I was.

No, not me.

Tempestra.

I can't allow myself to get bogged down by thoughts that aren't mine. But it's hard to define those edges. Shared moments blur together, two songs in harmony, a story remembered two different ways. I will not let that muddle me; I am Lys, even if I am Tempestra now too. At least for as long as it takes to get Nolan back, and then you are getting the fuck out of my head, Mother.

*Lys . . .*

I see it.

Osiron seems to rally, getting to their feet again, though with obvious effort. A look of new-parent pride flashes. Then they see us, and it turns into something I'm overjoyed to see: fear. "What . . . what have you done?"

"Same thing as you." I raise the sword, feel my power swell. "What we had to."

Then the floor shifts like sand beneath me, opening and closing just as fast, locking me in place. Oh, please. I push back, give Tempestra rein. The rock moves, not as freely, but enough to release us. I climb out of the ground. Something punches me in the chest—a spear of twisted iron—throwing me back into the apse of bones. I only laugh. The blow would have pulped a normal person's innards, put a Potentiate down for at least a few minutes.

I barely felt a thing.

*Do you grasp my power now—*

Shut up.

I rise again, blade still in hand, waiting for the next blow to fall. Instead, there is a rumbling. The Whisperer's attention isn't on me anymore. Their eyes are raised to the ceiling, to the arches above, as if in prayer. Too late, I realize what is coming.

Osiron can't win, but they can do the next best thing.

I throw myself against the back wall as the Cathedral begins to split and crumble, raining down. I deflect, push it all away, but Tempestra's hold over the world is clunkier, less precise. Debris collides with my newly healed flesh, enough that it actually hurts, actually *damages*, no matter that the power rises to fix those wounds almost immediately.

I . . . we . . . cannot escape the barrage. The whole of our existence turns toward survival, while around us, the world fills up with darkness.

Lys.

I wake entombed.

It hasn't been long, but by the time I dig out from beneath the stone and wood and tile and glass, I am already fully aware that Osiron and Nolan are gone. The sensation of the new deity still tickles at the edge of my perception, but it's only a piece of knowledge, not a compass. And Osiron might as well be a ghost.

What is left is left in pieces, illuminated by the sunlight streaming through the broken remains of the roof. Gold. Bones. Bodies and blood. The Cathedral is in ruins. The Enduring Flame, extinguished.

And I failed. Nolan is still enthralled. Maybe lost forever.

*No. Find them. Stop them, before it's too—*

Shut up, Tempestra.

I know what I have to do.

# *Epilogue*

I DIG THROUGH CORPSES AND debris until I find what I am searching for.

Then, it's only a matter of patience.

Some hours after Osiron and Nolan disappear, Morgan wakes, deathly still one second, gasping back into the living world the next. She draws one desperate breath after another, as if unconsciousness had been some sort of drowning. Finally, she gathers herself enough to take in her surroundings and spot me waiting nearby, settled upon the toppled statue of one of my chil—of one of our honored blood brethren.

"Hey," I say. "Knew you were too fucking stubborn to die."

Her mouth gapes open. Closes. Which is so satisfying, because I catch the moment she sees—really *sees*—who is sitting in front of her. I've been looking forward to it for hours.

"So," we say, because in this we are in agreement, "still interested in being Executrix?"

## ACKNOWLEDGMENTS

First thanks go to my agent, Laura Zats, for nearly a decade of support and hustling for my projects (can't believe it's been that long!) as well as her agency partner, Erik Hane, and their excellent podcast, *Print Run*, which helps keep both me and countless writers informed, sane, *and* entertained about this roller coaster of an industry.

Endless thanks to my editor, Nivia Evans, for helping make this book shine, and for giving me the opportunity to work with Saga Press, thus allowing me to check that particular goal off of my writer bucket list. And thanks to Jela Lewter, too, for all your input and hard work during the editing process.

I cannot imagine having a better cover for this book, which is thanks to Galen Dara's absolutely stunning art and Math Monahan's fabulous design. And thank you to the entire Saga team who made this book happen. (Special shout-out to the production folks, who never get enough love.)

Nothing I've published would have happened without the help of my amazing writing group, B-Spec, to whom this book is dedicated. Thank you to Kyle W. Kerr, Gillian Daniels, Clare Fitzgerald, Jess Barber, Andrea Martinez Corbin, Robert Davis, Lauren Barrett, Emily Strong, Caitlin Walsh, Elizabeth (E.A.) Brenner, Eric Mulder, Julia Gilstein, Caleb Slowinski, Rae Zakuta, Victoria Sandbrook Flynn, Jay O'Connell, Kat Black, and, of course, Tristam Chad Chadwick III (also known as Trip). As I'm writing this, it is with the exhilarating (and still partially secret) knowledge that more of our works will be making it onto bookstore shelves. Hopefully by the time this is published, even more additions will be on the way!

Jaz, my favorite ghoul—thank you for always getting when I need an encouraging word, a chance to vent, a cocktail, or all three at once.

If there is one thing I am blessed with an abundance of, it's amazingly supportive (and geeky and talented) friends. Thank you Brandy, Jerry, Sam, Adam and Amy and Chief, Bobby, Alyssa, Alan, Adina, Cheryl, Joseph, Jason, Jeffrey, and all of the rest of the Boston geeks. (Donuts all around.) Also, shout-out to fellow authors Anna Rae and Cat Scully for both their writerly camaraderie and general awesomeness.

Thank you to my family, for continuing to support my books even though I hope they never read a single word of them. Lane, you are still my favorite nephew.

Lastly, for as long as I'd been working at being an author, I had Nico, my best feline friend of nearly nineteen years, by my side. This was the last book I ever got to work on with him curled up next to me or, less helpfully, with his head resting on my hand as I tried to type. So, though I can't exactly thank him for his contribution, he was, and always will be, a very good cat.

# AUTHOR INTERVIEW

*What was the first book that made you fall in love with the SFF genre?*

*The Lion, the Witch and the Wardrobe*, although it probably wasn't the first SFF book I ever read. At some point when I was very young, I saw a few minutes of a cartoon version and was *entranced*. It imprinted so hard that later, in elementary school when we read the book, I realized what it was and fell in love with the series, as one inevitably does. (Ironically, I had no idea it was inspired by religion until the teacher of my extremely disliked Catholicism classes informed me, while also scolding me for reading when I was supposed to be listening.)

*Where did the initial idea for* The Lost Reliquary *come from and how did the story begin to take shape?*

I'm sure I definitely knew at some point, but have mostly forgotten. I do remember I had finished writing a book draft with multiple third-person POVs and wanted to try something different; I'd never written a full novel in first person before. Plus, Lys's rebellious, sarcastic personality was very different (and refreshing) compared to the characters I'd recently been writing.

Also, pretty sure I'd been stuck on certain elements at the time, like the idea of avatars and why people believe what they believe (still stuck on that, given real life as of late). And reliquaries. They can be so cool and weird and gross, all at the same time. Seriously, who came up with the idea of centering a whole religious experience around, like, a preserved tongue or a shriveled toe?

*What was the most challenging moment of writing* The Lost Reliquary?

Well, there's one section that I rewrote significantly, probably four or five times at least, that will remain unnamed. (There's *always* that one section in every book, I swear.)

*Your novel is set in a secondary world inspired by living gods. What was your approach to bringing this world to life? Is there a world-building element that you're particularly proud of?*

I liked the idea of a story where the gods of the land are known to be real and also fully present, because it upends the concept of faith. Real-life religion comes with zero proof, so how would religion function with 100 percent validation, especially when there's a choice of deities? Like, what is faith in something you definitely see and feel, but otherwise don't have a true understanding of?

Element-wise, the sepulchrae are my favorite part, since they remain as constant reminders that most of the gods are dead but their power remains, in some form. (Which keeps the faith in them alive.)

*The characters in* The Lost Reliquary *are incredibly compelling and sympathetic. If you had to pick, who would you say is your favorite character? Who did you find the most difficult to write?*

I'm not sure I can decide between Lys and Nolan. They are both so different in their beliefs and so similar in their conviction, which made them super fun to play off each other. I also have a love for minor, secondary characters, and though she doesn't appear much in this book, I have a soft spot for Morgan.

Nolan was probably the most difficult to write, since he goes through various shifts in the novel, and it was a little bit of a challenge to make sure there was still a connecting line through all the points of him.

*Who are some of your favorite authors and how have they influenced your writing?*

Diane Duane, whose Young Wizards series was formative. (Also, she's lovely in person, a far superior author of teen wizards compared to some others.)

Stephen King, mostly because every voracious tween reader in the '80s and '90s inevitably ended up reading his books for some reason. (*The Stand* and *Night Shift* are particular favorites. Love when the horror is as much human as supernatural.)

Terry Moore, for being able to write so very, very human characters, good and evil and in-between. His *Strangers in Paradise* comic series is one of my all-time favorites.

And more recently: N. K. Jemisin (for being able to blend SFF and beautiful prose in a way I can't even begin to aspire to), Marjorie Liu and Sana Takeda (*Monstress* is sooooo good), and Tamsyn Muir (for giving me the exact blend of weird, epic, and fantastical I *crave*).

*Without giving too much away, what can readers expect in the sequel?*

Angst.

*And, finally, if you could visit one of the gods' sepulchrae, which one would it be?*

Definitely *not* where the Salt Goddess fell. Dead things in water is a very specific fear of mine. (Lys handled it way better than I would have.) Probably Novena would be the safest, even if it's super creepy. Or the Shadowed Valley (though I may feel differently after the sequel).

## ABOUT THE AUTHOR

**LYNDSAY ELY** is an author of science fiction and fantasy across YA and adult categories. Her debut, *Gunslinger Girl,* was a YA genre-bent dystopian Western. She has also published an *Overwatch* tie-in novel, *Deadlock Rebels*; is a contributor to *Overwatch 2: Heroes Ascendant: An Overwatch Story Collection*; and authored the interactive adventure novel *Five Nights at Freddy's: Escape the Pizzaplex.* She currently resides in Boston.